TENDER TEACHING

Elizabeth's eyes opened widely as Strong Heart turned her on her side to face him. He gazed at her naked splendor; then he looked into her eyes.

"Say that you want me," he said, tracing the line of her jaw with his finger. "I must hear you say it. I must know you want it as badly as I."

"I'm not sure what want is," Elizabeth said. "I have never loved before."

"Listen to your body," Strong Heart said, his one hand now slowly caressing her. "Do you feel it? The ache? The passions that need to be answered with mine?"

Desire shot through Elizabeth as his fingers so skillfully awakened her body to newer, more wondrous sensations than ever before. She closed her eyes and threw her head back, sighing.

"Yes," she whispered. "I do feel it. Please, oh, please, I do need you . . ."

As the rain poured against the tent and the thunder boomed, shaking the very earth beneath them, Strong Heart reached for Elizabeth and began his lesson of love. . . .

WILD EMBRACE

by

Cassie Edwards

A TOPAZ BOOK

TOPAZ
Published by the Penguin Group
Penguin Books USA Inc., 375 Hudson Street,
New York, New York 10014, U.S.A.
Penguin Books Ltd, 27 Wrights Lane,
London W8 5TZ, England
Penguin Books Australia Ltd, Ringwood,
Victoria, Australia
Penguin Books Canada Ltd, 10 Alcorn Avenue,
Toronto, Ontario, Canada M4V 3B2
Penguin Books (N.Z.) Ltd, 182–190 Wairau Road,
Auckland 10, New Zealand

Penguin Books Ltd, Registered Offices:
Harmondsworth, Middlesex, England

First published by Topaz, an imprint of New American Library,
a division of Penguin Books USA Inc.

First Printing, June, 1993
10 9 8 7 6 5 4 3 2 1

 Topaz is a trademark of New American Library,
a division of Penguin Books USA Inc.

Printed in the United States of America

With affection I dedicate
Wild Embrace to:
Sheila Bilbrey
Marion Campbell
Kathy Stone
Stella Alexander
Aurora Gonzalez
Damita Lewis

also: Bruce and Ruth
and Mike and Nancy Girot

I thought you savage
You thought me uncaring,
Desire has a mind of its own
As passion brings forth sharing.

Your hands so strong upon me
Warm and gentle as they seek,
A desperate quake begins within me
I stand vulnerable and weak.

You proceed to imprison my heart
All my resistance is torn asunder,
I can see only you before me
And hear your voice, that sounds like thunder.

To you, I will constantly come running,
Of shame, I have not a trace.
Your open arms are a haven,
I cherish the feel of our wild embrace.

—SHEILA BILBREY,
a fan, poet, and
sweet friend

1

No soul can ever clearly see
Another's highest, noblest part,
Save through the sweet philosophy,
And loving wisdom of the heart.
—PHOEBE CARY

The Pacific Northwest
September, 1875

A fireplace dug out in the middle of the planked floor of the longhouse reflected the wavering light of its fire onto cedar walls hung with mats and various cooking and hunting paraphernalia, and onto sleeping platforms spread with several layers of bark, and soft, furry pelts. Overhead, berries and fish hung to dry from the crossbeams under the rafters. The smoke from the lodge fire was spiraling slowly toward the open cedar boards overhead, its gray wisps escaping upward, into the morning sky.

Chief Moon Elk rearranged his robe of black sea otter fur more comfortably around his lean shoulders, and pulled up his legs and squatted close to the fire. His steel-gray eyes were not large, but were bright and steady in their gaze, the skin of his copper face was fine in texture, although age and weather had wrinkled it.

"Remember always to walk softly, my son," Chief Moon Elk said as he peered at Strong Heart, who sat beside him feasting on a bowl of soup made from clams and wild vegetables. "While you are helping Four Winds escape from the white man's prison in Seattle, you must not shed blood. No good ever comes of kill-

ing whites. Our Suquamish people always suffer in the
end.''

Strong Heart paused momentarily from eating.
''This I know,'' he said, nodding his head with grave
dignity. ''And no blood will be shed. I would do nothing to lead trouble to our village. By choice, our clan
of Suquamish have kept ourselves from those who were
tricked by the white man's treaties and promises. Because of this, ours has been a peaceful existence. So
shall it continue to be, Father.''

Chief Moon Elk's gaze moved slowly over Strong
Heart, admiring his muscular son attired in fringed
buckskin. ''Your plan is to dress as a white man during
the escape, and you will ride your horse instead of
traveling by canoe to Seattle?'' he asked, wiping his
mouth with a cedar-bark napkin, his own stomach
warmed comfortably with soup.

''*Ah-hah*, yes, that is my plan,'' Strong Heart said,
leaning closer to the fire to ladle more clam soup into
his elaborately carved wooden bowl. The ladle was
decorated with the crest of his family: the red-tailed
hawk.

Strong Heart began eating the soup again, needing
his fill now, for he was not planning to stop for anything until he reached the outskirts of Seattle. His plans
for Four Winds were several sunrises away. He had
other chores to do before freeing his friend from the
cruel clutches of the law.

Moon Elk studied his son for a moment without offering a response to what Strong Heart had said. It
was like seeing himself in the mirror of the clear rivers
and streams those many years ago when he could boast
of being his son's age of twenty-nine winters. Moon
Elk had begun to shrink with age, so he was no longer
as tall as his son. Strong Heart was more than six feet
in height, a giant among his Suquamish people, and
most whites.

And not only was his son tall, he was powerfully built, broad shouldered, thin flanked, and lithe. His light copper-colored skin was smooth, with muscles that rippled beneath the flesh. He wore his dark brown hair long and loose, past his shoulders, and his gray eyes held strength and intelligence in their depths.

Ah-hah, Moon Elk thought proudly, there was a steel-like quality about his son.

His son was a man of daring and courage.

"My son, not only will the color of your skin give away your true identity, but also your dignified gracefulness. You are a noble man who towers over the white man," Moon Elk said. "This can perhaps betray your plans, my son. No white man walks with the dignity of my son, nor carries within their hearts such compassion."

Moon Elk leaned closer to Strong Heart and peered into his eyes. "My son, is Four Winds worth risking your life for? The world would be void of a much greater man should *you* die."

Strong Heart was unmoved by his father's steady stare, or his words. "Even now I am sure the white people are building a hanging platform for my friend, Four Winds," he said flatly. "My friend will *not* die with a noose around his neck. Do you not recall *his* dignity, Father? Being caged and awaiting his death, his dignity has been taken from him. And *I* see his life as no less valuable than mine. I will set him free, Father. And do not fear for my safety. I have faced worse odds in my lifetime than a *cultus,* worthless sheriff, who is blinded by the power he feels by caging men the same as some might cage a bird for entertainment's sake. It is *he* who should be caged, and put on display in a white man's circus!"

"Such a bitterness I hear in your voice," Moon Elk said, shaking his head sadly. "Now, when the autumn salmon harvest is near, and when your heart should be happy and your very soul should be filled with song, you are filled with bitterness over another man's misfortunes. That is *me-sah-chie*, bad, my son! *Me-sah-chie!*"

"*Ah-hah*, it *is* regrettable, yet is it not as regrettable that Four Winds was arrested unjustly?" Strong Heart said, setting his empty bowl aside. "You, as well as I, know his innocence. Although we have lost touch these past moons after his Suquamish clan moved north to Canada's shores, I know that his heart remains the same toward life. He could never ride with outlaws, killing and stealing! Never!"

"Who can say what drives a man, even to insanity?" Moon Elk rumbled. "The same could apply to a man who takes up the ways of a criminal. Is it not the same? Men are driven by many things to become who they are. As I recall him, Four Winds seemed a driven young man. You did not also see this, my son?"

Strong Heart arched an eyebrow and fell deep into thought as he peered into the flames of the fire. He was remembering many things about his friend Four Winds from when they were youths together. Some good. Some *me-sah-chie*, bad.

Strong Heart had overlooked the bad, for Four Winds's goodness had always outweighed his shortcomings.

"*Ah-hah*," Strong Heart finally said, looking back at his father. "I remember that Four Winds was in a sense driven, but not much more than I, Father. In games of competition, we *both* strived to excel."

"Do you not recall the times he would avoid you for days after losing at games with you?" Moon Elk persisted. "*This* is why I fear he may have changed now into someone you do not know. Or should not risk your life for."

"Father, this is not at all like you," Strong Heart said, rising. He then knelt on one knee before his fa-

ther and placed a gentle hand on his shoulder. "Trust
my judgment, Father. Never before have you doubted
me."

Moon Elk turned his eyes to Strong Heart and placed
a hand over his son's. "It is not you I doubt," he said
softly. "It is Four Winds. Remember this, my son, as
you take the long ride to Seattle. I trust your judgment
in all things. It is only that I worry too much over my
son who is destined to one day be a great chief. Remember always the importance of being a *tyee*, chief.
He is a man whose opinion carries more weight than
his fellow tribesmen."

"I remember all of your teachings, Father," Strong
Heart said, rising to his full height. "And I understand
the importance of being a *tyee*. But that is in the future. I must do what I must now for a friend."

Moon Elk rose to his feet also. He walked with his
son to the large cedar door and swung it open. Together they stepped outside to a blossoming new September day, the air heavy with the sweet fragrance of
the cedar-and-pine forest which lay just beyond the
village.

Moon Elk walked Strong Heart toward his *san-de-
lie*, horse, a magnificent roan. "You will also search
again for Proud Beaver, your grandfather?" he asked,
his face drawn. "Your mother still grieves so over him,
fearing that her father is dead."

Strong Heart turned and saw his mother coming toward them, having left the longhouse so son and father
could speak in private about things that would only
trouble her. She had busied herself by going to the
river for water and walked with a huge earthenware
jug balanced on her right shoulder.

It saddened Strong Heart to see his mother's change
since the disappearance of her father. Her eyes were
no longer filled with laughter. She scarcely ate, and
had become frail and gaunt.

Then Strong Heart smiled as he looked at her pert nose. It had remained the same—tiny and *toke-tie*, pretty—the reason her parents had called her Pretty Nose on the day of her birthing.

Pretty Nose set her heavy jug on the ground and went to Strong Heart. Tears filling her eyes, she embraced him. "My son, return safely to me," she murmured. "This that you do is courageous, yet I cannot say that it pleases me. Courage is just a word. It cannot fill my arms if you are dead!"

"Mother," Strong Heart said, placing his hands at her tiny waist, holding her away from him so that their eyes could meet. "You worry too much. This son of yours will return soon. And I promise to search for Grandfather. I shall go back once more to our ancestral grounds where our village once stood. We all believe that is where Grandfather went when he disappeared a moon ago. He felt as if the spirits of our dead ancestors were beckoning him there. He spoke of that often to me."

Strong Heart lowered his head momentarily, then looked back at his mother. "Had I heeded the warning in his voice and words, *never* would he have left our village. I would have kept watch. I would have stopped him."

"Do not blame yourself, my son," Pretty Nose said, gently placing a hand to his cheek. She looked adoringly up at him. "How could you know that his mind was aging more quickly than his body? We have not lived beside the waters of Puget Sound for *many* moons now. Many moons ago, even before Chief Seattle signed treaties with the white people, our people took money from white people for their land. Those who did were ignorant enough to think the value of the money was worth more to them than the land. It was a mistake. It ate away at your grandfather like an open wound festering with disease. His regrets turned him away from us. *Ah-hah*, it has surely carried him 'home,' to our ancestral burial grounds.''

She flung herself into her son's arms and clung to him, sobbing. ''Please find him, Strong Heart,'' she whispered. ''Please?''

''I shall try is all that I can say,'' Strong Heart said, easing her from his arms. He framed her face between his hands. His mouth went to her lips and he kissed her softly.

Then he turned and, with an easy grace, he mounted his horse, settling himself comfortably on the saddle stuffed with cottonwood and cattail down. He reached for his rawhide reins, and took a last look at his village before leaving. Rectangular houses built solely of cedar wood without the benefit of nails sat side-by-side facing the Duwamish River. All were supported by frameworks of massive posts and planks. The large, gabled houses were adorned with carved house posts and door poles, painted with the owners' crests, the animal spirit guardians and ancestors of each clan. Lines of totem poles stood before the houses, those dramatic columns of carved animals and birds.

Strong Heart then shifted his gaze to the saddlebags on his horse, his thoughts sorting through what he had packed to ensure the success of this venture that he was embarking upon. He was taking a change of clothes which would give him the appearance of a white man—a flannel shirt, leather breeches, and jacket, and high-heeled boots. He was carrying a pair of Colt revolvers with seven-inch barrels and pearl handles. A sombrero hung from the saddlehorn.

Ah-hah, he thought smugly to himself. All of this would be used when the time came for his masquerade.

Strong Heart patted the knife sheathed at his waist, then placed a hand on the rifle that was resting in its holster at his horse's flank. He valued this repeating rifle as if it were his right arm. It had gotten him through many scrapes when gangs of bandits had lurked beside the trails, waiting to attack any traveler who looked as if he might have something worth stealing.

Until recently, when they had been forced to go into hiding due to the many posses chasing them, the desperadoes had swarmed the countryside, attacking stations along the trail where travelers stopped to exchange tired horses for fresh ones for the next lap of their journey.

The robberies had lessened at the same time of Four Winds's arrest, yet Strong Heart still would not believe that his friend had any connection with the outlaws. It was surely a case of mistaken identity that made the posse think that Four Winds was a desperado.

Strong Heart looked at his parents, seeing the concern in their eyes for the dangers of his mission. Yet not even this could change his mind.

"I must go now," he said.

"Strong Heart, take many braves with you," Moon Elk said, in a final plea to his son. "They will ride beside you. They will help you."

"Father, as I have told you before, I must ride alone," Strong Heart said shortly. "Less trouble comes with lesser numbers. Many braves would draw attention—not avoid it. I, alone, can move about without being noticed."

Moon Elk nodded in acquiescence. Pretty Nose stepped closer to Strong Heart. Tears streamed from her dark eyes as she reached a hand toward him. "*Klahow-ya*, good-bye, my son," she said, sobbing. "*Hyak*, hurry! Make haste in returning to me!"

"I will, Mother," Strong Heart said, then urged his horse away in a gallop, not looking back. He kept his eyes straight ahead as he left his village behind him, savoring the wild, deep free feeling of being alone on a journey of the heart. He loved the quiet power of it.

He soon forgot the heartache that he had left behind and enjoyed this land that was precious to him. It was a wild yet peaceable land, sunny and quiet. Strong Heart urged his horse in a steady pace along the trail. The wind was soft today, and the mountains beyond were misted and breathtakingly beautiful. There was fullness to everything.

When the haloed fire of the setting sun was fleeing before an ashen dusk, Strong Heart rode through familiar terrain. With his horse breathing heavily, he topped a rise.

Drawing rein, he took in the familiar sight. Out of the east rose the mighty Cascade Range, shawled in a dark-green weave of cedar, hemlock, and firs, dominated by the eternally white cone of Mount Rainier.

Below, the city of Seattle stretched out before him. He recognized Skid Road, a steep slope along the Seattle waterfront where logs were skidded to waiting ships, and where brothels and saloons did a roaring business.

Looming high above Seattle on another slope of land, yet just below where Strong Heart stood, was a long, ugly and ramshackle wooden building, with the name COPPER HILL PRISON written on a large sign at the front. He squinted his eyes, watching the men hammering outside the prison, the tell tale signs of a hanging platform taking shape.

Heaving a long sigh, Strong Heart shifted his eyes to where the Sound lay. He knew that among its sheltered coves and winding channels, salmon were swimming peacefully through the kelp forests. Soon they would be making their journey upriver. He would be there waiting for them, meeting them at the canyon for the autumn harvest.

Then something else caught his eye: a huge, four-masted ship approaching Seattle. He watched its movement through the choppy waves made by the cool northwest breeze. He always felt awe for these large vessels with their white sails catching the wind. He could not help but wonder whom this ship carried to the land that once belonged solely to the Suquamish.

His jaw tight, he wheeled his horse around and followed the slope of land that took him away from Copper Hill Prison.

Tonight and tomorrow he would renew his search for his grandfather.

Then he would return to study the prison, and how often people came and went from it.

2

We have made no vows, there will be none broken.
Our love was free as the wind on the hill.
—ERNEST DOWSON

The wind was damp and chilly as it blew across the
deck of the four-masted schooner, whipping Elizabeth
Easton's elegantly trimmed black cape about her ankles. Her luxuriantly long, red hair whispered in the
breeze around her face. Her impudent green eyes
watched the ship pass Seattle, to go to a private pier a
mile or two down the Sound.

Elizabeth clutched her gloved hands to the ship's
rail, and although it was growing dusk, she was able
to study the city. From this vantage point, she could
not deny that it was a lovely setting. Seattle was framed
by mountains and water, the dark forest crowning the
hilltop above the city. If she inhaled deeply enough,
she could smell the mixed, pleasant fragrances of
roses, pine, and cedar. If she could forget her resentment for having been forced to come to the Pacific
Northwest with her father, she would regard the land
as nothing short of paradise.

In the dimming light of evening, her eyes locked on
something that gave her a feeling of foreboding. She
had been told about the prison, its reputation having
traveled as far as California.

"Copper Hill Prison," she whispered, shivering at
the thought of the kinds of criminals that were known
to be incarcerated there. She feared that this city of
Seattle might be even worse than the one she had left
behind, San Francisco.

As the moon rose bright and beautiful in the sky,

Elizabeth turned her attention from the city, and watched the land creep by on her left. Soon she would be reaching the place that she would call 'home.' She didn't look forward to it, for she had not wanted to leave her home in San Francisco. But leaving San Francisco had been a part of her father's plan for more than two years now. He had gone on many scouting expeditions in the Pacific Northwest, searching for just the right spot to build his fishery. After much study, he had found that the area around Seattle abounded in shellfish and other fish, making it possible for him to procure fresh fish year round for his planned business.

He had heard that much profit could be made in salmon, which were in abundance in the autumn. He planned to double his wealth on salmon alone, by exporting packed salted salmon to all corners of the world.

Elizabeth grasped the rail harder as the ship edged close to a pier. The water was deep enough here so the ship could dock without the need of longboats to carry cargo and passengers to shore.

In a flurry of activity, Elizabeth was whisked along with the others to the pier. She watched guardedly as her trunks were being taken from the ship and brought to land.

She sighed heavily, still not believing that her father was not going to take the time to go up to the house with her. Instead, he was going to join the ship's crew to help unload his own supplies to begin constructing his fishery tonight. Once he began, she knew not to expect his company, except for short visits, until it was completed.

Except for Frannie, her devoted maid, Elizabeth would be spending her every moment alone. Long ago, Elizabeth's mother, Marilyn, had fled the life Elizabeth's father had given her, leaving behind much bitterness and hurt. Elizabeth didn't think that she could forgive her mother, ever, yet deep down inside she had feared that when she and her father left San Francisco, it would cut the ties with her mother forever. If her mother decided to return, to be a part of the family again, she would not know where to find them.

And Elizabeth knew that she should not care. She had been eight when her mother had left her. She was now eighteen and had learned, in the many absences of her father, to fend for herself.

If she allowed herself, Elizabeth could understand why her mother had left to seek a new life elsewhere. Elizabeth had felt the same abandonment many times. Surely her mother had felt the same, when her husband had traveled the high seas.

A slim, muscled arm slipped around Elizabeth's waist as her father stepped to her side. She stiffened as she was encouraged to lean against him. These rare shows of affection were always brief. She was well aware that her father only paid her these attentions because he knew that it was expected of him, not because he actually wanted to be open with his feelings. He was one who shied away from revealing feelings of any sort. He had become a cold, embittered man since his wife's departure.

"So, daughter, do you think you can survive the transition without your father?" Earl asked, hugging Elizabeth to him. He looked down into defiant eyes, yet shrugged it off because he did not wish to take the time to question it. Though Elizabeth was petite, she was not frail and could withstand any change without his pamperings.

"I'll never understand why you had to move to what I feel is the end of the earth," Elizabeth said, drawing away from him. "Father, that is the only description that comes to mind when I try to describe this wretched place. And you aren't even going to take the time to go to the house with me. Just how long would that take, Father? But I'm wasting my breath, aren't I? You are determined to leave me to find my own way in this new place, and in a strange house, no matter what.''

"Elizabeth, if I'm ever to succeed in my new venture I must get right to constructing the fishery,'' Earl said, clasping his hands behind him. "Try to understand, Elizabeth. Although I won't be suppin' with you each night, I'll always be near. Soon we'll get acquainted with our house and land together.''

"Yes, soon,'' Elizabeth said, her voice bitter. She hugged herself, her gaze sweeping around her. The moon was high now, lighting everything with its silver light. Elizabeth could see that the whole face of the country seemed covered with trees, with huge, looming bluffs making up the sides of the Sound.

Her gaze shifted upward and she shivered when she looked at the monstrosity of a house that she would soon be entering. Tremendous in size, with its towers and turrets and rough stone construction, it stood high on a cliff, protected by a grotesque, iron fence.

Its great stone edifice overlooking the waters of the Sound looked like some unblinking, unmoving sentinel. She had been told that it had survived Indian attacks, two earthquakes, and a fire.

Trees crowded around the dark bulk of the house, crackling in the wind.

"I know the house seems grim,'' Earl said, following her gaze, then looking back at her again, seeing her disapproval—even traces of fright in her wide, green eyes. "But it has to do for now. One day soon we'll replace it with a new one. But first, let me make this the greatest seaport in the Pacific Northwest.''

Elizabeth moved her eyes to her father, wondering about a man who already had so much money he could retire to live comfortably for the rest of his life, yet hungered for more. Anyone that looked at him could see that he was a man of wealth. Tall and thin, he wore his clothes well. Tonight he sported a tan suit with a gold satin, embroidered waistcoat, and a white ascot with a diamond stickpin in its velvet folds. His golden brown hair was clipped immaculately to his collar line, his golden mustache was bold and thick, hiding his upper lip.

His eyes were the same soft green coloring as hers, yet in them were no warmth—no feeling.

"Elizabeth," he said, nodding toward the Sound, "there's no other place like this on the face of the earth. The water's alive with fish. And as I've told you before, salmon is the prime catch. We'll pay the Indians to catch 'em, and we'll sell 'em at a greater profit."

"Father, what if the Indians don't agree to catch the salmon for you?" Elizabeth asked softly. "They will surely look to you as an intruder. Most are still angry over having been forced to live on reservations."

"Not all Indians live on reservations," he said matter-of-factly. "There are some who weren't tricked by treaties. It's these free Indians that I plan to approach—that I plan to take my offer to."

"That doesn't seem like good logic, Father," Elizabeth argued. "If they couldn't be paid off then, why would you think they could be paid off now?"

"Things were different then," Earl scoffed. "It's a new day, a new time. Surely the Indians are more sensible in their thinking now and will be able to see a good way to make a profit when it is shown to them in black and white. All men want to make money, even Indians."

Elizabeth didn't respond, having never won an argument with her father in her entire life. She could not help but think that he was perhaps the most bullheaded man in the world.

"I hope you're right," she said sullenly. "I've sacrificed enough for this new idea of yours that is supposed to make you wealthier. I found it very hard to say a final farewell to my friends in San Francisco.''

Earl embraced Elizabeth again. "Baby, you're going to inherit all of this one day,'' he said huskily. "It'll be worth the sacrifice of leavin' friends behind.'' He patted her on the back. "You'll see. You'll see.''

Elizabeth slipped her arms about him, this time relishing this moment of closeness. She knew that it would be short-lived. She had seen her father looking nervously at the activity of the crew on the ship and the pier. He wanted to join them.

"Perhaps something good will come of this move after all, Father,'' she murmured. "If you establish a business here on land, you won't be out at sea as often. I so worried about you when you took those long sea voyages. I'm glad you are no longer planning to carry cargo as far as China. Now the ships will come to you.''

"Baby, had I not gone to China, how could you have boasted of having some of the finest silk dresses in San Francisco?'' Earl teased. He pulled away from her arms. "You know there won't ever be as fine a fabric hauled aboard my ship again, don't you?''

"Yes, I know,'' Elizabeth said, slipping her hands inside her cape, to smooth them along the skirt of her silk dress. "But I truly don't care. I'd much rather have you than any foolish silk fabric brought from China.''

She wanted to shout at him, saying that had he not gone to all corners of the world, neglecting his wife for his business, his wife might have never fled for a better life elsewhere. Her mother was surely with a man who now catered to her every whim. As Elizabeth could recall, her mother had been absolutely, ravishingly beautiful.

But Elizabeth thought better of mentioning her mother now, seeing no need to spoil her father's mood.

She had already done that, time and time again.

Earl cast another nervous glance toward his ship and his eager crew. He watched as the last of the trunks were placed on the pier.

Then he again looked into Elizabeth's troubled eyes. "Baby, I really must get back to the ship. The men are awaiting my orders. They are almost as anxious as I am to begin building the fishery. We are going to begin as soon as the supplies are sorted out and ready." He placed a gentle hand on Elizabeth's cheek. "I'll be gone more than I'll be seein' you, but I'll be up at the house lookin' in on you from time to time."

He grew frustrated when he could tell that she still did not understand any of this. Why couldn't she see that it was imperative to get his fishery built as soon as possible?

"But, Father, even after you go and make the Indians an offer, what will happen if they don't agree to catch the salmon for you?" Elizabeth asked, fear gripping her when she gazed up at the massive fence that had been erected around the house. Indians were the cause. Elizabeth's father had told her that many years ago a whaling captain had been determined to have his house on this land that overlooked the Sound. For some unknown reason the Indians had not wanted the house built on that site. They had first killed several of those who had built it, and then had tried to burn it.

The captain had not let anything, even Indians, stop him.

Now another man, just as determined and stubborn, had taken possession of the house and land, and Elizabeth had to wonder what she truly had to fear, since she was this man's daughter and had to live there, also.

"Indians are driven to find means of survival just the same as the white man," Earl said, shrugging. "Most are dirt poor and will surely be happy to hear the clink of coins in their pockets after I pay their wages. That will keep 'em in line. You'll see.''

Earl went to his waiting servants. He eyed them speculatively, then began handing out orders. One by one they turned and began dragging their trunks up a briar-laden path that led to the house.

Earl singled out a hefty, towering black man and ordered him to take Elizabeth's trunks to the house. Earl had left his own on the ship, knowing that he would be spending more time there than in the house.

Then Earl gently took an old black woman by an elbow and took her to Elizabeth. ''Frannie, you see to Elizabeth while I'm busy building my fishery,'' he said to her. ''See to it that she's made comfortable enough to forget San Francisco, her friends, and her damn mother.''

''Yas, suh,'' Frannie said in a slow, calm drawl. ''My baby'll not want for a thing.''

Earl gave Elizabeth a troubled, yet stern stare. ''Elizabeth, I don't want to receive word that you've left our estate grounds, unescorted,'' he said flatly. ''This is a wild land, filled with savages and ruthless desperadoes. Let's not tempt any of them with your sweet, pretty face, do you hear?''

Elizabeth gave him a long and frustrated glare.

Frannie locked an arm through Elizabeth's. Short and plump, with tight gray ringlets of hair framing a fleshy face, and dark, sparkling eyes, she looked up at Elizabeth. ''Come along, honey chil','' she soothed. ''Let your papa go and tend to his business. We've lots to do ourselves. But first, when we get to the house, I'll draw you a warm, comfortable bath. We'll get that saltwater washed clean outta yo' pores and hair. Then we'll see what we's can do to make your room pretty and delicate like you'se is.''

Understanding what Frannie was attempting to do, and appreciating the effort, Elizabeth smiled down at her. Then she looked sullenly over her shoulder at her father as he lumbered back toward his ship. He was in another world now—one that no longer included her.

Sometimes as a child, she could hardly bear moments like this. But now, all grown up, she had learned to bear anything. Even this move to a new land and a new life. She would cope, or die trying.

"Miss Elizabeth, we must hurry on to the house," Frannie encouraged, tugging on Elizabeth's arm. "You'll get a death of a chill. Bes' forget your papa for now. He'll check in on you from time to time. He promised, and Massa' Easton do keep his promises to his daughter."

Nodding, Elizabeth followed Frannie, half stumbling. The steep path leading up to the house was not a path at all. It was a maze of vines and briars, and it took all of Elizabeth's concentration to make her way through them. As the briars annoyingly grabbed her cape and pierced it, she jerked it free.

Ignoring Frannie's heaving breaths brought on by the climb, Elizabeth stubbornly moved onward, not wanting to look behind her again. Without looking, she knew that the shoreline was way below her now, the slap of the waves sounded like a great heartbeat, alive and threatening. She shivered as the hissing whine of the night wind swept about her, chilling her to the bone.

The fence now loomed high before her, morbid in its scrolled details and with its spikes lining the top. Behind it stood the mansion outlined against the moonlit sky, as if it were some dark, sinister monster ready to swallow her whole.

"Not to show disrespect to your papa, Miss Elizabeth, but I don't think I'm goin' to enjoy livin' in that house," Frannie said, suddenly clutching one of Elizabeth's hands. "It looks too ghostly to be lived in. How long has it been vacant?"

"I'm not sure," Elizabeth said, squeezing Frannie's

hand reassuredly. "But we must make the best of things, Frannie. We shall make this house a grand place in which to live."

She eased her hand from Frannie's. Her fingers trembled as she gave the gate a shove and it squeaked as it slowly opened. She gazed once again at the monstrosity of a house, then walked through the gate. Frannie hesitated behind her. Elizabeth ignored the other servants who had arrived at the house before them, hovering together at the foot of the steps.

"Come on, Frannie," she said softly. "Let's get this over with."

Frannie scurried to her side.

Elizabeth proceeded to walk toward the house, grimacing as she made her way through a thick tangle of trees and brambles. Her father had not said how long it had been since the house had been occupied, but it did seem to have been quite a long time.

Perhaps it should be even longer, she thought bitterly to herself. As far as she was concerned, she would as soon dive into a sea of sharks than live in this gloomy house.

Elizabeth stopped at the steps that led up to a leaning porch, and looked upward. She felt overwhelmed by the size of the house. The wind sounded lonely as it whistled around its corners. Shadows and silence seemed to close in on her. And then a shutter banged, causing her to start.

Swallowing back the fear building inside her, Elizabeth climbed the rickety steps and went to the massive wooden door with its ornate brass ornamentation, and found it ajar. With her heart pounding, she pushed the door open, squeaking hinges greeting her, echoing into the house.

Elizabeth and Frannie entered and searched for candles and matches. Elizabeth finally found a branch of candles on a table and lit several white tapers. She then looked slowly around her.

She was standing in a huge foyer that led to an ornately carved archway and down a broad, columned corridor that was broken at intervals by doors, and a wide, winding staircase that led upward to the second and third floors.

Elizabeth shuddered, feeling a sense of evil lurking inside the house. The corridor held too many dark shadows.

"This ain't a fit place to be," Frannie said, her eyes wide as she looked cautiously from side to side. "It ain't a place to be at all."

Elizabeth breathed shallowly. The house smelled dank and musty. The walls were paneled with dark wood. The beamed ceiling rose dim and high above her. The oaken floors were bare, and silky with age.

Determined not to let a mere house intimidate her, Elizabeth jerked her cape from around her shoulders and lay it across the back of a sheet-shrouded chair. Then she walked boldly toward the staircase, the skirt of her dress rustling in her haste.

"I ain't goin' up there," Frannie said, staring with fretful eyes up the dark staircase.

"Hogwash, Frannie," Elizabeth said, casting Frannie a quick glance over her shoulder. "Come on. Let's find a room that I can call mine."

Frannie hurried to Elizabeth's side. They ascended to the second floor, and walked slowly from room to room until they found one that was less dismal than the rest.

Yet even in this room the plaster had crumbled off the walls, showing the white laths behind it. The only furniture was an iron bedstead painted white, a nightstand on one side, and a washstand with a chipped China basin on the other. A cracked chamber pot peeked out from beneath the bed.

Frowning with distaste, Elizabeth went to the only window in the room. It was curtainless, small, and barred, and spotted on the outside with bird droppings. It looked out onto a gray gulley in the roof. Yet beyond, Elizabeth could see the estate grounds.

As she peered from the window, a movement from below, beneath a tree, drew her attention. She removed a handkerchief from her dress pocket and rubbed it over the pane of glass, removing enough of the filmy dust to enable her to see better.

Leaning closer, she peered intently toward the spot where she had seen the movement, thinking that perhaps it had been one of the servants exploring.

Again she saw movement beneath the trees, and with the aid of the bright moonlight, she was able to see that it was no one she knew. Her heart skipped a beat when she realized that she was staring down at an elderly Indian clutching a tall staff in his right hand.

"An Indian!" she gasped quietly, placing her hand to her throat, recalling the tales of the Indians' hatred for the house. She had hoped that those troubles would remain in the past.

Yet, it seemed not. Elizabeth watched, stunned at how quickly the Indian disappeared from sight.

"Who?" Frannie asked, edging close to Elizabeth, trying to also see from the window. "Who might you be seein', honey?"

"An Indian," Elizabeth stammered. "An old Indian. And he was carrying a staff."

Frannie gasped and placed her hands to her cheeks, her dark eyes wide with fear. "An Indian?" she cried. "Lord have mercy, Elizabeth. Has he come to take our scalps?"

"I don't know why he's here," Elizabeth murmured.

When she realized how frightened Frannie was, she turned to her and drew her into her arms. "It's best not to tell anyone about this,'' she softly warned. ''I don't need a whole household of servants too frightened to sleep at night.''

''You'd best tell your father,'' Frannie said, pulling away from Elizabeth. ''He'd do away with that Indian real quick like.''

''No, I'm not going to tell Father,'' Elizabeth said, turning to the window again. Her eyes scanned the land for signs of the Indian, yet didn't find any. ''No. Don't tell Father. He's got enough on his mind. Let me take care of this.''

''But how?'' Frannie cried. ''It's too dangerous! What if the Indian sets fire to the house?''

Elizabeth turned back to Frannie and took her hands. ''Frannie, if this Indian had wanted to burn the house down, he'd surely have done it long before we arrived,'' she said, her voice much calmer than her insides. She could not deny that she was afraid, yet she was also intrigued. Perhaps a little bit of excitement was what she needed to fill her days. She would try to find the mysterious Indian and discover why he was there.

3

If ever any beauty I did see,
Which I desired, and got,
'twas but a dream of thee.
—DONNE

The next day Elizabeth slipped into her dress of pale green cotton organdy with its embroidered designs of white lilies on the skirt. Her lovely breasts swelled above the low, round neckline.

Standing before a full-length mirror, she began pulling a hairbrush through her long red hair. She yawned. She had spent a restless night hearing creaking sounds in this strange house, and listening to the surf pounding against the walls of the bluff below her window.

Wondering again about the mysterious Indian, she turned and walked to the window. Raking her gaze across the land below her, searching again for any possible signs of the elderly Indian, she lowered her hairbrush to her side. She knew that she should be more afraid of the Indian's presence than she was, but for some reason she was more curious than frightened.

And he had seemed harmless enough. He was an elderly man, surely only wandering aimlessly about because he had nothing else to do.

Through the filmy haze on the window, Elizabeth peered into the distance, thinking that anything as beautiful as this land could mean nothing but a peaceful existence for its new inhabitants. She admired the forests of white pines and hardwood sweeping down the flanks of the mountains, and saw by the water, the dark green leaves of white birches trembling in the morning breeze.

She stretched onto her toes to look at the brilliant sunlight flickering on the waters of the Sound.

"My, oh, my, Elizabeth, I thought you were going to sleep the mornin' away," Frannie said, as she came into the bedroom. She puffed and fluttered around the bed, fussing over the blankets. "Honey, you'd best get yo'self downstairs and get a warm breakfast. This mausoleum of a house makes one's bones ache somethin' fierce."

Elizabeth turned a warm smile to Frannie and lay her hairbrush on the nightstand beside the bed. "Frannie, it's still early," she said, securing her hair back from her face with a pale green satin ribbon. "What did you do? Get up at the crack of dawn?"

"Earlier than that," Frannie said, giving Elizabeth a frown. "The noises in this place kept my eyes wide open mos' the night. I'm sure the house is haunted, Elizabeth. You watch yo'self. Somethin' might grab you as you go explorin' from room to room."

Elizabeth giggled as she swung away from the window and began walking toward the door. "Frannie, you seem to have survived the morning without being assaulted by ghosts," she teased. "And I would wager that you have already been in all of the rooms, cleaning. It's not like you to let anything go long without a thorough dusting."

Frannie pulled the last of the blankets up over the plumped-up pillows. Then she went to Elizabeth and gave her a soft swat on her behind just as Elizabeth started to step out into the corridor.

"Get on with you," Frannie said, chuckling. "And I must admit, honey chil', you'll soon see that things don't look all that bad. Now that I've seen the rooms in the daylight, with the sunshine comin' in at all of the windows, and with the dustcovers removed from the furniture, I think we can be comfortable enough here. The furniture is plush and the hardwood floors will be beautiful once they get a good polishing.'' She clasped her hands. ''And the rooms is grand.''

Frannie then thrust her hands inside her apron pockets. ''But it's still too cold for my liking,'' she said, giving a glance toward the marble-faced fireplace in the room. ''But once we get all of the fireplaces goin' with a fire, I'm sure it'll soon be warm enough.''

Elizabeth gave Frannie a hug. ''Frannie, you know that you'd be happy anywhere as long as you had a roof over your head and me to spoil,'' she said, laughing softly. ''I love you, Frannie. I don't know what I would have done without you after . . . after Mother left.''

Frannie patted Elizabeth's back. ''Now, now,'' she murmured. ''Let's not get to talkin' about your mother. She's a part of your past. Let it go, honey. Let it go.''

Elizabeth stepped away from Frannie. She nervously ran her hands down the skirt of her dress. ''Just when I think I have forgotten her, she's back on my mind again,'' she said cheerlessly. ''I have never given up hope that Mother would return and my life would be normal again. But that is such a hopeless thought—I must stop thinking it.''

''Yes'm, you must,'' Frannie said, then placed her chubby hands at Elizabeth's tiny waist and led her into the corridor. ''Now you go on and eat some breakfast. There are plenty of eggs, bacon, and biscuits. And I unpacked a jar of honey just for you. That'll sweeten your thoughts if nothin' else will.''

Elizabeth turned and planted a quick kiss on Frannie's cheek. ''You're such a dear,'' she said, then bounced down the staircase.

When she reached the first floor, she was amazed at how much of the mustiness of the house had already cleared. The house now smelled of clean linens and furniture polish.

Before going to the kitchen to eat, Elizabeth went

from room to room, smiling when she saw how Frannie had already made them presentable, even inviting. Even the shadows seemed to be lifting.

And Frannie had been right. The furniture was plush. And someone had paid a lot of money for the fancy tapestries that hung along the walls with the many gilt-framed portraits.

Elizabeth then went to the library and stopped short, appalled by the array of horns bristling on the far wall, overwhelming the rows of books that lined the room on three sides.

As Elizabeth looked slowly from horn to horn, she recognized those of the deer, antelope, and longhorn steer. Then she paled and placed a hand to her throat when her gaze found a perfect specimen of a bobcat. It was perched on a stand, as if ready to pounce on her.

She grimaced, thinking that the taxidermist who had prepared this animal for viewing had been quite skilled and exact. The eyes of the animal were gleaming into hers, and its sharp teeth were glisteningly white and bared.

She could not help but feel threatened by this room that reeked of death and danger, so she fled to the parlor and felt no less unnerved. No matter how much Frannie had tried, this room retained its mustiness, the sweet fragrance of the furniture polish unable to overcome the stale aroma of cigar smoke and smell of mildew that hung heavily in the air.

"This won't do," Elizabeth said. "This won't do at all."

She walked briskly to first one window, and then the next, lifting them open so that the room could have an airing.

A brisk, chilly breeze blew in, ruffling her dress and the bow in her hair. She hugged herself, shivering.

Yet she did not want to close the windows until the

room smelled better. So she turned and eyed the fire-place. Wood was stacked neatly on its grate, old and yellowed newspapers wadded between the logs, to be used to help start the fire.

"That's what I'll do. I'll build a fire," she whispered to herself. "That might also help lift the rank odor from the room."

Spying matches on a table, Elizabeth picked up a few and took them to the fireplace. She knelt down before the hearth and struck a match and held the flickering flame to the newspapers until several of them caught fire. Then she stood, patiently waiting for the flames to ignite the logs.

Once they did, she turned to go get the breakfast that awaited her.

But she didn't get far. She was stopped by billows of smoke quickly filling the room. The smoke from the fire wasn't drawing up the chimney. Instead, it was escaping into the room in great puffs of black.

Elizabeth realized that the chimney must be clogged with something, more than likely a bird's nest. Her eyes burned from the smoke. Her throat was closing up with it.

Coughing and choking, she tried to feel her way to the door that led to the corridor, to escape to the outside. But before she reached the door, her hand touched something—*someone*.

Startled, she looked up and peered through the screen of smoke and found herself face-to-face with an Indian. And it was not just any Indian. Nor was it the elderly Indian that she had seen the previous night.

This Indian was handsome. His piercing steel-gray eyes mesmerized her as he stared back at her with what seemed as much surprise at seeing her, as she had at seeing him.

Her sight swept quickly over him, seeing how muscled he was in his clinging buckskin attire, and how tall he was.

Her gaze returned to his face. She was struck speechless by his handsomeness. She had heard that there was such a thing as love at first sight, in which one look weds two souls in everlasting devotion. She wondered if she was now experiencing such a phenomenon.

He *was* causing strange sensations to flood her insides.

Stunned by her reaction to the Indian and where her thoughts had taken her, Elizabeth remembered the past history of the house. How the Indians had obviously hated it.

She took a quick step away from the Indian, his handsomeness not enough to quell her fear of him.

"Who are you?" she managed to ask. "Why are you here?"

Strong Heart was shocked, having never expected to find a lady in the house. From a nearby high bluff he had watched the activity on the beach. He had seen the moored ship, and several white men erecting some sort of building on the beach. He had thought that all of the white men were there, having not suspected that someone else might be here—in the *house*.

When he had looked toward the house and had seen the smoke billowing from the windows, his first thought was of his grandfather, and that he may have finally found him. His grandfather could have set fire to the house to keep the intruders on the beach from living in the old house that sat on the hallowed grounds of the Suquamish. Strong Heart knew that many years ago some of his ancestors had tried to burn the house down, but white people had stopped them by slaughtering them.

Since then, none of Strong Heart's people had tried to rid the land of the house. They had found peace and harmony elsewhere, on land far from this place of death and sadness.

Only recently had Strong Heart become acquainted with the house and grounds, when he had returned to search for his missing grandfather. But the house had been empty the other times Strong Heart had gone through it.

Now it seemed it was lived in again.

And, he thought to himself, the house was now inhabited by someone as entrancing as the roses that grew wild in the forests.

The woman's hair was as red as the most lovely of the wild roses. Her eyes were as green as the grass that blanketed the earth and the sides of the bluffs. Her cheeks were as pink as the interior of the conch shell that could be found along the shores of the Sound.

He looked down, seeing the swell of her breasts and the way they were heaving. She seemed to fear him. That he regretted, for he had not come to harm her. Nor would he ever.

She was not the sort of woman any man could harm.

His gaze lifted and he saw such innocence in her eyes and delicate face.

Then his mind returned to sanity. He must ensure his safety. Fearing that the white men on the beach might also be drawn to the house by the smoke, and not wanting to be seen there, Strong Heart knew that he must leave.

But first he would remove the lovely lady from the smoky house, no matter that her mere presence on this hallowed ground should anger him.

When would the white people ever realize that this land could never belong to anyone but the beloved dead of the Suquamish? When would they ever realize they desecrated this land?

But having fought this battle inside his heart more times than he wanted to count, and never winning,

Strong Heart cast the sorrowful thoughts from his mind and whisked Elizabeth up into his arms and carried her outside to the porch.

Breathless, and aghast at what the handsome Indian had done, Elizabeth pushed at his chest. "Let me go," she cried. "What on earth do you think you're doing?"

Strong Heart didn't set her to her feet right away. Instead, he stood there and stared at her face. Elizabeth swallowed hard, wondering if he was going to carry her away, and hold her captive, perhaps even for ransom.

And then suddenly Strong Heart released her and fled into the deep shadows of the forest.

Elizabeth was breathless from the experience, in wonder at this Indian who had appeared out of nowhere, and who had left just as quickly and mysteriously.

And it was obvious that he had meant her no harm. He had actually carried her from the house.

Had he thought that it was on fire, she wondered? Had he thought that he was saving her?

She wanted to run after him and demand that he tell her why he was there, and why he had felt the need to rush away so quickly.

But she did not have the opportunity.

Her father was suddenly there, winded from running.

"Good Lord, Elizabeth," Earl said, gasping for breath. "I saw the smoke. I thought . . . I thought—"

"No, Father, the house isn't on fire," Elizabeth said, interrupting him. "I'm sure it's just a faulty flue. I imagine a bird's nest. I wouldn't be surprised if all of the flues aren't the same." She laughed softly. "Imagine how Frannie will be fussing over the damage the smoke has done to the parlor."

"To hell with the parlor," Earl said, wiping beads

of sweat from his brow. "Just as long as you're all right."

"I assure you I am just fine," Elizabeth said. Her heart was pounding recklessly within her chest, but not from danger. It pounded from the excitement of having been with the Indian, even if for only a few moments.

"I'm damn glad that everything is okay," Earl said. Then he shifted his feet nervously, his eyes not meeting hers. "Baby, I . . . uh . . . was coming to the house for another reason," he said with a stammer. "I've got several dependable men working on the fishery. I feel that I can leave for a spell without being here to oversee every nail pounded into wood . . ."

Before he could finish, a stocky man, with brindled sidewhiskers, sporting huge pistols holstered at each hip, came and stood beside Earl.

Earl swung an arm around the man's hefty shoulder. "Elizabeth, this is Morris Murdoch. You know. I've talked about him often enough. He's my partner in the fishery venture," he said, a smug smile across his face. He nodded at Morris. "Morris, this is my daughter, Elizabeth. Isn't she everything I bragged about?"

"And even more than that," Morris said in a flat drawl. He cocked his wide-brimmed hat aggressively at Elizabeth, then reached out to shake hands with her. "Pleased to meet you, Ma'am."

Elizabeth stared down at Morris Murdoch's huge pistols, stiffened, then looked up at him as she reluctantly shook his hand. When he released it, she wiped her palm on the skirt of her dress. Morris's hand had been so clammy and cold.

She nodded at him, not wanting to say that she was pleased to meet him, for, in truth, she wasn't. She *had* heard her father speak often of Morris Murdoch, ever since her father had chosen Seattle for his fishery.

But this was the first time she had met him and she could not help but take an instant dislike to him. A tall man, surely over six feet in height, he had eyes of a peculiar shade of blue that glinted menacingly down at her.

She could not help but equate such eyes with those of a killer. Then she shrugged off such a thought. She knew her father would not align himself with a man of questionable reputation.

"Elizabeth, what I was saying, is that I'm too eager to wait any longer before going to speak to the Indians," Earl said, interrupting her wary thoughts. "Morris and I are going to leave now, to talk business with the Indians—*salmon* business."

Elizabeth gasped at the news as she turned her eyes back to her father. First he had dumped her on these faraway shores, and now he was going to travel to unknown territories, leaving her alone, waiting to see if he returned alive or dead.

She feared that he might not return one day from his reckless adventures. This could be the time, the worst time of all for her to be left without a father. Without a protector.

But she was silent. She had said all that was possible that could be said to such a father. She would have to wait again to see what fate handed him—and in turn, her.

She watched disbelievingly as Everett, their black groom, brought two saddled horses to the outside of the fence, dutifully holding them by the reins at the gate. Bulging saddlebags were on each of the horses. Her father was leaving her so soon, and she knew that he planned to be gone for several days and nights.

An emptiness filled her, the same feeling that she had always felt at her father's departure on his lengthy journeys.

Earl turned and followed Elizabeth's stare, then

smiled when he saw the readied horses. "Ah, I see that my orders have been promptly followed," he said, glancing over at Morris. "Are you ready to ride, Morris?"

"Anytime," Morris said, his voice a silken, lazy drawl which rankled Elizabeth's nerves.

Earl turned back to Elizabeth and took her hand in his. "Baby, please understand why I must leave," he said. Elizabeth recognized the words he always spoke before heading out on an adventure. "It's business, Elizabeth. Business."

He cleared his throat nervously when he saw her set jaw and her eyes fill with defiance.

"I'll be gone for several days," he said, releasing her hand, not wanting to feel her reaction when he gave her a particular order that he knew that she would resent. "Elizabeth, I don't want you leaving the premises under any circumstances while I am gone, unless escorted by one of the servants. Do you hear?"

Elizabeth tilted her chin stubbornly, not wanting to give him the satisfaction of agreeing to anything he asked of her at this moment.

And what did it matter to him, anyway, she wondered. Surely if something happened to her he would be better off. He would be free to do as he damn well pleased without having to offer awkward apologies or explanations to anyone.

She knew that she should have told him about having seen the two Indians, but she was glad now that she hadn't. She had something of her own that she could keep from her father. The secret about the Indians.

No. She would not tell him anything. He didn't deserve knowing her secrets—intriguing secrets that she could fill her lonely hours with. She would search for both Indians, to see why they were on the property that was now owned by her father. Although she knew that she might be placing herself in danger, she felt an excitement that she had never felt before at the thought of seeing the handsome Indian again.

"I understand your silence," Earl said. He looked with wavering eyes at his daughter for a moment longer, then spun around and walked hurriedly to the horses.

Flicking a tear from the corner of her eye with a finger, Elizabeth watched her father and Morris ride away on their horses. She watched them until they were no longer in sight. Then she looked with interest at the dark, silent forest. She quickly decided that this was the perfect opportunity to go exploring, hoping to find clues as to where the Indians had come from, and why—especially the young Indian.

Frannie came lumbering from the house, coughing and wiping at her dark eyes. "There you is," she said, moving to Elizabeth's side. "Lordy, lordy, I neva' thought I'd eva' get that room cleared of smoke. That fireplace needs a cleanin' bad. Don't neva' lights a fire in it again, honey, until we sees that it's cleaned first."

Elizabeth laughed softly. "I don't think you have to worry about that," she said, again studying the forest. The chill of the morning breeze caused goosebumps to rise on her flesh, as well as the apprehension she felt at wandering alone where she knew that she shouldn't. She shivered.

Frannie placed a chubby hand on Elizabeth's arm. "Come back inside the house," she said, trying to move Elizabeth along. She tilted a heavy, gray eyebrow up at Elizabeth when she refused to budge. "Elizabeth, honey. You come in the house. You gonna catch a chill standing out here without a wrap."

"I'm fine," Elizabeth said, easing from Frannie's grip. She gazed down at her sweet and caring friend. "I'm going exploring, Frannie. This is my new home—one that has been forced upon me, so it is my decision to acquaint myself with it and the grounds that surround it. I can't be expected to sit in that dreadful house every day and night, rotting away doing nothing.''

"You ain't goin' nowheres," Frannie fussed, again grabbing Elizabeth's arm, " 'cept in the house with me, where you belongs.''

Elizabeth detached her hand again. "Frannie, I'm not going inside the house until I'm good and ready," she said stubbornly. "I'm going exploring. That's final!''

"It ain't safe," Frannie grumbled. "It just ain't safe for a young lady to be wanderin' alone away from home. If you insist on goin', then ol' Frannie goes with you.''

"No, Frannie, you're not," Elizabeth argued, her patience running thin. "But you can go and fetch my shawl. It's apt to be much colder in the forest than here. I would prefer my wrap, if you please.''

"If you please," Frannie echoed, angrily folding her arms across her thick bosom. "If you do as I please, you'd stay here with me and not out there where Indians can take your pretty hair from your scalp.''

Elizabeth paled somewhat at these words, having read many novels in which Indian scalpings had been described in gory detail. But all that she had to do was remember the handsome Indian, and his gentle arms and eyes, to know that she surely had nothing to fear from him.

Especially being scalped!

"I'll get my wrap myself," Elizabeth said, wanting to end this debate with Frannie.

"There ain't no need in that," Frannie said, sighing resignedly. "I'll fetch it. But mark my word, Elizabeth, if you don't get back home when I'm expectin' you to, I'se comin' after you. Does you understand?''

Elizabeth placed a gentle hand to Frannie's fleshy cheek. "Yes, I understand," she said, filled with much love and gratitude for this woman who had become a substitute mother to her. "I'll try not to stay long. I don't want to worry you."

"Huh! If you don't want to worry me none, you stay home with me," Frannie said, then shook her head and marched inside the house for the shawl. When she saw the stubbornness in Elizabeth's eyes, she knew that it was useless to argue with her. She had never seen anyone as stubborn as Elizabeth, except perhaps Elizabeth's mother. Now that was one redheaded stubborn woman who knew her mind better than she should have. She had walked away from her daughter because of her stubbornnesses.

Frannie took the shawl back outside to Elizabeth and devotedly placed it around her shoulders. She then watched with a heavy heart as Elizabeth began making her way through the brambles that stretched out across the lawn to the grotesque fence. She watched Elizabeth until she was out of sight. Then she moved back inside the house, unable to shake a feeling of doom that seemed to have suddenly come over her. She wanted to run after Elizabeth and beg her to return to the safety of the house, yet she knew that would be a futile attempt.

Frannie had to accept that although Elizabeth loved her, the child had her own mind and would do as she wanted, for, in truth, Frannie was only Elizabeth's maid, not her keeper.

Holding her shawl securely around her shoulders, Elizabeth moved into the deeper gloom of the forest, where the musty aroma of rotted leaves arose to her nose, stinging the tender flesh of her nostrils. She looked guardedly from side to side, everything too eerily quiet, as if she had stepped into a tomb. Except for herself, there seemed to be no life in this section of the forest. No birds sang and no squirrels scampered about collecting acorns for the long, cold winter vigil that was just ahead. She felt as if she might be intruding on some deep, dark secret, and that the trees surrounding her resented her presence.

She saw a break in the trees up ahead, which could mean that she had reached the Sound. Welcoming anything besides what she had found so far in her explorations, Elizabeth hurried her pace. As the sunshine began spiraling more vividly through the umbrella of trees overhead, and she could see even more light just up ahead, she began softly running toward the opening.

But when she finally reached the cleared land, where the sun drenched its warmth on all sides of her, what Elizabeth saw made her heart leap into her throat, and her mouth go dry. She stopped and stared at the many posts that had been driven into the ground, skulls topping each one of them, their eye sockets all facing her, as if looking at her accusingly.

Finding the courage to move again, Elizabeth edged her way around the skull-crowned posts, her heart pounding.

As she circled the hideous sight, she was able to think more clearly. She guessed that she had just found the graveyard of some Indians—burial grounds she may have desecrated by her intrusion. Burial grounds that were much, much too close to her house for comfort.

Breathing harshly, Elizabeth turned and fled onward, toward the welcome sight of a grass-covered bluff that overlooked the Sound. When she arrived there, she tried to blot the horrible sight of the skulls from her mind by looking at the beauty of the view.

She stepped closer to the edge of the bluff, gazing down at the thundering surf. But there was something foreboding in the rhythm of the waves and their steady splashing seemed for a moment to mesmerize, then disorient her. She found herself weaving, feeling as if she were going to fall. Then she cried out with alarm when she felt strong hands on her waist, stopping her.

When those powerful hands drew Elizabeth away from the edge of the bluff and turned her around, she was stunned to find herself again looking up into the steel-gray eyes of the handsome Indian. Although she knew that she should be wary of him, a stranger—she could not deny that being near him again made her heart take on a crazy, erratic beating.

His hands on her waist were like fire, scorching her clothing, burning her flesh.

Elizabeth shivered from the boldness of his hold. Then she found the strength to speak to him. "Thank you for stopping my fall," she murmured. She glanced down at his hands which still held her, then looked up at him. "You can let me go. I'm . . . I'm safe enough now. I've regained my balance."

"Your husband is *pel-ton,* foolish, to allow you to move about alone on land that is not familiar to you," Strong Heart finally said, scowling down at her from his tall height. "Does your husband not know about the bandit gangs and warrior bands that are known to roam the forests and the unguarded valleys? These men stop at nothing to get their pleasures and lusts fulfilled."

Elizabeth cast her eyes downward, her face coloring with a hot blush.

Then she boldly lifted her chin and met his steady stare with one of her own. "I'll have you know that I answer to no husband, because I have none. And under normal circumstances I am capable of taking care of myself," she blurted. "Furthermore, I have the right to wander on property that is owned by my father. Why are *you* here? Do you make it a habit to trespass, to go where you do not belong?"

When he did not answer her, she saw anger in his eyes, which changed quickly to pain. She wished that

she could erase all that she had just said. Again she
reminded herself that this land had once belonged
solely to the Indians. This man's very ancestors might
have lived here.

In truth, she was the intruder. In truth, all white
people were the intruders.

"I'm sorry for being so abrupt . . . so thoughtless,"
she said in a rush of words. "Please allow me to once
more thank you for being so caring that you would
rescue me twice in one day."

Strong Heart was surprised that the white woman
had apologized for having spoken harshly to him. She
seemed to be a lady with compassion.

And he could not deny that he was glad that she was
not married. Although he saw her as an interloper on
what was once his people's land, he could not stop his
eyes from devouring her loveliness.

Her luminous green eyes stirred feelings within him
that he had willed himself to ignore when in the presence of women whose beauty captivated him. His goal
in life was to prepare himself to be a great chief, like
his father. A commitment to one woman had been the
last thing on Strong Heart's mind.

It still was, yet the longer he was with this intriguing
woman, the more he felt his reserve weakening.

Then he remembered the reason he had come to the
bluff. It had been to watch the white men who had
gone to the house to check on the smoke. When they
had left on horseback, he feared they had gone after
him. Surely this woman had told them about him. Yet
they had traveled away from the mansion and the
Sound, as if not in search of him but something else.

"Did you tell those two men that I was at the
house?" he asked quickly.

"No, I did not see the need," Elizabeth said slowly,
not sure if she should trust him enough to be this

truthful with him. She still did not know his intentions. She feared to ask him.

What if he was there scouting the place, to take back the news to his people that there were white people who should be slaughtered and a house to be burned?

What if she was falling into a trap by innocently befriending him?

Her father had always told her that she was the sort who trusted too easily.

At this, Strong Heart arched an eyebrow, again surprised by her. "Why did you not see the need?" he asked, watching her expression. "Did you not see me as the enemy?"

"How could I see you as the enemy when only a short while ago you thought you were saving me from a house that was on fire. And now? To have rescued me from a fall?" she offered quietly. She swallowed hard. "As for why I did not tell my father, I . . . I . . . am not quite sure, myself."

Frannie's voice reached up to the bluff and broke the spell that had captured Elizabeth and Strong Heart, causing Elizabeth to jump. She turned away from Strong Heart to peer down at the old house whose roof towered high above the treetops, knowing that it was best that Frannie didn't see this new Indian. She had been too upset over the other Indian the night before.

Her eyes wide with the wonder of having met the young Indian again, Elizabeth turned back to question him, but he had fled into the forest. Then she heard a horse's hoofbeats, and knew that the Indian was gone. She realized she had missed her chance to find out who he and the elderly Indian were, and why they were there. Apparently Frannie's voice had frightened him away. Perhaps she would never see him again, and that filled her with regret. She had not had the chance to tell him why she was there, or what her father was constructing on the beach.

She decided it was for the best. She did not know what his reaction would be if he ever found out. She feared that no Indian would be happy to know that her father was going to interfere in their lives for his own personal gain.

She then recalled the horrid skulls perched atop the poles. Perhaps she had found the graveyard of this handsome Indian's ancestors.

Frannie's voice called to Elizabeth again, this time filled with anxiety. Elizabeth fled from the bluff and hurried through the forest, avoiding the burial site, and, breathless, met Frannie at the fringes of the forest.

"Elizabeth Easton, I told you not to stay in the forest so long," Frannie scolded as they walked toward the house together. "You done went and frightened ol' Frannie outta ten years of her life! You ain't goin' alone into the forest again. No sir, honey chil'. Neva' again!"

Elizabeth listened patiently, yet not hearing, for her thoughts were on the Indian. She could not help but feel that something unspoken had passed between them, and somehow, some way, she had to find out exactly what.

She went back inside the house, and Frannie followed, still chastising her.

4

Her face, it bloomed like a sweet flower
And stole my heart away complete.
—JOHN CLARE

Another long night of restless sleep had passed. Bored
and frustrated, Elizabeth had a buggy readied, and
ignoring Frannie's pleadings against journeying away
from the house again alone, she was now traveling
toward Seattle, to acquaint herself with the city. As
the horse trotted in a leisurely fashion along the dirt
road, the sun shone brilliantly in the midmorning sky.
Elizabeth sat comfortably on a cushion in her buggy,
the brim of her lace-trimmed bonnet shading her
eyes.

The day was warm. The air was perfumed by roses
and wild flowers blooming alongside the road. A mon-
arch butterfly drifted past overhead, riding a south
wind. The white branches of sycamores broke the
dense green foliage of the towering hardwood forest,
and a symphony of birdcalls pervaded the leafy halls.

Elizabeth smiled, thinking that this day, indeed, was
perfect for an outing. Yes, it *was* another day. Another
adventure!

She had been torn between whether to return to the
bluff and, perhaps, meet the Indian again, or to go on
into Seattle and see the sights.

She had decided to take advantage of her father's
absence while she could, and had chosen Seattle for
this day's explorations. Anyway, she scoffed at the
thought of the Indian reappearing, especially after he
had fled so quickly the previous day.

Twice he had disappeared as if no more than a mysterious apparition. He would surely not materialize all that quickly again—for her or anyone else.

"In time," she whispered to herself, "I surely *shall* see him again. In time. For he *was* real—*very* real!"

And what she had seen in his eyes told her that he had been as intrigued by her as she had been by him.

Foreign feelings that felt oddly delicious swept through her as she recalled her two encounters with him, being so near to him . . .

Lifting the reins, and slapping them against the back of the gentle mare, Elizabeth urged her horse to hurry onward, anxious now to get to Seattle. She had not been able to see all that much from the ship's deck, but from afar it had been lovely. She knew to not expect it to be any sort of paradise, for its reputation was not that much better than San Francisco's. She knew she would find many saloons, and wild and rough men lounging outside them, and also the bright skirts and painted faces of fallen women.

She feared none of it. She had learned to cope with almost anything while living in San Francisco. In truth, nothing much was left to shock, or frighten her.

A turn in the road brought the horse and buggy alongside the Sound, the rocky beach only a slight drop from the road. Elizabeth squinted her eyes against the glare of the sun as it shone brightly in the water.

Something drew her attention to the water, and what she saw gave her cause to straighten her back.

It was the strange sight of a young woman walking into the waters of the Sound. Elizabeth wondered why the woman seemed so intent on wading this morning, fully clothed. She was looking straight ahead, her gait determined.

And although the day was warm, Elizabeth realized the water had to be cold. No one in their right mind would go wading today. No one in their right mind would go wading *any* time in their clothes, whether it was summer, *or* autumn.

Elizabeth knew in a flash what the woman's intention was. She was going to walk until there was no bottom. She was planning to kill herself by drowning.

Elizabeth tightened the reins and drew her horse to a quick halt. She tossed her shawl aside as she scrambled from the buggy. Running toward the water, she began waving her hands and shouting at the young woman, who ignored her.

At the water's edge, Elizabeth shivered as the breeze blew damply against her face, her heart thumping inside her chest as she watched the woman go farther. Then she suddenly dropped out of view, her body now immersed in the water.

"Good Lord!" Elizabeth said, paling. "I've got to do something!"

She untied her bonnet and threw it aside. Without thinking about the danger, or the cold temperature, she began running into the water.

When she reached the deeper depths, Elizabeth began swimming steadily toward the victim. The woman was now splashing around, screaming for help, having suddenly changed her mind about wanting to die. She screamed and floundered wildly in the water, calling out that she could not swim.

Elizabeth reached the woman and tried to grab her, to tow her back to land. The young woman panicked and desperately clawed at Elizabeth, her eyes wild with fright.

Elizabeth tried to fight off the woman, realizing that if she allowed her to get a firm grip in her struggles to be saved, she would, instead, pull both of them to their deaths.

But the young woman's fear gave her frightening strength. She succeeded at wrapping her arms around

Elizabeth's neck, pulling her beneath the water with her.

Swallowing great gulps of water, Elizabeth fought harder so that at least *she* could get back to the surface. Already her lungs felt as though they were going to burst. She felt light-headed, as if at any moment she might pass out. She was losing the battle of survival.

Suddenly Elizabeth was aware of a third person in the water beside her. She felt, and welcomed, strong arms around her waist. She and the other young woman were drawn to the surface.

Elizabeth clung to the muscular arm that held her in place against a hard body. She coughed and spewed water from her mouth, until she could breathe. Her eyes cleared of their watery haze.

When she turned to see who was holding her safely from the depths of the Sound, she was stunned.

"You!" she managed to gasp, her voice weak from her ordeal. "Again, it . . . is . . . you who saved me?"

Strong Heart was just as stunned to see whom he had rescued from drowning.

The same woman that he had carried from the house that was smoking, but strangely not burning.

The same woman he had saved from toppling from the high bluff into the Sound.

It seemed to him that she was the most accident-prone person that he had ever encountered.

And he wondered if it was fate that caused him to rescue her again.

He gazed into Elizabeth's eyes, ignoring the other woman.

Yet that one, the total stranger, did seem to be the most helpless of the two as she clung to his arm with a wild desperation.

Still his attention remained on Elizabeth. "Are you all right?" he asked softly. "Are you able to swim to shore?"

"Yes, I'm sure that I can," Elizabeth said, nodding anxiously. She trembled, now quite aware of how cold she was. It felt as if she were immersed in a tub of ice water.

She glanced over at the young woman, remembering what she had shouted while flailing her arms in the water. "*I* can swim to shore," she quickly said. "But this young lady will need your assistance. She can't swim. Please take her to shore. I shall be right behind you."

"*Kloshe*, well enough," Strong Heart said, releasing his hold on Elizabeth. He noticed the blue tint of her lips, now realizing the cold temperature of the water. "But *hy-ak*, hurry. It is *me-sah-chie*, bad, to stay in the water much longer. Go to shore. I shall lend you and the woman a blanket to warm you."

"Thank you," Elizabeth said. "That would be very kind of you."

She was already swimming alongside him, yet found it hard to keep up with him. Although slowed from transporting the woman, this handsome Indian's strong body seemed unaffected by its burden. In a matter of moments he would be on dry land.

Elizabeth envied the woman, and how the Indian held so possessively to her as he took her to shore. Elizabeth recalled the strength of his arms, having now been held three times in their steely grip. If not for the emergency of each of these times, she could look upon them as sheer heaven. This was how the Indian affected her—as no other man had, in her entire life.

Glad to have finally reached shore, Elizabeth rose shakily to her feet and stumbled out of the water. The breeze nipped at her wet flesh like clawing, icy fingers and her wet dress clung to her, causing her to shake and tremble.

Strong Heart thought her just as lovely soaking wet, as dry. His loins stirred as his gaze moved from her enchanting eyes and face, to her breasts that were so evident under the wet dress. He could even see the outline of her dark nipples, and he had to look away, for he could not help but want to possess such breasts with his lips and tongue.

He cast such thoughts aside, knowing that this was not the time, or the place, if there ever would be one.

Elizabeth glanced over at the young woman, seeing how purple her lips were, and how she was shivering uncontrollably herself from the chill.

Elizabeth went to the frail young woman, thinking her perhaps only sixteen years old, yet well grown for her age. Her large swell of breasts heaved as she breathed hard and coughed into her hands. "Everything is going to be all right now," Elizabeth tried to reassure her, glad when the young woman gave her a flicker of a smile.

Elizabeth wanted to ask the young woman why she had tried to kill herself, but the Indian was there suddenly with his offering of blankets. He slipped one around Elizabeth's trembling shoulders, and then the young woman's.

Clutching the blanket closely around her, Elizabeth smiled up at him, and again thanked him. It seemed that he was giving her many reasons to repay him for his kindnesses. She wondered how this could ever be possible.

Strong Heart stood over Elizabeth, and their eyes met. "Do you think you can get home all right?" he asked, a hint of amusement in the depths of his intriguing, gray eyes. "You have yet to prove that you are capable of taking care of yourself. You did say that you were able to, did you not, after I saved you from falling from the bluff?"

Elizabeth was embarrassed by his teasing, yet more relieved at him having been there again for her. And though she was captivated by him more than ever, she knew that she must return home quickly for a change to warm clothes. She was already tempting fate by lingering even this long drenched to the skin.

Pneumonia was the last way she wanted to spend her time in this land that now held such a fascination for her.

Not the *land*, she corrected herself. The man. The Indian.

"I can make it home just fine, thank you," she said politely, swallowing hard as he continued giving her a quiet, lingering stare.

Then he spoke slowly and eloquently to her. "When a favor is shown a white man, he feels it in his head and his tongue speaks," he said. "When a kindness is shown to an Indian, he feels it in his heart and the heart has no tongue."

He gazed at her a moment longer, then turned and walked away from her, leaving as abruptly as he had the other times.

Shaking from both the chill and her latest encounter with the handsome Indian, Elizabeth watched him ride away on a lovely roan horse. Yes, he was mysterious, but not at all dangerous.

He had proven more than once that he was a compassionate, caring man—and ah, so exquisitely handsome!

Then she wondered about his riding a horse. The Indians around Seattle were known as 'canoe Indians,' for most of their travel was done by canoe.

And, again she wondered about his name. Why did she always forget to ask him his name?

The young woman's coughs drew Elizabeth's thoughts from the Indian. Seeing that the young woman was as cold as herself, she went to her.

"Allow me to take you home," she offered. "You should get out of those wet things as quickly as possible."

Dark brown eyes, veiled with even darker, thick lashes, peered up at Elizabeth, tears springing forth in each. "I . . . I . . . have no place to go," the young woman said, a sob escaping from her throat.

Elizabeth was not surprised by this confession, realizing that anyone who had chosen to take their own life could not have a loving home with caring parents. It was plain and simple: She was alone.

"I'm sorry," Elizabeth soothed, placing a comforting arm around the younger woman's shoulders. "Then come along with me. I shall share my home with you. We shall both get into warm clothes and Frannie will prepare bowls of soup for us. Soon we shall forget about ever being in that dreadful, cold water."

The woman's eyes wavered. "I'm not sure if I should," she said, in hardly more than a whisper. "I . . . I . . . don't want to intrude."

"I insist that you come with me," Elizabeth said, guiding the girl by an elbow to her horse and buggy.

After the buggy was turned around and headed back toward home, and blankets were wrapped not only around their shoulders but also their laps, Elizabeth studied the young woman.

"Do you want to talk about it?" she blurted out. "Do you want to tell me why you had decided to end your life? Surely you have someone, somewhere, that cares about what happens to you."

"Yes, I do have someone," the young woman replied. "But not here. My parents live in San Francisco."

Elizabeth's eyebrows shot up. "Then why on earth are you here in Seattle?" she asked, glancing at the road, then again at the woman.

"I was wrong to come," she whispered, casting her eyes downward in shame. "Had I known . . . had I known . . . what I know now, I never would have come."

"Known what?" Elizabeth prodded. "What happened to make you leave home, and then want to kill yourself? Did someone take advantage of you? Is that it?"

"In a sense, yes," the young woman said, nodding.

There was a brief pause. Then Elizabeth reached a hand to the young woman and took her hand. "Well, no one is going to take advantage of you again," she reassured. "I'll see to that. You can stay with me as long as you wish. We've plenty of room, and I'm new in these parts and quite lonesome."

"You'd do that for me?" the young woman gasped. "You'd be that kind?"

"It'd be my pleasure," Elizabeth said, not venturing to guess what her father would think about bringing a total stranger into the house. He was never home to lodge a complaint, anyway. "My name is Elizabeth Easton," she offered, smiling at the young woman. "Care to tell me yours?"

"Maysie," she said softly. "Just Maysie."

"No last name?" Elizabeth asked, again raising an eyebrow.

"Not one I feel free to use right yet," Maysie said, giving Elizabeth a cautious glance. "Please just call me Maysie."

"All right, Maysie," Elizabeth said. She patted Maysie's hand. "But one day I hope you'll tell me everything." She paused, then added, "Like where you've been living since you left San Francisco, and who has put such fear in your heart."

Maysie ducked her head and swallowed hard, then turned blinking, apologetic eyes to Elizabeth, as though what she wanted to tell her was too shameful to share.

Strong Heart rode onward to the outer fringes of Seattle. He made his way up the butte to his camp where he could continue to watch and study the activity at Copper Hill Prison below.

After securing his horse where it could graze peacefully beneath a towering oak tree, Strong Heart changed into dry buckskins. He was disappointed that he had not found his grandfather, yet he had not actually thought that he would. The old Indian was too elusive for his own good, it seemed. So tomorrow he would go for Four Winds.

But tonight he would think about the lady whose name he had not asked. It would have allowed her to ask too many questions about him, and he had already drawn too much attention to himself in meeting her and the other woman.

He settled down on a blanket and drew his knees to his chest, hugging them, smiling as he continued thinking about the lady whose hair was the color of a flaming sunset. Yes, she was worth taking risks for. Even though he did not approve of her living on Suquamish soil, the woman had fascinated him from the first moment they had met.

And today, he had been a witness to her courage. He had seen her fiery spirit, which matched the color of her hair.

And her eyes! They were as green as the panther's that stalked the trails of the forest. Somehow he had to find a way to meet her again—when danger would not overshadow their meeting.

He must learn her name, and soon. It must have been their destiny to meet. Chance had thrown them together now not only once, but three times.

Yes. Sometimes destiny worked in strange ways, he mused.

The dried buckskin warm against his flesh, Strong Heart glared down at Copper Hill Prison and thought, first things first.

He *had* come to Seattle for a purpose.

5

They spoke as chords do from the string,
And blood burnt round my heart.
                    —JOHN CLARE

Dwarfed by the many monumental totem poles that
stood on all sides of them, Earl and Morris entered
the Suquamish village. Their horses moved in a slow
lope between two long rows of Indians who stood with
spears in their hands, apprehensively watching their
arrival.

Earl and Morris exchanged troubled glances, then
looked guardedly at the Indians, most of them men
dressed only in loincloths. The women and children
seemed to have disappeared into thin air—the village
seemed void even of dogs.

And then suddenly, at the far end of the double row,
a single man stepped out from the others and stood
with his arms folded tightly across his chest, his jaw
set, and his eyes narrowing as the horses bearing the
white men came closer to him.

Earl gave Morris a quick look. "I think we'd best
dismount and go the rest of the way on foot," he said,
his voice a whisper. "I think we're just about to make
acquaintance with the chief. And what I see doesn't
make me feel too confident about our mission. I'd be
surprised if we don't end up as that damn Indian's
dinner. He looks like he'd as soon eat us as look at
us."

"He's not a bad sort," Morris tried to reassure him.
"From what I've heard about him, Chief Moon Elk's
one of the most congenial of the chiefs in the area.

That's why I suggested that we come to him first. He'll listen to reason. You'll see.''

''I sure as hell hope so,'' Earl said, wiping nervous perspiration from his brow. ''And soon. I'm not as confident as you are about these transactions. This is my first experience with Indians. I'll take the Chinese over Indians any day.''

''The Chinese don't fish for salmon,'' Morris grumbled, ''so keep your mind on who does. The Suquamish.''

Earl nodded, then slipped easily from his saddle. He walked on wooden legs beside Morris until they reached the chief. Then he let Morris make the introductions.

''Chief Moon Elk, my friend and I have come in friendship to have council with you over an important matter,'' Morris said, his eyes steady on Chief Moon Elk. He extended his hand to the chief, then lowered it slowly to his side when the chief refused to shake it.

Chief Moon Elk looked sternly from Morris to Earl, then back at Morris. Then he turned and nodded for them to follow him.

Earl stayed close to Morris as several Suquamish braves fell in step beside them, their spears still clutched threateningly in their hands. His thoughts went to Elizabeth, hoping that she had obeyed him and hadn't wandered alone from the house. At this moment he knew the true dangers. He could see such hate and mistrust in the eyes of these Indians. It was enough that *he* was having to deal with them. He wanted to make sure that his daughter had no dealings with them, ever. With her brilliant red hair, she would be a novelty for them.

Earl and Morris were ushered inside a large, cedar longhouse, the interior lit by a crackling fire in a firepit in the center. They were offered seats on mats of

woven grass. The chief sat down on a platform opposite them, keeping the fire between them.

Earl swallowed his rising fear as several Suquamish
braves positioned themselves behind him and Morris.
Then his full attention was on the chief as a brave
brought the man a robe of black sea otter fur, and
placed it devotedly around his lean shoulders.

Chief Moon Elk studied the white men suspiciously.
He had had no close connection with white people for
many moons now. Chief Moon Elk had broken away
from those who had agreed to live on reservations and
that had earned him much respect among the white
community. They left his people in peace, to live their
lives as they would have it—away from the rulings of
the great leader that the white people called their
"president."

"And what brings you to my village?" Chief Moon
Elk asked. He pulled up his legs and squatted on his
platform. "Do you bring tidings from your president?"

Earl and Morris exchanged quick looks. Morris
nudged Earl in the side, prompting him to speak now—
to explain their plan to the chief while he was willing
to listen.

Earl cleared his throat nervously and crossed his
legs, resting the palms of his hands on each knee. "We
have come to talk business with you," he said, his
voice sounding foreign to himself with its frightened
timbre.

He could not help but be unnerved. The chief's eyes
were bright and steady in their gaze, seeming to see
clear through Earl. He was afraid that the chief could
even see his fear.

"Business?" Chief Moon Elk asked, lifting a
shaggy eyebrow. "What business could white men and
Suquamish talk about? We mind our own business. It
is best that you mind *yours*."

"I know that is the way it has been between the white men and the Suquamish for many years, but now it is time for change—a change which could be profitable for your people," Earl said, his fingers now digging into his knees, his fear changing to determination. He had come for a purpose, and he could not fail. Nothing, and no one could thwart his dreams. Especially not a dumb, savage Indian chief, he thought smugly to himself.

But the look of defiance in the chief's eyes was telling him that he may have come up against a brick wall—a wall that Earl would somehow have to tear down.

"My people do not seek change," Chief Moon Elk growled. "Especially changes suggested by white men. Our lives are filled with enough purpose, without any interference from white men!"

"But what I have to offer could make your people have more purpose in life," Earl softly argued. "At least listen to what I have to say. Think it over. Once you do, you will see that what I offer is good for your people."

"Nothing any white man has ever offered to the Suquamish has ever been good for them," Chief Moon Elk answered. "*Nah,* look here! If that is why you have come to have council with Chief Moon Elk, the meeting is now over. *Kla-how-ya,* goodbye!"

Not to be dismissed that easily, Earl rose to his feet. Morris scrambled to his feet beside him. "We will leave and *soon,* but I first will quickly tell you my plan," Earl said in a rush of words. "Please allow it. What can it hurt just to listen?"

"*Kloshe,* well enough," Chief Moon Elk said, standing, also. He nodded. "Speak. *Hy-ak,* quickly. Then be gone with you."

Earl explained his plan—that the Indians would use their skills at catching the salmon for him, and he, in turn, would pay them a high price. He also told Chief Moon Elk that he would like to hire several of his braves to work in his fishery, and that he would pay them well for a day's work.

After Earl had given his presentation, there was a long pause before Chief Moon Elk offered any response.

The chief moved around the fire and stood eye to eye with Earl. "Many moons ago my people labored for the white man, catching and selling salmon to them, but they were cheated. Now my people catch salmon only for themselves. My people rely on salmon for their main food. They share with no one!"

"That was unfortunate that your people dealt with men who cheated them," Earl said, becoming unnerved again by the chief's steady, penetrating gaze, and by the presence of the braves as they moved closer behind him. "But that wouldn't happen if they were under my employ. I cheat no one. I give you my word."

"A white man's word is no better than that huge boulder that perches on the edge of the butte close to our village. It threatens to fall at any moment and crush my people beneath it," Chief Moon Elk said, his voice tight. "No. I will not allow my people to participate in this white man's venture. My people will continue to catch salmon, but only for themselves."

Earl was at a loss for words. He looked over at Morris for support, but the chief began speaking again.

He turned his eyes to Chief Moon Elk, seeing his hopes in his fishery venture fading. There weren't that many Suquamish who had chosen to live away from the reservations. It was imperative that he convince *this* chief, for he was the most important and admired of those who chose to live a free existence.

"*Nah*, look here," Chief Moon Elk said, his voice taking on a softer tone. "The salmon to the Suquamish

are what the buffalo once were to the plains Indians.
If angered, the spirits that control the salmon will
cause a failure of this autumn's run. It would anger the
spirits if white men joined with the Suquamish in the
salmon run.''

Earl tried to dissuade him. ''I'm sure your spirits
would understand that there is more than enough
salmon for everyone. Your spirits will see that my plan
will help the Indians. Those who work for me will
have a steady income.''

''I have spoken,'' Chief Moon Elk said, lifting his
chin proudly, and folding his arms across his chest.
''My people will remain free like the *mee-gee-see,* eagle. The Suquamish people's lives and religion are tied
to the salmon, whose migrations mean sustenance.
And the salmon's autumn arrival is sacred. I will not
take that away from my people—now or ever!''

Morris nudged Earl in the side again, and nodded
toward the door. ''We'd best leave,'' he whispered in
Earl's ear. ''But don't fret. I've my own plans. Chief
Moon Elk will change his mind. You'll see.''

Earl gave Morris a harried look. He looked one last
time at the chief then turned and walked from the
longhouse, escorted by the braves. Disappointed,
frustrated, and angry, he mounted his horse and gladly
rode away from the village. Usually, he was able to
convince anyone of anything. He was known as a
wheeler and dealer.

But he had never met anyone as stubborn and strong
willed as Chief Moon Elk. He wasn't quite sure now
how to deal further with him, but he must. He would
not give up hope this quickly. He had not become a
rich man by allowing himself to be stopped by dis-
couragement and doubts.

''You sure are a quiet one,'' Morris said, edging his
horse closer to Earl's as they rode beneath a massive

umbrella of trees. "The chief's got you tongue-tied, eh? Well, that won't be for long. I've got a plan."

Earl glowered at Morris. "It's a little late for that, isn't it?" he spat out. "I could've used a little support back there in that damn Indian's longhouse. You just sat like a bump on a log, letting me do the pleading. Damn it, Morris, you're my partner. Why didn't you act like it back there when you saw me cornered? You've got a big mouth, usually. Did you lose your nerve, or what? Did the spears at your back make you yellow? Damn it, I don't need no partner that don't know how to think under pressure."

Morris's face became red with anger. His cold, blue eyes flashed into Earl's. He said in a low and controlled voice, "I'd watch my mouth if I were you. You wouldn't want me to back out on my deal. Without me, it's no deal at all. And just because the chief got the best of you, don't give you the right to jump on my ass about things. Just let it lay, Earl, or you'll have more than you bargained for."

Earl paled, not liking the implication behind Morris's threat. Morris was absolutely necessary for his fishery.

Yet, Earl was not sure if his choice had been a wise one. He had not been able to find out much about Morris before agreeing to a partnership with him. His credentials had been sketchy. Earl suspected that Morris had a dark side, but he did not want to find out what it was.

"All right, so I mouthed off a bit too much," Earl conceded. "Just forget that I did and tell me what you meant back there. How are you going to convince the chief to join up with us? What's on your mind, Morris? Tell me about it."

"There's no need in my going into detail about it," Morris said, shrugging casually. "Just relax. Things have a way of working out." He swung his horse away from Earl's. "This is where I leave you, my friend, to find your way back to Seattle alone. I've something to do—someone to see."

Morris rode away without further explanation. Earl headed in the direction of Seattle. His future seemed bleak. He had wanted the fishery for Elizabeth. Although, she did not know it, he was driven to succeed only because of her. She was all that was left in his life that was important to him. For her, he must succeed.

"Elizabeth," he whispered to himself. "I wonder what you're doing right now?" He smiled. "Frannie is probably fussin' over you, makin' you beautiful."

Elizabeth snapped the reins, goading the horse to hurry its pace. Her wet clothes were not only cold, but made her skin itch. She looked over at Maysie, whose shoulders were still weighted with her secret shame.

"I'm sorry for acting as though I don't trust you," Maysie suddenly blurted. "There is no need, whatsoever, in you not knowing my last name—or why I am in Seattle." The girl paused, then continued in a rush, "My name is Maysie Parker. I'm sixteen. My parents are poor. There was hardly ever enough food on the table for me and my five brothers and sisters. I came to Seattle after I read several leaflets that had been handed out in San Francisco—saying that the opportunity for young women in Seattle was great. I sneaked aboard a freighter and came here hoping to make my own way in the world. Hoping to make lots of money. Once here, I discovered that the leaflets had been distributed by brothel and saloon owners. The opportunities that lured me here were nothing more than having to live as a whore, to make enough money to exist from day to day."

The shock of this revelation showed on Elizabeth's

face. She remained speechless as Maysie went on telling her sad tale of a young life in trouble.

"I grew tired of selling my body," Maysie said, lowering her eyes. "But with no hopes of ever being able to do anything better with my life, I . . . I . . . decided to end it."

Maysie looked up quickly, and met Elizabeth's pitying eyes. "This sort of thing happens to many innocent girls and women of Seattle," she softly explained. "Some have ended up in Copper Hill Prison for killing the men who led them into a life of prostitution. I could not bear ever to think of . . . of . . . being in a prison. Once there, one rarely ever leaves alive."

"Well, you are one young lady who will never have to worry about that," Elizabeth said, squaring her shoulders. "I will see to that."

Elizabeth was glad when, through a break in the trees, she caught sight of the old mansion. She had never thought that she would be glad to see it.

But now was different. After hearing Maysie's sad tale, Elizabeth knew just how lucky she was. Even though her mother had rejected her all those years ago, she at least had a father who kept her clothed and fed—and sometimes loved her.

Not everyone was this fortunate.

Her thoughts returned to the handsome brave, wondering what sort of life *he* led, and if there was someone who saw to his every wants and needs—a wife, perhaps?

The thought of a woman being a part of the Indian's life made a keen jealousy stab at her heart.

6

A day of days!
I let it come and go,
As traceless as a thaw of bygone snow.
—CHRISTINA ROSSETTI

The next day, her stomach warmed with oatmeal, Elizabeth took another slow sip of steaming tea, marvelling over the brim of her cup at how Maysie still continued to eat. Maysie, her hair drawn back from her pale face with a blue satin ribbon, was scooping up big bites of egg, and stuffing her mouth with jellied biscuits as if she hadn't eaten in days.

And last evening, when Elizabeth had offered Maysie a bath and perfumed soap, and then a fresh, clean dress with frilly laces at the throat and at the cuffs of the sleeves, Maysie had looked as if she thought she had entered Heaven.

At that moment, Elizabeth had almost understood why Maysie had stooped to selling her body for money. Just as Maysie had said, she had found it the only way to survive in a world that had forgotten she existed.

Elizabeth's heart went out to Maysie, hoping that it was not too late for the young woman to begin a new life of decency.

Frannie entered the dining room in a flurry, huffing and puffing, a scarf with bright designs wrapped around her head. She was carrying a huge bowl of fruit, which she set down on the middle of the table.

"Help yo'selves to the fruit," Frannie said, stopping long enough to place her hands on her hips, to give Elizabeth an annoyed stare and then a slight nod toward Maysie.

Elizabeth smiled weakly up at Frannie, realizing that Frannie did not altogether approve of her having brought home a total stranger to stay with them. Elizabeth had tried to explain Maysie's plight, but couldn't tell Frannie that Maysie had been living the life of a prostitute. Elizabeth had just told Frannie that Maysie was homeless.

Elizabeth understood that it was not so much that she had brought home a stranger that Frannie was concerned about. It was Elizabeth's father and his reaction to Elizabeth being so free in offering her charity.

"I done been to the market this mo'nin'," Frannie said, untying the scarf from around her head and laying it across the back of a chair. "This city boasts of its fine apples. I can see why. They are plump and they smell delicious."

"Thanks, Frannie, I believe I'll have one," Elizabeth said. She was glad when Frannie left after giving Maysie another troubled glance.

Maysie wiped her mouth clean with a monogrammed napkin, washed down the last bites of her food with a large glass of milk, then leaned back in her chair and sighed. "I haven't eaten that good since I left San Francisco," she murmured, lowering her eyes timidly. "My mama, when she had the makings, she baked the most delicious biscuits. But . . . but . . . we never could afford jams and jellies to eat on them. Nor could we afford butter."

Then Maysie's eyes looked up. "I can't thank you enough for taking me in," she said. "But what about your papa? When he comes back home, will he turn me out?" She glanced toward the door. "Your maid, she . . . she . . . doesn't like me. Perhaps your father won't either."

Elizabeth took an apple from the bowl, then shoved the bowl toward Maysie, silently offering her one. "It's not that Frannie doesn't like you," she tried to explain. "It's just that I've never brought strangers home before. She's finding that hard to accept. And don't fret about my father. At first he may behave gruffly, but deep inside his heart he will understand and allow you to stay for as long as you wish." She paused, then added, "He will, Maysie, because that is what I want, and he owes me, Maysie. He owes me."

Elizabeth took a bite of her apple. Maysie only eyed those left in the bowl, her mind elsewhere. "I wish everyone could be as lucky as me," Maysie said. "The poor women at Copper Hill Prison never had this sort of chance. I'm so, so lucky. I'm so grateful."

She leaped from her chair and gave Elizabeth a hearty hug. "Thank you from the bottom of my heart," she whispered. "Thank you, thank you."

Elizabeth lay her apple aside and rose from her chair. She embraced Maysie, then placed an arm around her waist and walked her out of the dining room to the sitting room. Elizabeth chose a plump, over-stuffed leather chair before the roaring fire in the fireplace and sat down. Maysie chose the divan.

Elizabeth shook her hair back from her shoulders. The fire cast a golden glow on her face, and her bare neck. Her yellow dress was cut low in front, emphasizing her soft swell of breasts. The bodice was softly pleated to the tight waist and the skirt billowed out in yards of luxuriant silk.

Elizabeth turned and silently admired Maysie. She was a lovely girl, one could see, even though she was now much too pale and wan looking. Elizabeth had chosen a silk dress from her wardrobe for Maysie and it fit her perfectly as it clung to her large bosom and tiny waist. The full gathered skirt spread out on the divan on each side of her.

"Tell me more about Copper Hill Prison," Elizabeth said.

"I've visited the women at the prison as often as I

could," Maysie answered softly. "Whenever it was possible, I'd steal some fruit at the market, or from apple trees in people's yards, and take it to the women prisoners. They never get decent food there. Just . . . just watery soup with no meat in it, and barely a trace of vegetables. With the sort of . . . profession that I was in, I met many of the women before they ended up in Copper Hill. They are mostly God-fearing women who had nothing in life, and no one who cared about what happened to them."

Maysie paused, then added, "They are the victims of the evil men who misused and abused them. Now they are with men who taunt them endlessly, and not only the sheriff and his deputy. Some are also at the mercy of the male prisoners whose cells they are forced to share when the prison is too crowded. These women are treated like animals—animals!"

Elizabeth listened sadly, finding it hard to accept that in any civilized community women could be treated so callously. It gave her a helpless, sick feeling at the pit of her stomach. Then her eyes brightened with an idea.

"Perhaps you and I could do something that could help lessen the women's burdens," she said, smiling at Maysie. "Of course I know that we can do nothing about their actual incarceration, but we *can* take them fruit. And books from my personal library to help while away their lonesome hours."

Elizabeth felt somewhat guilty for her suggestion, for she knew that she was not thinking only about the women's welfare, but also her own. Spending time helping them would give her something to do.

Maysie scooted to the edge of the divan. "You would do that?" she breathed, touched to the core by the generosity of this woman who had only yesterday been a total stranger.

Elizabeth pushed to her feet, the skirt of her dress

rustling around her legs. "*We* shall do that, *together*,"
she said, going to Maysie. She placed an eager hand
to Maysie's elbow and urged her up from the divan.
"Come on. Let's choose which books we can take to
the women. They are still in packing crates. I have yet
to take the time to place them on shelves in the library.
Then we shall ready a basket of fruit and be in Seattle
before the dinner hour. Isn't it exciting, Maysie, to
think that we might help lessen the women's misery
somewhat?"

Maysie pulled away from Elizabeth's grip. She began slowly shaking her head, a guarded fear in her
eyes. "I shan't go with you," she said, her voice
breaking. "I'm . . . I'm still tired and weak from my
dip in the Sound. Please. Please go on without me."

Maysie looked away from Elizabeth, for she knew
that she was not being altogether truthful. Deep inside, where her darkest fears lay, she was afraid of the
man who had employed her at the brothel. She was
afraid that Frank might see her and drag her back with
him, or worse, throw her in prison for running away
from him.

No, Maysie thought sullenly, she had best not be
seen by anyone for a while. While she was safely away
from the city, she had best stay hidden.

Elizabeth drew Maysie into a gentle embrace. "I
should've known that you wouldn't be up to traveling
into Seattle just yet. You stay here and rest. I shouldn't
be gone long."

Maysie slipped from Elizabeth's arms. "I'm not sure
you should even go to the prison," she said, her eyes
averted. "Elizabeth, the sheriff, Jed Nolan, can't be
trusted. What if . . . what if . . . he tries to accost
you? He's a despicable man with no morals. If he tried
to rape you, there'd be no one there to stop him. If his
deputy is there, he'd just laugh, any maybe even take
a turn once the sheriff was through with his fun." She

began to wring her hands. "No, Elizabeth. I don't think it's good that you go. You wouldn't be safe at all."

"Go wheres?" Frannie said from behind Elizabeth, her voice so loud that Elizabeth jumped as if she had been caught stealing cookies from a cookie jar.

"I didn't know you were standing there," Elizabeth said, nervously smoothing the front of her dress.

"And what if I was?" Frannie said, giving Elizabeth a look of impatience. "What is you plannin' behind my back, Elizabeth Easton?"

"So you *didn't* hear all that was said," Elizabeth said, trying to hold back a sigh of relief. Yet she knew that Frannie would have to be told, no matter that she might scream and yell, that she would not allow it.

"I hears enough to know that you're up to no good. Don't you get it in your head that you're leavin' this house again unescorted." She gave Maysie a haughty glance, then peered up at Elizabeth. "Who's to say what you'll be draggin' in the house the next time if you is allowed to run loose like, like, a trollop?"

That word made Elizabeth blanch and glance at Maysie. When she saw the look of shame in Maysie's eyes, she looked angrily back at Frannie.

"Frannie, I don't know what has got your dander up this morning," she scolded. "It can't be only because I felt compelled to bring Maysie home. What else has rattled your nerves, Frannie? Was it something you saw while you were in Seattle? Did someone scold you for something? If so, tell me who, and I will see to it that this person never does it again."

Frannie wrung her hands, then answered somberly. "It ain't nothin' anyone said to me. It's . . . it's what I *saw*."

"Well? What did you see?" Elizabeth said, her voice filled with impatience.

"It was high on that hill close to that prison," Frannie said, her eyes wide. "They was buildin' a hangin' place, they was. I ain't neva' seen such a sight. To think that soon a man will hang there, with a noose chokin' the life from him. I don't likes it one bit. Livin' near a city that has criminals bad enough they must be hanged."

Her words sent involuntary shivers through Elizabeth, especially now that she had decided to go into Seattle, *to* the prison. She was having second thoughts, yet she knew that if she put off going now, she more than likely never would.

And the idea of going to the prison to share some of her blessings with the women was too compelling not to do it.

But how was she going to tell Frannie? Especially since Frannie was so obviously frightened of the place. Yet she had never kept secrets from Frannie. Nor would she now.

"Frannie, would you prepare me a large basket of fruit for traveling?" Elizabeth asked, deciding on a direct approach. The sooner she got this settled with Frannie, the sooner she could leave and begin her mission.

Frannie seemed taken off guard. She raised her eyebrows. "A basket of fruit? What evah for?"

"I've decided to take fruit and some of my books to the women prisoners at Copper Hill Prison," Elizabeth said nonchalantly as she walked past Frannie into the corridor. She winced and tightened her jaw as Frannie fell into step beside her.

"You ain't goin'," Frannie said angrily. "You ain't goin' nowheres. You're going to stay put beneath this roof until your father returns. Then you tells *him* this crazy plan of yours. He won't allow you to go near that prison and you knows it! Lordy, lordy, Elizabeth, why would you even want to?"

Elizabeth went into the library, where stacks of

boxes awaited her. Lowering some boxes that were marked hers to the floor, she opened one and began sorting through it. "There are many less fortunate than I," she said calmly, laying books aside in two separate piles—those she would take, and those she would keep. "I intend to share my fortune with others." She rested a book on her lap and gave Frannie a stern look. "And, Frannie, I'm not about to wait on Father for anything. He is doing his work. I shall do mine."

"Elizabeth, the dangers," Frannie said in a whine, bending to place a gentle hand to Elizabeth's cheek. "Honey, don't do it. The hangin'. What if they hang the man while you're there? Does you want to see a man take his last breath? Does you?"

Elizabeth swallowed hard and blinked her eyes nervously, knowing that, no, that would not be something that she would ever want to witness. Yet, she had a mission, and she would not allow anything to stand in the way.

And, she thought with a rush of passion—she might at least catch a glimpse of the handsome Indian. She seemed to have a better chance of that in Seattle than here in the house.

"I'm going, Frannie," she said firmly. "No matter what you say—I'm going."

Frannie shook her head helplessly. She knew from Elizabeth's eyes, there was no use arguing. With a sigh, she left Elizabeth alone.

Maysie came in and knelt beside Elizabeth. "Perhaps she's right," she ventured. "Elizabeth, what you're doing is generous to a point—then it becomes dangerous."

Elizabeth smiled weakly at Maysie. "I know," she admitted. "I know."

They gazed at length at one another. Then Elizabeth returned to sorting through her books. Her heart beat quickly at the prospect of perhaps seeing the Indian again, and the danger that she might be facing to chance it.

Strong Heart had eaten pemmican for breakfast, a food that required no fire for cooking. It was dried meat pounded fine and mixed with melted fat. To this he added fresh apples that he had picked from an orchard not far from where he had made camp. He changed slowly and methodically into clothes that would help him to blend in with the white men on the streets of Seattle. He would look more like a white man on horseback than an Indian. Along with the white-man clothes, he would wear a bandanna to hide his face and a sombrero to hide his long, brown hair during the escape.

His effects gathered up and secured in his saddlebags, he slapped a gunbelt around his waist and fastened it, and pulled the brim of his hat low over his gray eyes. Then he swung himself into his saddle.

Pausing for a moment, he stared down at Copper Hill Prison. Then he began making his way down the side of the hill which would lead him to the city.

While inching his horse down the steep grade of land, memories of the green-eyed seductress plagued Strong Heart. He recalled her ravishing curves as her wet dress had clung so sensually to her body when she had stepped out of the water yesterday. She had disturbed him in many ways that were dangerous to him.

Yet he knew that he would search her out again, one day. He must have her. He *would* have her!

7

Wait not till tomorrow—
Gather the roses of life today.
—RONSARD

The sky was gray and the air damp as Elizabeth rode into Seattle in her buggy. With one hand she held on to the horse's reins, with the other she secured her fringed shawl more comfortably around her shoulders and adjusted her lace-trimmed bonnet. All the while her gaze swept around her, this being her first time in Seattle.

While on the ship she had not been able to see the tawdriness of the city—the saloons and gambling establishments, and the houses of ill-repute blossoming, it seemed, at every street corner. It was a bawdy seaport town, well known to sailors, loggers, and transients.

Holding the reins with both of her gloved hands, she directed her horse down First Avenue. At first she thought it was snow lying along the ground. Then she realized that it was, instead, piles of sawdust that had scattered and blown there from nearby Yesler's Mill.

This reminded her that Seattle was a lumber town. Every building, even the large public structures such as Squire's Opera House and Hotel were constructed from wood.

As she rode onward, she noted that among the commercial establishments were several miners' stores, ready to outfit prospectors bound for the new gold strike on the headwaters of the Skagit River.

On the left side of the road hung a sign advertising spring beds, a retail enterprise undertaken by two morticians. On the right was Yesler's Hall, where town meetings were held.

Her inspection was broken as several men loitering on a street corner began jeering and tossing leering remarks her way.

Insulted by such behavior, Elizabeth impudently thrust her chin up and snapped her horse's reins, setting her sights on the prison. She was anxious to get there, do her good deed, and return to the quiet and safety of her house. She could now see why her father had forbade her to go to the city alone. If he ever heard that she had, and that she had even gone to the prison, she guessed that he might even lock her in her room and throw away the key.

When a man dressed in buckskin rode past her on a black mustang, she was struck by memories of another man in buckskin, whose eyes, whose handsomeness, had mesmerized her.

How could she have forgotten for even a moment that he was also her reason for coming so boldly alone into Seattle?

She had hoped to see him again, perhaps to find out his name at last.

She wanted him to know *her* name.

For a moment she studied the buckskin-clad man, until she determined it wasn't him. Then she looked at the men on horseback who rode past her, and at the men trodding along the wooden walks of the city.

She also squinted at the men leaning against the buildings. Yet she saw no one who even remotely resembled the Indian.

In fact, as far as she could tell, there were no Indians to be seen in the city at all. As if they were forbidden to enter here. Which puzzled her, since the city had been named after a powerful Suquamish Indian Chief—Chief Sealth. His name was misinterpreted as Seattle by those who had founded the city.

The mysterious, handsome Indian seemed to go and come as he pleased.

Or had he not gone into the city after rescuing her from the Sound, she wondered. If not, then what had been his destination?

More taunts and insulting remarks coming from the boardwalks and the shadows of the buildings caused Elizabeth to urge her horse into a faster gait. They turned a corner, and the horse and buggy now climbed a steep road—the road that led to the prison.

Elizabeth felt the strain of the buggy, and heard the wheels groan frighteningly the farther the horse traveled up the grade. She paled, fearing to look over her shoulder, realizing that if the wheels slipped, or the horse faltered, the backward plunge would take her straight into the waters of the Sound.

But soon that fear was replaced by another. The sound of hammers striking wood came to her.

Her eyes widened and she gasped when she first caught sight of the hanging platform that Frannie had spoken so fearfully about. It was being built directly in front of a long, dreary wooden building—Copper Hill Prison. Forests towered way above the site as far as her eye could see.

Her heart pounding, as though an echo of the hammers, Elizabeth was at least glad that the steep grade of land had leveled out. She was now driving along a level, narrow street that soon took her to the prison.

After climbing from her buggy and securing her horse's reins to a hitching rail, Elizabeth tried to will her knees not to shake, and her pulse not to race so fast, but failed. Being there made her realize the danger she was in. The men working on the hanging platform had caught sight of her, and one was lumbering toward her, a cigar hanging limply from the corner of his wide lips, his eyes raking her body.

"What do we have here?" the man said, circling

Elizabeth, not allowing her to reach for the huge basket of fruit and books at the back of the buggy. "Come to see the hanging? It's not 'til sunup tomorrow. Want some entertainment to pass the time whilst waitin' to see the Injun hang? I can offer some mighty interestin' entertainment, if I do say so, myself."

"Indian?" Elizabeth said, even more fear gripping her heart at what he had said. They were planning to hang an Indian. She felt anxiety at the pit of her stomach.

For she knew only one Indian.

Surely he was not the one to be hanged, she despaired to herself. In her mind's eye, she saw the handsome Indian's body hanging from the gallows, spinning slowly in a dance of death.

"Sure," the man said, guffawing. He yanked the cigar from his mouth and spat across his shoulder. "An Injun called Four Winds. And it's about time we hung the renegade. He's been stinkin' up our prison long enough."

"Just how long has . . . has . . . he been incarcerated?" Elizabeth dared to ask, feeling the sudden tightening in her throat at the possibility that the condemned man was *her* Indian!

"Weeks," the man said, shrugging.

Elizabeth sighed, knowing that *her* Indian was not going to hang. He had been free yesterday, to save her from the Sound. He was surely as free today.

She started to ask the man about the prisoner, wanting to know what he had done to deserve hanging, but he had been called back by the others. She watched, wide-eyed, as he helped secure the rope and its noose on the cross beam. Her insides rebelled at the sight and what it meant—that soon a man would die there, and not only a man, an Indian! No wonder she hadn't seen any Indians in Seattle today. Being there was dangerous.

Elizabeth was jarred out of her unpleasant reverie when the man who had talked with her mounted a horse, and began riding away with the others. She stiffened when he yelled something over his shoulder at her—that he would look her up later, and he would like to "acquaint" himself with her body.

"The pig," she whispered, cringing at the thought of this crude man's rough hands on her.

Yanking the heavy basket from the rear of the buggy, Elizabeth stomped up to the prison door, then stopped and took a nervous breath before placing her hand on the latch.

When she composed herself she lifted the latch, and took a shaky step across the threshold. What she encountered made her want to turn around and seek the haven of her home as quickly as possible. Never had she seen such filth and gloom as crowded this small, outer room. A bearded man sat behind a crude desk piled high with yellowed papers and journals, his booted feet resting on the edge.

She grimaced when their eyes met, and she felt ill when he leaned his head sideways and spat a long stream of chewing tobacco into a large and tarnished brass spittoon that had strings of tobacco dripping down its sides.

Elizabeth stood stiff and unresponsive to how this man was looking at her as he slowly pushed himself up from his chair. He hooked his thumbs through red suspenders that held up soiled, black, baggy breeches. A red-plaid shirt was stuffed loosely into the waistband.

Elizabeth looked slowly around the room, at the peeling paint of the walls, and at the one filthy window that failed to let in any light through its dirt.

Her gaze stopped at the many small pegs along one of the walls. Keys hung from each.

She then saw a closed door, which surely led to the

back where she would probably find the cells in even worse condition.

Her nose curled at the foul odor emanating from the sheriff as he stood before her, blocking her view. His beady eyes squinted above a thick, dark mustache that had chewing tobacco clinging to the tips.

"What's your business here?" Sheriff Jed Nolan asked, his voice a growl. He glanced down at the basket clutched in Elizabeth's right hand. "What's in that basket? Somethin' to help you break out one of your gentlemen friends, huh?"

Elizabeth didn't get a chance to reply. The sheriff grabbed the basket from her and threw the cloth aside, and peered down at the books and fruit.

Then he looked slowly up at Elizabeth. "Books?" he said, tossing the basket aside, spilling its contents. "Fruit? Who are you, anyhow? What do you want here?"

Elizabeth stared blankly down at the spilled contents of her basket. Then a slow burn began within her and she turned angry eyes up at the man. "You had no right to do that," she said, placing her fists on her hips. "I came here out of the goodness of my heart to help lighten the burden of those less fortunate. I pity those who are under your care. You don't deserve the title of sheriff. I would think it would have to be earned. What have you done, sir, to earn it? But I'm sure I don't want to know the answers. Such a man as you gets what he wants by—"

Elizabeth's words were cut short when Sheriff Nolan grabbed her by the wrists and quickly wrestled her to the floor, where he proceeded to straddle her. "What are you doing?" she screamed, squirming to get free. "Let me up, do you hear? Let . . . me . . . up!"

The sheriff brushed her lips with a wet kiss, his body holding her in place as one of his hands went to the swell of her breast and began mashing it through the silk fabric of her dress. "You've got a big mouth," Sheriff Nolan grumbled, staring down at her with lustful blue eyes. "Let's see what else you have that I might find more pleasant."

Elizabeth managed to get a hand free, raised it and slapped him across the face.

She sucked in a wild breath of air when she saw a sudden angry fire leap into his eyes. He in turn slapped her across the face, and followed by crushing her mouth with his hungry, wet lips. His tongue assaulted her as it pressed in and out between her unwilling lips.

And then, as quick as lightning striking, someone else was there in the room. Elizabeth saw a man, whose face was partially hidden behind a bandanna, strike the sheriff over the head with the butt of his pistol.

The sheriff collapsed unconscious on top of her. Elizabeth screamed and began pushing at his chest. The stranger yanked the sheriff off, tossing him away from her.

Elizabeth scrambled to her feet. Then she realized that she should still be afraid. It was apparent from his mask that the stranger who had saved her was not there for any good reason. When he stepped closer to her, she quaked.

Elizabeth stared at the hooded eyes above the bandanna, seeing something familiar about them. And when he told her in a whisper to leave, there was something about the voice that compelled her to want to see his face.

Without thought of the outcome of her action, Elizabeth yanked the man's bandanna down, revealing his face. She became weak in the knees when she saw that it *was* whom she had thought it to be: The handsome Indian!

Sighing resolutely, Strong Heart pushed the brim of

his sombrero back from his brow with the barrel of his pistol. "What you have done is *me-sah-chie*, bad. You shouldn't have interfered," he said with annoyance. "Now that you've seen me, I have no choice but to take you with me. I can't leave you behind to describe me to the authorities. Why didn't you leave when I told you to?"

Elizabeth was numb from the discovery. She didn't understand when Strong Heart told her to get the keys from the sheriff's pocket, then take them to the cells, and release the Indian, Four Winds.

When Elizabeth did not obey him, Strong Heart took a step closer and gestured toward the sheriff who still lay unconscious on the floor. "*Hy-ak*, make haste," he grumbled. "Get the keys from the *cultus*, worthless man."

"I can't do that," Elizabeth said, her voice quavering. "That would be breaking the law. I would become a criminal." She gave him a glare. "Just like you. You're a criminal, aren't you? A renegade Indian, just like the Indian you want me to set free."

"*Nah*, look here," Strong Heart answered, bending to get the keys himself, "this is not the time to discuss who I am, or why I am here." He turned his gray eyes up at her as he handed her the keys. "If we don't get out of here soon, the deputy will arrive. I would soon be hanging alongside Four Winds. Is that what you want? That I die, also?"

The keys seemed like hot coals burning her palm. She glanced down at them, then up into Strong Heart's eyes as he rose slowly to his feet.

Then, knowing from the depths of her heart that she wanted nothing to happen to him, she spun around and moved quickly toward the closed door that led to the cells. Strong Heart was suddenly there, opening the door for her. She stopped long enough to look deep into his eyes. She felt as if she were drowning in them, they were so dark with feelings that she knew were for her, for he had looked at her in the same way before.

"Set Four Winds free," Strong Heart said, his voice soft, yet commanding.

Elizabeth swallowed hard and nodded her head, then stepped into a gloomy corridor lined with a long row of cells which housed both men and women. Hands reached out for her. Women cried and wailed as they saw her, begging her to set them free. Men cursed underneath their breaths. Then she caught sight of one who stood quiet, his eyes probing hers.

Elizabeth knew that this was Four Winds, for he was the only Indian inside this horror chamber. She stared at him, thinking that he looked no more dangerous than the other Indian. Yet being in jail was proof that he was a criminal—a criminal awaiting his death at the end of a rope.

Suddenly his face was replaced in Elizabeth's mind with the handsome Indian's. It was *he* who was hanging from the platform, not Four Winds. It was him swaying in the gentle breeze, the flies crawling on his dead eyes.

The vision spurred Elizabeth into quick action. She went to Four Winds's cell. Clumsily she tried one key after another, sighing with relief when she finally found the one that fit, and set him free.

Many cries and jeers followed Elizabeth and Four Winds as they fled to the outer room. Elizabeth dropped the keys on the desk, turned and stared up into the handsome Indian's face which was alight with admiration and gratitude. Then all three hurriedly left the prison.

Elizabeth didn't object when she was placed in the handsome Indian's saddle. She knew that she had no choice. She didn't object when he swung himself into the saddle behind her, his arm circling her waist to hold her as he and Four Winds rode away.

Again, she had no choice.

She couldn't believe this was happening.

These Indians were surely part of an outlaw gang.

Never would she have believed that he, this *compassionate*, caring man, could be an outlaw!

Strong Heart led his horse away from the streets of Seattle, and they were soon thundering through the dark reaches of the forest.

Suddenly Elizabeth panicked and began struggling to get free, but the more she squirmed, the harder the Indian held her. "Why do you insist in taking me with you?" she cried. "I can't tell anyone your name. I don't even *know* it. And after saving me from harm the other times, why would you harm me now?"

"*La-daila*, do you make it a habit to search for trouble?" he shouted over the sound of his horse's hooves. "First I find you choking to death in a house filled with smoke, then almost toppling off a bluff. Then I find you half drowned in Puget Sound. And now I find you in a hellhole of a prison. Why is that, *la-daila*. Why is that?"

"What is this *la-daila* you call me?" Elizabeth shouted back. "That isn't my name! My name is Elizabeth. Elizabeth Easton."

His chuckle made Elizabeth turn to stare up at him. "What do you find that's so amusing?" she asked heatedly. Yet, again, his handsomeness nearly stole her breath away. "At least I have no secrets about who I am. You have yet to tell me *your* name."

"Secrets?" Strong Heart said, smiling down at her. "My *la-daila*, which means 'woman,' I have no reason now to keep secrets from you. My name? It is Strong Heart. I am Suquamish. My father is Chief Moon Elk."

"Does your chieftain father know that his son has turned into a renegade who sets hardened criminals free?" Elizabeth taunted. She was now his captive but she decided that she would not cooperate with him one bit!

"*Ah-hah,* my father knows of my plans to set Four Winds free, and he approves," Strong Heart said, giving her a stern look. "For you see, Four Winds is innocent of the crime he is accused of."

Wanting to believe Strong Heart and not wanting to think he was just a criminal lying to her to make his escape from Seattle easier, Elizabeth turned her eyes away in confusion.

But she did know that she was now a captive, something that even Strong Heart could not deny, for it was he who was her captor.

She glanced over at Four Winds, his shoulder-length brown hair flying in the wind as he leaned low over his horse. She had to wonder, what sort of crime had he been accused of? How could she not think that he might be capable of anything?

She looked away, fear freezing her thoughts. Strong Heart could be a liar. Although she had never seen him be cruel, she did not really know him. He could be a renegade.

If so, what would become of her?

He seemed adamant against setting her free. How long would he force this upon her?

What if it was . . . forever?

She had fantasized about being in Strong Heart's arms. But not under these conditions. The fantasy had lost its sweetness, as she was taken farther into the unbroken wilderness, a mist rising eerily from the floor of the forest.

8

My heart has left its dwelling place,
And can return no more.
                    —JOHN CLARE

Bone tired from the long ride, Elizabeth was relieved
when Strong Heart and Four Winds finally stopped
for the rest of the night. Embarrassed that she had
been forced to go into the bushes to take care of her
most private needs, she strolled back to the campsite
and ignored Strong Heart as he glanced her way.

Yet she had no choice but to sit down beside him on
a blanket spread across a patch of soft moss.

Still not giving him the slightest inkling that she
knew he was there, sitting so close to her, Elizabeth
sat stiffly against a big, downed sycamore tree which
was half buried in the ground. Her eyes feasted on fish
skewered on sticks over the hot coals of the fire that
Strong Heart had built. She had watched in awe as he
started a fire without matches. He had used a flint and
a stone to strike with and a spongy piece of dry wood.
She had sat, shivering from the damp chill of night,
as he had struck the flint against the rock until a spark
flew out igniting the wood.

Then Four Winds fashioned a spear from a tree limb.
His fisherman skills honed as a child became quickly
evident after he had smilingly brought a string of fish
to the campsite for their supper.

The aroma wafting from the fish cooking slowly over
the fire caused Elizabeth's stomach to emit a low, lazy
growl.

This had drawn both silent Indians' attentions to her.
Embarrassed, she turned her eyes away and tried to

focus her thoughts elsewhere—especially away from Strong Heart and how he sat so close to her, so close that if they should turn to face each other, their breaths would mingle.

But it was hard not to think about him. And although she was angry at him for having taken her captive, she could not deny that the excitement of the adventure of being with him was giving her strange, glorious feelings that until tonight she had never experienced.

But now she was in the wilderness, free from her father's watchful eye, and stern, commanding voice, and having been attracted to Strong Heart from the first made her fear her feelings for him. She was glad that Four Winds was a part of the group. For, if she were totally alone with Strong Heart, she did not know what she might expect from him, or herself.

She already knew the wonders of his touch, of being held in his strong arms, and the thrill of the heat of his breath on her face and lips. Alone with him, she might forget all that she had been taught about being a lady. She would perhaps learn what it meant to be a *woman,* with needs of a woman.

Shocked at where her mind had wandered, Elizabeth again tried to change her thoughts. It was a cool September night, with lightning flashing luridly over the mountains in the distance. Elizabeth gazed around her at the groves of tall, slim pines which stood majestically sprinkled with stars. Only a few feet away, a swift-running, sweet-singing trout stream coursed. Strong Heart had chosen this beautiful campsite which seemed like a woodland cathedral, roofed by the open skies, and where wave and rock and tall pine met.

It was a place of serenity, yet Elizabeth could not feel that serenity within her heart, for again her thoughts had traveled back to Strong Heart and the dilemma in which she had found herself.

Strong Heart had not said much to her during their flight from the prison. She had to wonder if he was reconsidering keeping her captive.

The thought that he might set her free frightened her, for they were now many miles from Seattle, and she would not be able to find her way back alone.

And he did not dare return with her, for surely a posse had been formed to search for him and Four Winds and herself. It was possible that she was considered an accomplice. The sheriff would not know the truth, for he had been unconscious.

Elizabeth started when a stick with cooked fish at its tip was thrust toward her. She turned and looked up at Four Winds, who was offering it to her.

"Eat," was all Four Winds said.

Elizabeth accepted the skewer and nodded a silent thank you. Four Winds had been quiet since his release. He and Strong Heart had not even discussed the escape. There seemed to be a strain between them, and Elizabeth could only surmise that it was because Strong Heart and Four Winds were not so much friends as allies in crime. Surely if they were close friends, they would have been warmer to each other.

At the moment she only truly cared about the hungry ache in her stomach. Elizabeth tore at the fish with her teeth, giving Strong Heart a sideways glance as he also began eating from his stick.

When he looked her way, she turned away from him, embarrassed by how her hunger was making her forget her table manners. She was so hungry, she yanked the fish from the stick and began stuffing it into her mouth with her fingers, then blushed when she found two sets of eyes on her. She offered Four Winds and Strong Heart a weak smile.

Having eaten all of her fish, Elizabeth wiped her mouth free of grease with the back of her hand, then opened her ears to the conversation that had started between Strong Heart and Four Winds.

Four Winds squatted before Strong Heart and placed a heavy hand on his shoulder. He began earnestly, saying, "Strong Heart, *mah-sie*, thank you for what you have done for your childhood friend. Your silence since the escape proves that you do not yet fully trust that I am free of guilt for that which I was about to be hanged. Trust that I am. Feel good in your trust."

"My silence was caused by many things," Strong Heart said, giving Elizabeth a quick glance, then focusing his attention on Four Winds. "Many things trouble me, and, *ah-hah*, part of that is my doubt about your innocence. But knowing you from childhood, I cannot see you as anything but innocent. When I spoke with my father about breaking you free, he hesitated, yet agreed with me that you should be saved. Prove to me, old friend, that you have earned our trust. Do not allow yourself to be taken prisoner again by the white man. The hangman's noose would not go empty a second time, for this friend of yours would no longer be a friend."

"Four Winds will remain your friend, for Four Winds will never give you cause again to risk your life for his," he said, humbly lowering his eyes. Then he raised them and looked into Strong Heart's. "I must now go my way alone. I will flee high into the mountains until I feel it is safe to surface again. This I do not only for myself, but also for you. As long as I am with you, your guilt in helping me escape could be proved. Without me, you are just another Indian to the white man, for no one witnessed your part in the escape."

Four Winds's eyes focused accusingly on Elizabeth, then turned back to Strong Heart. "This woman's presence with Strong Heart can also prove danger-ous," he said, his voice barely a whisper. "Her being with you could be proof enough of your guilt, not only for having aided an accused criminal in an escape from prison, but also for abducting a white woman. Once the sheriff regains consciousness, he will remember, and recognize her if his posse finds you.''

Strong Heart rose to his feet. He placed a hand at Four Winds's elbow and led him toward the grazing horses. ''*Ah-hah*, yes, it is best that you leave,'' he murmured. ''As for the woman, she stays.''

''But do you not see the danger in that?'' Four Winds persisted, untying his horse's reins from a tree stump. ''She can be the cause of *you* being taken to the hanging platform.'' He placed his free hand on Strong Heart's shoulder. ''Consider carefully your decision about this woman. Is she worth the risk? Is she?''

''I have learned many ways of being elusive,'' Strong Heart said, setting his jaw. ''No posse or sheriff will find me.''

He glanced over his shoulder at Elizabeth. Her beautiful eyes unnerved him. There was no denying the true reason why he would not set her free now that he had her to himself. It was for his own selfish needs that he held her in bondage. She was the embodiment of all temptation. And he never would allow her to leave.

Never.

Not even his father could shame him into releasing her. She had stolen his heart, a heart which until now beat for no woman.

Only her, only Elizabeth, who was now his *la-daila*.

Strong Heart turned his attention back to Four Winds. He squared his shoulders proudly. ''You say that it is dangerous for the woman to be with me,'' he said, stubbornly. ''The chances are worse for me if I set her free. She knows too much. And I cannot *kill* her to silence her. Do you not recognize me still as a man of honor?''

Four Winds could remember very well his childhood with Strong Heart, and could see that he had not changed. Strong Heart was still a bullheaded, stubborn man. Four Winds knew not to argue with Strong Heart when he had his heart set on something.

Four Winds looked over at the woman, seeing her loveliness, and was convinced now that his friend's heart was set on the white woman. Four Wind had seen how Strong Heart had looked at her, and had seen the gentleness with which he had treated her.

Four Winds knew that Strong Heart saw her as special, perhaps special enough to take as his *la-daila*, and there was no arguing with that, once *any* man chose the woman of his heart.

"*Ah-hah,* yes, Four Winds knows that Strong Heart is a man of honor, and Four Winds will say no more about your decision concerning the woman," Four Winds said, dropping his horse's reins as he stepped close to Strong Heart. He embraced Strong Heart. "*Kla-how-ya,* good-bye, my friend. Again, *mah-sie,* thank you."

Strong Heart embraced his friend, then stepped back and watched Four Winds mount his horse. They exchanged looks filled with deep emotion. Then Four Winds swung his horse around and rode away in a brisk gallop.

Strong Heart watched Four Winds until he was lost to the night, then turned slowly around to Elizabeth. She had drawn a blanket around her shoulders, and was staring into the dancing flames of the fire. Strong Heart's breath caught in his throat as once again he looked on her loveliness. His loins ached for that which he would deny himself until she invited him into her blankets.

9

Give all to love,
Obey thy heart. . . .
—EMERSON

Now that they were alone, Strong Heart did not know
what to expect from Elizabeth. Would she demand to
be set free? He moved cautiously to the blanket and
sat down beside her. When he looked at her, she did
not follow his lead and raise her gaze to meet his.
Instead, she stared into the flames of the fire, her jaw
set, her eyes filled with a defiant anger.

Even when Strong Heart began talking to her, she
did not budge, nor did she show any sign of even hearing him. When he called her by the Suquamish term
for 'my woman,' he thought he noticed a flicker of
reaction, but just as quickly it was gone.

"*La-daila*, there is much to be said between us,"
Strong Heart began, his voice soft, yet measured.
"Please listen while I tell you the truth about every-
thing. Then if you condemn me, so be it."

A dull knot ached within Elizabeth's chest, she so
wanted to be able to turn to him and tell him that she
would willingly talk with him, that being with him was
thrilling her through and through. But for too many
reasons she did not feel free to speak her mind. Just
the thought of Strong Heart being no better than the
man he had set free from prison made her heart silently cry out to him in pain. For she had discovered
this side of him just when she had begun to believe
that she was falling in love with him!

Before the encounter at the prison, before she realized what he was capable of, she had loved the way

his mere presence caused her heart to beat so erratically. Even now, while he was so close, she could not deny the wondrous, strange sweetness that seemed to be pressing in on her heart. And the more he spoke—the more sense he made, giving her cause to hope that perhaps all of these wrongs could be made right between them!

But how could he? she despaired to herself. He could never deny having helped an outlaw escape from Copper Hill Prison. She could never forgive him for forcing her to participate, then abducting her, an innocent bystander.

"*La-daila,* for so many years Four Winds and I were the best of friends who knew all the secrets of the silent forest; who, together, heard when the bluebird sang his wildest, clearest notes; knew where the scarlet wing hung his nest in the river rushes; and knew why the yellow beak sang his most beautiful song in the springtime."

He paused to place another log on the fire.

Although Elizabeth did not reveal to Strong Heart that she was listening, she was, intently, never offering him a nod or a glance. Her pulse raced and she was feeling more hopeful by the minute that he was that man of compassion she had first thought him to be. And perhaps she *could* forgive him, but only if he would escort her safely back home, she thought bitterly to herself, knowing how unlikely that was.

Strong Heart resumed his place beside her and she listened even more raptly, desperately wanting to believe him.

"As youths, Four Winds and I shared everything," he said softly. "We shared the hunt, bringing home to our clans our prizes of the day, boasting of each other's catch to our chieftain fathers. We are of two separate clans of Suquamish, and as we grew older and had to become more diligent in learning the ways of our fathers, we had to give up our childish friendship for the more serious side of life.''

Again he paused, his eyes melancholy as he looked into the flames of the fire.

Elizabeth was touched by the sincerity of his words, and the emotion in his voice, yet she still did not reach out to him with words, or a gesture of sympathy.

When he began talking again, and gave her a slow glance, she jerked her eyes around, not wanting him to know that she had been studying him and imagining her flesh being warmed by his touch.

She swallowed hard and concentrated on his words.

''Four Winds and I meet from time to time, sharing talk and dreams of our futures,'' Strong Heart said, again turning his eyes away from Elizabeth, not sure if he was reaching her with his explanation. She was stubbornly hiding her feelings, whether they were in his favor or against him.

''But after Four Winds's clan of Suquamish moved far to the north toward Canada, we broke all our ties,'' Strong Heart continued. ''Then I received word that Four Winds had been arrested for riding with criminals—something I could not, *would* not allow myself to believe. I decided to set my old friend free from the prison, having hoped—no, having *known,* without a doubt—that Four Winds had been accused unjustly, for I know the honor by which Four Winds guides his life.''

Strong Heart's brow furrowed into a deep frown. His eyes narrowed as he spoke in almost a snarl. ''The white men who imprison my people would cage eagles, chain the wolf, corral the moose!'' he said sharply. ''The white race is unable to order their lives into ways of peace and freedom, not knowing an innocent man when they see one, for most white men are guilty of one or more crimes against nature or humanity. From the Indian, the white man stands aloof, scarcely deigning to speak or touch his hand in human fellowship. He calls the Indian *savage*, meaning that he believes we are low in thought and feeling, and cruel in acts; and that we are incapable of a philosophical understanding of life and life's relations.''

Elizabeth was stunned by the strength in his words, and his intense feelings against the white race, yet it did not show in how he treated her. He had risked his life more than once to save her. How could he have, when he obviously hated the white people so much?

And, oh, what he had said was so true! She had always been aware of the injustices against the plains Indians. She had never thought to consider that it was the same for those who lived elsewhere, such as here in the Pacific Northwest. Now, she realized that her father's hopes of winning the Suquamish over to his side must surely have been dashed when he met with them about his proposals.

Strong Heart moved to his knees before Elizabeth, blocking her view of the fire. He placed a finger under her chin and elevated her eyes to meet his. "Have you listened to what I have said?" he asked, his voice filled with kindness; filled with gentleness. "The white people are wrong about the Suquamish. Among my people there are many men of vision. There is great honesty and loyalty, noble sacrifice, unselfishness, and devotion to peace. Tell me that you hear me and understand, that you *believe*."

Elizabeth felt deeply touched by his words, and overwhelmed with relief that she had *not* been wrong about him. He was a man of compassion, of deep understanding, a man of clear vision and intelligence.

And she could not control the beating of her heart when she gazed into his steel-gray eyes, his lips so close—his voice so suddenly soft and sweet.

"I have heard you," she murmured. "And . . . and
. . . I believe you. Truly, I do."

"Do you understand now why I set my friend free?"
he asked, leaning closer to her, placing his hands on
her shoulders, drawing her nearer to him. "While
caged, Four Winds was the *mee-gee-see,* the eagle, his
wings no longer able to spread and fly. He had to be
set free, for to cage an innocent man is a crime against
all humanity!"

"I'm trying to understand everything," Elizabeth
murmured, blinking her eyes nervously. "And I think
I do. But please, Strong Heart, set *me* free. While you
hold me captive, I too am like the eagle. You must
allow me to return home, where I belong."

"You belong with *me,* not in the white man's
world," Strong Heart said, drawing her even closer to
him, their lips only a breath away. "Do you not see
that? Do you not feel it? Your heart no longer beats
only for yourself. It also beats for me, the man you
are meant to be with."

A great heat rose to Elizabeth's cheeks; she was
speechless over what he had just said. She knew she
should be frightened of his declaration, yet how could
she be, when she had such strong feelings for him?

She wanted to make her own choice, not be forced
to be with a man—no matter how wonderful he made
her feel.

"I cannot allow you to go free, and not only because I have never felt this way about any other
woman," Strong Heart said. "I am to be chief of my
people one day. I cannot allow you to jeopardize this
that I have prepared for all my life. If you were to
point an accusing finger at me and have me caged by
the white man, I would not be the only one to suffer.
Many Suquamish people would be punished."

His fingers dug more tightly into her arms. "No,"
he said determinedly. "I cannot let you go."

When he saw a defiant anger enter her eyes, he grabbed her wrists and lowered her to the ground before she had the chance to rise and run away from him.

"Everything that I have told you is true," he said, leaning in close to her. He feathered soft kisses along the lovely contours of her face. "Trust me. I mean you no harm. Remember that I gave you the chance to flee at the prison, after you stripped away my mask and discovered my identity. If I had meant you harm, I would have never given you the chance to leave. I would have taken you then as my prisoner, without any questions asked, or apologies for having abducted you."

Elizabeth could scarcely listen to his words as her senses were swept away by his lips and the press of his body against hers. She lay on her back on the dew-dampened grass, drinking him in, and her anger slowly waned. "Are you apologizing for having abducted me?" she asked, their eyes locking.

"If that is what you want, *ah-hah*, yes, I apologize," he said thickly.

"If you apologize so easily, why don't you let me go?" she asked, her pulse racing as his lips came close to hers again. "I promise never to say a word. Truly . . . I do."

"I'm sorry, *la-daila*, but your promises alone are not enough protection against being hunted down and arrested," he said, again brushing a kiss across her beckoning lips. "Did not the sheriff see you just prior to my arrival at the prison, and only moments before I knocked him unconscious?"

"Yes," she said, her voice weakening, the building passion making her feel crazed and confused.

"If you were to return to Seattle, the sheriff would ask you many questions," he said, urging her to appreciate the danger. "Under pressure, you might break down and tell everything."

He paused, every fiber of his being tense and poised for her response.

"Are you never going to allow me to return home?" she asked, her voice breaking.

"It's not possible," he said too matter-of-factly, bringing Elizabeth abruptly back to her senses. She began shoving at him, trying to push him away from her.

But the more she shoved, the more tightly he held her.

"You are more beautiful than all the skies," Strong Heart whispered passionately against her cheek, and when his lips came to hers, she forgot everything but how her body thrilled to his kiss.

Her breath quickened and she tilted her face back, letting herself feel the strange sinking downward, the wondrous swirling sensation deep within her. When his hands sought her breasts and kneaded them through the fabric of her dress, she felt aflame with desire for him. Blind to every risk, she melted against him and twined her arms around his neck, returning his kiss with complete abandon.

A great clap of thunder drew them apart. Elizabeth winced when a bolt of lightning split the sky above them, followed by another boom of thunder. When a few desultory raindrops began to fall, Strong Heart rose quickly to his feet and went to his belongings and began setting up a tent.

When the tent was erected and Strong Heart returned to Elizabeth, offering her his hand, she accepted it. He led her to the tent, her knees weak and her heart pounding, not knowing what would happen next, and afraid of how she might respond.

She was baffled when he left her at the flap of the tent and returned to his bedroll beside the fire. A part of her wished that he would stay with her; another part of her was glad that he hadn't.

Struggling with her feelings, she entered the tent and stretched out between the blankets, wondering about this man she could not help but love with all of her heart.

"Heart," she whispered to herself. "Strong Heart. What a lovely name."

She moved to her knees and crawled to the tent opening. "I adore your name," she said, glad to have something to say to break the silence between them.

Strong Heart rolled over to his side and smiled at her. "*Mah-sie,* thank you," he murmured, blinking raindrops from his lashes as the storm began to thicken the air. "The name means courage."

"My name also has a special meaning," Elizabeth said, glancing up at the sheets of gray falling from the sky. "My mother told me many years ago that my name means consecrated by oath to God."

They exchanged warm smiles and she returned to her blankets.

Strong Heart wondered about her name, and her god. He had always felt that God was where one finds him. And her god had most surely thrown away the mold when he had made her.

Elizabeth listened to the rain hitting the tent with such great force, she thought it might collapse on top of her.

But it was not herself she was concerned about. It was Strong Heart, still lying in the open, surely becoming drenched to the bone!

Determinedly, Elizabeth went to the tent opening again. "Please come in out of the rain," she said, wiping sprays of water from her face as she held the flap aside. "Strong Heart, there is room in here for both of us. Come on. There is no need for you to stay outside. You will catch a chill at the least."

Dripping and cold, Strong Heart went to the tent. Once inside, Elizabeth wrapped a dry blanket around his shoulders. "You must get out of those wet clothes," she said, blushing at the thought of him undressing in her presence. "I . . . I . . . shall turn my head. Please do it quickly, Strong Heart. You don't want to become ill."

Amused, Strong Heart watched her turn her head from him, then dropped the blankets away. Swiftly, he yanked the clinging white man's clothes off and tossed them from the tent. They were of no further use to him. He would dress in buckskin tomorrow for his journey through the forest toward his home. He was glad to be returning to his people and his familiar ways.

He drew on the blanket, wrapping it snugly around his body. "You no longer have to keep your eyes from me," he said lightly.

Smiling abashedly, Elizabeth turned her face back to him. She blushed again when she saw him dressed in only the blanket. "Are you warmer now?" she asked softly, sitting down on another blanket, wrapping it around her shoulders.

"*Ah-hah,*" Strong Heart said, settling down beside her.

"Well, I . . . I guess we'd best get some sleep," Elizabeth said, her eyes wide, wondering if he could hear the thunderous beating of her heart. She could feel it in her ears, pounding like a thousand drums.

"*Ah-hah,*" Strong Heart said, easing down onto his side, so that she would have plenty of room to lie down.

She followed his lead, stretching out beside him.

When another great clap of thunder shook the ground beneath her, she jumped with alarm and welcomed a comforting arm around her waist, yet knew the dangers in even this minimal contact.

She closed her eyes tightly, to try and block out the

desire that made her ache for the feel of his lips on hers, his skin against hers.

And, as if he read her mind, he slowly turned her to face him, and she allowed it. . . .

10

In one another's being mingle;—
Why not I with thine?
                    —SHELLEY

His long lean fingers weaving through Elizabeth's hair,
Strong Heart drew her lips to his. Never had she felt
such bliss as when he began kissing her, his free hand
at her waist, urging her closer to him, pressing her
hard against his body—which was now nude, the blanket having dropped away from him.

Her senses reeled as he prolonged the meltingly hot
kiss, his hand skillfully unfastening her dress at the
back. She watched, feeling as if she were in some sort
of magical trance, as he leaned away from her and
slipped the dress over her shoulders, and down the full
length of her.

She did not protest when he continued, not even
when she was totally disrobed and could relish the feel
of his skin on hers as he again drew her fully against
him.

His hands were on her flesh, searching, caressing,
fondling, causing Elizabeth's breath to catch in her
throat. Just when she thought she could bear no more,
Strong Heart's lips explored her body for her most sensitive pleasure points.

She stretched out on her back and closed her eyes,
giving herself up to the rapture, fighting off the urge
to tell him to stop—tell him that what she was allowing
was surely wicked.

All rational thoughts she easily cast aside, having
never been lectured against this beautiful thing that
was happening between herself and the man she loved.

Her mother had not been there to explain this side of life to her.

Her father had never been able to speak of such things around her.

What she had learned had been from novels, and now, tonight, Strong Heart was her true teacher.

And, ah, how skilled a teacher he was. His tongue and lips were like flames against her flesh, scorching . . . burning. Desire rose high within her as he showered heated kisses over her taut-tipped breasts, his mouth sweet and hungry as he then kissed her lips with a lazy warmth that left her weak.

And then she became aware of something else. A thick shaft resting against her thigh, pulsing it seemed, with a life of its own.

Curious, she drew her lips away from Strong Heart's and peered down at him, blushing when she gazed upon this part of a man that she had never seen before.

She was not as embarrassed as she was intrigued.

She slowly reached a hand toward the swollen shaft, Strong Heart's fingers circling hers, guiding her hand to his throbbing member.

"Touch it," Strong Heart said huskily, his heart thundering within his chest, desire filling him now as never before in his life. "Caress me. There you will find the center of my passions . . . my passions aroused by you, my *la-daila*. Only you."

Her pulse racing, every nerve ending within her feeling the exquisite tension of the moment, on fire with needs that were new to her. Elizabeth looked shyly up at Strong Heart.

Then, without losing contact with his eyes, she circled her fingers around the thickness of his manhood.

She was fascinated at how when his lean, sinewy buttocks began to move, he caused his manhood to move within her fingers.

But this seemed to cause too much pleasure for

Strong Heart, for too soon he moaned throatily, then placed his hands at her shoulders and urged her away from him.

He drew her against him again, cradling her in his arms, the heat of his passion now pressing into her abdomen.

Holding her tightly, he turned her to lie again on her back. Brushing some strands of her hair back from her brow, he gazed at her with a look of possession in his eyes. "My love for you is new, yet strong," he said passionately. "My *la-daila,* tell me that it is the same for you."

"I have never loved before," Elizabeth said, pleasure spreading anew through her body as his fingers gently kneaded her breasts. "But I know it, now that I am experiencing it."

She framed his handsome face between her hands and drew his lips close. "Yes, Strong Heart," she whispered. "Although new to me, my love for you is strong. It steals my breath away, this love I have for you. It is a wonderful feeling, as if I am suddenly wrapped in a cocoon of deliciously warm cotton, my whole body responding to yours. You are lying with me in this cocoon, your body awakening mine to pleasure."

She clung to him as once again he kissed her. She felt a soft probing at the juncture of her thighs— something hot, something wonderful, and then she understood exactly what was trying to make entrance where no man had been before: His manhood.

One of his knees moved her legs apart, and then again she felt the probing. She closed her eyes tightly and clasped her arms around Strong Heart's neck, opening herself to him, making it easier for what he sought. Yet he pulled away, stopping what he had begun and she had agreed to.

Elizabeth's eyes opened in surprise as Strong Heart

rolled away from her, his hands still at her waist, turning her on her side to face him.

He gazed at her naked splendor, his eyes filled with a drugged passion, then he looked into her eyes.

"Say that you want me," he said, tracing the line of her jaw with his finger. "I must hear you say it, before our bodies become as one. It is important to know that you understand this that we do, and want it as badly, as I. I want you to love me forever, my *ladaila*. Not just tonight."

"I'm not sure what want is," Elizabeth said, innocently. "As I said earlier, I've never been in love before."

"Listen to your body—the ache, the passions aroused within it," Strong Heart said, his one hand now at the core of her womanhood, slowly caressing it with his fingertips. "Do you feel it? The passions that need to be answered with mine?"

Desire was shooting through Elizabeth as his fingers so skillfully awakened her body to even newer sensations. She closed her eyes and threw her head back, sighing.

"Yes," she whispered. "The passion. Oh, such passion. I do feel it. Please, oh, please. I do need you, Strong Heart. Forever I will need you."

Strong Heart drew her beneath him. He bent down and kissed her, his palms moving softly and arousingly over her as he once again parted her legs with his knee and began pressing his manhood slowly inside her yielding folds.

Gently he entered her. When he reached that shield that stopped his entrance, he held her tenderly to him and kissed away her pain as he made the plunge that finally made her wholly his.

The pain was only brief, causing Elizabeth's body to wince, and then the pain smoothed out to something deliciously sweet.

She twined her arms about Strong Heart's neck and circled her legs around him, locking them at the ankles, and rode with him, taking from him all that he offered, his strokes within her a steady rocking movement now.

As Strong Heart's breathing quickened, he moved his mouth from her lips and pillowed his cheek against her full bosom. He closed his eyes and plunged ever more deeply within her, his fingers digging into the flesh of her hips, pulling her tightly against him.

The soft, melting energy was warming him, spreading throughout his body.

Overcome by the unbearably sweet pain, Elizabeth began rolling her head from side to side, the whimperings that came to her ears, her own. She trembled with excitement as Strong Heart began sucking one of her nipples, then flicked his tongue around its hardness.

She drew in her breath sharply and gave a little cry as he gave one last, hard thrust, his manhood filling her—oh, so magnificently filling her—causing the passion to spill over within her.

She strained her hips up at him when she felt a great shuddering in his loins, thinking that surely meant that he had also reached the same pinnacle of ecstasy that she had just climbed.

Breathing hard, Strong Heart's body subsided exhaustedly onto hers. He lay there for a long moment with her, stroking her womanhood, that still pulsed from the aftermath of her rapture.

And then he rolled away from her. His hands found the soft swell of her breasts. She arched toward him, her parted mouth and closed eyes an invitation to kiss her again.

With a groan he pulled her against him and kissed her, their tongues touching, their bodies straining together.

As she clung to Strong Heart, his kiss dizzying her, Elizabeth moved her body sinuously against his, feeling his renewed desire as his swollen shaft once again pressed into her warmed flesh.

In what seemed a dream, Strong Heart had her positioned above him and magnificently filled her again with his powerful need. As she straddled him, leaning back, her red hair streaming long and gleaming down her back, she rode him as he lifted himself into her with his thrusts. She awakened anew to the smoldering desire that she had discovered tonight with this man that she adored—that she loved.

As the rain poured against the tent and the thunder boomed, shaking the very earth beneath them, Strong Heart reached for Elizabeth's waist and urged her beneath him again. As he entered her and began his steady strokes, they once again found paradise together, their bodies locked together in a fierce, fevered heat.

And then they lay side by side, their hands entwined, their breaths mingling as they stared with bliss into each other's eyes.

"You now understand the meaning of want?" Strong Heart whispered, his one hand gently caressing one of her breasts.

"Yes," she breathed, her face flushed from the drunken pleasure that she had just experienced. "Oh, yes. I understand. Oh, so very much, my darling."

"Your needs were answered . . . fulfilled?" he prodded. He could feel her tremble sensually when he flicked his tongue out to again taste the sweetness of her breast.

"Yes, yes," she said, shivering with delight when he moved to his knees and bent over her, kissing the pleasure points of her body. "You are a masterful lover. So . . . so . . . very skilled."

She wove her fingers through his long, brown hair

and brought his lips to hers. She kissed him softly, then sighed languorously when he moved away from her and lay on his back beside her.

"Come," he said, beckoning with a hand toward her. "Lie within my arms. Let me sing you to sleep, my *la-daila*. Listen. Relax. Enjoy. Sleep and dream of this man who loves you."

Smiling sleepily, Elizabeth snuggled into the warm nest of blankets with him. She moved into his arms and lay close to him, having never felt so much at peace with herself and her world.

And as he began to sing to her, he pulled her deeper and deeper into loving him.

"What did you think when you saw the trail we took?" he sang in a soft and lulling voice. "What did you think when you saw the trail we took? My dearest one, I thought of you when I saw the trail we took. I thought of you."

He paused before starting his next song. He glanced down at Elizabeth and smiled to himself when he saw her eyes were closed, sleep coming easily to her tonight, as it would to him. He was in a world now that transcended all troubles and pain. He was in a world that belonged only to him, and his *la-daila*.

He began singing again:

"I saw the moon rise tonight and my thoughts went to you.
I saw the moon rise tonight and my thoughts went to you.
Beloved, I wish I were there with you.
I saw the moon rise tonight and my thoughts went to you.
My beloved, I wish I were there with you."

Cradling Elizabeth protectively, he closed his eyes, a smile on his face.

11

Too late I stayed—forgive the crime,
Unheeded flew the hours.
—WILLIAM ROBERT SPENCER

Elizabeth's eyes flew open and she bolted to a sitting position. Then she paled and drew a blanket around her nakedness as she slowly looked around her, her sight stopping on Strong Heart. She remembered the previous evening as she looked at him lying so close beside her, his breathing slow as he soundly slept, his blanket having fallen aside.

Elizabeth could not deny the passion that flooded her when she regarded his nude body, seeing that part of him that had made her body thrill with pleasure.

Her heart beat wildly at the memory, yet now she regretted her wanton behavior with Strong Heart.

Last night it had seemed so right.

Today—she was confused about how she should feel!

She loved Strong Heart, yet a part of her tormented her, telling her that what she had done was wrong.

What she had done had surely been because she was under his spell. Strong Heart's presence had bewitched her from the moment they had met.

Even now, she felt it, the way he made her feel—oh, this wasn't her!

He turned on his other side, his face now away from her, his breathing still, even, and soft, indicating that he was still asleep. Elizabeth recalled something else—how he had said that he would never allow her to return home. How he seemed to want *total* possession of her.

She wanted nothing more than to be with him, forever. Yet there was this thing called "freedom" that nagged at her mind. She did not want to be anyone's captive. She wanted him to understand that if she stayed with him, it was because *she* had decided to—not because *he* had made the choice for her.

Yet, he had seemed so determined in his decision, she saw no other option but to try and escape, even if it meant losing him. *And* the special love that he had introduced her to.

As her gaze lingered on his muscular body, every beat of her heart told her that she wanted to stay with him.

Yet these strong feelings for him were another reason she must try and escape from him. She did not see how a love between them could work. She began crawling on her knees, gathering her clothes into her arms. Then she scurried outside where she could dress without awakening him.

As she slipped into her clothes, she looked around her, and was glad to see that the morning mists had vanished. The sun was clearing the horizon, the dew sparkled on the grass.

She peered warily into the depths of the forest, a rush of fear stopping her. She wondered that even if she did escape from Strong Heart, could she, in truth, find her way back to Seattle?

There were no true roads. There weren't even any paths. And she would be at the mercy of all the animals roaming the land, four-legged and two-legged.

The thought terrified her, yet she saw no other choice but to take her chances.

Her future must be *hers,* not something planned and mapped out by someone else.

Finally she was fully clothed. She groaned as she glanced down at her silk dress and saw how wrinkled and stained it had gotten on her flight from Seattle.

And it was less than suitable for the return journey.

Its yards of silk would constantly impede her movements. It was not the attire to wear while riding a horse.

"A horse," she whispered to herself, blanching. "I must steal his horse."

She glanced back guiltily at the tent. If she stole the horse, Strong Heart would be stranded without any transportation.

She set her jaw. It would serve him right! He had not thought of her welfare when he had abducted her. Nor would she his!

Relieved that the air was warm, *that* at least in her favor, Elizabeth began moving toward the roan that grazed close beside the river. When she reached the lovely animal, she grabbed for the reins, then she felt a movement behind her.

Turning with a start, she gasped when she saw Strong Heart running after her, having not taken the time to dress when he had found her gone. She watched his muscular, copper body and recalled with a rush of passion how it had felt to be pressed against it. Then she shook herself free of her trance and again grabbed for the horse's reins, knowing that this was perhaps the only chance, ever, for her to win her freedom.

Her fingers worked clumsily with the knot of the rawhide reins, unable to untie them.

She glanced over her shoulder just in time to see Strong Heart lunge for her. Her breath was momentarily knocked out of her when he threw her onto her back on the ground.

"You leave me?" he said, holding her wrists to the ground as he straddled her. He thrust his face into hers, peering down at her angrily. "Why do you? You professed to love Strong Heart. You professed to *need* me!"

Elizabeth did not know how to explain to him why she was leaving him, for deep inside, where her desires dwelled, she knew that she was going against everything that her heart was telling her to do.

The sudden screech of a hawk overhead, and its loud flapping of wings as it dipped low, barely missing Strong Heart's head, caused him to flinch and loosen his grip on her wrists.

Taking advantage of his loss of concentration, Elizabeth jerked her wrists free and gave him a hard shove on his chest.

Wild-eyed, she watched him fall away from her. Then he grabbed her at the waist, bringing her along with him as he rolled threateningly close to the river.

"Let me go!" Elizabeth cried, struggling to get away from him.

But he was determined not to let her go. He rolled her over and started to straddle her again, then lost his balance and started slipping sideways into the water. At the last moment he grabbed her hand, pulling her into the water with him.

Stunned by the spill and the intense cold of the water, Elizabeth's wits were momentarily stolen away. When she regained her bearings, she found herself floundering just beneath the surface of the river, the sun pouring through the water like bright lamplight.

A muscular arm circled around her waist. She tried to pry it away, then rose with Strong Heart to the surface, coughing fitfully. He held her close to him as he stood, his feet planted firmly on the rocky bottom of the shallows. She again struggled to get free, slapping at his arms and chest.

"I can't believe this!" she shouted, coughing and gasping for air. "Let me go, do you hear? Haven't you done enough?" A shiver coursed through her. "I'm freezing. Let me out of this water!"

"Not until you tell me that you are sorry for planning to leave me," Strong Heart said, his grasp strong as steel, his face leaning into hers. "Only then will I let go of you."

"You will have to hold me in this water until it freezes over then," Elizabeth cried, wiping wet strands of hair back from her eyes. She shivered and shook and her teeth chattered from the frigid cold.

Strong Heart's eyes bored into hers. He saw how purple her lips were, but he still would not allow her to leave the water.

"When the waters turn to ice in the dead of winter, then both of us shall become lodged within it," Strong Heart said stubbornly. "I mean to have you. And I shall."

He lowered his face closer, smiling. "You are already mine, you know—body and soul. Why do you fight it? It is useless, this decision of yours to turn your back on Strong Heart. Because I know that it is not what you truly want. I shall not allow it. Ever!"

"No one wants to feel imprisoned, by *anyone*," Elizabeth cried, hugging herself with her arms. The silver minnows in the water seemed puzzled as they swam in circles around her and Strong Heart.

"You are not the only one held captive," Strong Heart said, his eyes flashing into hers. "Strong Heart is also a captive—of your heart. Even if I would allow you to ride away from me, or I from you, *I* would *never* be free. Do you not understand this? Do you not believe it? As long as I have breath in my body, I am yours. Totally."

Frustrated, Elizabeth lowered her eyes. "Oh, Strong Heart, please don't confuse me any more than I already am," she said softly, her voice catching in her throat.

When his finger lifted her chin upward, and their eyes met, she even became more confused between loving him, and wanting not to.

But when his mouth came to hers, and he kissed

her, everything began to fall back into place within her heart and mind.

And when he wrapped her within his powerful arms, the coldness of the water was forgotten. All that she felt was the heat of his flesh. She knew what she wanted.

To be with Strong Heart. *He* was her heart. Her soul. Her entire being.

She knew at this moment that she could never leave him—not as long as he wanted her with him.

She hungrily returned the kiss, moaning as his hands slipped from her waist up to her breasts, stroking them through the clinging wetness of her dress.

"I do need you," she whispered, as she pulled her lips away from his. "I do want you. I love you, Strong Heart. I no longer want to flee from you. I want to stay. I love you. I adore you."

Strong Heart framed her face between his hands and smiled down at her. Then he placed his arms beneath her and swung her up into them, and carried her from the water, his lips again sending her into a whirlwind of desire as he kissed her until they were inside the tent.

"Your wet clothes," Strong Heart whispered as he slid his lips down to the hollow of her throat. "You must get them off."

"So I won't come down with pneumonia?" Elizabeth said, her eyes twinkling into his as she raised her arms, allowing Strong Heart to pull the clinging dress over her head.

"I do not wish to see you get ill," Strong Heart said, tossing the dress aside. His long, lean fingers finished undressing her. "But the main reason for disrobing you is so that I can give you more cause to not want to leave me. Perhaps last night was not lesson enough. Today I will make love to you so that you will

never, for even a moment, forget my feelings for you—
and yours for Strong Heart.''

Now splendidly nude, Elizabeth drifted into Strong
Heart's embrace. His flesh quickly warmed hers as he
held her and kissed her.

Then he led her to the blankets, spreading her out
on top of one, while he drew another blanket over
them, so that as they made love, the heat of their bodies
would be warmer than the flames of any fire.

Elizabeth's breath quickened with yearning as Strong
Heart's lips brushed her throat. His hands moved over
her silky, satiny flesh, stroking her, teasing her.

Then he took her mouth by storm and engulfed her
in his muscled arms. She trembled with readiness as
she felt the probing of his manhood at the juncture of
her thighs, then arched and cried out as he drove in,
swiftly and surely, his body soon moving against hers.

She absorbed the bold thrusts, his lips drugging
her, the intoxication of his kiss, and the caress of his
hands, causing her to be overcome by an unbearable,
sweet agony that was pressing in on her heart.

When he slithered his lips down her neck, and he
flicked a tongue around one nipple, and then the other,
she gave herself up to the ecstasy. She clung to him,
her fingers grasping his long, wet hair, and then down
his back. Then she splayed her fingers against his buttocks and wrapped her legs around his waist and thrust
her pelvis toward him, drawing him more deeply into
her. He pressed endlessly deeper, his mouth moving
back to her lips, their tongues tangling through parted
lips. Tremors cascaded down Elizabeth's legs.

Strong Heart paused and looked at her, their eyes
locked in an unspoken understanding, and promise of
rapture.

Then Strong Heart gathered Elizabeth to him, feeling the pleasure mounting within him, ready to go over
the edge.

One last, deep plunge inside her, and the spinning sensation rose up and flooded him. He felt the intensity of his passion exploding through every cell of his body.

A surge of tingling heat spread through Elizabeth. Her head rolled and she emitted a cry of joy as the fire began exploding within her.

Afterward, they clung to each other, breathing hard, sweat pearling their bodies.

"I'm no longer cold," Elizabeth whispered, placing a gentle hand to Strong Heart's cheek. "I feel as if I'm on fire, my darling. What I just experienced with you was agony *and* bliss. How can that be?"

"Who can explain the wonders of the body when in love?" Strong Heart said hoarsely, leaning over to kiss the pink tip of one of her breasts. "Just accept it. Just enjoy it."

"I do love you so," Elizabeth said, snuggling closer to him. Then she gazed up at him and smiled. "Do you think it's time we ate something, then went on to your village?"

Strong Heart smiled back at her and nodded. "*Ah-hah*, it is time," he said, then grabbed her more tightly into his arms and kissed her heatedly, hungrily.

"But first, let us make love again," he whispered to her. "Then, my *la-daila*, I shall give you dry clothes to wear for the rest of the journey. It will not be any that you are used to. You will wear one of my buckskin outfits."

She nodded her approval, then lost herself in sensual frenzy again as he lowered himself onto her and began moving, loving her slowly and leisurely this time.

12

And now on the sky I look,
And my heart grows full of weeping.
—MRS. CRAWFORD

Disgruntled, and his clothes snug after shrinking from riding in the rain, Earl stomped into his house, slamming the large oak door behind him.

Dropping his saddlebags to the floor, he stared down the long corridor that led to the grand staircase, then at the doors which led from the corridor to the other rooms on the lower floor, anxious to find Elizabeth. Had she behaved while he had been gone? The long ride into the wilderness away from her had made him realize just what she meant to him. He had sworn to himself that he would pay more attention to her—make her feel more loved, more wanted. He had lost a wife due to his business concerns. He did not want to lose his daughter's love, as well.

"Elizabeth!" he shouted, smoothing his hands through his golden hair as he began walking down the corridor, toward the staircase, thinking that perhaps she was in her room this time of day, napping or sewing. "Baby, I'm home. Elizabeth, do you hear me? I'm home."

When he got to the foot of the staircase, he heard footsteps above him. He smiled and looked up, expecting Elizabeth to be there, glad to see him home safe and sound.

But his smile quickly faded and his mouth gaped open when he did not find Elizabeth there. Instead, a young lady—a total stranger—stood at the head of the staircase, looking down at him with an awkward smile.

Then Frannie stepped to this stranger's side, herself looking no less nervous as she twisted and untwisted the strings of her lace-trimmed apron as she peered down at him, her eyes wide.

"Frannie, who is that young lady and where is Elizabeth?" Earl demanded. When Frannie did not answer immediately, he began to feel unnerved.

He glanced from the young lady, back to Frannie, then doubled his fists at his sides. "By God, Frannie, explain this lady's presence here. Tell me why Elizabeth is not here to greet me," he said between clenched teeth. "If you have allowed my daughter to leave this house unescorted, so help me, Frannie, you may have to swim all the way back to San Francisco, for I doubt if I would be able to tolerate such foolery from you."

Frannie glanced at Maysie, then with a pounding heart she looked back down at Earl. "This here is Maysie," she said, her voice pitched high from fear. "Elizabeth . . . Elizabeth invited her to stay with us for a while. Our sweet Elizabeth done saved Maysie from drowning in the Sound."

Earl's eyebrows rose. "Drowning?" he said with a gasp. "Elizabeth risked her life for a total stranger? How, Frannie? When?"

Frannie twisted her apron strings more as she cast her eyes to the floor, fearing to tell him the whole truth. What she had told him already had condemned her.

Earl stomped up the stairs and when he reached the second-floor landing, he towered over Frannie and glowered at her. "So help me, Frannie, if you don't tell me what this is all about, I'll horsewhip you," he said, his voice edged with anger and frustration.

He glanced toward Elizabeth's door. It was open and he could see that she was not there.

Then he gave Frannie an uneasy look. "Damn it, Frannie, where is Elizabeth?" he half shouted.

Tears streamed in silver rivulets down Frannie's dark face. She looked slowly back up at Earl. "Massa' Easton, she's gone," she sobbed. "After Maysie here told Elizabeth about the poor women locked up in that prison in Seattle, Elizabeth, with her big heart an' all, she done take books and fruit to them women."

His shock was so keen, Earl had to reach for the bannister to steady himself. He clutched it, speechless for a moment. Then he forced himself not to shout at Frannie again. Right now all that was important was to get answers—answers about his beloved daughter. A frantic, hysterical Frannie would not be able to help.

He placed a trembling hand gently on Frannie's thick shoulder. "Hush up your crying," he said. "I'm not going to ship you off. I'm sorry I frightened you. Now tell me how long Elizabeth has been gone."

Frannie burst into loud wails, shaking her head frantically. "For too long, Massa' Easton," she cried, now looking pitifully up at Earl. "Too long. She left yesterday mornin' and hasn't returned. I sent Everett to look for her. He didn't find her. When he went to the sheriff to see if he'd seen her, the sheriff made no sense. He'd been hit over the head earlier by someone who helped turn the Indian loose from the prison. He was still not talking right when Everett asked him about Elizabeth. Seems no one knows about her, Massa' Easton. Oh, lordy, lordy, what has become of our Elizabeth?"

Earl's face twisted into a grimace, frightened by Frannie's words. There had been an escape at the prison, and the sheriff had been injured during it. If Elizabeth had been there at the time of the escape. . . .

"God," he said beneath his breath, panic filling him. He began running down the stairs. "I'm going to Seattle to find Elizabeth. I've got to. Surely some-one's seen her!''

His horse was still saddled from his journey. Earl quickly mounted and sunk his heels into the flanks of the animal. Snapping the reins harshly, he urged the stallion into a hard gallop. Something terrible must have happened to his daughter for her not to have re-turned home by now. If anything had happened to her because of her foolish do gooding, he would have no one but himself to blame—and he would never forgive himself. He shouldn't have given her cause to be rest-less. He should have spent more time with her.

And Frannie had said Elizabeth had saved the strange girl while wandering about the Sound. Who was to say where Elizabeth had wandered in his ab-sence?

His jaw tightened and his eyes became lit with fire. ''Damn it, Frannie,'' he grumbled to himself. ''I thought you had more hold on her than that.''

But he knew that he could not blame Frannie for any of it. Frannie had tried with all of her might to keep Elizabeth in line. Even in San Francisco, Eliza-beth had given him and Frannie fits at times. Frannie had never been unable to stop her. His daughter had a mind of her own. She was even more stubborn than her mother had been.

And that gave Earl much cause for concern.

The ride to Seattle seemed to take forever, but fi-nally he was riding up the steep hill that led to the prison.

When he arrived at the ramshackle building, he dis-mounted, his eyes locking on the swaying noose on the hanging platform. An involuntary shudder coursed through him at the sight. He had seen many hangings in his lifetime.

But the worst sight of all for him had been when he had been in China. The Chinese did not hang their condemned. Instead, they lined them up in a row in the center of the city, and chopped their heads off.

Shaking the memory from his mind, Earl walked quickly to the prison, and marched into the office. The sheriff was sitting with his feet propped up on the desk. What Earl saw on top of the desk made him pale and feel light-headed.

"Elizabeth's books," he gasped, knowing them well, for he had bought every one of them for her during his travels. He now knew that she *had* been there.

She *had* brought the books to the incarcerated women, as Frannie had said. But what then had happened to her?

"What'd you say about those books?" Sheriff Nolan said, rubbing the raw, aching knot at the base of his skull. "Do you know the woman they belong to?"

Earl sighed heavily as he shifted his gaze to the sheriff. "More to the point," he said dryly, "do *you* know her? Do you recall her being here?"

"Who wants to know?" Sheriff Nolan asked, rising slowly from his chair. He ambled out from behind the desk and stood eye to eye with Earl.

Earl squared his shoulders. "I'm her father," he said, leaning his face into the sheriff's, repulsed by the foul odor of chewing tobacco and rotgut whiskey. "Now you tell me. Where is she? She didn't make it back home after comin' here with her books."

"Oh? Is that a fact?" Sheriff Nolan said, resting his hands on the handles of his pistols at each hip. "Describe this daughter to me and I'll tell you whether or not she's been here."

"Damn it, Sheriff, I already know she's been here," Earl said. He nodded toward the books. "Those are hers. You don't look like the sort that reads, or pays for books."

Sheriff Nolan shrugged and went to his desk, lifting

up a book and slowly turning the pages. "She's an educated redhead, is she?" he asked. He recalled yanking her basket from her and wrestling her to the floor. Right after, he had been knocked unconscious. Ever since he had regained consciousness he had thought of hardly anything else but the redhead and that she had probably participated in the escape. She had been the distraction, and it sure as hell had worked.

Sheriff Nolan quickly decided not to let Earl in on his assumptions about Elizabeth. He had his own score to settle with the slut.

"So you *did* see my daughter?" Earl said, impatient with the sheriff's vagueness.

"Yeah, guess I did at that," Sheriff Nolan grumbled, slamming the book back down on his desk. "But that was short-lived. Soon after our introduction, someone knocked me out." He shrugged. "As far as I can figure, she's been taken captive by whoever hit me and set the Injun loose from his cell. Yeah, that's how I see it."

On hearing the sheriff say that Elizabeth had been abducted, the reality of the situation hit Earl hard. It was as if someone had slapped him across the face. He tottered, feeling a sudden queasiness. His sweet, his precious daughter's life was at the mercy of hardened criminals, one of them an Indian condemned to die!

It was hard for him to bear—the possibility of having lost his daughter forever.

Then he came to his senses, realizing that something had to be done.

A posse. Yes, a posse had to be formed. Why was the sheriff here when Elizabeth had to be found?

The sheriff moved behind the desk again and slouched down into his chair. He reached for a fresh plug of chewing tobacco and bit off a large wad, stuffing it into one corner of his mouth.

Earl had to work hard at controlling his temper at the sheriff's indifference. He leaned his hands on the desk and looked the sheriff square in the eye. "You say my daughter has been abducted and you just sit there twiddling your thumbs and chewin' that damn tobacco?" he said, his voice cold and steady. "Am I to expect nothing more from you? You allow an innocent girl to be abducted and you talk about it as if it is something that happens every day, and nothing to concern your ass about?"

"I wouldn't get myself riled up too much before knowing everything," Sheriff Nolan said, turning his head, to spit a long stream of tobacco juice into the stained spittoon. "There's a posse out there somewhere busy lookin' for the criminals, *and* your daughter. That's all that can be done at this point."

The sheriff leaned his elbows on the desk. "Now I'd suggest you go home and wait for the posse's return. Do you get my meaning? There ain't nothin' you can do here, 'cept get me riled, and I don't think you want to get me riled, eh? What did you say your name was?"

"I didn't," Earl said through clenched teeth, his eyes narrowed with anger.

"A name is needed if you want to know the results of the posse's findings," Sheriff Nolan said, smiling crookedly up at Earl, enjoying his fooling with the man. If the redhead *was* found, safe and sound, her father would be the last to know. Jed would take his turn with her before her father had a chance to even realize that she was alive. What he had planned for her would not paint a pretty picture.

She was worse than the outlaw who had been set free from the prison. She was a whoring seductress who had made a fool out of him. And no woman made a jackass out of Sheriff Jed Nolan and lived to tell it, he thought darkly to himself.

Earl wasn't quick to respond to the sheriff's command, seeing too much about the man that did not ring true. He seemed an untrustworthy sort. Earl was amazed that such a man had been elected to be sheriff.

Yet too often in bawdy seaport towns, these were the kind of men in power that he had run into. And he had no choice but to trust that this lawman would do right by his daughter.

"My daughter's name is Elizabeth," Earl said, his voice guarded. "Elizabeth Easton." He reached a hand to the sheriff. "I'm new in town. I'm establishing a fishery down the Sound a mile or two. At the old Pike Mansion. I'm sure you've heard about it. I'm Earl Easton."

Before accepting Earl's handshake, Sheriff Nolan turned to the spittoon and spat out another long stream of juice.

He wiped his mouth and mustache on the back of his right hand, then offered it to Earl. "Nice to make your acquaintance," he said, chuckling beneath his breath when he saw Earl grimace as he took the hand with traces of tobacco juice on the fingers.

Earl wiped his hand on the leg of his pants, then glowered down at the sheriff. "I'll be waitin' to hear from you," he warned. "If I don't hear soon, I'll take out after the damn outlaws myself."

"That wouldn't be wise," Sheriff Nolan said, placing his fingertips together before him. "You'd just complicate things. Let the professionals do the job. You just get back to your fishery. I'll send word as soon as I know."

Hesitating, yet knowing that he was only one man and did not know the countryside as well as those who made a living hunting outlaws, Earl nodded and left the prison.

With a heavy heart, he mounted his stallion and headed back for home. His thoughts were on Elizabeth, and how it had been between them through the years—how he had been the one to hold back on love.

It was her mother's fault. If Marilyn had not fled to parts unknown, Earl would not have had the need to reject his daughter.

He hung his head. He knew that he should hate his wife for having deserted him, yet he knew that he was the cause. Just as now, as he was the cause for his daughter's life to be in peril.

Before he realized it, he was home. The miles had been eaten up while his mind had been absorbed by thoughts of the past and the future.

He gave his horse's reins to Everett. Then he went inside the house, where he was met by an anxious Frannie.

"Elizabeth?" Frannie said, her eyes wide as she followed Earl toward the parlor. "Do you know any more about Elizabeth?"

Earl stopped and turned and gave her a watery stare. "As far as anyone can tell, she's been abducted," he said, his voice breaking.

Maysie stepped beside Frannie, just in time to hear the disheartening news. Her knees grew weak and she felt a desperation rising within her. Guilt pressed on her heart.

"No!" she cried, placing her hands to her cheeks, tears flooding her eyes. "Elizabeth has been abducted? No! Please, no! Oh, God, I'm to blame. If I'd never told Elizabeth about the women at the prison, she'd have not gone there! Who abducted her? Who?"

"Apparently the man who set the Indian free from prison," Earl said. Then he took a step toward Maysie and glared down at her. "And, yes, young lady, you *are* to blame. If not for you, my daughter would be home now, *safe*!"

Maysie stared up at Earl with stricken eyes. Then she bolted up the steep staircase, wailing distraughtly.

Frannie went after her, also wailing.

Earl hung his head, and went into the parlor. He walked lifelessly to a window and drew the sheer curtain aside, staring into the trees.

His beloved daughter. Where was she?

He tried to distract himself from his anguish with other thoughts. He knew he must go back to the Suquamish Indian village. He had to convince them that what he offered was for their best interest, as well as his own.

"My fishery," he muttered to himself.

He wondered how he could make plans for the future now, when he did not know if it would include his daughter?

He was ridden with guilt for having neglected her.

First his wife, and now his daughter.

He had never been a God-fearing man. But now he could not help but think that God was punishing him for all of his transgressions against humanity, especially his own kin.

13

Ah!—With what thankless heart
I mourn and sing!
—BARRY CORNWALL

The sun was splashing the sky a brilliant crimson as it lowered behind the mountains in the far distance. Elizabeth sat in the saddle behind Strong Heart, clinging to his waist, apprehensive about soon entering his village and meeting his people, especially his parents. She knew Strong Heart's bitterness over white people well enough. Surely his people's feelings were even stronger against white people.

If so, they would not take to their chief's son having fallen in love with a white-skinned woman. Her mere presence might make life awkward for Strong Heart, and that was the last thing that she wanted.

Yet he was strong willed. Perhaps he would overlook any resentment toward her.

She glanced down at her clothing. The fringed buckskin outfit fit her loosely. A rope around her waist held the breeches up. She had rolled up the legs so that she would not trip over them as she walked, and she had rolled up the sleeves of the shirt to her elbows.

Although she knew that she must look comical, at least it had made traveling on horseback with Strong Heart more tolerable.

Strong Heart noticed hawks circling in the air up ahead. They must surely be flying above his village. It would soon be within sight once they rode up a slight butte. His roan's footing was sure on the loose and crumbling rock.

His keen senses picked up a faint odor of smoke and ash, sending a warning to him that all was not right.

He surveyed the soaring hawks, realizing that they only flew like this in a group, if death was on the trail. Or in a village, he thought grimly.

Elizabeth could feel how Strong Heart's muscles had suddenly tensed. His breathing had quickened and he was concentrating strangely on several hawks in the sky.

"What is it, Strong Heart?" she asked, clutching even more tightly around his waist as he kicked his moccasined heels into the flanks of his horse and sent it up the rise, to the top.

Strong Heart had not heard Elizabeth. All that he heard was the crying of his heart as he peered down and saw the destruction of so much of his village. Half of its cedar homes had been burned to the ground. The burnt totem poles listed crazily. The sight chilled his blood.

The devastation was everywhere.

He could see the people of his village roaming about, their heads bowed, their wails reaching clear into his soul. While he was gone, tending to his own affairs, his village had caught fire, somehow. And by the sound of the wailing, several of his people had died.

"Mother!" he gasped. "Father! Are *they* allright? *Aieee*," he cried with a shrill yelp, sending his horse into a hard gallop toward the remains of his village.

When he arrived, he dismounted in one leap, and forgetting Elizabeth, began running toward his father's longhouse. It still stood proud and untouched by the ravages of the fire that had swept through the village.

As he continued to run, he also saw that *his* longhouse still stood, saved by the people who loved him and his parents so much. They had probably allowed their own dwellings to burn in order to save their chief's, and the one who would next be chief.

He was followed by many people who reached out for him, crying his name. Strong Heart did not stop until he came to the entrance of his parents' lodge. Then he hurried inside.

What he saw made him teeter, for his father was lying on his sleeping platform, his eyes closed, otter fur pelts drawn up to his chin. "Father," he cried out, rushing to kneel beside the sleeping platform. He could not understand how his father had been harmed when his dwelling had been saved. Unless, unless, being the kindhearted man that he was, he had gone to help the others, and perhaps falling debris had struck him.

Strong Heart's mother came into the longhouse with a jug of water balanced on her shoulder. When she saw Strong Heart, she sat the jug down and went to kneel beside him.

When Strong Heart felt her presence, he turned to her and, with tears splashing from his eyes, he quickly embraced her. "You were not hurt by the fire?" he asked, holding her tightly to him, her usual scent of sweet grasses now ruined by the stink of smoke.

"Your mother is well enough," Pretty Nose murmured, then coughed fitfully. She eased from Strong Heart's arms and covered her mouth with her hands, continuing to cough until she was red in the face.

When she finally stopped, she cleared her throat and gazed sadly up at her son. "The smoke," she said hoarsely. "It entered my lungs. Still I cannot rid myself of the burning feeling left by the smoke."

Strong Heart stared with pain for a moment at his frail mother. Then he looked at his father again, whose eyes were now open, watching Strong Heart. When his father's hand reached out, Strong Heart circled his fingers around it and clung to it.

"My father, how are you?" Strong Heart said, seeing much pain in his father's eyes. He wanted to believe that part of that pain was from the loss of some of his beloved people, and the devastation the fire had caused.

"Your father has a heavy heart," Chief Moon Elk mumbled. "So much hope was taken from me yesterday."

"Yesterday?" Strong Heart said, recalling the fierceness of the thunderstorm as he and Elizabeth had clung to one another beneath the protection of their tent. "You say this happened yesterday. Was it lightning, Father, that caused the fire?"

"No, not lightning," Chief Moon Elk said somberly. "The fire was set by—"

Chief Moon Elk stopped in mid-sentence and looked fiercely into Strong Heart's eyes. "Four Winds?" he asked, his voice low and threatening. "You set him free? He is free to roam and do as he pleases now?"

"*Ah-hah,* that is so," Strong Heart said, puzzled by his father asking about Four Winds. What could Four Winds have to do with the fire?

If it had not been started by lightning, then by what? Or by whom?

"He is with you now? He has come to our village before riding on to his village in Canada?" Chief Moon Elk asked suspiciously.

"No, he did not come here. Once free, he rode separate from me," he said. His eyes widened when he remembered that, in his haste to check on the welfare of his parents, he had left Elizabeth alone. He wanted to rush to her now, but the matters of his people came first. Especially now that so much *me-sah-chie,* bad, had befallen them.

"That is as I thought," Chief Moon Elk grumbled, turning slowly away from Strong Heart. "He was probably among those who came and ravished our village. He was not recognized, but it was renegades like

Four Winds who rode side by side with the white men as they tossed torches on our people's dwellings. They sent many of our people to their deaths with sprays of arrows and bullets.''

Chief Moon Elk's eyes flashed with anger as he threw aside the otter fur pelts, and revealed a gunshot wound in his right leg. ''Four Winds may have even sent the bullet into your father's leg!'' he shouted.

Strong Heart sat there, aghast and speechless over what had happened while he had been gone. Chief Moon Elk drew the pelts back in place again and turned his eyes from Strong Heart.

''My son, you should have let the white man hang Four Winds,'' he said bitterly. ''Four Winds is *me-sah-chie,* to the core!''

Pretty Nose placed a gentle hand on Strong Heart's arm. ''My son, it is best now that you let your father rest. His wound has been treated well enough by me, but his heart—it still pains him, terribly.''

She flung herself into Strong Heart's arms. ''My son, it is so good that you are home again,'' she cried. ''Pay no heed to your father's anger about Four Winds. I believe that you would not have allowed him to be set free just to come and harm us. I truly do not believe that Four Winds had any part in the attack on our people. It is just someone for your father to blame, so that he does not feel so to blame, himself, for our tragedy.''

Strong Heart held his mother close. ''If anyone is to blame,'' he said thickly, ''it is I. I should have been home, protecting our people, instead of—''

He closed his eyes tightly, trying to block out thoughts of where he had probably been at the very moment of the attack. In Elizabeth's arms, his people and their concerns far, far from his mind. While he was making love to his *la-daila,* his people had needed him.

And he had not been there for them.

Pretty Nose pulled away from Strong Heart and peered up at him. "My son, you are only one person," she tried to reassure him. "You cannot be everywhere at once. No one expects you to be." She paused, then added, "While in Seattle, you did not find your grandfather? He is dead, is he not, my son? Your grandfather is surely dead!"

Strong Heart held her face between his powerful hands and leaned down and kissed her on her pert nose. "I searched and I did not find," he said. "But I do not allow myself to think that he is dead. I shall return to Seattle when I can, and search again, Mother."

Then his thoughts flew again to Elizabeth, seeing her sitting on the horse, afraid, as his people surrounded her. Perhaps they had even pulled her from the horse. She was white. And white men, accompanied by Indian renegades, had only yesterday come to their village and wreaked havoc in their lives! They could suspect her because her skin was white.

Without further words, Strong Heart left the longhouse at a run, then stopped in dismay when he did not find Elizabeth anywhere. His heart pounded as he looked in all directions. Seeing his longhouse, he wondered if she could be there.

With swift strides, Strong Heart went to his longhouse. He found Elizabeth inside sitting beside a fire. There was even a pot of soup hanging over it.

Strong Heart's eyes went to the Indian who was kneeling beside the fire, slowly stirring the soup. It was Many Stars, a lovely, petite Suquamish maiden who served Chief Moon Elk and his son devotedly. Although the same age as Strong Heart, she had been widowed twice. She now spent her time helping others, warding off any man's attempt to court her. She had declared that she would never love again. She had experienced the pain of too many losses already.

When Elizabeth saw Strong Heart standing in the doorway, she bolted to her feet and ran to him. She flung herself into his arms and clung to him. "Thank God you've come. If not for Many Stars, I may have been slain. She grabbed me away from several of your people. They see me as the enemy, Strong Heart. They hate me."

Many Stars smiled up at Strong Heart. "It was just a few who reacted foolishly to seeing Elizabeth on your horse," she said, rising to her feet, her eyes as dark as midnight as she gazed up at Strong Heart. "I guessed she was your woman since she was riding on your horse, and wearing your clothes. I brought her to your lodge. I knew that was what you would want."

Strong Heart reached a hand to Many Stars's soft, copper cheek. "*Mah-sie,* thank you," he said softly. She was comely as always, in her mountain sheepskin dress that was beautifully ornamented with quill beads. Her hair was neatly plaited in large braids that hung down over her breasts. "Now return to your parents. Help them build a new dwelling. I saw that their long-house was among those that burned, yet I was thankful to see that your parents were among the survivors."

Many Stars nodded. "*Ah-hah,* they survived and I will return to my chores alongside them. We were the lucky ones. We still have one another, while others have lost loved ones."

Guilt flooded Strong Heart's heart again, for having not been there to look after the welfare of his people.

Yet he felt blessed that it had not been worse than it was. All of the village could have been destroyed and all of his people could be dead.

His thoughts went to Four Winds, also wondering about his innocence or guilt in this. Yet it was just not logical to think that Four Winds would repay Strong

Heart in such a way for having helped him to escape from the prison.

No. Four Winds could have had nothing to do with this. Strong Heart would keep that thought while trying to find out who *did*.

"Go with care," Strong Heart said to Many Stars as she slipped outside.

Elizabeth eased from Strong Heart's arms. "Your parents?" she queried softly. "Are they all right?"

"Both are alive, but my father lies with a leg wound."

"I'm sorry about your father," Elizabeth responded. "I hope it's not serious."

"In time he will walk again," Strong Heart said sourly. "But for now, when he is needed the most by his people, he is incapacitated. He needs my leadership now. I will lend it to him to lessen his burden. I will be his legs. I will be everything for him."

"How can I help?" Elizabeth asked, almost afraid to hear the answer. For that brief moment, when her life had been threatened by those few Suquamish, she had seen just how much she could be resented by the Indians. In truth, she was quite shaken by the incident. But for Strong Heart, in his time of need, she would have to brush her fear aside.

"It is perhaps best if you return to Seattle," Strong Heart said. Saying this to her made it feel as if a knife were cutting into his heart, for he never wanted to let her go. But for now, he had to put his people before his needs.

Elizabeth paled. "You no longer want me?" she said, gasping. "Now that I want to be with you . . . you will send me away?"

Strong Heart softly held her shoulders. "My *ladaila*, I have much to make right in my world. That includes *you*. I should have never taken you against your will. You are free to go. And I have much to do.

I must help set things right for my people. And I trust you now, my *la-daila*. I know that you would never lift an accusing finger at me. I know that you love me too much to ever want harm to come to me.''

''If you know that I love you, and I know that you love me, why then do you still send me away?'' she pleaded.

Strong Heart placed a finger to her lips to silence her. ''Listen to what I have to say,'' he said quietly. ''*Ah-hah*, our love is strong between us. But there is more in life, than love between man and woman. I have always aspired to match the deeds of my father. I have spent much of my time hunting, fishing, wrestling, and swimming—preparing my mind and body for a worthy life, the life of a *leader*. So many of my people are now in their death sleeps due to the vile actions of the renegades and outlaws. I must guide those who are still alive!''

He paused, then added, ''I must see to my people's burials, then go and try to find the ones responsible for the raid and deaths. Then I must help prepare my people for the salmon harvest.''

Elizabeth was reminded of her father, and what he had planned for the salmon run. She suddenly felt protective of Strong Heart and his people, not wanting her father to come *here* with his hopes for his fishery! These people had already suffered enough at the hands of intruders.

''I would like to stay and help you in any way that I can,'' Elizabeth reasoned. ''There are many ways that I could help. And, darling, must I remind you that if I do return home, it would be as you had earlier worried—the sheriff could come to me and question me about what had happened. He would order me to describe the man who had knocked him unconscious. The sheriff surely knows that I had to have seen you.

And how could I explain my absence—where I have been since then? And with whom?''

The memory of the hanging platform was embedded in her mind. She must, at all costs, make sure that Strong Heart was never accused of any crime. She knew that the hangman's noose was always ready for the neck of an Indian, no matter if they were guilty or innocent.

Strong Heart nodded. ''*Ah-hah,* what you say is true. It is best that you stay. I will welcome anything that you might do to help lessen the burden of this grief.''

''Thank you, darling, for allowing it,'' Elizabeth said.

But Strong Heart's mind was elsewhere. It seethed with anger at who might have done this thing to his people. His tribe lived separate from others because they wanted to live in peace.

Strong Heart pulled Elizabeth close to him. She could feel his sorrow and anger lessening, and she was glad. She knew that he had to be strong to live through the days ahead as he buried so many of his people and guided the living toward hope again.

''Such pain burns within my heart,'' Strong Heart whispered to Elizabeth, his voice choked with despair.

''My darling,'' Elizabeth comforted him. ''My poor, sweet darling. I'm so sorry about everything. So very, very sorry.''

As Earl stood dejectedly at the window in his new office in his fishery, he almost did not hear someone enter. When he looked up and found Morris there, his eyes narrowed in anger.

''Where the hell have you been?'' he yelled. ''Why has it taken you so long to get back here to see to business? We're partners, or do you find that hard to remember?''

"You'd better hope I never decide to forget," Morris said, coming to the desk and running his hands over the smooth texture of the oak finish. "I'd say my money even paid for this desk, wouldn't you?"

Earl's face flushed. He tried to ignore the constant reminders that Morris offered of who did not have the money to back this project and who did.

"How's it all look to you?" Earl asked, shaking off his anger and his worry about Elizabeth.

Morris sat down behind the desk, as if he belonged there. He smiled smugly up at Earl. "I'd say it's as fine as it ever will be," he said, chuckling. "And don't you worry about Chief Moon Elk either. Things have turned around in our favor. Let's go full speed ahead with the fishery. We'll wait a few days and go and talk with the chief again. He'll place his 'x' on the dotted line. I'm sure of it."

Earl lifted an eyebrow, wondering exactly what Morris would do to convince the chief, yet his thoughts were interrupted by a sight from the window of the office. He saw Maysie riding at the back of a wagon that was headed into Seattle.

He smiled to himself. Maybe she was gone for good. He hoped.

"And how's Elizabeth?" Morris asked, rising from the chair, to place an arm around Earl's shoulder.

Earl looked at Morris. The empty feeling rushed back. He had no answers at all about his darling Elizabeth.

Maysie clung to the wagon as it rattled along the dirt road. She had gotten permission from Everett to go with him into Seattle. Unable to bear being at Elizabeth's house in her absence and feeling guilty because of it, Maysie had decided to leave. She didn't believe that Elizabeth would ever return. She had been gone for too long. There were too many wicked men

in the world to believe Elizabeth would come out of
this abduction alive.

She sat listlessly on the tailgate of the wagon, wondering how she was going to live. It was better to die
than to return to her former life! She could walk into
the Sound right now, and no one would save her. She
would not allow it!

Making her decision, she jumped from the wagon
and ran toward the crashing waves of the Sound. She
walked into the water without looking back. But again
a voice yelling to her caused her to stop. She remembered how Elizabeth had yelled at her, and had then
risked her life to save her.

She could not resist turning around, to see if it could
possibly be Elizabeth.

The sky was darkening overhead, dusk coming on,
so Maysie could not tell whether or not it was Elizabeth. But the hair coloring of the lady standing beside
a fancy carriage was identical.

Hoping that somehow Elizabeth *was* there, safe and
sound, Maysie worked her way back to the shore. She
walked, breathlessly toward the road. The lady came
forward to meet her.

"Child, why on earth would you want to kill
yourself?" the woman fussed, lifting her shawl from
her own shoulders and placing it around Maysie's.
"You come with me. Let me get you warmed at my
house and then we can talk this over."

Maysie was disappointed that she wasn't Elizabeth.
But she was stunned by the resemblance. This lady
was as beautiful as Elizabeth. Her hair was stunningly
red. Her eyes were a soft, captivating green. Their
faces were almost identical, yet this lady had to be at
least twenty years older than Elizabeth.

No matter how much Maysie wanted it to be Elizabeth, she had to accept that someone besides Elizabeth
had saved her this time. She couldn't find it in herself

to try again. And this lady seemed just as kind as Elizabeth.

The woman placed an arm around Maysie's tiny waist and led her to the fancy carriage, helping her inside. Once they settled on the plush cushions, the woman commanded the driver to return to her house "promptly."

Maysie shivered and accepted a blanket around her shoulders. "You are way too kind," she said, her teeth chattering. "Thank you."

"My name is Marilyn," the woman said softly, smoothing a stray lock of dark hair back from Maysie's brow. "Care to tell me yours?"

Feeling that she could trust this lady, Maysie replied, "Maysie. You can call me Maysie."

"Well, Maysie, it's good to make your acquaintance." Marilyn ran her hand down her fully gathered, silk dress. Its shade of green matched her hat trimmed with flowers at the brim.

Maysie smiled meekly at Marilyn. Then, so quickly it seemed, the buggy had come to a halt. "We're at my house," Marilyn announced, nodding a thank you to the driver as he opened the door and stepped aside. "Come. Let's see to getting you warmed."

Maysie started to leave the carriage, then stopped in confusion when she recognized the mansion. She remembered it well from when she had envied those women who worked there instead of in the tawdry places along the waterfront. She had heard that this brothel was the best in Seattle, its furnishings and its women breathtakingly beautiful.

But she no longer wanted such a life. Not after having met Elizabeth, and seeing her wholesomeness.

No. She would definitely die first!

"Why do you hesitate?" Marilyn asked, drawing Maysie's attention.

"Ma'am I don't want no part of a brothel," Maysie said, swallowing hard.

"Yes, I do manage a brothel," Marilyn said, placing a gloved hand to Maysie's cheek. "But that doesn't mean that you have to work in it just because I bring you here to make you warm and comfortable. You don't have to do anything you don't want to."

Marilyn gazed admiringly at Maysie's well-endowed figure, then at her angelic face. This young lady could bring top dollar from the men callers.

But Marilyn would never force this life on anyone—a life that even she did not totally approve of. She, herself, no longer took gentlemen to her bed. She supervised, only supervised.

"If you are sure," Maysie said, still hesitating.

Marilyn drew her gently into her arms and gave her a motherly hug. "Positive," she murmured. "Absolutely positive."

Maysie clung to Marilyn, her eyes filling with tears, grateful, yet afraid to totally trust again.

14

How many days, thou dove,
Hast thou been mine?
—BARRY CORNWALL

It was late afternoon. The sun dipped low in the sky as the muffled beat of ceremonial drums filled the air. The burial rites for the Suquamish dead had just begun. The survivors of the massacre stood on a butte that rose high over the Duwamish River. The cremated remains of the many dead were in one large communal jar. Some would be tossed into the river; the rest would be spread across the land.

Attired in a fringed buckskin dress decorated with seashells that Many Stars had sweetly lent her, Elizabeth stood among the Indians, with Strong Heart's sanction.

She had felt awkward until Many Stars had come to stand by her to give her moral support. Elizabeth gave Many Stars a grateful glance.

Elizabeth did not think that the lovely maiden was befriending her only because Strong Heart wanted her to. Many Stars sincerely seemed to care for her, even though Elizabeth was white-skinned, and red-haired, and quite different from anyone Many Stars had ever known.

Elizabeth gave Many Stars a warm smile. She was warmed through and through when Many Stars smiled generously back at her. At this moment, Elizabeth could feel that she belonged in this new world, in this new place with its foreign customs.

Chief Moon Elk was carried through the throng of people, his wife walking beside him, and carefully

placed on a pallet of furs at the front of the assembly.
Elizabeth could see Pretty Nose's devotion to her husband as she made sure he was completely covered by
the furs before settling down beside him.

Elizabeth swallowed hard as she stared at Chief
Moon Elk's wounded leg as he eased it from beneath
the furs and stretched it out before him. His wound
was covered with some sort of ointment that was green
in color. Elizabeth hoped that it would heal quickly.
At least then there would be one less burden that
Strong Heart would have to carry.

When Strong Heart stepped before the crowd of silent people, Elizabeth melted inside at his noble appearance. A robe of sea otter pelts was hung from his
broad shoulders. It did not hide the heavily beaded,
fringed shirt that he wore beneath, nor the leg bands
of shredded bark that were twisted about his fringed
breeches.

When he began speaking from the heart to his people, his father and mother looked proudly up at their
son. Elizabeth recalled what Strong Heart had told her
just before the burial ceremony.

He had told her that today's ceremony was not the
usual kind for those who had died. Today there were
too many dead to eulogize individually.

And since most of the deceaseds' houses had been
burned during the raid, it was impossible to perform
a main part of the ceremony.

Under normal circumstances, the individual bodies
would have been first wrapped in cedar-bark mats for
burial. The relatives, torn between grief and fear of
his ghost, would have removed the body from the
house as soon after death as possible. The exit of the
body was through a hole specially made in the wall so
that the living would not have to follow the path of the
dead as they walked in and out through the main door.

The body would then be placed in a canoe that was

usually raised off the ground on a scaffolding, or placed in the limbs of a tall tree. The bow always pointed toward the setting sun which would light the way for the dead. The personal possessions would be placed with the dead or burned.

"Do you hear Strong Heart and what he says?" Many Stars whispered as she leaned closer to Elizabeth, her English quite proficient. The tribe had dealt with white men for many years. "He will one day make a great chief. I have known him since we were children together. Neither of us had brothers or sisters. I became his sister. He became my brother. I watched him as a boy. He out ran, out swam, and out wrestled all of his playmates. He also spoke well before people. Even when he was only fifteen winters of age, he practiced the art of speaking well. Then many of his speeches were devoted to restraining our people and allies from declaring war on the settlers. Today he again speaks to his people, sad though it is that he must."

Many Stars took Elizabeth by the hand. Elizabeth felt their bond of friendship strengthening. She squeezed Many Stars's hand in response. Many Stars further encouraged, "Listen to this man whose heart you now hold within your soul. Listen well, and you then will see how lucky you are that he has chosen you to be his *la-daila*."

Feeling so grateful for so much, and at the same time feeling sad for these people and their losses, Elizabeth could not stop tears from springing in her eyes. She gazed proudly at Strong Heart. His words, translated by Many Stars, touched her deeply. He was skilled at making it seem that he was speaking to each individually.

She had never seen this side of her beloved. She felt filled with more love than she ever thought possible.

She leaned forward and soaked up his every gesture.

The ceremonial drum still beat softly somewhere behind her. Many Stars's voice murmured in her ear.

"My people, the spirits of our dead have drifted onward, to the 'Land of the Dead,' " Strong Heart was saying. "What remains here with us today are pure white ashes, the essence of the good in those who have gone on before us. I shall fling the ashes to the winds and the waters. I shall scatter them on the rocks, the pines, the ferns, the sands, and the wild flowers. Forevermore, they will blend with the things that we all love so well. Would we not all want the spring rains to bathe us? To awaken to the fragrance of the forest, to the call of the birds from out of the sky, and to the lapping lullaby of the river? Would we not want to experience forever the leap of the frog and fish in the stillness of the dawn?"

He paused and smiled from person to person, stopping longer at his parents. Then he shifted his eyes slowly to Elizabeth, causing her heart to lurch as she met his steady, loving gaze.

Then he continued his speech, still commanding complete silence from his people. "Our departed loved ones will still be warmed by the summer sun. Be as one to the joy of life and love, to the wonders of a canoe skimming between towering bluffs crowned with emerald and jade. They will still be able to experience the thrill of swimming in golden waters, surrounded by the trees and rock giants, and to know the serenity of twilight, and the infinite mysteries of night. It is with these thoughts that you watch as I scatter the ashes. Then your grief will be lifted to the sky, along with the spirits of those who have loved you while living."

Elizabeth's eyes widened as she watched Strong Heart reach into the white ashes. She sucked in a wild breath of air as he released the ashes into the river. Then he began walking along the bluff, spreading the ashes onto blossoming wild flowers, along the granite rock, the green grass, and into a brook that flowed down the sides of the bluff.

When the ashes were all scattered, Elizabeth stood mute as everyone returned to their dwellings, except for Strong Heart. He removed his sea otter robe, and dove into the Duwamish River, looking like a graceful eagle as he soared through the air, splashing into the sparkling clear waters.

Preoccupied with watching Strong Heart swimming masterfully in the water, Elizabeth did not hear the soft footsteps behind her. When a hand touched hers, she turned with a start, then swallowed hard when she found Strong Heart's mother standing there.

"My son will be a while," Pretty Nose said, glancing down from the bluff, watching Strong Heart taking wide and even strokes as he swam in the bone-chilling waters of the river. "He is saying his last good-byes to those whose ashes are now a part of the river. It is his farewell to friends and comrades. Come. Let him do this without an audience."

Elizabeth blushed, now thinking that she had been intruding on a private ritual. "I'm sorry," Elizabeth apologized. "I . . . I didn't know."

"No one expected you to," Pretty Nose said, urging Elizabeth to walk beside her as she moved slowly down the slope toward the village. "It is true that your customs differ much from ours. If you stay among us, you will learn quickly enough, for my son is a great teacher of many things."

Elizabeth was in awe of the kindness of these people, after having recently suffered so much at the hands of their enemies.

But she knew that Strong Heart had spoken with his mother and father about her, which might have made their acceptance of her more coerced than actual.

Elizabeth went with Pretty Nose to the longhouse of

the chief and accepted a place beside where the lodge
fire was blazing. Gazing across the fire at Chief Moon
Elk who reclined on the platform piled comfortably
with pelts, she smiled weakly as he offered her no
more than a nod of welcome.

She then eased down onto a pillow pad of shredded
bark. With a quiet nod of thank you, she accepted a
makuk of roasted fish that Pretty Nose had taken from
a flat tray of wood.

With a large bone spoon, Elizabeth attempted to eat
the fish. She wished that she had a fork, which would
have made it much simpler.

Pretty Nose sat down beside her and began eagerly
eating. Elizabeth attempted to continue eating, but her
heart wasn't in it. Today's rites had made her hunger
wane. All that she wanted was to be with Strong
Heart—to have his comforting arms around her again.
Only then could she for at least a little while forget the
savagery that had been done against his people.

She looked around her, examining the way in which
the chief and his wife lived. It was quite simple, yet
much better than she would have expected the Indians
to live. The household furnishings were made of wood,
or woven of cedar bark. She could see masks and ritual
paraphernalia hanging on the walls. There were furs
and clothing, trade blankets, and prized oils rendered
from candlefish and whale blubber stored on low
shelves.

At the far end of the large room, a rolled-up skin
curtain revealed a large bunk covered with several layers of furs and blankets of mountain goat wool. Blad-
ders of whale oil, and long strings of *hiaqua* shells,
considered money here, hung from the overhead rafters.

There were crest designs painted on everything, like
the ones she had seen carved on the totem poles out-

side. Even the troughlike dishes, hollowed out from blocks of alder, were painted with these designs.

Elizabeth's attention flew quickly to the door when Strong Heart came into the longhouse, dressed in only a breechcloth.

He came to her and held out a hand, beckoning for her to come to him. She lay down the large wooden dish and took his hand, inhaling the heady fragrance of pine emanating from his muscled body. Strong Heart had dried himself with pine needles and the smell clung wonderfully to him.

Strong Heart offered his parents only a silent nod each, then walked with Elizabeth out of their long-house to his.

After they were inside the privacy of his dwelling, Elizabeth noticed that the lodge was lit not only by the fire in the firepit, but also by several "candlefish," that were so rich in oil that a dried one with a wick threaded through it burned like a candle for hours.

Many Stars had been there in their absence. Clean grass had been spread on the floor and over this, rugs of rawhide were thrown, hair side up. Soft buckskin pillows with cottonwood floss lay beside the fire, and painted bags and clothes containers decorated with brightly hued quillwork hung against the walls of the home.

"The day was long," Strong Heart said, stroking Elizabeth's cheek with his hand. "The day was hard. But now it is night, and the night belongs to you and me. Love me, my *la-daila*, so that I may only think of now—of us. Today was sad. It is hard to shake away the sadness. Except with you, my *la-daila*. Except with you."

Overwhelmed by the joy of being with him again, his eyes mesmerizing her anew, Elizabeth stepped away from him and slowly began undressing herself.

She watched with a tremulous excitement as he also began undressing.

When they were both nude, their hands reached out and touched, and caressed. Elizabeth crept closer and molded her body against his as he held her and lowered her to a thick bed of pelts beside the fire.

As Elizabeth lay there, Strong Heart leaning over her, she ran her fingers over his finely chiseled copper face, along his bold nose, his strong chin, and the line of his hard jaw.

She then ran her fingers over his wide shoulders, across the expanse of his sleekly muscled chest, and then smoothed her hands down and across his hard and flat stomach.

As she smiled up at him, she found his eyes smoky and dangerous, as her hand paused before going on. She could already feel the throbbing hardness of his shaft as it lay thick and heavy against her thigh, and to go on with her exploration of his body meant that was the place to touch next. She was reminded of the other time that she had touched it, and how it had felt the moment he had pressed it inside her.

The pain had been brief. The pleasure had been blissful.

"You stop now?" Strong Heart said, his eyes dancing. "You have yet to touch the center of my passion, and you stop?"

"A part of me is almost afraid to," Elizabeth murmured, her face flushing with a building arousal as Strong Heart cupped one of her breasts and circled his thumb around her taut nipple. "I'm not sure if I can stand such rapture again, Strong Heart. It stole not only my breath away, but also my senses. Surely there is danger in that."

"The only danger is in not answering the need that I have awakened inside you," Strong Heart said, his hand leaving a heated path in its wake as it moved from her breasts, across her stomach, causing her body to tremble with pleasure. Then his hand reached the juncture of her thighs where he began stroking her.

When he thrust a finger inside her, he smiled at how she moaned and how her eyes rolled with the pleasure. "Never deny yourself this that I so freely offer you," he said huskily. "Who is to say what tomorrow brings? Did you not see how quickly life was snuffed from those whose ashes I spread today? One can never be certain of tomorrow. So it is only right to take from life today, as it is being offered you."

Elizabeth's head swam as he lowered his lips to hers and gave her a fiery kiss. She returned the kiss and moaned against his lips as she felt the thrust of his hardness as he entered her, and then arched her hips to meet his steady strokes within her. His mouth urged her lips open as his kiss grew more passionate and demanding, his fingers teasing and stroking the supple lines of her body.

Her world melted away as his fingers moved purposely slow in circles around one of her breasts, then swept down her spine in a soft massage.

Elizabeth's pleasure bubbled from deep within as Strong Heart enfolded her in his solid arms and showered heated kisses over one breast and then the other. Anchored fiercely against him, in an embrace long and sweet, she was soaring—she was thrilling. She reached around and placed her fingers on his muscular buttocks, and urged him even more deeply within her.

And again he kissed her—a blazing, searing kiss that left Elizabeth weak with a delicious languor. She clung to him now in a torrid embrace, the air heavy with the inevitability of pleasure.

Tremors ran down Strong Heart's back and perspiration laced his brow, the bliss drenching him with warmth. He moved in steady strokes inside her, feeling the tightness of her encircling his throbbing member.

It was that tightness that he was answering, sending him to a world that was far from the sadness of this land of sudden heartache and death. He was delirious with sensation, feeling the last vestige of his rational mind floating away.

He pressed himself closer to her moist body and plunged more deeply inside her. Soon their bodies jolted and quivered, then grew quiet, yet still entwined.

"We are the only two people in the universe tonight," Elizabeth whispered, her hands skimming his perspiration dampened back. "There is no one else, Strong Heart. No one."

Strong Heart looked down at her, smiling. In the light of the fire, her body gleamed golden. He ran his hand across her curves. "If I died tonight, it would be with a smile on my face," he whispered, then again drew her into his arms and gave her a soft kiss. Their tongues touched as Elizabeth slightly parted her lips.

The moon was casting shadows across the land as Earl looked from the window. He felt the strangest, God awful loneliness tonight without Elizabeth. He had gone to the prison today and had checked with Sheriff Nolan, and the posse had still not returned with any sort of answer.

Hope was dwindling within Earl's heart that she would be found alive. And he felt as though he had let her down by not having searched for her himself. He had probably been wrong to listen to the sheriff's advice.

The sound of a horse approaching drew Earl away from the window, and he rushed to the door and swung it open. His heart pounded and his mouth went dry when he recognized Sheriff Nolan riding toward him.

Surely the sheriff had some kind of news about Elizabeth, or why else would he be way out here this time of night?

Earl stood on the porch, clasping and unclasping his hands as he waited until the sheriff reined in and dismounted. Nolan ambled toward him, his hands resting on the heavy pistols at his hips.

"Posse's returned," Sheriff Nolan said, as he came eye to eye with Earl. He spat a long stream of tobacco over his right shoulder, then turned his gaze back to Earl. "They've given up. There's no sign of your daughter *or* the escaped renegade anywhere. Sorry, but the men refuse to look any longer. Those who have wives have gone home to them. Those who are itchin' to bed up with a whore, are probably smellin' their cheap perfume even now. I thought I owed it to you to come and tell you the news. Now I'd best get back to more important business." He turned and began to saunter away.

Anger quickly welled up inside Earl. He stomped to the sheriff and stopped him, swinging him around so that their eyes met again. "More important business?" he said, his voice threatening. "You call my daughter unimportant? You give up on finding her this easy? I think you'd best rethink things, sheriff, or I'll—"

Sheriff Nolan sneered at Earl and knocked his hands away from his shoulders. "Or you'll what?" he said, thrusting his bearded face into Earl's.

Earl swallowed hard and took a step back. "Surely there are other men that you can get together to continue the search? I'll personally lead the posse. I've got to find my daughter. If you can spare the men, I can damn well spare the time!"

Sheriff Nolan pulled his beard thoughtfully, then nodded. "That's fine with me. Come into town first thing in the morning. I'll see what I can do."

Sighing heavily, Earl nodded. He wiped the perspiration from his brow as the sheriff rode away. Then he turned with a start when Morris came out of the shadows, his gaze on the sheriff's back.

"I heard everything," Morris said, turning his eyes to Earl. "I don't think you have any business leadin' a posse. You'll never find your daughter, and might even get yourself killed in the bargain."

"I'm going to go, so save your breath," Earl said, turning to walk back up the steps. He stopped and gave Morris a stern stare. "And I expect you to cooperate. While I'm gone, I'm leavin' the business in your hands totally."

Morris didn't answer.

15

Come, live with me, and be my love!
—MARLOWE

Several days later, with everyone's feelings still raw since the burial, Strong Heart felt that it was still too soon to take warriors to seek vengeance for the devastation and deaths at the hands of the raiders.

But the village was being restored quickly, with all of the braves who were healthy enough working.

Elizabeth stood near Strong Heart as he helped construct a longhouse. She watched several young men carve figures into six-foot-tall cedar logs to support the roof.

"You are admiring the handiwork of my people?" Strong Heart said, moving to Elizabeth's side. He leaned on a tall, heavy wooden mallet that he had been using to pound cedar poles into the ground. "Some are carving the legendary guardian spirits of our tribe. Others are carving the cedar log into a story pole, which records the history of the Suquamish to instruct future generations."

Elizabeth glanced from one pole to another. On some of the poles were a number of carved toads, bears, blackfish, and other spirit guide symbols. But the ones that showed a red-tailed hawk, carved in detail at the top, drew her most keen regard. They looked real, as if they could take flight.

Strong Heart also admired the hawk. Above everything, he admired those whose hands were skilled enough to make the hawks look so alive, as if more than mere wood.

"These story poles are being built to replace those that were burned," Strong Heart quietly explained. "They are to remind our youngsters of their heritage. The hawk is the crest of my family, and thus of this clan. It is the heraldic emblem of nobility."

He glowered as he looked around at those totem poles that had been ravaged by the recent fire. "It was *me-sah-chie,* bad, that the raiders saw fit to destroy that which is so precious to the Suquamish," he grumbled. "But soon the desecration will be gone. These new story poles will not be robbed of their future teachings as those others have been. Warriors will forever guard our village now. It is understood that there will always be someone who chooses to be the enemy of the Suquamish. Those who do, will die."

Hearing Strong Heart talk in such a way, his words filled with such venom, caused an involuntary shiver to course through Elizabeth. She hugged herself and watched Strong Heart as he directed his eyes to something else—some*one* else.

In Strong Heart's eyes she could see pain as he stared at an elderly man. The man was reclining on the ground close to those who were laboring, too old to help with the regrowth of his village.

Elizabeth wondered what Strong Heart was thinking about the old man. His eyes were filled with longing.

Strong Heart was remembering another old man. He thought of his beloved grandfather who was still missing. His grandfather had often placed a hand on the ground, saying that the Suquamish sat in the lap of their Mother when they sat upon the earth. He could even now hear him saying, "From her, our Mother Earth, we, and all other living things, come. We shall soon pass, but the place where we now rest will last forever."

"What is it, Strong Heart?" Elizabeth asked, placing a hand on his arm. "What are you thinking about?"

"My grandfather," Strong Heart said, a haunted expression crossing his face. "He, in his beautiful eagle-feather headdress so long ago, taught me many things—how Indians loved the earth and all things of the earth."

With a nod of his head, Strong Heart motioned toward the elderly man. "See that Suquamish elder?" he said softly. "See how he lies upon the ground? It is with a feeling of being close to a mothering power that he does this. My grandfather, my mother's father, told me as a child that it is good for the skin to touch the earth. The old people like to remove their moccasins to walk with bare feet on the sacred earth. My grandfather told me that earth was the final abiding place of all things that lived and grew. He taught me that soil was soothing, strengthening, cleansing, and healing. When he sat or lay upon the ground, he could think more deeply and feel more keenly. He could see more clearly into the mysteries of life and come closer in kinship to other lives about him."

"That's so beautiful," Elizabeth said. Then she jumped when Strong Heart suddenly threw his wooden mallet to the ground.

When he turned to her and clutched her shoulders with his fingers, she looked wide-eyed up at him, seeing a determination in his eyes, replacing the haunted look that had only been there a moment before.

"I must go and find my grandfather," Strong Heart blurted out. "He deserves to know that so many of his beloved have passed away. It is my place to carry this message to him. It is *my* responsibility, for I am his only grandson."

"You have never mentioned your grandfather before," Elizabeth said. "Where is he? Why is he gone?"

"Over a moon ago, he disappeared from our village and no one knows where he went, or why," Strong Heart said, his voice filled with emotion. "I have searched for him more than once, but still I have not found him. It is my duty to search again, and *now*. He *must* be allowed to mourn the dead with the rest of our people."

"Where will you look for your grandfather?" Elizabeth asked slowly, afraid that he was planning to leave her behind in the village. Although she had made friends here, she did not relish being among those who still were suspicious of her.

"The first time we met," Strong Heart said, reaching a hand to her cheek, softly touching her, "I was searching for my grandfather. You see, your house sits on the hallowed ground of my tribe. It once belonged solely to our people. Where your house sits once housed many Suquamish longhouses. Close by, in the forest, are our burial grounds. It was my assumption that my grandfather had gone there to make peace with the spirits of the dead who were deserted by our people when we were forced to move north, away from land that was no longer ours."

Elizabeth listened with a pounding heart, now understanding so much. She now knew why the Indians had tried to burn down the old mansion in the past, and rid the land of any white intruders.

Then she suddenly recalled the old Indian walking outside her house with a staff in his right hand. It had to be Strong Heart's grandfather.

"Strong Heart, I wish you would have told me this earlier," she said eagerly. "Strong Heart, more than once I saw an old Indian close to my house. He carried some sort of staff. But he disappeared as quickly as he appeared, so I never did get to question him."

Strong Heart's eyes widened. He clutched Elizabeth's shoulders, almost desperately. "You . . . saw

. . . an elderly Indian?'' he gasped. "It was surely my grandfather! I must go now and find him! Come. Come with me. We shall search for him together!''

"Return with you?'' she asked, searching his eyes. "Now? Have you forgotten why you took me away from Seattle in the first place?''

Strong Heart eased his fingers from her shoulders and dropped his gaze to the ground. There was danger in returning to Seattle so soon after the escape. And, especially, with Elizabeth.

"*Ah-hah*, yes, it is dangerous,'' he conceded, turning his eyes to Elizabeth. "But, *ah-hah*, yes, I still plan to go. This is the first time I have ever had true hope that my grandfather is still alive. I must go and search for him now, not later, no matter the risk.''

Elizabeth stroked her fingers through her long hair as she pondered what to do.

She thought of her father, Frannie, and then Maysie. It was not at all fair for them not to know that she was alive.

And although she knew the risk of returning to Seattle, she saw that she must. She would just have to make sure she wasn't seen by the sheriff. She would not go into Seattle under any circumstances.

She must not be the one to lead the sheriff to Strong Heart. She knew what Strong Heart's fate would be, if she did. The memory of the gallows stayed in her mind.

"Yes, I will accompany you on this venture of the heart,'' Elizabeth decided. "While there, I must see my father, and others who are important to me. I must let them know that I am alive.''

She paused, then added, "My darling, in no way will I endanger your life. If I am cornered by the sheriff, I will lie to save your life. In my eyes, you are innocent of any crime. I will not be the one to cause you to pay for a deed that even I see as being right.''

Strong Heart took her elbow and they walked away from the workers to the edge of the forest. He drew her into his embrace, his eyes burning down into hers. "My *la-daila*, I do not want you to be forced to lie for me, ever. And I do not want you to leave me, ever. Once you see your father and reveal to him that you are alive, I want you to return with me to my village and become my wife. Share my blankets with me forever, Elizabeth. My people are impressed with your gentleness, intelligence, and beauty. They would accept you as my wife."

Elizabeth was not surprised by his proposal. She was thrilled, yet wondered how this could be arranged. "Strong Heart, I want nothing more than to say yes to your proposal. But how can I? If my father knows about you, he will also have to know how I happened to know you. It could prove dangerous."

He dipped his head and smelled the sweetness of her hair. "If your father loves you," he whispered, "*truly* loves you, he will do nothing to endanger your life. Bringing the sheriff to arrest Strong Heart would threaten your life. No, I do not think a father would do this to a daughter."

And then he paused, remembering that through all of the confusion of these past days, he had not thought to ask her about her father—why he had come to the Pacific Northwest in his great ship, and what he was building on the shores of Puget Sound.

He quickly asked her now.

Elizabeth paled, not wanting to reveal the full truth to her beloved, fearing that it would cause a confrontation between her father and the man she loved. Strong Heart could not afford an argument with any white man now that he was a fugitive.

"My father?" she said, easing from his arms. She turned her back to him and plucked a leaf from a tree. Nervously, she began shredding it into tiny pieces.

"My father came to Seattle because he was no longer planning to travel the seas with his ship. He found the Pacific Northwest a perfect place to enjoy fishing."

She turned quickly to him and looked innocently up into his eyes. "Yes," she said, her voice lilting. "That's why he came to Seattle. To enjoy fishing."

Strong Heart lifted an eyebrow as he regarded her, feeling that she was not being altogether truthful. But he did not want to think that she would lie to him.

"I will help you search for your grandfather, and then go alone to speak with my father," she said. "Perhaps it . . . it would be best for you to come back to the village alone, just in case my father doesn't react favorably to the news. I will come to you later, when I am certain that it is safe."

Strong Heart did not respond quickly. He mulled it over, then said, "That is not the way I want it to be, but if you feel that is best for *you,* then I will agree."

"Strong Heart, you have searched for your grandfather before and did not find him," Elizabeth said, as he placed an arm around her waist, walking her back toward the village. She gazed up at him. "What if you still cannot find him?"

Strong Heart frowned down at her. "Perhaps I will not be able to find him this time, but I *will* find him some day," he vowed. "It seems that my grandfather has learned the art of being invisible. Strong Heart hopes to find out why, and *how.*"

In Elizabeth's mind, she was recalling the times that she had seen his grandfather, and how quickly he had faded from sight. And the mere fact that he had chosen to return to the grounds of his ancestors, gave her cause to be afraid for her father. What if the old man decided to set a torch to the house to finish what his ancestors had not been able to?

What then not only of her father, but of Frannie and Maysie?

Maysie, she thought suddenly. Elizabeth wondered if Maysie had stayed on at the house, or had been forced to leave. Perhaps to return to a life of sin again—or to die in the Sound?

Yes, Elizabeth decided. It *was* best that she return home, to tie up some *very* loose ends.

16

Love's wing moults when caged and captured,
Only free, he soars enraptured!
—Thomas Campbell

As the sun was setting beyond the ever purple ridges of the distant bluffs, the crackling fire of lightning forked across the heavens above Elizabeth and Strong Heart as they dismounted. They looked warily at the display.

Elizabeth moved to Strong Heart's side and jumped with alarm as the cannon roar of the thunder reverberated all around her, the ground shaking ominously beneath her feet. "I have never seen such weather as I have found in this country," she said, shuddering. The heavens darkened to an inky blackness as the storm clouds moved in rapidly. "On our way to your village we were almost drowned by rains, and now, on our way back to Seattle, it storms again?"

She turned her green eyes up at Strong Heart. "Is the weather always this temperamental, Strong Heart? Or am I just worrying too much?"

Strong Heart placed a comforting arm around her waist, and gazed at Mount Rainier in the distance as lightning danced and played around its peak. "Rain is a natural thing in our land of trees, mountains, and rivers," he said, his voice hushed. "But thunder and lightning do not always accompany the rain. You have cause to be alarmed over the repeated storms. It is the spirits of the mountains that cause storms. They are angered. The spirits of the mountains speak of this anger tonight."

He paused and turned his eyes back to Elizabeth.

"My people have long pictured the spirit of the storm as a huge bird known as the Thunderbird, flapping its wings, causing the sound of thunder. The lightning is the flash of its eyes. This bird is never seen, only talked about. It is known to live in a cloud above the highest peak that our tribe can see—which to us is *Dahkobeed*, Mount Rainier."

"I have heard about the Thunderbird. I have read about it. Thank you for sharing this with me, Strong Heart. I want to know everything about your culture, about your beliefs. It will make my being with you as your wife more complete."

The sky seemed to open up as rain began to fall in torrents, quickly drenching them.

Strong Heart grabbed a blanket from his saddlebags and held it over Elizabeth. He turned and searched quickly around him for a place to go for shelter.

When another lurid flash of lightning lit everything around them, he caught sight of a cave not that far from where he and Elizabeth stood.

"Come," he said, taking her by the elbow with one hand, and grabbing both horses' reins with his other. "Over there. We shall seek shelter in the cave. The spirits are kind to us. They have lit the sky enough so that I could see the protective sheltering of the cave."

Trembling from the cold of the rain, her buckskin dress clinging wetly to her skin, Elizabeth walked briskly beside Strong Heart as the horses followed. She sighed with relief when they stepped into the cave.

Hugging herself, her teeth chattering, Elizabeth watched Strong Heart quickly unsaddle the horses, tossing the saddlebags toward her.

"There is another blanket inside my bag," he said, running his hands down the flanks of his roan, settling him down as another crash of thunder echoed into the cave. It was as if someone had pounded a giant drum within the close confines.

"There is a change of clothing for you in your saddlebag," Strong Heart called, above the sound of the thunder. "Many Stars packed not only one clean buckskin dress in your bag, but two. Change into one. As soon as I get the horses settled down, I shall search for wood inside the cave, then build a fire."

Elizabeth was too cold to answer him. She fell to her knees on the damp ground of the cave. With trembling fingers, she opened his saddlebag and grabbed a blanket from inside it. She wrapped it around her shoulders, savoring its warmth.

She then reached inside her own bag and felt the softness of the buckskin dress and also some moccasins that Many Stars had been thoughtful enough to provide.

Elizabeth clutched the moccasins to her chest, and smiled, filled with such gratitude and love for a friend as kind as Many Stars.

Her smile wavered. She hoped that she would be able to see her again. This journey back to Seattle had many risks for Elizabeth—and her future with the Suquamish.

Before she was able to change into the dry dress, Elizabeth was amazed to see that Strong Heart had found enough wood and had a fire going. Its warmth touched her flesh like a soft hand.

She drew the wet dress over her head and lay it aside. Again she quickly drew the blanket around her shoulders to warm her nakedness.

While slipping her wet moccasins off, she peered up at Strong Heart as he hurriedly yanked his wet clothes off. Then he stood close to the fire, absorbing the warmth into his gleaming, copper body, his back to her.

Elizabeth felt wanton when her heart began to beat at the mere sight of his nudity. Never before in her life had she hungered after a man as she now hungered for Strong Heart.

It was a fact that he was in her blood. Her very soul cried out for him at this moment.

She looked at the planes of his shoulders, his straight back, slim hips, and muscled buttocks, recalling the rapture she had felt when she had explored every inch of his body with her fingers.

Her gaze caressed him now.

As Strong Heart turned to place his back to the fire, to warm it as well, the muscles moved down the length of his lean body, and his eyes caught Elizabeth's.

Elizabeth blushed. She was afraid that he could read her mind—her thoughts of wanting to go to him and run her hands down the full length of him, and then gather his manhood within her hands, to stroke it. She felt strangely light-headed.

Strong Heart reached a hand out toward her, beckoning her to come to him. She hesitated for a moment, then rose slowly to her feet and went.

When she reached him, she blinked her eyes nervously. Her heartbeat almost swallowed her whole as his hands went to the blanket around her shoulders and tugged at it.

He began pulling on both corners of the blanket, drawing her with it against his hard body. Both of them were enfolded within the warmth of the blanket. Elizabeth closed her eyes in pleasure. Never had anything felt as wonderful as to be with him in such a way, the blanket and their fiery need for each other warming them.

As he held the blanket in place, Elizabeth snuggled against him. Her arms wrapped around him, hugging him tightly.

Standing on tiptoe, she pressed her lips to his. He answered her silent invitation by crushing his mouth down upon hers, his tongue surging between her teeth, exploring the depths of her mouth. She melted into him, grinding her body against his, her breasts pressed hard into his chest.

Not even knowing how the transition had been made, just knowing that her back was now pressed hard against the cave floor, the blanket beneath her, his body warm against her as he nudged her legs apart with his knee, she welcomed the floating sensation as his hands stroked her sensitive flesh.

Breathless, longing to have him inside her, to fill her with his magnificent strength, Elizabeth opened her legs willingly to him and arched her hips. She moaned with pleasure against his mouth as he entered her with one, quick thrust.

Strong Heart began his even strokes within her. Her body moved with his, rising and falling as he plunged deeply in and out.

Elizabeth's hands thrilled at the mere touch of him. She reached down and touched his manhood as he withdrew it from her, circling the shaft as he paused before his next thrust, allowing her to give him this sort of pleasure for a moment.

As Elizabeth moved her hand on him more quickly, more determinedly, Strong Heart slipped his mouth down to the hollow of her throat and moaned against it.

She could feel his body stiffening with his building pleasure. And when he reached down and moved her hand away from his throbbing hardness, and once again buried himself deeply within her, she tossed her head in excitement. Then the thrashing stopped when he caught her face between his hands and he kissed her.

Strong Heart was no longer aware of the lightning, the thunder, nor the torrents of rain that were falling just outside the entrance of the cave. All he could concentrate on was this vision that lay beneath him, her lovely red hair spilling away from her face, spread out beneath her like a fiery halo. Her flawless features were vibrant and glowing, her slim, white thighs now clutching to him as she locked her legs around him.

His hands framed her face as he smiled down at her, feeling he was drowning in passion, hardly able to hold back any longer.

His lips brushed the smooth, satin skin of her breast, and then again he kissed her lips.

As he thrust his tongue teasingly into her mouth, so did he press his manhood endlessly deeper within her moist channel. He could tell by her harsher breathing that she, too, was ready to ascend that same plateau as he, where a joyous bliss was awaiting them. He could feel the excitement growing, growing, growing.

And then his body jolted and quivered as for a moment he lost all sense of time, place, or even of being. All that mattered was that wave that rose through his whole body, making it fluid with fire.

Elizabeth sucked in a wild breath of air, then let herself go, to experience the ecstasy. It flooded through her, it seemed, with sweet agony.

Afterward, they lay together, their bodies still throbbing with the afterglow of love.

Then Strong Heart rolled away from her and drew the blanket over them again. "You are no longer cold?" he asked, his eyes smiling into hers.

"No," Elizabeth said, softly giggling. "I feel as though I'm burning up inside."

"It is a good feeling?" he asked, flicking his tongue across one of her breasts as he bent beneath the blanket.

Elizabeth closed her eyes and shivered. "Yes, a good feeling," she whispered. "As is what you are doing right now." She placed a hand to his head and urged his mouth even more closely to her breast. "My darling, how wonderful you make me feel, *always*."

He moved his lips back to her mouth, yet did not kiss her—only whispered against it. "Remember what you just said, that when you reach Seattle and are tempted to stay behind, to live the life that you are more familiar with," he said huskily. "Remember that, my *la-daila*, always remember that."

"Always," she whispered. "How could I ever forget how you make me feel? I could never live without you, Strong Heart. You are my very reason for breathing—for getting up each morning. It is you I wish to see upon my first awakening. Only you."

"That is *kloshe*, good," he whispered back against her lips. "That is very good."

He kissed her softly, his hands plumping her breasts.

She slung a leg over him and trembled with pleasure as his manhood found her open and ready for him again.

Earl was cursing as he yanked off his wet clothes. "This damn weather," he grumbled. Members of the posse stood around the campfire in the cave, also taking off their drenched clothes. "I've never seen anything like the weather here. Why does it have to rain so often?"

"We're lucky we found this cave," one of the men said, totally naked and drying himself off with a blanket before the campfire. "So quit grumblin', Earl."

Another of the men came up next to Earl—a Suquamish Indian who had taken more to the life of the whites', than the Indians'. "You have angered the mountain spirits by traveling too far into land that one time only knew the footsteps of the Suquamish," Joe Feather grumbled, squeezing water out of his waist-length black hair. "That is also why your horse took a spill, and even now limps on its lamed leg. It would be better if you would shoot the horse. If you continue riding him, your journey back to Seattle will be slowed, and then you will have to shoot him anyway.''

"We don't have any spare horses and I'm a damn sight better off riding my own steed, than saddling up with someone else,'' Earl snarled. He reached into his saddlebag and pulled out a dry change of clothes. "And don't fill my head with any more nonsense about the mountain spirits. I've had enough of your mumbo jumbo for one day. If you still believe in so many of the Suquamish customs, why the hell are you riding with the white men, as though you're one of them? Or don't you know where you fit in best? Huh?''

Joe Feather frowned at Earl as he stepped out of his fringed breeches, and then into dry buckskin. "A lot of me is still Suquamish,'' he said, his voice void of emotion. "*That* part of me speaks of spirits whenever it seems fit to do so. And tonight, when the storm warriors are throwing their lightning sticks to earth, I remember my beliefs.''

"Save me from a lecture about Indians,'' Earl retorted, even though he wished that he knew of a secret potion that he could use on Chief Moon Elk, to sway him over to his plans. "I've got one Indian on my mind tonight. That's enough.''

Earl buttoned his fresh, dry shirt, then stepped into his breeches and fastened them. Disconsolately, he sat down on a blanket close to the fire, wondering where Elizabeth was.

The search was going badly.

And now, with his hobbled horse, it would take him much longer to return home to see if any word had arrived there about her whereabouts.

Joe Feather sat down beside Earl. He drew his knees to his chest and hugged his legs. "There are many beliefs about why there are fierce storms,'' he said, ignoring Earl's agitated sigh. "One belief is that there are warriors who live in the sky who dash about on their spirited horses during a thunderstorm, their lances clashing with the thunder, and glittering with the lightning. Lightning does no harm to most Indians. Whenever it comes too close, the mothers of the tribes put cedar leaves on the coals of their fires, and their magic keeps danger away.''

Earl turned angry eyes to Joe Feather. ''Will you just shut up?'' he growled.

''This cave that we are in?'' Joe Feather said, looking over his shoulder, toward the darker depths of the cave. ''It has another opening, on the far end. Would you want to go and see what might be at the other end?''

Earl glowered at Joe. ''I like this end just fine,'' he said, his teeth clenched.

Joe Feather shrugged, then stretched out on his side, his eyes soon drifting closed.

Earl sighed heavily. ''Finally,'' he whispered to himself. He had not been sure how much more of the damn Indian that he could tolerate.

He glanced over his shoulder at the darker depths of the cave. ''Another entrance, hogwash,'' he said, soon forgetting about it.

17

The sun was low in the sky. The shadows lengthened around Strong Heart and Elizabeth as they rode silently through the forest. Up ahead, Elizabeth's house loomed through a break in the trees.

Elizabeth gave Strong Heart a downcast look. She was weary not only from the long travel, but also from searching for hours in this forest for where Proud Beaver might be hiding.

Elizabeth's muscles were sore from the many hours in the saddle, even though the Indian saddle was stuffed with thick layers of cottonwood and cattail down. She was not used to this sort of life—this life of adventure.

And although it meant being parted from Strong Heart, she looked forward to telling her father about her upcoming marriage to the handsome Suquamish brave. It would be a reprieve before she would have to make the long journey back to Strong Heart's village.

She glowed inside, thinking about what would happen once they were back at his village. She had agreed to be his wife. From that time on, they would never have cause to be separated. It would be like living a dream, to be with the man she loved from morning 'til night.

"The sun soon sleeps as the moon replaces it in the sky," Strong Heart said, drawing his reins and stopping his horse. Elizabeth followed his lead and her horse stopped beside his. "It is best that we give up the search for my grandfather. He knows the art of elusiveness too well. He does not want to be found. So be it. There is only so much a grandson can do for a grandfather. Now I must return to my people, to my duties to *them*.''

Elizabeth reached a hand to his bronze cheek. ''Darling, you do understand why I won't be returning with you right now? That I must make all wrongs right with my father? I've been selfish until now to only consider my feelings. Although he does not always show how much he loves me, I am sure he does and is very concerned over my welfare.''

''What man could not love you?'' Strong Heart said, taking her hand, kissing its palm. ''My *la-daila*, I am fighting jealousy over you putting another man before me. But I know that loyalty is owed to parents. This lightens the burden of jealousy within my heart. Go to your father. Stay as long as it takes to make him understand. Then return to me. I have been careful to map the way for your return. But do not travel alone. If your father is at peace with this that you wish to do, and has agreed, ask him to accompany you to my village. There I will pay him gifts for you. There he will join our wedding celebration. It will be a good time of camaraderie and understanding, this time spent with our people and your father.''

Elizabeth smiled weakly at Strong Heart, easing her hand from his. ''You make it sound easy,'' she murmured. ''I shall try, Strong Heart. But if I do not return soon, please come for me. No matter if my father understands or not, I want to be with you. Come and take me back with you. Please?''

Strong Heart reached for her and placed his hands at her waist. He lifted her from her horse and placed her on his lap facing him.

Breathless from the surprise of what he had done, Elizabeth then laughed softly as she twined her arms around his neck, drawing his lips close to hers. ''How foolish of me to even ask if you would come for me,'' she breathed, as he brushed her lips with a teasing kiss, his hands on her breasts, massaging them through the soft buckskin of her dress. ''I'm surprised that you are allowing me to part from you for even one second. Our time together is so wonderful, Strong Heart. So wonderful.''

She looked at him, a pout on her lips. ''I'm going to miss you so much,'' she complained. ''I'm not sure I can stand being away from you.''

''Then do not stay behind without me,'' Strong Heart urged, his hands now at the fringed hem of her dress, pushing it up her legs. ''Return with me. Forget your father.''

Elizabeth's face flushed hotly and she flung her head back so that her hair hung in silken red streamers down her back as she felt him slip his manhood into her. He began the sweet rocking rhythm.

Elizabeth moaned as she clutched Strong Heart about his neck. It felt wicked making love on a horse. Wicked doing it so close to her father's house, where he might even now be pacing the floor in worry about her.

But her insides were burning from the passion that her beloved always evoked in her. She knew that this was his way of saying good-bye. Strong Heart was such a sensual man, such a splendid, romantic lover. He had awakened in her feelings that surely no other man could have ever awakened.

Now, as she rode him, his body thrusting his satin shaft within her, so pleasurably filling her, she could not deny that he was the answer to all of her tomorrows—her need for him perhaps even stronger than his for her.

Yes, she would return to him, for without him, she would be only half a woman.

But first, she must see her father. She could not

forget that without her, her father was alone. She hoped that he could bear his loss.

Then she felt foolish for thinking that, knowing that his business was all of his tomorrows—not her.

The heat building within her made Elizabeth feel euphoric. She could tell that Strong Heart was feeling the same, for his moans of pleasure filled the air, echoing into the forest that lay on each side of them.

And then that peak of bliss was reached.

Afterward, they clung to one another, Elizabeth still straddling him, their cheeks pressed together.

"You still say good-bye to Strong Heart?" he asked throatily, as he placed a finger to her chin and directed her eyes up to his. "I have not persuaded you to return with me?"

"Your ways of persuasion are unique," Elizabeth said, laughing softly. "But, darling, I still must stay and talk to my father. Please tell me that you understand."

"*Ah-hah,* I understand," Strong Heart said, tracing a finger down one of her cheeks. "And in your absence I will do what I must, to make things right for my people. As soon as I return to my village, I will get many braves together and leave to search for the culprits responsible for the raid. And this must be done soon, for the autumn salmon run must be prepared for. Without the salmon, the lives of the Suquamish are not as easy. *Ah-hah,* and when it comes time to participate in the harvest of the salmon, it will be done with you at my side as my wife."

Elizabeth sighed and hugged him. "It sounds so magical. I so want it to be that way."

"And why should it not?" Strong Heart challenged, again holding her away from him so that their eyes could meet.

"Strong Heart, I'm not able to forget the threat that lies over your head, should you be suspected of having

set Four Winds free,'' Elizabeth said, her voice trembling. ''That, alone, clouds my hopes for the future,
Strong Heart. What if the sheriff discovers that I am
home, and questions me? Will he be able to tell that I
am lying when I tell him nothing about you? I have
never been skilled at lying.'' She cast her sight downward. ''Never before have I had *cause* to lie.''

He placed a finger to her chin and brought her eyes
to his again. ''Knowing me brings too much pain in
your life,'' he said sadly. ''I am sorry for that.''

''Never be sorry for this that you and I have found
together,'' Elizabeth said, then kissed him softly and
sweetly.

She drew away from him. ''I must go now. The
sooner I get on with this thing that I must do, the
sooner we will be together again.''

''That is so,'' Strong Heart said, nodding. He pulled
her dress down, then lifted her over onto her horse. ''Go.
I shall watch until you are safely at the house. Then I
shall search awhile longer for my grandfather. But only
for a short while. My people await my return. I must
not worry them needlessly.''

Tears misted Elizabeth's eyes as she gave Strong
Heart a lingering look, realizing how slim the chances
were that they might be together again. Danger seemed
to be lurking everywhere, not only for her, but also
for the man that she loved. He could fall victim to evil
white men and Indian renegades. She wondered if Four
Winds was a man who could be trusted. What if he
was a renegade, guilty of all sorts of horrendous
crimes? Would he go as far as committing a crime
against his own people? Against his friend?

Shaking these thoughts from her mind, afraid that if
she thought much more about it, she might return with
Strong Heart after all, and her father would forever
worry about her. That was not fair of her, she decided
firmly.

"I shall see you soon," Elizabeth said, tears rushing from her eyes. "Please ride with care, darling."

"*Kla-how-ya*, goodbye, my *la-daila*," Strong Heart said, placing a fist over his heart. "My *tum-tum*, heart, already misses you."

Elizabeth brushed the tears from her cheeks, gave Strong Heart a feeble smile, then wheeled her horse around. Without looking back, she urged her steed into a hard gallop away from him.

When she rode through the open gate, she continued until she reached the stables behind the house. Dismounting, she led her horse inside the stables, and then jumped with alarm when Everett stepped from the darkness into the dim light of a lantern that hung just inside the door.

"You frightened me," Elizabeth said, placing a hand to her throat.

Everett took the lantern from its nail on the wall and held it above him, walking slowly toward Elizabeth. "You frightened *me*," he said, his dark eyes wide. "You're the last person I expected to see. Your father is leadin' a posse even now, searchin' for you."

"Father is-is a part of a posse?" Elizabeth said, paling and looking past Everett, to the darkness outside. Her thoughts went to Strong Heart, now fearing more than ever for him. If a posse was out there somewhere searching for her, Strong Heart might come right into the midst of them!

Then she willed her heart to stop its racing, reminding herself that no one in the posse knew of Strong Heart's role in Four Winds's escape, or her abduction. Strong Heart would be just an innocent traveler on his way home.

No, she tried to convince herself—she had nothing to fear. Strong Heart would be all right. He would be all right.

Then she noticed Everett staring at her attire. He

shifted his eyes slowly to the Indian saddle on the horse. Her heart plummeted to her feet, knowing those things were enough to reveal to anyone that she had been among Indians. And that might be fatal.

Trying not to show her uneasiness, Elizabeth went to the saddle and removed it from the horse. Boldly, she turned and handed it to Everett. "I want you to hide this for me," she said crisply. "And, Everett, if you value your position with my father, you will never tell anyone about the saddle. Do you understand?"

Everett gulped hard as he sat the lantern aside and took the saddle. "Yes'm," he said, nodding his head. "Whatever you say, ma'am."

She slowly ran her hand down the buckskin dress. "And don't you breathe a word, either, about this dress that I'm wearing. It is nobody's affair but my own. Do I make myself clear, Everett?"

"Yes'm," he said, again nodding. "I won't say a word. Not to no one."

"Thank you," Elizabeth said, exhaling a long breath and relaxing her shoulders. "I truly thank you."

She turned and left the stables, dreading having to meet Frannie and her curiosity when she saw how Elizabeth was dressed.

But Frannie had to know, as did her father, eventually. For now, she had been given a reprieve. Hopefully she would at least get a night's sleep in her bed before her father arrived home and she would have to face him.

18

How can I live without thee?
How forego thy sweet converse,
and love so dearly joined?
—MILTON

The sun poured through the bedroom window in streamers across the drab furniture and hardwood floor. The forest beyond was alive with the music of birds. The pulse of the waves crashing endlessly against the beach below seemed to echo Elizabeth's heartbeat.

As she brushed her hair in long strokes, Elizabeth stared at her reflection in the mirror. She had changed overnight, it seemed, to the person she had always been. She no longer wore a buckskin dress or moccasins. Today, for her planned outing on the beach, she had chosen to wear a light blue, eyelet wrap dress with white cotton-eyelet pantaloons and petticoat with crocheted trim.

"No matter what I wear, my heart will forever be changed," she whispered to herself. "Strong Heart, darling. Oh, how I miss you."

She shifted her gaze and looked with melancholy at the buckskin dress that she had laid ever so gently over the back of a chair the previous evening. Frannie had peppered her with questions as to where she had got the dress, and why she had been wearing it.

Elizabeth was silent, refusing to answer any of Frannie's questions. So Frannie's conclusion, that Elizabeth had been with Indians, had made Frannie almost faint with fright. She had grabbed the dress and announced she would burn it.

Elizabeth took back the dress and told Frannie that this dress belonged to a sweet Indian maiden, someone who was Elizabeth's friend.

But she hadn't explained any more to Frannie. That would have to wait until Elizabeth had been given the chance to first talk with her father. Once he understood that she was in love, then she would tell Frannie her secret. But not until then.

Elizabeth's thoughts went to Maysie. "Sweet Maysie," she whispered to herself as she lay the hairbrush aside. "If only I could go search for her."

When Frannie had told her that Maysie had left without telling anyone, a sudden ache had risen in Elizabeth's heart.

But she knew that she couldn't go into Seattle for anything, not even to try and find Maysie. Yet Elizabeth could not stop thinking about that day when she had found Maysie walking into the Sound, and had discovered Maysie's life of prostitution.

"And so's you still determined to keep that dress I sees," Frannie said, entering the bedroom with an armful of fresh linens. She laid the linens on the bed and turned to Elizabeth, folding her arms angrily across her thick bosom. "You still too stubborn to tell ol' Frannie where you've been these long days and nights?"

Elizabeth went to Frannie and placed a gentle hand to her plump cheek. "Isn't it enough for now that I am home safe?" she asked softly. "Please don't ask any more questions until I am ready to tell you everything. First, I must talk to Father."

Elizabeth turned and walked to the window and looked down at the yard below. "Father hasn't returned yet," she said, her voice full of concern. "I wonder what's taking him so long?"

She was worried not only about her father's delay,

but also about Strong Heart's welfare because of it. What if they had met on the trail?

What if her father somehow knew of Strong Heart's guilt, and even now was ushering him into a cell at the prison?

Her imagination worked overtime. She felt that she must think of something else or she would go insane from worry. Elizabeth turned abruptly and walked determinedly toward the door.

"I need a breath of fresh air," she said, grabbing a shawl from a peg on the wall. She wrapped the shawl around her shoulders. "I'm going to take a stroll on the beach, Frannie. I shan't be too long."

Frannie rushed after her and grabbed her by the arm, stopping her. "Don't goes nowhere today, honey," she pleaded. "Stay in the house where's you'll be safe. Ol' Frannie don't trust this land, nor nobody. Lordy, Elizabeth, ain't you glad to be home, in the safety of your house? Why on earth would you trust leavin' it again, no matter that it's only to take a walk on the beach? Anything could happen to you. Anything!"

"Frannie, please quit worrying," Elizabeth said, taking Frannie's hand, clasping it tightly. "I'm not going to do anything to put myself in danger. All I want to do is take a walk and clear my head of a few things. Start my breakfast. I'll be back to eat it before you can flip a stack of flapjacks onto my plate."

Frannie sighed heavily and shook her head, then pulled her hand from Elizabeth's. "If that is as long as you plan to be gone, I sees no true harm in it," she said, her dark eyes concerned. "Go on. The sooner you get your strollin' over with, the sooner you'll be back here with me so's I can keep my eye on you."

"Frannie, I don't need anyone keeping an eye on me," Elizabeth said. "I can take care of myself."

"Hah!" Frannie said haughtily. "You sure do have strange ways of provin' it."

Elizabeth looked down into Frannie's face and tried to smile. "I'm here, aren't I?" she asked in a light-hearted manner. "I'm all right, aren't I?"

"For now," Frannie said, giving Elizabeth a disapproving stare. Then she walked past her and went downstairs with heavy footsteps.

When Elizabeth reached the first-floor landing, she took a straw hat from a hat rack and placed it on her head, tying its satin bow beneath her chin. Then without the usual spring in her step, she went on outside.

She crossed the estate grounds, through the wide gate, and walked toward the beckoning waves of the Sound. When she reached the steep incline that led down to the beach, she stopped momentarily to look at the large building that would soon be processing salmon for export.

Today there were men busy putting finishing touches to the building. She could even make out Morris Murdoch among them. She realized that he would have to have stayed behind instead of joining her father on the posse. He seemed to be enjoying having full control in her father's absence as he shouted curse words to the workmen.

Recalling his cold, blue eyes, and how being around him gave her a sense of discomfort, Elizabeth shivered with distaste. She was careful not to be seen as she moved down the rocky slope, and sighed with relief when she reached the sandy stretch of beach.

The wind was warm and soothing, the sprays of water from the Sound were salty on her lips as she began walking aimlessly along the beach. Her eyes looked across the water to the mountains in the distance. She recalled how the lightning had played across the peak of Mount Rainier, and how the thunder had shook the earth on her journeys with Strong Heart.

She remembered how wonderful it had been to lie

in Strong Heart's sheltering arms during the storm after having just made maddening, exquisite love.

"This isn't making me forget anything," she murmured, feeling frustrated. She stopped and turned her
face toward the sun, closing her eyes as she absorbed
its warmth. The skirt of her dress lifted in the gentle
breeze.

"Strong Heart, I wish I were with you now," Elizabeth whispered longingly. "Father, where are you?
Please come home soon so that I can rejoin the man I
love!"

She resumed walking, then sank down onto the soft
sand and scooped up a handful, watching it run
through her fingers. Time. Today it was dragging so.

Watching the sand as it collected in peaks beside
her, she was reminded of when she was a child in San
Francisco, and how her mother had taken her to the
beach and had taught her how to build sand castles. It
seemed as if her mother was there even now, laughing
and playing with her. She remembered that there had
only been the two of them, the rest of the world held
at bay.

Smiling at the memory, she tossed her shawl aside,
and without the aid of a bucket, she used her hands to
scoop out a hole in the sand. Then she made a foun-
dation for her sand castle with the moist sand she had
dug out.

Skillfully, she formed pancake-shaped layers of
sand, piling them up to make a dome. The secret was
to keep the sand good and wet so that the castle did
not topple.

After the dome had reached the desired height, it
was time to carve the architectural details and add
flourishes like winding staircases and graceful arches.

Pleased with how things were progressing, and how
the castle looked so far, Elizabeth rose to her feet. She
moved along the beach looking for small pieces of

driftwood and tiny twigs for sculpting and smoothing the walls and carving everything from doors to balconies.

Bright sea shells and pebbles would be used to line the walkway. A handful of seaweed would be planted for the lawn.

Her arms and the pockets of her dress crammed full with treasures for her castle, Elizabeth turned to go back to her sand castle, then stopped. She dropped everything from her arms when she saw Sheriff Nolan standing beside her castle, his eyes glaring at her.

"You . . ." Elizabeth said, frozen to the spot. "What are you doing here? I-I didn't hear you."

"No, I guess you didn't," Sheriff Nolan said, taking a plug of the ever-present chewing tobacco from his shirt pocket and pushing it into a corner of his mouth. "Your mind is elsewhere, I'd say, Red."

Elizabeth swallowed hard, knowing the danger of revealing too much to him—not only by her words, but by her actions, as well. If she behaved guiltily, then he would have reason to suspect her. She had to act normal, as if seeing him didn't matter one bit.

She tried to act nonchalant as she gathered up her treasure and willed her feet to take one step after another until she reached her sand castle. The sheriff hovered over it like a monster ready to step not only on the castle, but also its sculptress.

"Pardon me," Elizabeth said, giving Sheriff Nolan an annoyed glance as she tried to make him step back.

When he did not budge, she gave him an icier stare. "If you please?"

"If I please what?" Sheriff Nolan grumbled, spitting sticky tobacco juice over his left shoulder. His blue eyes gave her a steely cold stare.

"Please step aside," Elizabeth said, trying to keep her voice steady. "I would like to resume what I was doing before your rude interruption."

"Red, I didn't come here to play house with you," Sheriff Nolan said, not moving. He even placed a hand on Elizabeth's shoulder.

Elizabeth paled and her knees trembled as she looked up at him. "Why *are* you here?" she found the courage to ask. "I'm minding my business. Why don't you?"

"I'm making *you* my business this mornin', Red," Sheriff Nolan said, easing his hand from her shoulder. He rested it on one of his holstered pistols. "I've been keepin' an eye out for you for days. Today I lucked out. As I was riding past your house I saw you coming to the beach. Now ain't that perfect timin'?"

His smug, throaty laugh unnerved Elizabeth. "Oh, I see," she murmured. "Since my father is gone with the posse, you've been watching for my return so that you can send word to them to return home. That's good. Please do it soon. I didn't think my father would be gone this long."

"How would you even know how long he's been gone when you've been gone so long, yourself?" Sheriff Nolan asked with a growl. "Where've you been, Red, since the prison breakout? Who've you been with?"

Elizabeth stiffened. Even though she had expected him to ask her these questions, it did not make it any easier for her. If she answered them wrong, she knew what the consequences would be.

"Where have I been?" Elizabeth said, fighting not to stammer.

"More to the point, I want you to identify the man who knocked me unconscious just before the breakout," Sheriff Nolan said, taking a threatening step toward her. His large boot toppled the sand castle. "I know you had to see the culprit. You were there, damn it. Now you identify him to me."

"I can't," Elizabeth said, her voice breaking. "I . . . just . . . can't."

He reached behind him and took a pair of handcuffs from his back pocket, and before Elizabeth could even blink, he had her wrists handcuffed together. "You leave me no choice but to take you into custody," he said gruffly.

"What?" Elizabeth said, gasping. "You have no right. I am innocent!"

"You're no more innocent than Four Winds who escaped the hangman's noose," Sheriff Nolan said, yanking Elizabeth close to him as he pushed his face into hers. "You were in on the plot from the start, weren't you? You were used as a diversional tactic for the one who planned the escape. Why else did you disappear at the same time? Why else are you home now, safe and sound, as though nothing happened? A few nights in jail will change your mind about confessing the full truth. It will loosen your tongue, all right."

He straightened his back and jerked her to his side as he turned to walk up the hill to his horse. But he was stopped when he found Frannie there, a shotgun leveled at him.

"You let my Elizabeth go," Frannie said breathlessly. "I sees you come to the beach. I sees you place handcuffs on my little girl. Now you just takes them off her again and leave. If you do, I won't pull this trigger. If you don't, I'll fill your stomach full of holes."

Elizabeth became light-headed at the sight of Frannie going up against the sheriff. Not because of her courage to defy him, but more because she was a colored person and it was dangerous.

"Frannie, put down the gun," Elizabeth begged, cringing when Frannie determinedly took a step closer. Her eyes were wild as she peered at the sheriff. "Frannie, there is no need in you going to prison, too. I won't be there long once Father finds out. Please, Frannie, go back to the house. Please?''

Frannie's eyes wavered. ''Honey, I can't let this man takes you away like some . . . some . . . common criminal,'' she said.

''Frannie, I'll be all right,'' Elizabeth said softly. ''It's all a big mistake. One that Father will correct as soon as he returns with the posse. That will probably be today sometime, Frannie. I'll be home in my own bed tonight. I promise you.''

Frannie slowly lowered the gun.

Elizabeth saw the sheriff go for the pistol at his right hip. ''Please let Frannie go,'' she cried. ''Please don't blame her for wanting to protect me. I'm like a daughter to her. Please forget what she did. Let her go. Please?''

Sheriff Nolan eased his hand from the pistol as he glared down at Elizabeth. ''You've been lapse in teachin' that fat thing her place,'' he grumbled. ''You're lucky I don't blow her damn head off.''

Elizabeth sighed heavily. Ignoring Frannie's wails, she went with the sheriff. She had to protect Strong Heart at all cost—even if it meant the loss of her own freedom.

When they reached the summit, she took a last glance over her shoulder at the remains of the castle that she had been building. When she was a child, her sand castles lasted for days.

Today's castle had been crushed, along with her hopes for tomorrow.

19

Some fears,—a soft regret,
For joys scarce known.
— BARRY CORNWALL

The next evening, worn and weary from the unsuc-
cessful search, Earl rode his limping horse in a slow
gait through the open gate of his estate. He peered at
the monstrosity of a house. The window panes seemed
to be on fire from the reflection of the sunset.

He shifted his gaze to the heavy oak front door. His
shoulders slouched, knowing that if by chance Elizabeth had arrived home before him unharmed by whoever had abducted her, she would have already been at
the door.

A low whinny, filled with pain, drew Earl's attention
back to his horse. He would have to put the horse out
of its misery. The animal was no longer useful to him.
He felt lucky that the horse had gotten him back home
instead of leaving him stranded out in the wilderness
after Earl and the posse had parted ways earlier in the
afternoon.

The stables now in sight, Earl rode his horse slowly
onward, giving a mock salute to Everett when the black
groom came toward him.

Everett peered intently at the horse's lame leg, then
up at Earl. "He's doin' mighty poorly, Massa' Easton," he said, shaking his head. "Mighty poorly, indeed."

"Yeah, and I've been riding him for too long that
way, that's for sure," Earl said, yanking on his reins
to stop the horse. He slid out of the saddle, but did
not offer the reins to Everett. "Never mind about him,

Everett. I'll do the ugly task of shootin' him. You can have the job of getting rid of his body.''

Earl walked the horse toward the stables and gave Everett a sidewise glance. "I don't guess my daughter's arrived home yet, has she?" he said, his voice thin and tired.

Everett lowered his dark eyes to the ground as he walked into the stable with Earl. He did not reply, just busied himself removing the horse's saddle.

Earl went to Everett's side and placed a heavy hand on his shoulder. "Have you gone deaf?" he asked irritably. "I asked you a simple enough question. Has Elizabeth returned home?"

Before Everett could answer, Earl saw something half hidden beneath some straw in the corner, the light from the lantern spilling onto it.

"What the hell is that?" he said, for the moment forgetting Everett's strange silence. He sauntered over to the pile of straw and kicked it aside. His eyes widened when he discovered that it was a saddle—an Indian saddle.

His head jerked around, his eyes questioning Everett. "Where did that come from?" he asked. Then he saw an unfamiliar horse in a stall to his right. "That horse. It doesn't belong to me."

He stomped back to Everett and gathered Everett's shirt front into his hand and leaned into Everett's face. "If you value your job, you'd best begin talking," he said, his words hissing through his clenched teeth. "Whose saddle? Whose horse?"

"I was told not to tell," Everett managed to say, his eyes wild with fright. "If I do, she'd make sure I was let go."

Earl's heart skipped a beat. He dropped his hand away from Everett, placing it on the handle of his holstered pistol. "She?" he said, an eyebrow rising. "Who, damn you? Who?"

''She'll not like me tellin' you,'' Everett said, dropping his gaze to the floor.

At the end of his patience, Earl now grabbed Everett by the throat, half lifting him from the floor. ''If you don't tell me,'' he said, his eyes narrowing into Everett's, ''I'll not only be shootin' my horse this evening, I'll use one of my bullets on *you.*''

''Elizabeth!'' Everett shot out. ''She told me to hide the saddle. She came home the other night. She was ridin' that horse there. It was saddled with that Indian saddle.'' He swallowed hard, then said, ''And she was dressed in some kind of Indian dress!''

All of this was coming too fast for Earl. It was spinning around inside his head, not making sense. He jerked his hand away from Everett's throat and wiped it on his breeches. His breath came in short, raspy sounds.

''She's here,'' Earl mumbled, walking toward the door. ''That's all that matters now. My Elizabeth. She's home. She's safe.''

Everett hurried after him. ''Sir, you'd best not go to the house just yet,'' he said, his voice hushed. ''You'd best let me tell you what happened yesterday to Elizabeth.''

Earl stopped and turned to face Everett. ''What about Elizabeth?'' he said, his voice ominous. ''Damn it, what about Elizabeth? Tell me. What happened to her?''

Everett slipped his thin hands into the pockets of his loose, dark trousers. ''The sheriff came,'' he said thickly. ''He took her away. He arrested her. He took her to Copper Hill Prison.''

Feeling his knees close to buckling beneath him, Earl grabbed for the door jamb and steadied himself. He blinked his eyes nervously, finding it hard to breathe.

Then he turned his gaze back to Everett. ''Why

would the sheriff arrest Elizabeth?'' he said, his voice weak. ''Why?''

''He said that she was in on the recent escape,'' Everett said, shifting his feet nervously in the straw. ''He called her an accomplice, or something like that. He said she helped the renegade Indian escape.''

Again Earl felt a weakness sweep through him. He concentrated on the Indian saddle, and then on the strange horse. ''You say Elizabeth was using an Indian saddle on that horse, and she was dressed in Indian attire when she arrived home?'' he said, his mind conjuring up all sorts of nightmarish thoughts about what Elizabeth may have gone through after being abducted by the renegade Indian and his partner.

And now the damn sheriff had cooked up some cockeyed idea that she had joined the escape party? That she had actually had a helping hand in it?

The thought filled him with a keen revulsion for the sheriff and his idiot logic.

''You know as well as I that Elizabeth had no part in anything,'' Earl said, doubling his hands into tight fists at his side. ''She was taken captive.''

Then his eyes wavered. ''How'd Elizabeth look when she got home? Did she look as though . . . as though she may have been tortured by her abductors? Was she all right?''

Everett slipped a hand from his pocket and rubbed his chin thoughtfully. ''Come to think of it, she looked better than I've ever seen her,'' he said, nodding. ''There was something about her eyes—a happiness of sorts. No, I don't believe you have to worry about her having been tortured in any way. I'd say that someone took mighty good care of your daughter.''

Earl lifted an eyebrow at his response. Then he hurriedly took a horse from a stall, slapped his saddle onto its back and fastened it. ''I'm riding into Seattle,'' he said, stopping to eye his lame horse. ''Do what's required here.''

Everett nodded and went to grab a rifle that was propped against the stable wall.

Earl swung himself into his saddle and gave the Indian saddle another lingering stare. Then he slapped his reins and rode quickly away past the towering house and through the gate.

When the low blast of a rifle echoed from the stables, he flinched. Then he rode onward, not stopping for anything or anyone until he reached Seattle. He didn't slow his horse's gait as he made his way through the throng of traffic on First Avenue.

When he reached the street that led to Copper Hill Prison, he felt sick knowing that his sweet daughter was there among the most hardened criminals, at their mercy. He had heard tales of what happened to the women prisoners there:

They were used in every way unholy—they were used.

This torturous thought spurred him on. He didn't even notice the strain on his horse as it climbed the steep street. His eyes were set on the prison. If Elizabeth had so much as been touched by any of those vile men, he vowed to kill the sheriff. Then one day he would find the one who had made her life go astray—the outlaw who had set the Indian free, and taken his Elizabeth as captive.

Earl could not move fast enough when he reached the prison. He jumped out of the saddle, secured his horse's reins and rushed inside the prison. When he found the sheriff lazing behind the desk, chewing on his perpetual wad of tobacco, it almost threw Earl into a fit of rage. To think that this man could arrest his daughter without any proof of her guilt, then lock her up with the rest of the criminals, as though she was one, herself. . . .

Earl stormed to the desk and slammed his hands down on the paper-cluttered top. He leaned into Sheriff Nolan's whiskered face. "I hear that you have my daughter at this godforsaken place," he growled, his eyes red with anger. "You Goddamn idiot, go and set her free at once. Do you hear? Release her. Now!"

"That ain't possible," Sheriff Nolan said, turning his head so that he could let fly a string of tobacco into the spittoon. "She's there until her trial, and then we may have our first hanging of a woman in the history of Seattle."

Earl paled at the thought and his resolve weakened. "You can't be serious," he finally said. "My daughter isn't a criminal. And you know it. Why are you doing this? Why would you want to take your troubles out on an innocent woman? The fact that someone got the best of you that day of the escape is the only reason you've arrested my daughter, isn't it? You have to have a scapegoat. You're makin' her one."

"That redhaired vixen daughter of yours ain't as innocent as you want to believe she is," Sheriff Nolan said, rising slowly from his chair. He made a wide turn around the desk and stood eye to eye with Earl. "She was used as a diversion to what was ready to happen. She flirted with me and once she had me, hook, line, and sinker, I was hit from behind."

Sheriff Nolan slipped a hand inside his right pocket and took a ring of keys from it. He jangled the keys in front of Earl's eyes. "There ain't no rule sayin' you can't visit your daughter," he said tauntingly as he held the keys closer to Earl. "Go on. She's in the first cell. She's a lucky one. She has the cell all to herself. Most other prisoners are cooped up together. But none complain. They like it that way when the night gives them the privacy to do what they damn well please with one another."

Anxiety almost making him dizzy, Earl snatched the keys from the sheriff, then headed toward the door that led to the back room. He flinched when the sheriff stepped in front of him, and opened the door.

"You didn't think I'd let you go visit your daughter alone, now did you?" Sheriff Nolan said, chuckling. He nodded toward the interior. "Go on. Get in the cell with her. But don't forget, I'll be watchin' your every move."

Earl set his jaw, then walked past the sheriff. When he caught sight of Elizabeth standing in a far corner of a cell, his gut twisted and tears splashed from his eyes. "Elizabeth," he whispered. Just saying her name seemed to tear his heart to shreds.

He went to the cell. Elizabeth gasped when she saw him there. His fingers fumbled with the keys, trying to find the one that fit the lock.

She ran to the front of the cell. She clasped the bars. "Father, you've come," she cried.

She then stared icily at the sheriff who was mightily amused watching her father try to find the right key.

Finally a key turned in the lock. Earl slammed the door open and rushed inside the cell, embracing Elizabeth. "Are you all right?" he asked.

"No one has harmed me," Elizabeth said, giving the sheriff another cold glare. Then she pleaded, "Get me out of here, Father. I don't want to spend another night in this . . . in this hellhole. It's even worse than Maysie described. At night . . . at night—"

She stopped and turned her eyes away from him, haunted by the sounds that she had heard the night before. There were moans of pain, and many more of lusty pleasure. As the moonlight had filtered through the narrow windows, she had seen many varieties of sexual activity acted out before her. What she had seen had not only startled her, but sickened her as well.

Earl had seen and heard enough. He turned and faced the sheriff. "I demand you release her immediately," he said, his voice growing louder with each word. "She's no criminal and you know it. Set her free or I'll—"

"If you so much as even look like you're going to threaten me I'll lock you up with your daughter and throw away the key," Sheriff Nolan spit out between clenched teeth. He nodded at Earl. "Forget this foolishness of takin' your daughter with you tonight *or* tomorrow. When the judge arrives from San Francisco, she'll get her day in court. But until then, she's mine. Do you hear? Mine."

Earl's jaw went slack and his heart fell to his feet. He realized that no matter what he said to the sheriff, Elizabeth was to remain in jail.

He turned slowly to Elizabeth and drew her gently into his arms. "I've got to go," he whispered. "But I'll manage to get you out of here. Somehow."

"Please do," Elizabeth whispered back, feeling safe and loved because he had come.

But then Earl whispered something else to her, something that proved that he had little trust in her. That he might even believe that she was guilty of helping in the escape.

"Elizabeth, whose hide are you protecting?" Earl whispered, not allowing her to jerk free when she tried. "Where've you been? With Indians? I saw the Indian saddle. Everett told me that you wore an Indian dress the day you returned home. Tell me, Elizabeth, why?"

Elizabeth pressed her lips together, refusing to respond. She was glad when the sheriff's voice boomed from behind her father, making him release her from his tight grip.

"Come on, you've been in there long enough," Nolan barked.

Her father stepped away from her and gazed into her
eyes. She turned her back on him, dying a slow death
inside over the way he was looking at her—as if *he*
were the judge and jury, handing down a death sentence. Without her having even told him about Strong
Heart, he seemed to already know her secret—the secret that she had thought to have locked safely within
her heart.

Now what would he do? she thought despairingly to
herself.

Earl stared at Elizabeth a moment longer, then
stormed from the prison. He lifted himself into his
saddle. He was filled with anguish and doubt over
Elizabeth's part in the Indian's escape. Her silence was
troubling.

But how, he wondered? When would she have met
an Indian? It made no sense, no sense at all. Then he
recalled how she had somehow managed to get herself
involved with that young girl, Maysie.

He now had to believe that she had gone against his
orders more than once. She had wandered wherever
she pleased when he was not there to stop her.

The thought angered him. Yet, no matter what she
had done, no matter how defiant she had become, he
would do everything to free his daughter from prison.
Only then could he force the answers from her. And
this he must do. He hoped that what he would find out
would be less awful than it now appeared to be.

He sent his horse into a gallop away from the
prison, already devising a plan in his mind as to how
Elizabeth might be set free. Morris Murdoch. Morris
must have connections—he would surely know who
to cut deals with in Seattle to get Elizabeth out of the
prison.

"Yes, that's what I'll do," Earl said to himself as

he guided his horse through the town. "I'll ask for Murdoch's help. I'm going to ask him to use whatever influence he has to get Elizabeth back home with me."

He gave the prison a look over his right shoulder, then rode onward.

Elizabeth moved halfheartedly to the bunk in her cell and sat down on its edge, peering at the darkened sky through the window.

Another night.

Another hell.

When would it end? If ever?

20

I think and speak of other things,
To keep my mind at rest.
                    —JOHN CLARE

Discouraged over not finding the raiders after having
scoured the countryside looking for them, Strong Heart
sat beside a blazing fire in the newly constructed council house. Many braves around him were discussing
the matters of their village, especially their plans for
the upcoming salmon harvest.

Strong Heart was not only displeased about his un-
successful search, but also worried about his father.
He had not joined the council today. When he had
gone to his father's longhouse early this morning, his
mother had greeted Strong Heart at the door and dis-
suaded him from waking his father. His leg wound had
kept the old chief awake most of the night.

Guilt filled Strong Heart. Twice now he had let his
father down—the day of the raid Strong Heart had not
been there to fight for his people, and now he had not
found those responsible for his father's injury.

He had let his mother down, as well, by not being
able to find her father.

At least there was one thing that could bring some
sunshine into his heart as he sat listening to the other
braves debating. His *la-daila*. His Elizabeth with the
luminous green eyes and hair the color of flame.

Soon she would join him again and then his burden
would be lightened. She had a way of making his losses
bearable, giving him the strength to forge ahead to the
future.

Something one of the braves was saying brought him back to the present.

He listened intently, realizing that while he had been thinking he had missed something important.

"As we have discussed before, again I say that we should forget the salmon harvest this year," the brave was saying, shocking Strong Heart clear to his core. That any brave would ever think such a thing, much less speak it aloud!

Strong Heart leaned forward, his hands resting on his knees. The same brave quickly explained his reasons.

"I say let us catch the salmon for the white men and take the money they have offered instead of keeping the salmon for ourselves." The brave looked nervously over at Strong Heart, whose expression was stern and forbidding.

"I . . . I . . . would even accept their offer to work in their fishery," the brave continued warily. "Why should others have the money, when it could be ours?"

"This that I am hearing, from a brave who has always prided himself on living away from the ways of the white people, basking in the pride of being Suquamish, living only for the honor of being Suquamish, makes Strong Heart ashamed," Strong Heart scolded. His gaze roamed the circle of braves. "Are there others who feel the same? Would you rather work for the white men than your very own people? How could any of you forget the importance of the salmon to the Suquamish? It is what sustains us through the long, harsh winters. Without the salmon, many would go hungry!"

His eyes bored into the one brave that had spoken so favorably of working for the white people, becoming their slave as had so many of their forefathers so long ago.

"This that you bring before our braves today—this

talk of working for white men," Strong Heart said, his voice flat, "why do you?"

"Two white men came to our village while you were gone to set Four Winds free from the white man's prison," the brave said, his face flushing under Strong Heart's stare. "They sat in council with your father and made offers that sounded foolish until . . . until . . . after the raid, and I saw how quickly things could change for our people. In one instant, the salmon that we would harvest could be taken from us by fires set by evil raiders. Now I see the importance of learning ways to feed our people other than the salmon run each autumn."

Strong Heart rose slowly to his feet, towering over the braves in council. With his fists on his hips and his legs spread, he glared from man to man. "Who were these white men intruders?" he asked, his voice filled with wrath. "A name. Do you have names?"

"Morris Murdoch was the only name that stays in my mind," another brave said, looking sternly up at Strong Heart. "The other name has flown."

A smooth and clear voice suddenly spoke from behind Strong Heart, who turned in surprise. His father was limping into the council house with the aid of a staff. Strong Heart started to go to him and was stopped by what his father was saying.

"I, too, have forgotten the white man's name due to all that has happened since their visit," Chief Moon Elk said. "But, my son, while you were gone on your search for the raiders, I sent out scouts to see where the white men were building their fishery that they spoke so openly of—where they wish to enslave our people for what they call wages. This building in which salmon will be processed to sell to other white men sits on the shores of the Sound, close to the hallowed grounds of our people. The white man's house that also sits on our hallowed grounds is lived in by one of the men who came to us with cheap offers of the heart.''

Strong Heart's heart constricted and his throat went dry, stunned by what his father had said. In his mind, he saw that day when he had stood on the butte, studying the men working on the shore, erecting a building. He had wondered what it was for.

The realization of who the man was whom Chief Moon Elk was speaking of sent a wave of despair through Strong Heart, making him weave with the pain that the knowledge brought him.

The man was Elizabeth's father! It had to be.

His heart now beat rapidly with anger, as he recalled her explanation for her father's decision to move to the Pacific Northwest. She had spoken very skillfully around the truth—not actually lying to him, yet not being altogether truthful.

It sickened him to know that all along she had known of her father's schemes to entice the Suquamish into leaving their way of life to take up the white man's culture!

She had surely known, also, that her father had chosen *his* village to work his schemes on. And yet she had not admitted it to Strong Heart.

The thought that she could betray him in the slightest way tore at his very soul, making her betrayal lie heavy on his heart. He fell speechless in front of his father.

Chief Moon Elk went to the circle of men and sat down among them. Strong Heart silently followed and sat down beside his father.

Elizabeth! he despaired to himself. His *la-daila!*

Strong Heart would not allow himself to believe that she would betray him. Knowing her as well as he did, he had to believe that her purpose for lying to him had a good reason.

Ah-hah, he silently decided—yes, he would believe that his woman had lied for a good reason.

As his father conversed with the other braves, convincing them to stay with their people and participate in the salmon harvest only for their people, Strong Heart's thoughts turned elsewhere.

He began thinking about the timing of the white men's visit to his village with offers that they had, in turn, refused, and the massacre that had occurred shortly after.

He could not help but suspect that Elizabeth's father had led the raid in retaliation for the Indians' turning him down.

Would her father have planned the raid in order to frighten the Suquamish into bowing down to his wishes when he came back?

Strong Heart momentarily held his face within his hands, slowly shaking his head.

No! he cried silently to himself. It could not be. Elizabeth was too sweet—too wholesome—to have a totally monstrous father who would kill and maim innocent people.

His father's voice brought Strong Heart out of his turmoil. He turned to his father and listened to him be the leader who Strong Heart could remember from childhood. As Strong Heart looked slowly around him, he could see that what his father was saying was reaching the braves, persuading them to agree with his every word and command.

"I will listen to no more talk about assisting the white men," Chief Moon Elk said firmly. "Our people will fish the salmon as we always have. It is time to concentrate only on the welfare of our people. We must begin the preparations for the march to the canyon where we have always harvested the salmon in the autumn of the year."

Chief Moon Elk shifted his eyes to Strong Heart.

"My son, do you have anything to add?" he said, placing a hand on Strong Heart's shoulder.

Strong Heart felt proud of his father at that moment, and was relieved that his father was able to ignore the pain of his leg, and lead his people again.

The raiders at least had not robbed him of his strength of spirit.

"You have said it all quite eloquently, my father," Strong Heart said, placing a hand on his father's that rested on his shoulder. "There is nothing more that I can add."

When his father leaned over and drew him into a fond embrace, Strong Heart closed his eyes, reveling in this closeness between himself and his father. Strong Heart's place was here, at his father's side. He tried to force Elizabeth from his mind, yet she always seemed to return, haunting his every thought.

He knew that no matter how hard he tried to convince himself that he could do it, he would not be able to forget her all that easily.

The mountains were a hazy purple against the darkening sky. A deer roasted on a spit over a campfire, sizzling in its own juices.

Four Winds sat quietly in the growing shadows away from the other desperadoes and renegades, listening to Morris Murdoch tell the men about Elizabeth's imprisonment, and that her father wanted her set free.

Four Winds ran one hand along the cold steel barrel of a pistol lying in his lap. He had just cleaned its chambers and reloaded it with soft-tipped bullets. He wondered what he should do about this latest piece of news that could eventually involve his friend, Strong Heart. When had Strong Heart set the woman free? He had seemed determined to keep her as his captive.

No matter, though, Four Winds thought to himself, how she happened to leave Strong Heart. It was the fact that she was jailed in that miserable prison that bothered him.

Not because he was concerned about *her*. Strong Heart was his only concern. If the authorities managed to get information from Elizabeth concerning Strong Heart and Four Winds, they might join Elizabeth in jail and be hanged as criminals.

On the other hand, if the desperadoes went to the prison and broke her out, what then? If they let her return home, the sheriff would only arrest her again.

But if they did not return her home, where would they take her?

If she was not in the custody of Strong Heart, Strong Heart was in danger. It was Four Winds's duty to warn him, for Four Winds owed him a favor for having released him from prison.

Ah-hah, he had to warn Strong Heart of the danger that this woman posed for him—even though revealing this to Strong Heart, would also be revealing that he was not the innocent man that Strong Heart had thought. His best friend would know that Four Winds *was* a renegade, who had joined up with his old friends again. The excitement that riding with outlaws offered had become too thick in his blood to leave.

Four Winds rose quietly to his feet, making sure not to draw undue attention to himself. He continued to listen to Morris Murdoch, who was the leader of the gang.

"Men, let's go and get Earl's daughter out of prison," Murdoch urged. "What can it hurt? You need some excitement in your life now, don't you, since you've been forced to lie low in the hills. Staying away from raidin' until things cooled off a mite. Set his daughter free and we'll hide her someplace where the sheriff can't find her. Earl will have to accept that as a condition of her being rescued. And he will. The fool. He doesn't know that he doesn't have much time left to enjoy her. After everything is set with the Suquamish, I plan to kill Earl and take complete control of the fishery.''

Morris laughed throatily. "But all in due time," he said, sipping from a cup of coffee. "Everything good comes to those who wait."

As the men put their heads together and began making plans on how to break Elizabeth out of the prison, Four Winds slipped away unnoticed.

When he got to the horses, he went to his and very easily untethered it and launched himself into the saddle.

Knowing how to be as quiet as a panther in the night, he urged his horse in a soft lope away from the campsite.

Yet again he worried about telling Strong Heart that he was at heart a renegade—an outlaw. But his loyalty to his friend was much stronger than his fear of being condemned in Strong Heart's eyes.

When he was far enough away from the campsite, Four Winds bent low over his horse and sent it into a hard gallop across the land, hoping that he could get to Strong Heart's village in time. Strong Heart would have to make his own decision about what should happen to the woman.

21

A burden still of chilling fear
I find in every place.
　　　　　　　—JOHN CLARE

Elizabeth's cell was dark, with only thin beams of moonlight sifting through the bars above her bunk, where she lay in a fetal position. She clutched her arms around herself, shivering not so much from the chill of the night—but from the horror of everything that went on in the jail after the cloak of night had fallen. The moon had given off enough light for her to see bodies scrambling together, fulfilling their lusts once again, tonight.

And now everyone but her seemed to be asleep. Snores, groans, and women sobbing in their sleep reached Elizabeth's ears. Maysie had been right to have pitied the women in this godforsaken place. In the larger cells women and men alike were housed. Elizabeth had seen too many of the women bent to the wills of the men.

No matter what their crime might have been, only stealing a piece of bread to keep from starving to death, most of the women in this prison were treated like animals. Elizabeth wished that she could do something to help them, yet she could not even help herself!

Tears splashed from her eyes as she thought of Strong Heart. She could not expect Strong Heart to help her, for he did not even know that she was in the prison.

But her father! Why hadn't he gotten her out of this

hellhole? He had money, plenty of money. Surely he could have found a way to pay for her release!

The sound of the sheriff's office door opening startled Elizabeth. With trembling fingers she reached beneath the mattress and found the fork that she had hidden there after her evening meal. She didn't trust the sheriff, or his deputy. She had never forgotten how the sheriff had tried to rape her on her first visit to the prison on the day of Four Winds's escape.

To protect herself, she had managed to steal a fork from her dinner tray. She wasn't sure how much damage a mere fork could do, but at least it would give her a slim chance of protecting herself.

Her eyes wide, she watched a form moving in the dark toward her cell. She slid the fork beneath a fold of her dress, clutching desperately to the handle.

Her heart pounded as she saw the man take a ring of keys from his back pocket and sort through them, until he found the one that fit the lock of Elizabeth's cell.

The door creaked slowly open and she was finally able to see who it was now standing over her, slipping the ring of keys back into his pocket, his free hand at the fly of his breeches, eagerly undoing its buttons.

"Deputy Bradley," Elizabeth gasped, inching her way from the edge of the bunk, then hugging the wall with her back when she could go no further.

She still held the fork in her hand. Her throat was dry and fear gripped her hard in the pit of her stomach.

"Don't say a word, slut," Deputy Bradley said through yellow teeth, his coppery mustache twitching as he spoke. "Just keep still or I'll do worse than rape you. I'll save the judge a day in court. If you're dead, he won't have to bother with rulin' you innocent or guilty."

His words made Elizabeth feel as though ice water had been poured into her veins. She was shocked that this man could be this devious—this heartless. Until now, of the two men who controlled the jail, Elizabeth had thought that she could trust Deputy Bradley more. He appeared young and not yet as hardened as Sheriff Nolan.

When Deputy Bradley dropped his pants Elizabeth thought this might be her best opportunity to make her attack. But as she took the fork out from beneath her dress, the moonlight flashed on it, revealing it to Deputy Bradley. He jerked it from her hand before she could even plunge it into his face.

Deputy Bradley tossed the fork aside and quickly straddled Elizabeth. "Bitch," he said, holding her wrists to the bunk, one of his knees shoving her dress upward. "You think you can stop me? It's been too long since I've had me a woman like you to let anything stop me from gettin' what I'm after."

His lips crushed Elizabeth's with a wet, slobbering kiss as he started lowering his manhood toward her. Panic rushed in her like wild fires spreading through dry brush. Elizabeth raised one knee and hit him hard in the groin with it. He leaped away from her with a yowl and clutched himself where she had caused the damage.

Elizabeth jumped from the bunk and grabbed the fork from the floor and held it threateningly before her, her eyes flashing. "Get out of here and leave me be," she said breathlessly. She was stunned to see that he seemed unable to move as he still held himself, moaning and groaning.

Suddenly she was aware of something else. The commotion had awakened all of the prisoners. They were shouting and jeering and mimicking the deputy. The place was in an uproar.

Deputy Bradley glared at Elizabeth as he slowly leaned over to pick up his pants. Not bothering to put them on, he inched around her and left the cell. He stopped long enough to fish his keys out of his pocket, then locked the cell behind him.

Elizabeth breathed hard as she watched him limp away, tossing curses over his shoulder as the prisoners continued to jeer and mock him.

Then Elizabeth sank back down onto the bunk, fearing the rest of the days and nights of her incarceration, for surely the deputy would find a way to make her pay.

A movement in his longhouse awakened Strong Heart. He groped around until he found the knife that he always kept close beside his bed, and then bolted from his sleeping platform, the knife poised for its death plunge.

When Four Winds came out of the shadows and stood over the dying embers of the firepit, Strong Heart sighed and lowered the knife to his side.

"It is unwise, *me-sah-chie*, bad, to enter a dwelling unannounced, whether it is night or day," Strong Heart said, bending to place the knife back on the floor.

He then gestured with a hand toward Four Winds. "*Mitlite*, sit down, my friend," he said softly. "Tell me why you have come in the middle of the night to awaken Strong Heart. What news do you bring me?"

Strong Heart watched Four Winds carefully as he sat down, his dark brown hair held into place by a colorfully beaded headband. Strong Heart remembered his father suspecting Four Winds of being among their village's attackers. Strong Heart still could not believe his friend capable of such a fiendish act.

"There is not much time for talk," Four Winds said, his expression troubled.

"There is not time for you to tell me if you have rejoined your people?" Strong Heart asked, raising an eyebrow. "There is not enough time for me to ask of your people's welfare?"

"No," Four Winds said, placing his hands on his knees, leaning on them as he locked his eyes with Strong Heart's. "There is no time for idle talk of family. I have come with news of something other than my people, or yours."

Strong Heart's spine stiffened and his jaw tightened. "What news then is it that you bring me, that you find it important enough to awake me from my sleep?" he asked. "Tell me now, Four Winds. What is it?"

"It is because of the woman with the hair of flame that I come to you tonight," Four Winds said, seeing alarm enter his friend's eyes. "Strong Heart, she has been arrested. She is in Copper Hill Prison. She is accused of being a partner with the one who set me free which, of course, is you, my friend."

Strong Heart's mouth gaped and his heart seemed to stop beating, the shock was so quick and overwhelming.

Then he bolted to his feet and began scrambling around the longhouse, slipping into his buckskins and moccasins. With a growl, he grabbed his rifle and held it up in the air. "They shall die for doing this to my *la-daila*," he cried, forgetting all of his doubts about Elizabeth. At this moment, there was no doubt exactly what she meant to him, and always would. He must save her.

He turned to Four Winds as he rose to his feet. "You will ride with me?" he said, his eyes dark with emotion. "My friend, you will help me set her free?"

"This I would do gladly, except . . ." Four Winds said, lowering his eyes, for now was a time of truth between friends—a truth that might turn them into enemies.

"Except what?" Strong Heart dared to ask, seeing now that something was very wrong in Four Winds's demeanor. Instead of being proud for having brought such news to a friend, Four Winds was acting as one who had something to be ashamed about.

Strong Heart's pulse raced as he waited for Four Winds's explanation. They did not have much time to waste, when his beloved was at the mercy of too many whose hearts were black. He must *hy-ak,* hurry, and get to her before she was harmed by the *cultus,* worthless man, the sheriff.

Yet, because of friendship, he must wait for Four Winds to say his piece.

Four Winds looked slowly up at Strong Heart. "You did not ask me how I knew about the white woman being in the prison," he said, his voice quiet.

"I saw no need," Strong Heart said, his puzzlement deepening. "If Elizabeth is jailed, surely those in the city know, and such news spreads quickly."

Then Strong Heart was shaken by a thought. "But you, my friend, should not be near the city, or with those who would hear such news," he said slowly. "You should be with your people, or still be hiding in the hills."

Strong Heart walked around the fire and came eye to eye with Four Winds. "Tell me, my friend, how do you know about Elizabeth?"

Four Winds lifted his chin and folded his arms across his chest. "The news traveled to the band of outlaws of which I am a part," he said, holding his voice steady, although his heart was pounding like distant thunder within his chest. "Now you know that the law was not wrong about me. I *am* a criminal who enjoys raiding the white settlers. Elizabeth's father is friends with the leader of the gang. The father asked his help in setting Elizabeth free from prison. They are on their way even now, Strong Heart. We will not be able to reach Elizabeth before the gang gets to her. It is dangerous for you, Strong Heart, either way—whether she is in prison, or freed by the outlaws. If she is able to point an accusing finger at you for setting me free, *you* could be the one that will use the hangman's noose that has been readied for me.''

Strong Heart was silent and numb from Four Winds's confession. He recalled his ravaged village the day after the fatal attack on his people, and his father's thoughts about Four Winds's part in it.

He reached a hand to Four Winds's throat and sank his fingers in it. ''I do not know if I should call you *pelton,* foolish, or brave, for coming to my village tonight with the pretense of being my friend,'' he said, his eyes filled with fire.

Four Winds paled and his eyes widened. ''What do you mean?'' he gasped. ''What are you saying? I have done nothing to cause you to turn on me, my friend. I have come to you tonight, for payment in part for what you did for me. But, most of all, I have come because of our lifelong friendship. Why do you doubt me? Why do you treat me harshly, instead of as a friend?''

''By the cover of night you did not notice that my village is being rebuilt, and that some of the totem poles stand half burned by such raiders that you profess to being part of?'' Strong Heart hissed. ''Can you say that you do not know of the plight of my people? That you did not ride with your friends against my people? Against me?''

Four Winds tried to shake his head, the effort only causing Strong Heart's fingers to dig more deeply into his flesh. ''Believe me when I say that I know nothing of such a raid,'' he rasped out. ''And since my return to my comrades, there have been no raids, not even on the settlers. They are lying low, waiting for things to settle down since my arrest. They . . . they . . . are taking a chance riding into town to help the white woman escape. They do this because the man who is their leader asked them to, and owe him much. He keeps them in food and clothes in harder times. They did not notice when I slipped away to warn you.''

The thought again of Elizabeth in the prison caused Strong Heart to wince and his heart to cry out in pain. He dropped his hand away from Four Winds. ''We will talk later of these things that are new between us,'' he said thickly. ''For now, Four Winds, my heart and mind is full only of Elizabeth. Let us ride together as friends. Let us take this woman from the prison. Then, as friends, we will talk. You can explain to me why you have chosen the life of crime over the congenial life of the Suquamish.''

Four Winds nodded and they left the longhouse in a rush. He waited for Strong Heart to go to his parents to explain why he would be gone, and for Strong Heart to get his horse.

Soon they were riding hard beneath the moonlight, Four Winds giving Strong Heart questioning glances. ''This woman!'' he finally shouted. ''She means much to you? You find her special?''

Strong Heart turned flashing eyes on Four Winds. ''She is my life!'' he confessed loudly, his words echoing far across the land, through the forest, and to the sky.

22

Whatever on my heart may fall,
Remember, I would risk it all!
—ADELAIDE ANNE PROCTER

It had been a day's ride for Strong Heart and Four
Winds—a ride against time. Finally, at midnight the
next night, they arrived on the butte that overlooked
Copper Hill Prison.

Strong Heart glared down at the prison, seeing no
activity, or light glowing from any of the barred windows. The only light that was evident was in the sheriff's office, and even that was only a dim golden glow
as it shone through the glass panes.

Strong Heart gave Four Winds a quick glance. "You
know the dangers and yet you still come with me to
the prison?" he asked, his hand resting on the stock
of his rifle that hung from the side of his saddle. "We
could be hanging side by side on the platform tomorrow if we do not succeed in releasing my *la-daila* from
prison. You would risk that for my woman?"

"No," Four Winds said flatly, giving Strong Heart
a steely gaze. "I do it for *you*, my friend."

This proved many things to Strong Heart—the most
important being that Four Winds could not have participated in the raid against Strong Heart's people. It
would not make sense to go against Strong Heart one
minute, then ally himself the next.

He reached over and placed a firm hand on Four
Winds's shoulder. "Friends forever?" he asked, his
face questioning.

Four Winds placed a hand on Strong Heart's. "Forever," he said vehemently. "Now, and always!"

Strong Heart nodded, then dropped his hand back to his rifle, and quietly studied the prison again. He nodded once more toward Four Winds, then slapped his horse and began edging his way down the side of the butte. Four Winds followed him into the forest that bordered the prison.

When the prison was in sight through a break in the trees, Strong Heart felt a fever of anticipation building within him as he slipped easily out of the saddle.

Four Winds dismounted and soon they were moving stealthily through the forest. Their hands clutched their rifles, and their eyes darted about them, watching for any sudden movement.

"I fear that this is too easy," Strong Heart whispered to Four Winds, stopping at the edge of the forest, to stare at the door that led into the prison. "I see no activity—no people. Is everyone asleep?"

"It may appear so but I was housed in the prison long enough to know the nighttime activities there," Four Winds whispered back. "They are unpleasant, yet the sheriff and his deputies have a hands-off policy. Whatever happens in the shadows behind the bars is the business of the prisoners—and their victims. But *ah-hah*, this time of night the sheriff or whoever is in charge, sleeps. We shall enter the prison unnoticed. We shall leave just as easily."

What Four Winds had said about the activity in the cells after dark made Strong Heart feel ill. Who was to say what may have happened to Elizabeth?

His jaw tightened. If Elizabeth had been defiled or even so much as touched by any man in that prison, the man responsible would not live to see the next sunrise! Strong Heart would take much pleasure in plunging a knife into the man's dark heart!

Not letting his imagination distract him from his purpose, Strong Heart began running softly toward the door of the prison. His moccasined feet were as quiet as the pads of a cat. He glanced over at Four Winds, glad to be with his friend again on an adventure. As children, they had sought out the dangers of the forest beyond, enjoying the challenge of the bear, the panther, and the wolf.

Yet this that they were doing tonight was even more challenging than anything else they had done in the past. For Strong Heart's reward would be to hold Elizabeth in his arms again, to become her protector for all their tomorrows.

Looking warily from side to side, seeing no sign of anyone, Strong Heart and Four Winds stopped long enough to lean their backs against the prison wall, to get their breaths.

Strong Heart cocked his rifle and Four Winds cocked his.

They stared into each other's eyes, then nodded in unison, and crept to the door.

Strong Heart nodded at Four Winds, then nodded toward the door latch. He then stood aside with his rifle ready to fire as Four Winds followed his silent bidding and slowly opened the door.

Strong Heart looked inside the sheriff's office, and he could see that a deputy was there instead of the sheriff. The deputy was fast asleep at the desk.

Gripping his rifle, Strong Heart moved stealthily and quickly into the room, Four Winds behind him. Strong Heart rendered the deputy unconscious with a blow to his head from the butt of his rifle. The man never knew what hit him.

"The keys," Strong Heart said, standing guard beside the door that led to the cells. "Four Winds, get the keys."

Glancing over his shoulder at the deputy, Four Winds went to the pegs on the wall and slipped a ring of keys from them. Standing his rifle against the wall, he sorted through them. Soon he and Strong Heart were standing in the shadows of the back room, the moonlight sifting through the small windows of each of the cells the only light.

Everything was quiet, except for snores from the cells on either side. This made Strong Heart breathe easier, knowing that while everyone slept, his woman was safe from abuse.

Peering through the darkness, Strong Heart checked the cells, determining who was housed in them. His pulse raced.

The moon was shining on long and drifting red hair that hung over the side of the bunk in the first cell. Strong Heart recognized the exquisite creamy skin of Elizabeth's face as she lay asleep on her side, her dark brush of lashes on her cheeks.

Strong Heart was for the moment too overcome to move. Such a sight as this sent his heart into a tailspin of love for his *la-daila*. How could he ever live without her?

His gaze lingered on her lips, remembering how passionately moist they could become as he kissed her.

Then he lowered his gaze to where the tantalizing cleavage of her breasts could be seen where her dress dipped low. Her translucent body seemed to gleam in the moonlight.

He wanted to take her in his arms and press her against him and challenge anyone who might try to separate them.

Four Winds had stopped beside Strong Heart. He saw Elizabeth in the cell, then turned his eyes back to Strong Heart. He placed a hand on Strong Heart's shoulder. "We must *hy-ak*, hurry," he whispered. "The sheriff might come and check on things."

"*Ah-hah*," Strong Heart whispered back, shaken from his reverie. He realized how foolish it had been to allow his thoughts to interfere with his need to move quickly to get Elizabeth safely from this prison.

Four Winds went to the cell and slipped the key into the lock. The click of the tumblers echoed all around them, awakening not only Elizabeth, but some others.

Elizabeth sat up with a start, her eyes wide. She gazed in terror toward the open cell door. Then she gasped with surprise as she saw Strong Heart rush into the cell toward her.

"Strong Heart?" she said, tears spilling from her eyes as he gathered her into his arms and began carrying her from the cell. She looped an arm around his neck and clung to him. "I should've known that you would find out and would come for me."

When Four Winds moved past her and Strong Heart, toward the door that led to the office, her eyes widened. "And Four Winds is here also?" she asked, looking questioningly into Strong Heart's eyes. They stepped into the office, the shouts and cries of the other prisoners a loud rumble behind them.

She then paled as she looked down at the deputy with blood streaming from a gash at the back of his head. Strong Heart hurried toward the door that led outside. "Is he dead?" she asked, her voice hushed. "Did you have to kill him to set me free?"

"He is only slightly injured," Strong Heart said, heading outside toward the cover of the forest.

Elizabeth held on to Strong Heart as he carried her away from the awful prison. She pressed her cheek against his chest, then looked quickly over his shoulder. The wails of the women who had been left behind sent shivers up her spine.

"Those poor women," she cried, reaching a hand out toward the prison. "We must go back. We must set them free! You don't know how so many of them are forced to live! I was left alone. I was one of the lucky ones!"

"There is no time," Strong Heart said, running up to his horse and quickly placing her in the saddle.

He jumped before her into the saddle, then looked over at Four Winds who was astride his horse. "Four Winds, would you say that the town is deserted enough for us to make our escape through it?" Strong Heart asked, his horse pawing at the ground nervously. "Climbing the steep butte will slow our escape. I feel that it would be much faster to ride through the city and lose ourselves in that stretch of forest that is not so hilly."

"*Ah-hah*, I feel that you are right," Four Winds said. "And for the comfort of the woman, I think that escape is best."

Strong Heart nodded, then flicked his rawhide reins and sank his moccasined heels into the flanks of the roan, sending it out into the open, and down the steep grade of street beside Four Winds's horse.

When they reached First Avenue, they slowed their pace, not wanting to draw undue attention from those who still lingered along the boardwalks and those who swayed drunkenly outside the saloons.

Elizabeth clung to Strong Heart's waist, fearing capture. Then her attention was drawn to someone besides the loitering drunks. She drew in a breath when she recognized a young lady walking out of a saloon, steering a man who teetered alongside her.

"Maysie!" Elizabeth gasped, stunned to see how gaudily Maysie was dressed, and how thickly painted her cheeks were with rouge. The bright red dress that Maysie was wearing was cut short above her knees, with layers upon layers of lacy petticoats beneath it that bounced as she walked. The bodice was cut low, revealing all but the nipples of her breasts. Her hair was tied up in a loose chignon, with a few curls of hair that coiled down on each side above her ears.

Elizabeth's heart sank at the sight. It saddened her to see that Maysie had gone back to whoring. Yet she was at least relieved to know that Maysie was alive, if one could call that sort of life *living*.

Then Elizabeth's attention was caught when she heard Four Winds gasp as he saw Maysie being escorted from the saloon. She could hear him utter something under his breath as his eyes became filled with hurt, and she had to wonder what Maysie was to him.

Had they met in the brothel? Had he bought time with Maysie, and then fallen in love with her?

She dispelled these thoughts as she remembered the urgent matter of their escape. Strong Heart headed toward the forest, away from the direction of her house.

"You aren't returning me home to my father?" she asked, then realized how foolish the question was before he even answered her. If she returned home, the sheriff would come and get her again as soon as he knew about the escape. She had to hide from the sheriff. She was now a fugitive, along with Strong Heart and Four Winds.

She knew that a speedy escape now was of the essence, not only for herself, but for the man that she loved. He had risked his life again for her.

Oh, but how could she ever truly repay him? How?

Strong Heart looked over his shoulder at her. "You are going to my village again, and this time not as my prisoner, but as my beloved! I was foolish to leave you behind. This I will never allow again! You will be at my side at all times—even during those times I am called away to serve as speaker for my people. My *ladaila*, you will never be in danger again. Never!"

Tears streamed down Elizabeth's face and her eyes gratefully shone at Strong Heart.

Then as Strong Heart turned away from her, she hugged her arms more tightly around his waist, locking her to him. She pressed her cheek against his back, knowing that words were easy—but not always so easily kept.

Although Strong Heart was with her, that did not mean that she was safe. Should the sheriff form another posse and set out on a search for them, could they escape forever?

She closed her eyes tightly, trying to block out such fears.

At this moment she *was* safe, and she would revel in it. And she was with her beloved again!

23

Ah! What is love?
It is a pretty thing.
—ROBERT GREENE

The sun was just rising in a great splash of orange. The birds were waking in the trees overhead. Fish were fastened in strips to willow poles stuck in the ground near the campfire. The delicious aroma of the juices as they dripped into the flames, tantalized her as it filled the air. A spring, its bubbly water sweet and pure, flowed nearby.

Elizabeth was weary from the long ride from Seattle, and was feeling as if history was repeating itself as she sat beside the campfire, listening to Strong Heart and Four Winds discussing Four Winds's association with the outlaws.

When the words got heated, she looked guardedly from one to the other.

"Four Winds, when I set you free from prison, it was my sincere belief that you were not linked with the outlaws in any way," Strong Heart said, his jaw tight. "And now I discover that you are. Do you not see how foolish this makes me appear?"

Four Winds glowered at Strong Heart. "Had you known I was guilty of choosing my own way of life—the life of a renegade—you would have let me, your childhood companion, hang," he said dryly. "You would condemn me to death?"

"In my heart I would not want to," Strong Heart grumbled. "But, *ah-hah,* yes, I would have no choice but to allow the noose to be slipped over your head. What you stand for does not show a Suquamish brave well in the eyes of all who see you. As a renegade, you do not set a good example, Four Winds, for the children of your village or mine. Tell me, Four Winds, why did you choose this road that you have followed?''

Four Winds hesitated. He took a willow pole with its skewered meat from the ground and handed it to Elizabeth. He did the same for Strong Heart, then took some for himself. Yet he only stared at it, instead of eating.

''At first I thought what I was doing was best for our people as a whole,'' he mumbled. He looked slowly up at Strong Heart, who also was not eating. ''I saw the onslaught of white settlers as a threat to our existence. I rode with the desperadoes only to frighten the whites from our land.'' He lowered his eyes again, then said softly, ''After a while what I was doing was more for excitement than for our people. In a sense, I was free again, with no white authority dictating to me how I should live.''

His jaw tightened. ''It is good to be free,'' he said forcefully.

''Do you not see that Strong Heart is even more free than you?'' Strong Heart said, placing a hand on Four Winds's shoulder. ''You became the hunted the moment you raided and killed that first white settler.''

''You are now the hunted, also, my friend,'' Four Winds said, swallowing hard. He clapped his free hand onto Strong Heart's shoulder. ''And it is because of me that you are. It would have been best had you allowed me to die, Strong Heart. It would have been best for all concerned.''

Strong Heart turned his eyes to Elizabeth and gave her a lingering look. He knew that she would have been better off had she not become involved in these escapes, yet if she had not, they would have never known the wonders of the love they felt for each other.

And theirs was a special love—enduring to the end of time! For this, he turned grateful eyes to Four Winds and could not find it within his heart to totally condemn him.

"It is never too late for you to turn your back on this wrong life that you have chosen," Strong Heart said, dropping his hand from Four Winds's shoulder. Four Winds lifted his away.

"That is not what I wish to do," Four Winds said, his eyes holding steady with Strong Heart's. "It is still the life that I want. Do not fight me over it. I have my life. You have yours."

There was a strained silence between them. Four Winds turned his eyes away and began pulling meat from his stick with his teeth, slowly chewing it as he stared into the flames of the fire.

Elizabeth waited breathlessly for Strong Heart's next move, then relaxed when he also began to eat. Not taking her eyes off the two Suquamish braves, she also began eating, hardly tasting the food. The tension between Four Winds and Strong Heart seemed wound so tight it might snap at any moment.

Then Strong Heart spoke abruptly, breaking the silence with his forceful voice.

"Four Winds, I urge you to reconsider this choice that you have made," he said, laying his stick and half-eaten food aside. "It is time for you to choose sides—to live still as a renegade, or the life of a Suquamish brave who shares each and every breath and deed with his people."

"You ask the impossible of Four Winds," Four Winds grumbled. "I cannot do this thing you ask. I have already deceived my friends last night. I cannot do anything else against them."

Elizabeth's mind was spinning with questions about many things. How had Four Winds known about her?

Why had he cared? Why would he help release her if he was aligned with outlaws?

He had been motivated by friendship—friendship with Strong Heart.

But this was not answer enough for her. She would ply Strong Heart with many questions once they were alone.

"You are too hasty in your response tonight," Strong Heart said. "Because of what we were to each other as children, I will wait for you to think this through, this that I ask of you. Such a friendship as yours and mine cannot so quickly be cast aside, like something trivial and worthless. *Ah-hah*, I will await your response another day."

"*Kloshe*, good," Four Winds said, nodding, relief showing in his face. "*Ah-hah*, that is good."

"Four Winds, you said that you had nothing to do with the raid on my people, and I believe you. But I must ask you again if you think those of your outlaw band are responsible?" Strong Heart said, lifting up his stick and biting pieces of fish from it.

Four Winds took a bite of his own fish, then laid it aside as he looked at Strong Heart. "If I knew the answer, I would tell you," he said. "As I have told you, I did not return to my outlaw friends immediately after my departure from you the night of the escape. I went to the hills for two nights and two days. When I returned, they were also in hiding, and nothing at all was said about any raid on your people."

Strong Heart frowned as he thrust his stick into the flames of the fire and watched it catch fire and burn. "Of course, they would not mention it in front of you," he said in a low grumble. "You are Suquamish. They would expect you to still have some loyalty to our tribe. They would not want to give you cause to go against them, especially after hearing that it was your Suquamish friend who set you free."

"Perhaps so," Four Winds said, nodding. "But as far as I know, my friends are innocent of the crime."

Strong Heart turned his gaze to Elizabeth, now recalling that Four Winds had told him that her father was a friend to Morris Murdoch, the leader of the outlaw gang. His eyes narrowed, thinking about the two white men who had come to his village with proposals.

One was Elizabeth's father. The other was Morris Murdoch.

And now that he knew that Morris Murdoch was the leader, he suspected even more strongly that Elizabeth's father and this Morris Murdoch had played a role in the raid on his village. Either Four Winds was lying, or was innocent of knowledge.

But he would not mention this to Elizabeth just yet. She had been through enough without having to worry about her father's association with outlaws.

Ah-hah, yes, for now all that was truly important to him was that his woman was with him again and his people were readying themselves for the salmon run. Everything else would come later.

And it would come. Everything had an end—even the lives of those who were responsible for the massacre in his village.

"It is time that I part from you again, my friend," Four Winds said, pushing himself up from the ground. "Let nothing cause our friendship to end. To me, it is most valuable."

Strong Heart rose to his feet and went with Four Winds to the grazing horses. When Four Winds turned to him, Strong Heart hesitated, then flung his arms around Four Winds and gave him a tight hug.

"I will await word of your choice in life," Strong Heart said huskily. Then he stepped away from Four Winds and watched him climb into his saddle and ride away.

Strong Heart returned to the campsite and sat down beside Elizabeth. For a moment he stared gloomily into the fire, so many things troubling him.

Then he turned to Elizabeth and took her face in his hands, and gently drew her nearer.

"I can depend on you to always remain true to my heart?" he asked softly, his eyes searching hers for the answer that he sought.

"*Ah-hah,*" Elizabeth said. Her using the Suquamish word pleased Strong Heart. His smile broadened, causing Elizabeth's insides to begin a slow, sensual melting.

"Forever and always," she added softly, fastening her arms around his neck, urging his lips to hers.

As he kissed her, his fingers crushed her hair and his body pressed hers to the ground.

The kiss continued and his hands busied themselves with undressing her. Then he drew apart from her long enough to remove his own clothes. He knelt over her, the golden flames of the fire reflected on his body giving it a coppery sheen.

Elizabeth caught her breath when Strong Heart stretched out above her, bracing himself with his arms, his hands laced with hers, and holding them slightly above her.

With a knee he parted her legs and soon she felt the wonders of his manhood pressing gently into her soft folds.

Elizabeth wrapped her legs around him, her hips responding to his touch as she raised her pelvis toward him.

She drew in a breath of wild happiness as he entered her in one deep thrust.

Elizabeth moved her body sinuously against his and drew him more deeply into the warmth of her body, only half aware of her whimpers.

Then a rush of pure bliss flooded her senses and his

body jerked and spasmed into hers. She again knew
the true meaning of his wild embrace.

Sheriff Nolan walked listlessly into his office, his
jaw puffed out with a fresh wad of tobacco. Then he
almost choked on it when he discovered Deputy Bradley dead on the floor, a knife protruding from his back.
Then his own body jumped when someone stepped up
from behind him and knocked him unconscious with
the butt of a pistol.

A bandanna hiding his face, Morris Murdoch
slipped his heavy pistol back inside its holster and hurried to the door and looked toward the forest. He motioned with a wave of his hand for the other outlaws
to make a rush on the prison. He grabbed the keys and
went to the back room to set Elizabeth free. Then he
stopped in surprise. She wasn't there.

He stormed down the long corridor of cells. "Where
is she?" he shouted, looking from prisoner to prisoner. "Who took her?"

"Let us out of this hellhole!" was the response from
several prisoners who spoke almost in unison. "Who
cares what happened to that woman? Set *us* free, damn
it!"

Morris looked nervously from cell to cell. He
stopped a few times to stare at women who appealed
to him with their tearful eyes, their hands reaching
through the bars toward him.

Then he went to one cell in particular, glaring at the
man who stood close to the bars. He reached inside
and grabbed him by the collar. "I've come for only
one lady and by God, if you value your life, you'll tell
me who took her away," he said angrily.

The man made a strangling noise as Morris's fingers
twisted the collar. "It . . . was . . . dark," the man
said, gasping. "No one could see who took her. But

. . . it . . . was a man. He carried her away. That's
. . . all any of us know.''

Wondering who could have gotten there before him
and his men, Morris mouthed an obscenity as he released the man.

Several of the outlaws rushed into the back room,
then stopped and gawked.

Joe Feather went to Morris. ''You'd best get her and
let's get out of here,'' he said, his voice low. ''It's
almost daylight. Someone's bound to come and catch
us here.''

''She's not here,'' Morris grumbled, his brows
meeting in a frown. ''Goddamn it all to hell, she's not
here.''

''Where is she?'' Joe asked, tipping his hat back
with his forefinger.

''Who's to say?'' Morris said, shrugging. He stroked
his chin, looking at the prisoners.

''I'd say that's good,'' Joe said, patting his holstered
pistol. ''I didn't take much to this escape, anyhow.
What were we going to do with her once we got her?
She'd just draw the law to us, that's all.''

''If we don't do something about these prisoners,
the law'll get drawn to us now, no matter how you
look at it,'' Morris said, pushing aside Joe and stomp-
ing back to the sheriff's office. He gestured. ''Come
with me. We've things to do.''

Joe Feather scampered after him. They joined those
who were inside the office, their firearms drawn.

''Let's get a fire goin','' Morris said, his eyes
gleaming as he went to the desk and grabbed up several yellowed papers and began scattering them around
the room. ''Frank? You go start setting the prisoners
free. Panama? You stand guard outside and see to it
that no one sees what we're doin'. If someone comes
even near the prison, shoot 'em. We've got to make a

clean sweep of this mess we've made today. And we don't need no witnesses.''

Frank went to Morris, his pockmarked face wary. ''The prisoners?'' he asked in a monotone. ''Don't you think they'll be witnesses if any of them gets caught?''

''As I see it the community is going to be too busy fighting the fire to worry about catchin' escaped convicts. And these people aren't going to stay in these parts any longer than they can help it. They've already got a taste of what it's like to be here at Copper Hill Prison. They won't allow it to happen again. I'm sure they'd kill themselves before coming back. Why would they tattle on those who've been kind enough to set them free?''

''I guess you're right,'' Frank said, taking the keys Morris handed to him. He left, and soon there was a stampede from the back room as men and women ran from their cells, breathlessly free.

''Clear out of here!'' Morris shouted to his men. ''I'm going to set everything on fire!''

Soon flames were flickering from the barred windows and the panes of the front windows exploded, spewing glass everywhere.

''Get back to our hideout, quick!'' Morris shouted as he ran toward the forest for his horse. ''I'll meet you there later. I've things to do here in town.''

By the time Morris was riding nonchalantly down First Avenue, the fire wagons were already clanging and rushing up the steep hill toward the prison. Black smoke billowed up into the sky, darkening the heavens as if it were midnight, instead of early morning.

Morris rode onward, ignoring the clamor of people who were riding their horses toward the prison. He knew what they would eventually find—two bodies, not a hundred. And it would be hard for them to identify whether they were the sheriff and the deputy.

No one would ever know how it had happened, or who had caused it.

Or who had taken Elizabeth away? And why? Had they known about his plans? Or had it just been co-incidence that someone had gotten there before him?

In this life, there seemed to be nobody who could be trusted. No one!

He rode on to Earl's house and found him already at the fishery, getting an early start on the day. After securing his horse's reins to the hitching rail, Morris went inside the fishery and stood over the desk, where Earl was entering some figures into a ledger.

Earl looked up at Morris, his eyes eager. "Well?" he said quickly. "Did you find a way to free Elizabeth?"

"I didn't have to, it seems," Morris said, trying to fake concern. "When I got up this morning, I saw the flames shooting up into the sky from the prison. Earl, the fire wagons could do no good. By the time they got to it, it was gone."

Earl's knees weakened and his heart leapt into his throat. He started to rise from his chair, but he was too weak to stand. "Tell me," he said, his voice rasping. "What-what about Elizabeth? Did-did someone get her out before the prison burned?"

"Someone came and told me that everyone in the prison had been set free before the fire started, even Elizabeth," Morris said, seeing the relief in Earl's eyes. "As best they can tell, the sheriff and deputy perished in the fire."

"But Elizabeth?" Earl stammered. "What of my Elizabeth? Where is she? Who is she with? It's like before. She's been abducted! But by who?"

"Better she's been abducted, than dead," Morris said, shrugging. "And one thing for sure, Earl, there is something positive about this happening. Your daughter's name is now free and clear of any guilt.

The sheriff and deputy are dead. They were the two who was responsible for her being there. And all of the records that could show her as having been there, and why, have been destroyed in the fire.''

Earl nodded. Then he felt despair over losing his daughter again. He was beginning to think that he would never, ever, see her again, and felt that it was his punishment for having neglected her all of those years when he had been fortunate enough to have and love her.

He silently vowed to himself that if he ever had the opportunity to be her father again, he would make everything up to her. He would show her what a father's true devotion was all about.

24

All night upon mine heart I felt her warm heart beat,
Night long within my arms in love and sleep she lay.
—ERNEST DOWSON

Mount Rainier was rising through morning fog as
Strong Heart's village came into sight. Elizabeth clung
to Strong Heart's waist as his horse cantered slowly
across the land, her gaze drawn to the activity of some
Suquamish women on the sandy bank of the river.

Using wooden sticks bound loosely with a twist of
cedar bark, a young woman carefully extracted a hot
rock from a bed of coals. With the sizzling rock securely clamped in the tongs, the woman ran a few
steps across the beach to some women who were working around a big, square wooden box filled with
steaming water.

Quickly the girl dipped the hot rock in a small con-
tainer of water to rinse off the ash from the fire, then
dropped it into the box.

"What are those women doing?" Elizabeth asked,
her curiosity aroused. She was glad to have something
to say to break the silence that had fallen between her
and Strong Heart the closer they had come to his village.

It puzzled her how his mood had changed from being caring and loving the previous evening, to someone
distant now, as if he was carrying the burden of the
world on his shoulders.

She had to believe it was because many duties
awaited him helping his father prepare for the salmon
run.

Elizabeth prayed that his moody silence had nothing

to do with her. Yet, she could not see any reason why
it should. Nothing had changed between them that she
was aware of.

Strong Heart was silent for a moment longer, then
heaved a sigh and answered her. It seemed to her a
halfhearted explanation, as though it was bothersome
to him to answer. Again she was puzzled. Usually he
was anxious to explain the ways of his people to her.

Why would it be different now? she wondered, feeling unnerved by his attitude.

"The women are boiling whale blubber to extract
oil from it," Strong Heart said, gazing over at the
activity. "My braves must have found a whale washed
up on the beach at the mouth of the river, where the
river and sea join. You see, Elizabeth, my tribe does
not hunt whales, but we have learned to take advantage
of stray carcasses. This whale will provide our people
with much blubber, which can be used in many ways.
Our braves are always on the lookout for such a catch
as this."

"And soon you will participate in the salmon run,"
Elizabeth said. The thought of the salmon brought her
father to her mind. Again she had given him cause to
worry, perhaps enough to even forget about his fishery.

But she doubted that anything could cause him to
lose interest in his business. Not even her disappearance. His work was his life—not her. He would probably mourn her loss for a brief moment, then move
ahead with his plans.

And if he had loved her as a devoted father should,
he would have found a way to get her out of that dreadful prison.

As it was, only Strong Heart seemed to truly care
enough, and now even he was acting strangely.

She was disturbed by how he had called her by her
name a moment ago, instead of his *la-daila*.

Confusion flooded in, in greater intensity. She searched through the past few hours, to remember if she had said or done anything that might have angered him, yet was unable to find anything that was less than beautiful: The way he had held her. The way he had kissed her. The way he had made love to her.

It was all too perfect for him to be behaving so oddly now.

Strong Heart's jaw tightened at her mention of the salmon run, for it brought him back to why he was in such a sullen mood today. He had decided to confront her about her father as soon as they got settled at his longhouse. He would question her as to why she had found the need to lie to him about her father, instead of being honest with him.

Trust was needed in a relationship, and now it was evident that it was lacking between them.

Ah-hah, he had laid his anger aside long enough to rescue her from the prison, and even through the night as he held her in his arms, for it had been such relief to know that she was safe. During those special moments with her, when he was thankful she was alive, he had forgotten why he should be angry.

But now, it was different. He had to know the truth. For every time he held her in his arms, he did not want to think that he was holding someone who could be less than truthful with him.

He expected that the woman who was soon to be his wife should have no reason to feel that she had to lie to him.

He did not want to tell her that they could not be married—that she wasn't worthy of a man who would one day be a powerful chief.

Ah-hah, he would soon have this much needed talk with his woman.

Anger flared in Elizabeth when Strong Heart ignored her mention of the salmon run.

Well, she quickly decided, she had taken all that she could of his silent moodiness!

"Let me off the horse," she said, her eyes flashing into Strong Heart's as he turned his head quickly to look at her. "It is apparent that my mere presence is a bother to you, so stop your horse so that I can walk the rest of the way."

She glared at him defiantly. "Better yet, perhaps I should just turn around and start walking back toward Seattle," she stormed. "I don't want to be anywhere I'm not wanted, or be with someone who treats me as though I am nonexistent."

Strong Heart stared at her, stunned by her sudden rush of temper. Then, remembering his own reason for being angry with her, he turned his eyes ahead. He kept his horse going in a steady lope, refusing to allow Elizabeth to do as she wanted. At this moment, he was determined to have his way. She would not get away from his questions that easily!

He smiled to himself, though, thinking that perhaps she was even more beautiful angry—with her green eyes flashing, and her cheeks rosy with rage. It would be so easy to forget his suspicions and return to the way it had been between them before he had discovered that she had not been totally truthful with him. Instead of questioning her and finding out something that might cause a total estrangement between them, ignorance might be best.

But he was a man of truth. So his wife must be a woman of truth.

"Stop!" Elizabeth shouted, pummeling his back with her fists. "Let me down. If you don't, I'll jump."

Strong Heart wheeled his horse to a quick stop, then turned to Elizabeth and jerked her around, so that she was on his lap. He held her in place with his strong arm, and proceeded on toward his village.

"*Nah*, look here," he grumbled. "We are almost

at my village, and then we will go to my longhouse and talk. But until then, sit quietly and do not make a spectacle of yourself.''

''Why are you doing this to me?'' Elizabeth asked, angry tears spilling from her eyes. ''Last night, everything was so perfect between us. Today? You act as if you don't love me. Why did you set me free from the prison if . . . if . . . you don't even care for me anymore?''

''I will care for you until the end of time,'' Strong Heart said, his voice solemn as his eyes looked into hers. ''But there is something left unspoken between us. Today, before the sun dies in the sky, I will have the answers that I am seeking.''

''Answers?'' Elizabeth said, sniffling and wiping tears from her eyes with the back of her hand. ''Answers about what? You seemed content enough last night. Why now, Strong Heart? Why?''

''Last night was last night,'' Strong Heart grumbled. ''This is now. *Now* is when I want the answers. Perhaps I should have questioned you last night, but I didn't. So be it, Elizabeth. Just be patient with me. I have been, with you.''

Elizabeth shook her head slowly, her mind seething with frustration. ''Sometimes you talk and act in riddles,'' she murmured, turning her eyes from him. Her shoulders slumped dispiritedly. She knew she would feel better if she allowed herself to have a good cry.

But she did not have time to think further on it, for Strong Heart's horse had reached the outer fringes of the village and children were running toward them already, shouting Strong Heart's name, their dogs yapping at their heels.

Strong Heart smiled at them and kept riding on past the newly erected totem poles and into the village. Women sat outside their lodges, spinning the underside of the cedar bark which looked like flax, with

distaffs and spindles. Others wove it with strips of sea
otter skin on looms which were placed against the sides
of their houses.

When Strong Heart started riding past his parents'
large lodge, Elizabeth saw his mother step outside. A
smile of relief was on her tiny face as she gazed adoringly up at her son, a fist clutched over her heart as
she bid a silent welcome to Strong Heart. He returned
the welcome, in kind, and rode on, drawing rein before his longhouse.

Strong Heart eased Elizabeth from his lap until her
feet were placed firmly on the ground, then slid from
the saddle himself. Elizabeth stood with her arms
folded stubbornly across her chest as he secured his
reins to a post. She jerked away from him when he
reached for her elbow to escort her into the house.

"Don't worry," she said, her voice low, yet angry.
"I shall go into the longhouse without assistance."
She turned and stood on tiptoe, lifting her face to his.
"And I shall not make a scene. I'm just as anxious to
get this over with as you."

Then, her lips quivering, she reproached him. "I
hope to understand soon why you are behaving so . . .
so . . . cold to me. It wasn't my fault that I was taken
to the prison and jailed there."

She raised her eyes to his. "I didn't ask you to come
and get me either," she said, her voice breaking. "You
could have left me there just like my father. Why *did*
you come for me, if all that you had planned was to
chastise me for . . . for . . . only God knows what?
In truth, I am now no better than when I was in
prison."

Strong Heart's eyes wavered and a slow pain circled
his heart to see his woman tortured by what he was
forced to do.

He gestured with his hand. "Go inside," he said
softly. He followed her, then he pointed toward a soft

buckskin cushion filled with cottonwood floss. "*Mit-lite*, sit down beside the firepit."

Disconsolately, Elizabeth sat down on the cushion and crossed her legs beneath her skirt. She was suddenly mortified by the appearance of her dress. During their journey, she had not thought to be concerned about how disheveled she was after being imprisoned for so many days. Each evening she had been given a basin of water, with which she kept herself clean, but her clothes not only smelled of the jail cell, but now also of horse sweat.

As Strong Heart sat down beside her, and began building the fire in the firepit, Elizabeth watched him, her heart pounding. She was glad when the flames were curling around the logs, so that Strong Heart could say what he wanted to say to her.

When he turned her way and began talking, she turned pale and gasped. His question was proof of why he had been treating her as if she were no more important to him than a stranger.

"Elizabeth, it is *me-sah-chie*, bad, to tell lies, especially to tell a lie to the man you have professed to love," Strong Heart began solemnly, his gaze steady on her. "Why did you lie to me about why your father is in the Pacific Northwest?"

"How do you know about that?" she murmured, nervously brushing a strand of hair back from her eyes.

"Your father, along with another white man who is known by the name Morris Murdoch, came to my village just prior to the raid on my people," he answered. "I was not here. I had left to free Four Winds from prison. But my father and the other braves have told me why your father and Morris Murdoch were here—to trick my people with their white man promises to catch the salmon for them instead of for our people. And they urged our people to work in the fishery that they have built on the beach close to the hallowed land of the Suquamish. Why did you not tell me that your father was building a fishery, and for what purpose? Why did you not tell me that your father planned to come to my village and speak in council about the salmon? Why, my *la-daila*? Why?''

Elizabeth's mouth gaped, stunned by what Strong Heart had said. Her father had been trying to push his ideas on Strong Heart's people? She had not known exactly which Indians he had visited, and did not know why she had not considered this possibility before now.

But that Strong Heart saw her as a liar hurt more than anything had hurt her in her life, for she was not a liar. She had only told him a half-truth, hoping that she would never have to tell him the whole truth about her father. She had hoped that her father would make his contract with another village, leaving Strong Heart and his people in peace.

Elizabeth went to Strong Heart, bending on her knees before him. She held his face between her hands, feeling him grow tense at her mere touch. ''Darling, I told you a nontruth only . . . only to protect you,'' she pleaded. ''I didn't want my father and the man I loved to clash over differing ideals. Both of you have wills of steel. I . . . I . . . felt that if you fought with my father, *you* would be the eventual loser, and the hanging platform still haunts me. And, Strong Heart, I didn't know that my father was coming to *your* village. Please believe me. I didn't know.''

Strong Heart searched her eyes, and when he saw the apology and the hurt in their depths, he placed his hands at her wrists and drew her to him, holding her against him. He gazed down at her. ''I believe you did this from your heart,'' he said. ''I believe you did this for the man you love. I *do* understand your motive, but never lie to me again. I value honesty in everyone, especially the woman I love.''

He was very close to telling her the other thing about

her father, but something stopped him—perhaps feeling that enough conflict and doubt had been between them for today. Or perhaps he did not want to discover that her father was guilty of killing his people. This man that he doubted, would soon be his father-in-law, a man he wished to have peace with. For this man would one day be his children's grandfather, and it would not be good to have a grandfather who was despised by their father.

"Please never treat me so terribly again," Elizabeth mumbled, near tears. She flung her arms around his neck and drew his lips close to hers. "I love you so, Strong Heart. I would never do anything to hurt you. Surely you know that. I only want what is best for you—*and* your people."

"*Ah-hah*, yes, I believe that is so," he whispered, brushing his mouth across her lips, his hands eagerly undressing her. "But for now, my *la-daila*, do only what is best for me."

"You call me *la-daila* again instead of Elizabeth," she sighed, so glad to have the wrinkled dress off, and to feel the wonder of the warmth of the fire against her flesh. She giggled. "That proves that you are no longer unhappy with me."

Strong Heart pulled away from her and began to undress. "That is so," he said, laughing softly.

When he was naked, he reached for a basin of water fresh from the river. He took the basin over to Elizabeth and handed it to her. "Cleanse me. Then I will cleanse you," he said throatily.

Elizabeth picked up a buckskin washcloth, and then a piece of soap that Many Stars had placed there. It was quite a sacrifice on her part, for the chances of getting perfumed soap here in the wilderness were slim.

Meditatively, Elizabeth began to bathe Strong Heart, drawing a moan of pleasure from deep within him when she reached that part of his anatomy that was swollen and throbbing in her hand. She dutifully caressed it with fingers that were slippery with soap suds.

She continued caressing Strong Heart, watching his eyes become glassy with passion. He clutched his hands in her hair and he urged her lips where her fingers had just been. She scarcely breathed and her eyes widened, not sure of what he was asking of her.

But further urgings made her understand. Her pulse raced and her knees grew weak as she tasted him for the first time. The pleasure that she was giving was intense, for his body had stiffened and his eyes were closed, while soft moans rose from deep within him.

She pleasured him in this unusual way for a while longer. Then he placed his fingers to her shoulders and urged her down on her back on the soft cushioned floor. She became the recipient of the same sort of caresses as he took the soaped cloth and began stroking her all over as he washed her.

He knelt down over her, parting her legs, and he touched that most sensitive part of her with soapy fingers, where her heart now seemed to be centered. She closed her eyes, wishing that the pleasure would never end.

Then it seemed to intensify as she felt something even more wonderful caressing her swollen bud. Her whole body throbbed with pleasure. When she opened her eyes and gazed down at him, she was surprised to see that his mouth was the source of her pleasure, his tongue feverishly moving over her.

When she could not take much more without going over the edge into total bliss, Elizabeth took his face with her hands and urged him to move up. Soon his manhood was in rhythmic strokes within her, his lips on her breasts, moving from one to the other, setting her aflame with desire.

Moments later they reached that peak of passion they

had been seeking, taking from one another all that they could give. Then they lay together, their breaths mingling as they looked with rapture into each other's eyes.

"I could never have sent you back to your world, no matter if you had not had a good reason for lying to me," Strong Heart confessed. "My love is too strong for you to lose you."

"I would have never gone, had you even ordered me to," Elizabeth whispered back, leaning to flick her tongue into his mouth.

Earl lifted his saddle onto his horse, then gave Morris a frown. "I've lost the battle with my daughter," he said sadly. "But I won't allow it to happen between me and the Suquamish. By damn, I will have their support. I must. So, Morris, I'll be a few days tryin' again. You stay put and see to everything here at the fishery. Perhaps one man alone can do what two men together couldn't at the Indian village."

Morris smiled crookedly and gave Earl a mock salute as he launched himself into the saddle. "Good luck," he said, smiling smugly to himself. He had done his part by ordering the raid on the Suquamish. Now it was Earl's and Morris's time to reap the harvest of that raid.

25

When the praise thou meetest
To thine ear is sweetest,
O then remember me!
—Thomas Moore

Dressed in a soft buckskin dress, and having joined
Strong Heart's parents for breakfast the next day, Elizabeth sat beside Strong Heart in Chief Moon Elk's
longhouse sipping deer-bone soup from a wooden
bowl. She watched Strong Heart and Chief Moon Elk,
who were also eating breakfast. Pretty Nose was close
to the fire, already preparing frybread for lunch.

"You say that Four Winds is a renegade?" Chief
Moon Elk said, pushing his empty bowl aside. "My
son, did I not tell you that his blood is bad? Much
more pointed to his guilt than to his innocence."

"*Ah-hah,* yes, sad though it makes me to say it, I
now realize that, in part, you were right about Four
Winds," Strong Heart said, his face solemn.

"Four Winds is small in his shame," Chief Moon
Elk said, his eyes angry. He sat back against a willow
backrest. "He is a man who is hard to know, for his
blood is quick to turn bad. Why does he carry such a
bad heart for us, my son?"

Strong Heart placed his spoon into his empty bowl.
He gazed intently at his father. "Father, one thing that
I still see as a truth is that Four Winds had nothing to
do with the raid on our people," he said. "His heart
is *good* toward our people. It can never be any other
way."

Strong Heart gave Elizabeth an uneasy glance, still
having not told her all that he knew about her father

and his possible role in the raid. Each time, just as he would start to tell her, she would either hug him, or give him a sweet look that always held such tenderness for him.

He had not wanted to tell her anything that might cause her pain, or that might cause a strain between them.

She was home now, where she belonged—with *him*, and *his* people. She would soon forget her uncaring father.

And so would Strong Heart, for there was no actual proof that her father had had anything to do with the raid.

Pity the man, though, should Strong Heart ever learn the opposite. Strong Heart would stop at nothing less than squeezing the life from him with his bare hands. . . .

Before Chief Moon Elk responded to Strong Heart, a commotion outside the longhouse drew his eyes to the door. He then looked over at Strong Heart. "My leg still pains me too much to go and see what is causing the stir among our people," he said. "My son, go and see who it is."

Elizabeth rose to her feet and went to the door with Strong Heart. As he opened the door, she stopped. "My father," she said, as she watched Earl approach on his horse, with many Suquamish braves walking on either side of him. Their rifles were aimed at Earl.

Her anxiety was not caused as much by the sight of the weapons aimed at her father, but by the danger of him finding her there. Her presence would prove Strong Heart's guilt in helping her escape from the prison.

She would not allow any harm to come to him, even if she had to sacrifice telling her father that she was alive and well.

"Strong Heart, I must hide," she said, stepping back from the door. "That's my father. He must not be allowed to see me." She looked frantically around her. "Strong Heart, where can I hide? Where?"

Strong Heart was stunned to realize that the man approaching was her father. That he had the nerve to come to the village so soon after the raid was astounding.

Yet was that perhaps a part of his plan from the beginning? To come back to a weakened people who might then be willing to do anything to help put their lives back together again?

And then there was Elizabeth. *Ah-hah*, he knew, also, that it was best that her father did not see her there.

But now she might find out the ugly truth about her father, for Strong Heart was not going to spare questions once the man was sitting in council with him and Chief Moon Elk.

Strong Heart grabbed Elizabeth by the arm and quickly ushered her away from the door. Chief Moon Elk and Pretty Nose were watching with keen puzzlement in their eyes. He took Elizabeth behind a skin curtain that hung to the floor. Behind it were hidden the treasures of his father and mother in pits under wooden platforms.

"You stay here until he is gone," Strong Heart said, his eyes on hers. "My *la-daila*, soon you will hear things spoken to your father that may confuse or even hurt you. But these things must be said to him. Strong Heart needs answers about many things. I believe it is your father who can give these answers to me."

"Answers about what?" Elizabeth said, her pulse racing. "I . . . I . . . explained about the fishery. What else is there, Strong Heart? Tell me. I have the right to know."

"*Ah-hah,* and so you do," Strong Heart said, smoothing a lock of hair back from her brow. "And I should have told you sooner, rather than have you hear it now, in this way."

"Then tell me," Elizabeth said, tensing when she saw the stubborn set to his jaw. "Please, tell me."

"There is not time," Strong Heart said. Then he turned and left her with her eyes wide in confusion.

Strong Heart stepped outside just as Earl was dismounting. Strong Heart folded his arms across his chest, torn by feelings about this man that soon would be his father-in-law. He hoped with all of his heart that he was wrong about this man.

But so much pointed to Elizabeth's father's guilt, Strong Heart could not help but find himself already hating him.

Earl turned slowly around and faced Strong Heart, wondering who he was, and why he was standing at the door of the chief's house, as if guarding it. He swallowed hard, then extended a hand to Strong Heart.

"I'm Earl Easton," Earl said, his voice unsteady, as he felt the heat from the gray eyes that were boring into him. "I don't believe I had the pleasure of meeting you when I was here before?"

Strong Heart ignored the handshake and did not answer him for a moment. He was still studying this white man, trying to see if he carried innocence or guilt in the depths of his eyes. His eyes were the same color as Elizabeth's, which made him most definitely Elizabeth's father—and a man that Strong Heart did not want to hate.

When he saw that this brave was not going to take his hand, Earl slowly lowered it to his side. He cleared his throat nervously, glancing questioningly at the totem poles that were partially burned and then at the ones that seemed to have been newly erected and painted.

He then looked slowly around him, puzzled by the newness of many of the longhouses. What had happened here since the time he had come to talk business with the chief? It appeared as if some great fire had ravaged the village. Yet beyond, where the forest stood mighty and green, there was no sign of fire.

It made him uneasy, yet he again turned and faced Strong Heart. Nothing would dissuade Earl from his purpose for being here.

"I have returned to speak business with Chief Moon Elk again," Earl said, clasping his hands nervously behind him. "Would you please take me to him?"

Strong Heart stood there silently for a moment longer, then nodded toward the door. "Come with me," he said, turning and walking back inside the longhouse.

Earl followed him inside and stopped at Strong Heart's side. Earl's eyes widened as he stared down at Chief Moon Elk, whose one leg was stretched out before him, evidently wounded. Earl wondered how he had been wounded, and by whom.

Strong Heart gestured toward his father and his mother.

"My father, Chief Moon Elk, and my mother, Pretty Nose," Strong Heart said. "My father will speak to you again. I will listen, then speak to you myself as soon as my father is finished with you."

Earl paled and grew unsteady on his legs as he looked in surprise at Strong Heart. "You are Chief Moon Elk's son?" he said softly. "I did not know. You did not sit in council with your father and me before."

"That is so," Strong Heart said, glancing toward the curtain, knowing that this white man would be quite surprised to know that at the time of his last visit, Strong Heart had been with his daughter. This man would be even more surprised if he knew that his daughter was there even now, hiding from him in the Suquamish chief's longhouse.

It gave Strong Heart a smug feeling to keep these secrets from the scheming white man.

Elizabeth chewed nervously on her lower lip when she heard how wary her father's voice sounded. She was guilt-stricken over deceiving him. But the fact that he was there, instead of elsewhere with a posse searching for her, gave her cause to again doubt his love for her.

Tears flooded her eyes. She now understood why her mother had disappeared all those years ago more than ever before.

Wiping the tears from her eyes, she leaned nearer to the curtain and listened closely as Chief Moon Elk began to talk in a monotone to her father.

"*Mit-lite*, sit down," Chief Moon Elk said, gesturing toward a cushion on the floor opposite the fire from him. "You did not hear me well the other time you were speaking of fisheries and salmon to me. Did I not tell you that my people caught only for our village? Why do you waste your time coming again?" He looked past Earl, at the door. "And where is the man who goes by the name Morris Murdoch? He did not accompany you this time to hear a more determined no from my lips?"

"No, he did not come this time," Earl said, resting his hands on his knees as he crossed his legs. "He came the last time mainly to direct me to your village. I knew the way this time. He stayed behind and is tending to our business. I am the spokesman for the two of us now. I hope that you will give me another chance to explain the benefits to your people of working under my employ. Perhaps you have had time to

think about it? To see the worth of my plan, as I see
it?''

Earl glanced down at Chief Moon Elk's festering
wound again. ''You have had a mishap since I was last
here?'' he said, raising an eyebrow. He looked slowly
up at the chief again. ''How unfortunate. I'm sorry.''

Strong Heart went and knelt beside his father, gently
touching his father's leg, and glaring at Earl. ''*Ah-
hah*, my father is ailing,'' he said, glad that his father
was giving him the opportunity to speak as he sat in
stone-faced silence. ''Can you truthfully say that you
do not know the cause? Did you not see the burned
totem poles as you entered our village? Did you not
see the many new longhouses in my village? Of course
you could not see the ashes of many of our people that
have been spread across our land, and across the waters of the river. This has all happened since your last
council with my father. Can you tell me that you do
not know why this has all happened in our village?
Can you?''

Elizabeth blanched and she placed her hands to her
cheeks, her eyes widening in stunned surprise at what
Strong Heart was saying without actually accusing her
father. She shook her head, her thoughts flying, putting ghastly things together that she did not want to
believe or accept. She would not believe that her father
was driven by so much greed that he would have had
a part in the attack on this village!

Yet, she knew that was what Strong Heart was leading up to. And surely her father had guessed as much,
as well.

Her heart pounding, Elizabeth leaned her ear even
closer to the curtain, growing cold as she continued to
listen.

''What are you suggesting?'' Earl gasped, looking
quickly from father to son. ''What do you think I am
guilty of? Or should I even ask?''

"Your council with my father came suspiciously close to the raid on my people," Strong Heart hissed. "Can you deny that after my father turned your proposal down, you returned to our village and wreaked havoc on our people. To frighten us into doing as you ask, or to weaken us so that we would see no other way of survival except to take money earned from you? Do you think that we do not see right through such a scheme as this?"

Elizabeth quickly clasped her hand over her mouth and gasped. She swayed with a sudden light-headedness, to know that she had guessed right at what Strong Heart was thinking.

No! She would not allow herself to believe her father was guilty of such a heinous crime. He had never stooped to such tactics to get his way.

And why should he now? He was a rich man who did not need to go to such extremes as this to make more money for himself.

No. She could not, *would* not believe this of her father, no matter how greedy or ambitious he was.

Earl rose shakily to his feet, his knees weak with fright. "I am innocent of this that you are accusing me of," he said with a slight gasp. "I am not the sort to kill for my own gain. Please believe me. I did not even know of the tragedy, or I would have never come here. Especially alone. Doesn't that prove that I am innocent? I am not a foolish man. If I had any inkling of your having just suffered a raid, I wouldn't have set foot in your village, for fear that I would be accused of it. I value my life more than that. I am not the sort to take chances with it."

Earl's mind was calculating things, and his thoughts led him to what Morris Murdoch had said about having taken care of things. Could Morris have somehow attacked the village?

The thought sickened him, and now he wished that

he had investigated his partner's credentials more than he had. In truth, he did not know much about him, except that he had had the money to back up his desire to be Earl's partner in the fishery venture.

Strong Heart rose to his full height and began walking slowly around the fire toward Earl. "You must show me proof that you had no part in the raid," he said, his voice cold. "Your partner, Morris Murdoch? Did you not know that he is the leader of an outlaw gang? Do you deny aligning yourself with such desperadoes? Do you deny that you did not ride with them that day, side-by-side with your partner, purposely murdering my people?"

Earl took a shaky step backward, his heart thumping, his eyes wide. "Morris . . . is . . . the leader of a gang of outlaws?" he said, his voice thin. "God. God in heaven. No! I did not know. Tell me it isn't true. Tell me it is a ploy you are using to trick me."

An involuntary shiver coursed through Elizabeth, after learning the news about Morris Murdoch. But she wasn't truly surprised, when she recalled his eyes—how cold and empty they appeared.

And she could not help but feel sorry for her father, his voice revealing to her that he had not known this about Morris, and that he was most definitely innocent of everything.

Seeing that her father was concerned, she did not want the confrontation to continue. She feared what would happen to Strong Heart if her father ended up dead and the authorities were brought into the matter. Elizabeth saw no other recourse than to stop what had begun.

Elizabeth stepped hurriedly from behind the curtain and rushed toward her father.

Earl was shocked by her appearing from nowhere.

"Elizabeth?" he gasped. He placed his hands on her shoulders and held her at arm's length as he looked her up and down. "Good Lord, Elizabeth. What are you doing here? And why are you dressed in such . . . such garb as that?"

Then in a flash he remembered the Indian saddle that he had found hidden in the stable and the horse that had not been theirs. He recalled Everett telling him about Elizabeth wearing an Indian dress, and began putting two and two together.

"I'm safe, Father," Elizabeth said, her voice trembling. "That should be all that matters. Not how I happen to be here, or why I am dressed in such a way." She swallowed hard. "But that you are here, and that you are being accused of what I know you are innocent of is why I revealed myself to you. Otherwise, Father, I would have stayed hidden behind that curtain. It was my intention never to return home again."

Earl turned pale. "Never?" he gasped. "Elizabeth, why? Never is a long, long time. Have I been this unbearable to you? Did my neglect turn you totally against me?"

"It was not your neglect that made me fall in love with Strong Heart," Elizabeth said. "That alone is the reason I have decided to stay with Strong Heart—to be his wife."

Earl gasped and slowly shook his head. "No," he said thickly. "You can't be serious."

"Very," Elizabeth said, then turned her eyes to Strong Heart. "Darling, I grant you that my father is capable of many things, but he could never kill anyone. My father wouldn't come to your village, killing and maiming. Please believe me. Please don't harm my father." She swallowed hard again. "I know that he didn't know about Morris Murdoch. I could tell how shocked he was when you revealed this to him. He had no idea he had aligned himself with such a man as that. Please let my father leave the village unharmed. For me, Strong Heart? For me?''

Strong Heart and Chief Moon Elk exchanged troubled glances, then Chief Moon Elk broke the silence. "White man, you can go, but leave my people in peace," he said with a grumble. "Do not bring your words to us again. This is our life. We want to live it without your interference."

"I understand," Earl said, then reached for Elizabeth's hand. "Come home with me, baby. It's safe to now. The sheriff and deputy are both dead, and all of the records were burned in the fire that ravaged the prison. Come home with me, Elizabeth. Let me make all of this up to you. Take some more time to . . . to consider these plans to marry someone of such different customs. Please? For me? Give me another chance?''

"The prison caught fire?" Elizabeth asked, her eyes wide. "What of all those people who were imprisoned there?''

"It seems whoever set the fire also set everyone free," he said, then paled again as he realized that whoever had set Elizabeth free, had most probably set the fire. Yet she seemed genuinely surprised to know that the prison had burned.

"Thank goodness for that," Elizabeth said, sighing. "Those poor women."

"Come home with me, baby," Earl persisted.

Elizabeth was suddenly torn, fearing that rejecting her father might make him become bitter toward Strong Heart, making him do something foolish—like turn Strong Heart in to the authorities.

For this alone she knew what her decision must be.

She went to Strong Heart and took both of his hands in hers. "Darling, trust me when I say that I must return with my father for a while," she said softly.

She stood on tiptoe and leaned up near his ear, whispering, "After I am assured that I have made all the wrongs right between me and my father, I will return to you. We shall be married then. Trust me, darling. This is best for all concerned."

Strong Heart glowered down at her, silence like a wall between them as Elizabeth awaited his answer.

"I feel that what you are doing is wrong," he finally said. "But I will not stop you from going. Soon I will come for you, after the salmon harvest."

Tears welled up in Elizabeth's eyes. She flung herself into his arms and hugged him tightly, dreading leaving him, yet knowing that she must.

Always and forever she would do anything and everything to protect him.

26

Go from me, yet I feel that I shall stand
Henceforward in thy shadow.
— ELIZABETH BARRETT BROWNING

It had been a long journey, where feelings had been revealed between Elizabeth and her father that had never been aired before. She now knew that he sincerely loved her, and he knew the depth of her love for Strong Heart.

Sitting beside a campfire the night of their journey home, she had explained everything to her father— about the first time she and Strong Heart had met, and about the times he had saved her life.

Her father now knew that her time with him would be short, for she was going to return to Strong Heart soon. And her father had promised not to interfere.

Riding side by side toward the huge gate that led into their estate grounds, Elizabeth glanced toward the Sound, and then at the fishery. "Father, what are you going to do about Morris Murdoch now that you know of his involvement with outlaws?" she asked, shifting her gaze to her father. "Surely you will separate yourself from him. You don't actually need him. You have always done quite well for yourself without the aid of a partner. It should be no different now."

Earl gave Elizabeth an unsteady glance. Although she had been truthful with him about everything between herself and the Indian, he still did not feel that this was the time to reveal his financial status to her. He had hoped to turn everything around to his favor, before telling her about his bankruptcy in San Francisco.

And now, even though he had not yet found any Indians who would work for him, he still saw his fishery as something that could succeed. He had many men under his employ. Certainly they could catch enough salmon to turn over a substantial profit for him.

He decided he would wait and reveal his money problems to Elizabeth *after* he had solved them.

As for Morris Murdoch—the son of a bitch, he thought bitterly—he was still needed, no matter how he had accumulated his riches. Earl was depending on Morris's money for his survival until his fishery showed a profit.

"I don't want to rush into anything with Morris," he finally said, guiding his horse through the wide gate, Elizabeth's horse keeping stride with his. "If he's a criminal, I don't want to do anything that might get him riled up against us. Who knows what he's capable of? I think I'll feel him out—see if I can ease him out of the business, slowlike, so's not to have someone like him out for revenge later."

"Perhaps you're right," Elizabeth said softly, then her eyebrows lifted when she saw a fancy horse and carriage parked in front of the house. A footman waited beside the carriage.

"Whose carriage is that?" Earl said, studying it. "I don't recognize it. And who would come calling, anyhow?"

He paused, then looked over at Elizabeth. "Besides Maysie and Strong Heart, have you made an acquaintance you haven't told me about?" he asked.

"Father, I believe I've told you everything on the way back from Strong Heart's village," Elizabeth said, laughing softly. "There's nothing else to say, or anyone else to explain. I have no idea whose carriage that might be."

Her eyes lit up with a thought. "Except for May-sie," she said. "Could it be Maysie?"

Then she frowned, recalling the last time she had seen Maysie—how she was dressed and whom she had been with.

"No. I'm sure it's not her," she quickly added. "I doubt we shall ever see her again."

"I'm sorry about Maysie," Earl said, giving Elizabeth a heartfelt, apologetic look. "Sorry as hell."

He then slapped his reins and urged his horse into a gallop toward the house, Elizabeth following his lead.

When they reached the house, both dismounted and secured their reins to the hitching post, then took the stairs together up to the porch.

Before they had a chance to open the door, it burst open and Elizabeth found herself suddenly engulfed in a woman's embrace. Her father gaped openly at the affectionate scene.

Elizabeth stood, shocked to her core, stiff and silent. It was her mother! Her mother smelled sweetly of French perfume, and wore a soft mink wrap around her shoulders.

"Marilyn?" Earl finally stammered out, his surprise and shock immense. "My God, Marilyn!"

"Mama?" Elizabeth said, all of her resentment of her mother's abandonment overwhelming her.

Marilyn stroked her daughter's back through the buckskin fabric of her dress. "I'm here now, darling," she whispered. "Oh, Lord, Elizabeth, I'm so sorry for what I did. So very sorry."

Elizabeth's mind cleared and she recalled her mother's reasons for having disappeared in the first place. A warmth of love and understanding flooded Elizabeth.

With tears streaming from her eyes, she returned her

mother's hug. "Mama," she cried. "Oh, Mama. I've missed you so much!"

Earl cleared his throat and stepped up to Marilyn and tapped her lightly on the shoulder. "If I may interrupt this tender scene, I would like to know where you have been, and why you have chosen to return now," he said hoarsely.

Her brilliant red hair swirled into a chignon atop her head, her vivaciously clear, green eyes sparkling, Marilyn swung away from Elizabeth and smiled up at Earl. "Hello, Earl," she said, extending a gloved hand. "It's been a long time."

Earl gazed down at the extended hand for a moment, then lifted his hand and clasped his fingers around hers. "A damn sight longer than is decent," he said in a growl. Then he did something that made Elizabeth gasp. He gathered Marilyn into his arms and held her in a tight embrace. "Damn it, Marilyn, why'd you have to disappear on us? Did I make life that unbearable for you? If so, I'm sorry. Damn sorry."

Elizabeth placed a hand over her mouth, to try and stifle her sobs as tears washed across her face. For so long she had wanted her parents to reunite, but had never counted on it. Especially after they had moved from San Francisco. That Marilyn was now here stunned her. But the fact that both her mother and father seemed genuinely happy to see each other again seemed to make all the wrongs right.

Marilyn eased from Earl's embrace. She was still a beautiful woman. Her magnificent breasts strained against the silk fabric of her pale green dress, and the gathered full skirt emphasized her tiny waist. "There's so much to say," Marilyn said with a soft purr. "Let's go inside. Frannie has prepared tea."

Marilyn turned back to Elizabeth and placed her hands to her cheeks. "Darling, when I heard that you and your father had moved just outside of Seattle, and that you had been abducted, I just had to come and see your father about it,'' she said. ''A team of wild horses couldn't keep me away.''

Again she hugged Elizabeth. ''But you're all right,'' she whispered. ''My baby is all right.''

She stepped back and looked Elizabeth slowly up and down, puzzlement in her eyes. ''A buckskin dress?'' she asked. ''Isn't that what Indians wear?'' Her eyes focused on Elizabeth. ''Have you been with Indians, Elizabeth?''

''Yes, ma'am, I have,'' Elizabeth said, lifting her chin proudly. ''And, Mama, I'm soon to marry one.''

''What?'' Marilyn gasped, placing a hand to her throat. ''An Indian? You are *marrying* an Indian?''

''Don't make it sound like I'm about to commit a crime, Mama,'' Elizabeth said, her eyes flashing. ''If you want to talk about crimes, what you did—''

A sudden presence at the door stopped Elizabeth's outburst. She caught sight of Maysie, then rushed to her and hugged her. ''Maysie,'' she said, clinging tightly to her. ''It's so good to see you.''

''Your mother asked me to direct her to your house,'' Maysie said softly, smiling as Elizabeth stepped back and clasped one of Maysie's hands.

''Mama?'' Elizabeth asked, giving her mother a quick glance, then looking again at Maysie and seeing the modesty of her attire. It was not anything like the skimpy dress that Maysie had been wearing the last time Elizabeth had seen her. Today she wore a pretty cotton dress trimmed with eyelet lace. ''How do you know my mother?''

''I work for her,'' Maysie said matter-of-factly, smiling at Marilyn. ''She's given me a home, food, clothes, and a reason to continue living.''

Earl went to Marilyn and tilted her chin up with a forefinger. ''What does she mean?'' he said ominously. "Where do you live? And what sort of establishment do you run?"

Marilyn's smile faded along with her courage. "Please let us go inside," she murmured. "I . . . I . . . shall explain everything then."

Earl nodded, and placed a hand at Marilyn's elbow, ushering her past Maysie and Elizabeth, and on inside. Elizabeth and Maysie followed. They were soon sitting comfortably before a roaring fire in the fireplace, and sipping tea. Frannie stood by the door, marveling over Elizabeth being home again.

"Start from the beginning, Marilyn," Earl said, lighting a cigar, flicking the match into the curling flames of the hearth. "For years now my imagination has conjured up many things that may have happened to you. But never did I envision you living in Seattle. It's just recently become somewhat more civilized. Before, it was just men and whores in this town."

The cigar almost popped from between his lips as he spoke the word "whores." He blanched at the thought of what Marilyn might tell him.

He looked at her, marking that she had not aged hardly a year since he had last seen her. He remembered her in bed—how she had seemed to have experience way beyond what he had taught her—his virginal wife—on their wedding night. She had seemed to know skills of lovemaking that would make a church mouse blush.

He had to wonder if she had since improved her skills.

Now, after seeing her again, he knew that he still loved and adored her with all of his being, and he would have her back in a minute, should she offer herself to him.

Elizabeth sat with her back straight on the sofa, Maysie beside her, both listening intently as Marilyn started to speak. Elizabeth's heart cried out to her mother the more her mother tried desperately to explain.

"Earl, you know how it hurt me every time you left to travel to the Orient, and other strange places, leaving me behind to sleep alone at night," she began, giving Elizabeth an uneasy glance.

She cleared her throat nervously, then looked at Earl again. "Earl, you seemed to have forgotten that you had a wife," she said, near tears. "I couldn't bear those lonely nights any longer. I . . . saw . . . no choice but to leave. I came to Seattle to seek a new way of life and earned top dollar in a brothel. I saved my money to buy my own place. Earl, I am now madam of the classiest brothel in Seattle. Maysie works for me there."

There was a sudden silence in the room. Then Earl rose from the chair and went to the fireplace and placed his arm on the mantel, leaning his brow against it.

Wide-eyed, and choked up, Elizabeth watched as her mother went to her father and gently placed a hand on his shoulder. "Earl, it's not that bad," she said softly. "Please. It's not that bad. I am respected. Truly I am."

Earl turned slowly to face her, then ran a finger down the perfect outline of her face. "I'm sure you are," he said, his voice shaking. "And I am sure many have asked you to give up that sort of life, to become their wife. Did you tell them that you already had a husband? Or did I not exist for you anymore?"

"I have never forgotten you," Marilyn said, tears falling from her eyes. "It's just that I wanted what you did not give me. But I have never considered marrying anyone else. In my heart, I had . . . I had hoped that somehow you and I could eventually work things out. It's just that when I got involved in my business, making a success of it, the years seemed to slip by so quickly. And here we are now, much older, and hopefully wiser. I still love you, Earl. Truly I do.''

She turned her weeping eyes to Elizabeth. ''And look at our daughter,'' she said, a sob lodging in her throat. ''She's all grown up and so, so beautiful.'' She turned to Earl again. ''Thank you, darling, for taking such good care of her.''

Earl and Elizabeth exchanged quick glances, both recalling their conversations around the campfire. Then Earl turned his eyes back to Marilyn. ''I did the best that I could under the circumstances,'' he said, drawing Marilyn into his arms. ''It's so good to hold you again, Marilyn. There's been no other woman for me since you left.''

Elizabeth could not hold back a sob of joy when her mother and father suddenly kissed. Her whole world had suddenly turned right side up again!

Yet she was afraid to hope, to truly hope that just one kiss and a few words of apology could truly right things all that quickly.

She looked over at Maysie, and took her hands in hers. ''Tell me all about things,'' she murmured. ''Tell me how you met my mother, and then began working for her.''

Maysie explained about having contemplated suicide again, and how Marilyn had stopped her. She described Marilyn's house to Elizabeth, and how she happened to become a prostitute again.

''But I'm trying to change,'' Maysie quickly defended herself. ''Honest, I am, Elizabeth. In fact, I've fallen in love. Like you, I love an Indian. His name is Four Winds. He came one night with some white men for our services. Four Winds chose me. There has been only one time since then that I've slept with another man, and that was the night the prison burned. There was this fellow that I had been with before, who was down on his luck. I felt sorry for him. I went with him only to cheer him up. Since then, there has only been Four Winds. He sneaks into town as often as he can to be with me.''

"Four Winds?" Elizabeth gasped. She doubted his worth, yet knowing how special the love of an Indian could be, did not share her doubts with Maysie. "How nice, Maysie. I hope you'll be happy.''

"I hope to marry him one day," Maysie said, her eyes shining. Marilyn suddenly came over to them.

"Maysie and I really must go," Marilyn said softly. She bent over Elizabeth and placed a hand to her cheek. "I'll be back, if you wish me to.''

Elizabeth nodded as she looked wistfully up at her mother. "Please do," she murmured.

Maysie gave Elizabeth a hug. "I'll come also," she whispered. "That is, if you aren't too upset with me now that you know that I . . . that I have returned to prostituting.''

Elizabeth returned the hug. "I'm just glad that you are all right," she assured her, stroking Maysie's long, black hair. She leaned back, her eyes stern on Maysie's. "But be sure about Four Winds before marrying him. He seems to be a complicated man.''

"I think I know him better than anyone," Maysie said, smiling sweetly as they rose from the sofa.

Earl walked Marilyn to the door and stepped out into the shadows on the porch. He drew Marilyn into his embrace again. "I should hate you for whoring around," he said, gazing down at her with watery eyes. "But somehow that doesn't seem to matter. Come back soon, do you hear? Let's talk some more.''

"I'd love to," Marilyn said, her green eyes flashing up at him.

Earl lowered his lips to her mouth. She circled her

arms around his neck and returned the kiss. Then she broke quickly away from him and descended the steps as Elizabeth stepped outside on the porch.

Soon Marilyn and Maysie were in the carriage riding away, both waving out the windows.

Tears flooded Elizabeth's eyes, happiness warming her heart. She had seen her parents kissing. She saw the possibility of her childhood dream coming true— that her parents could be together again. They did seem to still be in love, no matter that her mother had lived the life of a whore.

Elizabeth knew that she was going to have to accept that, the same as her father. Perhaps her mother might not need to have a business much longer, if her mother decided to return to her father.

Dusk had fallen and the moon replaced the sun in the sky, casting long shadows in the forest beyond. Just as Elizabeth started to turn, to go inside the house, she stopped in surprise.

"Strong Heart's grandfather!" she said, in hardly more than a whisper. She had seen a fleeting movement within the forest. It was the old man with his staff. "My Lord, that has to be Strong Heart's grandfather."

Earl stepped to her side, following her gaze. "What is that you said about Strong Heart's grandfather?" he asked, glancing at Elizabeth.

"I know that I saw him," Elizabeth said, rushing down the steps toward the forest. "The old man with the staff? That's Strong Heart's grandfather."

"Elizabeth!" Earl shouted, racing after her, stunned to hear that she thought some old man she had seen lurking in the forest was related to Strong Heart.

Then he was taken by a quick thought. If this elderly Indian was Strong Heart's grandfather, and if he could help find him for Strong Heart, couldn't that work to his advantage? He could return Strong Heart's grandfather to the village and surely Chief Moon Elk would offer a reward.

The reward that Earl would ask for was what he had already asked for—cooperation with the salmon run, and his fishery!

"Stop, Elizabeth!" he shouted. "Wait up."

Breathless, Elizabeth stopped. When her father caught up with her, she continued running with him until she was through the wide gate and into the outer fringes of the forest.

She and her father searched for a while. When the moon was covered by dark clouds, and lightning began flashing overhead, they returned to the house, and went to their separate rooms.

Elizabeth was glad to find Frannie preparing a warm bath. As she undressed, she had to listen to Frannie's scolding about not letting Frannie know that she was all right.

Elizabeth sank into the bath, enjoying its warmth. Frannie quit her fuming and tenderly washed Elizabeth's hair. After Elizabeth ate supper she went to bed.

In the night, she was awakened by a frightful dream. Sweat pearling her brow, Elizabeth bolted to a sitting position. Her eyes wild, she remembered.

She had dreamed the house was on fire. She had dreamed that she had been trapped. She could even now feel the smoke stinging her throat and eyes, and her fingers felt raw from clawing at the door, trying to get it open.

"I'm afraid to go back to sleep," she whispered. She stepped from the bed into her soft slippers.

She pulled a robe around her shoulders and went to the window, peering through the sheets of rain that splashed against the pane.

She hugged herself, her mind whirling with many thoughts. She missed Strong Heart so much that her insides ached from longing for him.

Then the dream returned to her.

The fire! It had seemed so real.

Even Strong Heart could not have saved her, had he even been there.

Shivering, she turned and stared at the bed, then reluctantly went back and lay down. She willed her eyes to close, then found herself in another sort of dream—one which warmed her through and through, as Strong Heart held her close, telling her over and over again how much he loved her.

And then Strong Heart's face turned into the face of the older Indian, causing her to awaken again with a start, her eyes staring.

27

My face in thine eye, thine in mine appear.
—DONNE

Last night's nightmares were still haunting Elizabeth,
even though it was midmorning of a bright and clear
day, and the house was warmed by the sunlight
streaming through the windows. Delightful odors were
wafting from the kitchen, tempting her, but Elizabeth
grabbed a shawl from a peg on the foyer wall and went
outside and stood on the porch, to breathe the fresh
air.

As she peered into the forest, she tried to think about
her times with Strong Heart. Then the memory of the
elderly Indian with the staff intruded, bringing back
the nightmares again. The fire in her dream had surely
been set by the elderly Indian. She recalled with a
shudder how Strong Heart's face had turned into the
old man's.

Needing to find something that would get her mind
off her unpleasant and puzzling thoughts, Elizabeth
lifted the skirt of her cotton dress and descended the
steps. She gazed down the steep hill to the beach,
where there was not much activity, with the fishery
having been completed and ready for the salmon run.

"The salmon run," she whispered to herself, wondering if her father or Morris Murdoch would be vis-
iting Indian villages, seeking their assistance in
catching the salmon.

She heaved a deep sigh. At least Strong Heart's village was no longer the target for salmon discussions.
After their talk, her father had promised he would keep
his hands off.

She went through the wide gate and followed the steep path that led to the beach. Another unpleasant thought chased away the clinging memories of her nightmares: Morris Murdoch.

If her father had to explain to Morris why they were not going to pester Strong Heart's people again, it would lead to further conversation in which Earl might state exactly why he had chosen to leave them alone. Then Morris Murdoch might elicit more answers out of her father which could not only place her in danger, but also Strong Heart and his people.

She had to hope that her father's word was solid, and that his feelings for her would keep all conversations with Morris directed away from Strong Heart and her.

When she reached the beach, she walked past the pier. It was difficult to walk across the rocks on this stretch of beach. She slipped and slid, and was glad when she found more solid footing as she hurried on toward the huge fishery that loomed up from the land. Built of wood, with a shake roof, it was not an unsightly building, but she saw it as something ugly. Because of it and what it represented, many Suquamish had died.

She needed to see her father today, to ensure that things were still wonderful between them, so that she could make her plans to return to Strong Heart. Elizabeth quickened her pace. When she walked past an open window she heard her father and Morris Murdoch in a conversation that made her heart turn quickly cold. She stopped and moved closer to the window, hugging the wall with her back so that her presence would not be discovered. She leaned her ear closer to the window and discovered to her chagrin that her father *did* have a devious side.

Inside, she saw nets being woven. Earl and Morris discussed spreading these large nets across the shallow

parts of the river to catch the salmon before they had
a chance to get upriver to the canyon, where the Suquamish were known to fish.

Her heart pounded hard as she listened to her father
and Murdoch laughing together and boasting about
showing the Suquamish a thing or two. She listened to
them as they planned to place the nets in the water
before night fell.

This angered Elizabeth. She was hurt that her father
was not even considering her feelings in his plans. He
knew that she was going to return to Strong Heart, to
marry him—to *live* with him, and that the salmon harvest was a large part of his people's survival—which,
in turn, also meant hers.

Her mind spun with confusion as to what she could
do about it. She was only one person. There was no
way she could destroy the nets once they were placed
in the water. And she could definitely not destroy them
beforehand, for her father and Morris Murdoch would
not give her the chance.

"What can I do?" she whispered to herself, feverishly racking her brain. She felt bitter knowing that
her own father had lied to her and Strong Heart. She
could not help but believe that her father had planned
the raid on the village with Morris. She could not allow their scheme against the Suquamish to succeed.

She had to warn Strong Heart. But how? she despaired to herself. Although she had become familiar
with the forest, and the way to Strong Heart's village,
it was dangerous for her to travel alone through it.

She had to seek help from someone. But who?

Then the answer came to her. "Four Winds," she
whispered. "Yes, Four Winds!"

Maysie had said that Four Winds came often to see
her now. If Elizabeth went to her mother's brothel, she
could wait until Four Winds arrived, tell him about
the nets that would ruin the Suquamish salmon har-

vest, and see if he would take her to Strong Heart, and together they could warn him. Then Strong Heart could do what he must to save the harvest.

And this would be a way for Four Winds to prove once and for all whether or not he was a true friend of Strong Heart.

Her pulse racing, her knees weak from fear of being discovered before she reached the stables, she crept away from the fishery and made a turn which would take her out of view from the fishery.

She ran up the path, and once on level ground again, ran breathlessly to the stables.

Elizabeth was soon riding hard on the road toward Seattle, her red hair blowing loosely in the wind. Her shawl was tied securely around her shoulders, but gave her scant protection from the cool autumn air.

But she did not seem to feel the cold. Her thoughts were on her mother and where Elizabeth would have to go to see her again.

An involuntary shiver coursed through her at the thought of meeting her mother in the brothel. Her memories of her childhood, when her mother had been "Mama," made it hard to accept the kind of life that her mother now led.

In her house there were certainly no storybooks read to small children before bedtime.

Although it seemed to take forever, Elizabeth finally reached the city. The hardest part now lay before her—finding her mother's house.

Her horse walked in a slow gait down First Avenue. The skirt of her dress whipped above her knees as the breeze blew in from the Sound. Elizabeth blushed and smoothed her dress back in place when the men loitering along the thoroughfare began teasing and flirting with her.

Normally, she would ride on past, ignoring their taunts, but today she had to find answers that could help keep Strong Heart and his people fed for the long winter ahead.

And who but these brash, insulting men would know where the most lavish of whorehouses was located?

Although hating what she had to do, Elizabeth wheeled her horse around and headed toward a group of men. When she drew rein beside them, her face still hot from blushing, she summoned up the courage to talk to them. One man in particular stood out from the rest, his blue eyes as cold as winter as he ogled her.

She realized that these men must think that she was a loose woman, looking for a man who would pay her to lift her skirt for him.

The thought not only embarrassed her, but appalled her.

And the questions that she was finding hard to ask, the question alone would confirm what they thought of her—that she was, indeed, a prostitute.

"Might one of you gentlemen tell me where I can find the place run by Marilyn Easton?" she said. Those words were like stab wounds to her heart—words which joined her mother's name to a whorehouse. Elizabeth did not know if she could ever accept what her mother had become.

She stiffened, and she tightened her fingers around the horse's reins as the men did just as she had expected, treating her as if she were a whore. They said things to her that sent chills up her spine.

She bore all of their abuse and jokes until she got the directions to her mother's house.

She turned her horse around again, leaving behind the men, who still shouted filthy things after her. She was glad when a turn up another street took her away from them.

Soon she found herself staring at a large white house that looked innocent of its true nature. It was two sto-ried with black shutters and flower boxes at the windows and a white picket fence surrounding a yard that displayed varieties of roses in full bloom. A swing hung from a porch that reached around three sides of the house.

It looked like the house of a happy family—not the home of women who sold their bodies. It looked like the house where Elizabeth had been raised as a child, before her mother had fled.

Feeling suddenly dispirited, the past rushing in on her in waves, she drew rein outside the fence and slid from the saddle.

Staring up at the house again, she tied her horse next to other drowsing horses at a hitching rail, then took a deep breath and went on through the gate and up to the porch. With a trembling hand, she raised the large brass knocker and knocked.

Her heart pounded as she waited for the door to open. When it did, she found her mother standing there, ravishingly beautiful in a sleek, black satin dress with a low bustline which revealed the upper curves of her breasts. A diamond necklace sparkled against her lily-white throat, and her red hair was curled in a tight chignon atop her head. Elizabeth found herself at a loss for words.

Marilyn gasped, then took Elizabeth by the hand and ushered her into the house. "My dear, I did not expect you to come so soon to see your mother," she said. She drew Elizabeth into her arms. "Darling, thank you for coming. I . . . I . . . didn't sleep at all last night, for fear that you would not accept me as I am now. Your being here tells me that at least you are trying to understand."

Elizabeth wanted to shout at her mother, ask her why she was so concerned now over how her daughter would feel, when all those years she had not shown any caring—had not even let Elizabeth know where she was. Even on her birthdays, Elizabeth had not received a word from her mother.

But Elizabeth held her tongue, and checked her emotions. She must force herself not to allow any of the things that had lain heavy on her heart through all those long years, to ruin what might happen now. Her mother and father might become reunited.

Yet, she wondered, should she even wish for such a reconciliation? Her father had just proved to her that he did not deserve anything but loathing.

And Elizabeth had come to her mother's house today with other things than family on her mind.

Strong Heart. She had to help Strong Heart!

Elizabeth broke from her mother's arms and started to ask for Maysie but stopped when her eyes were drawn to the rich furnishings of her mother's house. Women lounged on the plush, bright red velveteen chairs and sofas, clothed in undergarments and their faces painted. She was aware of a man and a woman coming down the spiral staircase, arm in arm. The woman was giggling and the man seeming quite pleased not only with her, but also himself. He strutted down the steps in expensive clothes, sporting a sparkling diamond in the folds of his cravat.

Then Maysie came into view, thankfully alone. Today she was dressed in a simple cotton dress with a high neckline, her face bare of any paint.

When Maysie saw Elizabeth standing there, she lifted the skirt of her dress and ran to her, flinging herself into Elizabeth's arms.

"I'm so glad you came," Maysie murmured, clinging to Elizabeth. "I thought you might hate me after seeing that I had returned to the life that you tried to help me escape from. I'm so glad that you don't hate me. Oh, Elizabeth, I'm so very happy."

Elizabeth hugged her for a moment, then stepped back. "I could never hate you," she said gently, touching Maysie's cheek. "But I did not come to tell you that. I've come for something else. Maysie, I need to see Four Winds. Will you be seeing him soon? I very desperately need his help."

"What sort of help?" Maysie asked, clasping her hands behind her.

"Strong Heart," Elizabeth said, trying to ignore the boisterous goings on in the room as other men arrived to seek the pleasures of the women. "I've got to get to Strong Heart. It's very important. And I don't want to travel through the forest alone. I thought that Four Winds might go with me."

Marilyn paled and went to Elizabeth. "Darling, you can't be serious," she said softly. "You could be harmed going to see this Indian. Let him come to you."

"I can't wait," Elizabeth said with a sigh. "What I need to tell him can't wait." She was afraid to say anything else, for fear that her mother might not be quiet about it.

"And, Mother, please don't say anything to anyone about this," Elizabeth blurted out. "Even after Father finds me gone, and should he come to you, don't tell him where I've gone. It's of vital importance that he does not know."

"Elizabeth, it isn't right to keep secrets from your father," Marilyn said, then held her breath when she saw accusal flash in her daughter's eyes. Marilyn realized that she did not have the right to tell Elizabeth not to keep secrets, after she had kept so many for so long.

"Mother, you must promise me," Elizabeth said firmly.

"I won't say anything," Marilyn promised.

Maysie took both of Elizabeth's hands. "You're in luck," she said, smiling into Elizabeth's eyes. "I was just on my way to see Four Winds. I meet him from time to time, now that he no longer rides with the outlaws.''

''He's no longer with the outlaws?'' Elizabeth said, raising an eyebrow.

''For me, he has decided not to ride with them any longer,'' Maysie said, sighing happily at the thought. ''But he's laying low for now so the outlaws won't find him and kill him for turning on them. I know where his hideout is. Come on. I'll take you to him.''

Elizabeth hugged Maysie gratefully. ''Thank you,'' she said, a sob lodging in her throat.

''And he'll do whatever he can to help Strong Heart with whatever problem he has,'' Maysie said, stepping away from Elizabeth. ''He's talked to me at length about his feelings for Strong Heart. He said that he was willing to do anything for his friend.''

Elizabeth felt as if the weight of the world had been lifted from her shoulders. She was so relieved that she knew that she *could* count on Four Winds. She gave her mother a quick hug and kiss, then left with Maysie.

Soon they were riding through the forest, their horses lathered with sweat as they were pushed to go quickly. The women reached a meadow of blowing grass and wild flowers. Elizabeth's red hair was like flickering flame as the wind whipped it around her face; Maysie's was like trembling black satin as it blew and shimmered in the sun.

Elizabeth glanced at Maysie and felt warm inside, for she had never seen Maysie so alive and vital as now, and Elizabeth was proud to think that she was partially responsible for that.

Yet there was Four Winds. Elizabeth knew the power of an Indian's love. That it was special, and oh, so wonderful. Maysie was inspired now by such a love, which would lead her into a different life—a life of total caring and commitment, instead of one of degradation.

"Up ahead yonder," Maysie informed Elizabeth. "Four Winds is hiding in an abandoned mine shaft."

They rode onward, then dismounted when they reached the mine shaft. After securing her horse's reins, Elizabeth went with Maysie into the dark shaft, then stopped with a start when Four Winds stepped suddenly out of the shadows, blocking their way, a rifle aimed directly at Elizabeth.

28

Joy so seldom weaves a chain
Like this tonight, that O! 'tis pain
To break its links so soon.
          —Thomas Moore

Terrified, Elizabeth stood in the mine shaft, staring at the rifle, and at Four Winds's face that was distorted with hate. She grabbed Maysie by the hand and attempted to run away with her, but her feet seemed frozen to the ground, unable to move as Four Winds began pulling the trigger. . . .

Elizabeth awakened with a start, and looked anxiously around her, then sighed with relief when she realized that she had had another nightmare. Her dream was far from the truth of what had really happened. When she and Maysie had gone to Four Winds, he had quickly offered to take Elizabeth to Strong Heart. He urged Maysie to return to Seattle, promising that he would return for her later.

Elizabeth and Four Winds had ridden hard to reach Strong Heart's village, and as quickly as Strong Heart had been able to round up many braves, they had left by canoe on the river. Going by canoe would make it easier to remove the nets.

Elizabeth had fallen asleep on soft pelts on the floor of Strong Heart's massive canoe, snuggled beneath a warm bearskin. She lifted the bearskin aside, and rose to sit on the seat just behind Strong Heart. She felt his eyes on her as he turned to check on her welfare. She smiled at him, so glad that he had allowed her to come on this mission so she could settle the score with her father, herself. He was a man that she no longer knew—a man guided by treachery and greed.

It tore at her heart to know this side of her father, and she doubted that she could ever forgive him.

When Strong Heart turned his gaze back to stare down the avenue of the river, Elizabeth reached for the bearskin and wrapped it around her shoulders, content at least for the moment. For she had proven where her loyalties lay by having brought Strong Heart the news of the nets.

Four Winds had also proven his loyalty to Strong Heart, and now rode in a canoe that was moving beside Strong Heart's.

Driven by the sinewy arms of the oarsmen, the many intricately designed canoes pushed their way down the cold river that wound through the black forest and beneath the majestic bluffs, the long oars rising and falling in regular strokes.

The moon shone brightly onto the water, turning the tossing waves into flashing jewels. The wind soughed, and somewhere in the distance an owl hooted.

Elizabeth gazed at Four Winds's canoe. The moonlight revealed its decorations of sea otter teeth and the prow handsomely carved in the design of a whale. As were all of the canoes traveling the rushing waters tonight, the canoe that Four Winds commanded had been hollowed by fire and adz and was very sleek, designed for fast, silent travel.

Elizabeth looked down at herself. Many Stars had urged her to change her clothes before setting out on this journey. Elizabeth had had just enough time to change from her cotton dress into a fine, white buckskin dress, and comfortably soft moccasins. Many Stars had plaited Elizabeth's hair, so that it now hung in two braids down her back.

Elizabeth ran her fingers over the soft fabric of her buckskin dress, gazing at Strong Heart. His back was to her, she admired the definition of his muscles beneath the fabric of his own buckskin shirt. The fringes of the sleeves and his long brown hair lifted and waved in the breeze.

She looked down at the muscles of his arms, as they flexed and unflexed as he drew his single oar rhythmically through the water. She knew the strength of those arms, and desired to be held within his powerful embrace.

Then she stiffened and she grabbed ahold of the side of the canoe, for up ahead was a sudden cottony layer of fog which would hinder the view of the braves as they looked for the nets. It seemed as though her father had planned it this way—that he had the power of even changing the mood of the weather to suit his purpose.

But the steady movement of the oars did not slacken. They slid into the fog and as if guided by some unseen force, they did not crash into any floating debris, or the banks of the river.

The canoes kept a steady pace, the sound of the oars making contact with the water now almost eerie in the dim haze.

Elizabeth now felt strangely alone, for she could not even see Strong Heart through the denseness of the fog. It was as if she was the only person in the world.

Then the canoes slid from the screen of fog, and once more followed the moonlit path on the water until Strong Heart raised a fist in the air in a silent command for his braves to stop. As his canoe came to a halt in the water, so did those that followed.

Elizabeth's breath quickened as Strong Heart, along with the other braves, turned the direction of their canoes and paddled slowly toward shore.

Once there, they pulled their canoes ashore on a spit of sand. Elizabeth nodded a silent thank you to Strong Heart as he helped her from the boat.

It was then that she got her first look at the nets that stretched across this narrow span of the river, as if a monstrous spider had spun a web.

A tremor coursed through Elizabeth, seeing how completely the waters were covered by the vast nets. There were nets crisscrossing the water, her father and Morris having evidently not taken any chance that should one net fail to stop the salmon, the others wouldn't.

Knives flashed in the moonlight as the braves left their canoes and ran toward the nets. Elizabeth followed Strong Heart, slipping her own knife from a sheath that she had tied on her leg beneath the skirt of her dress—a knife that Many Stars had lent her.

With eager fingers and a building rage against her father, Elizabeth waded into knee-high water, and stood at Strong Heart's side as they quickly began cutting the nets to shreds. She was so determined to make things right for Strong Heart and his people, she didn't even notice how numbing cold the water was. The only thing that was important to her now was to help Strong Heart destroy the nets. Any day now the salmon would be appearing in hordes in these very waters.

They must become the harvest of the Suquamish, not her father and Morris Murdoch!

Just as the dark began to dispell with the sun's rising, the last net was cut loose. And with the same silence that had brought them there, the Suquamish braves entered their canoes and shoved off into the water. Only when they got several miles up the river did they let out shouts and whoops of victory, Strong Heart and Four Winds's the loudest of them all.

When Strong Heart turned to Elizabeth and motioned with a hand for her to come and sit beside him, she moved quickly to his side and snuggled against him.

"This thing that you have done for my people will

never be forgotten,'' he said feelingly. ''And that you brought Four Winds, so that he could prove his worth again to the Suquamish, and his devotion as a friend to me, warms my heart, my *la-daila*.''

''I'm so happy that everything turned out all right,'' Elizabeth said, her eyes shining at his. ''I even feel important now. Even your braves look at me with a different look in their eyes, as though . . . as though I now belong.''

''You do, and you always have,'' Strong Heart said, never missing a stroke with his oar. ''Have you returned to stay with me now, to be my wife?''

''*Ah-hah*,'' Elizabeth murmured. ''My life with my father as I have known it is now a thing of the past. I could not bear to even face him now, knowing what he is capable of.''

''My *la-daila*, forget your bad feelings,'' Strong Heart softly encouraged. ''Let us live for tomorrow. Today and forever throw all bad thoughts away!''

''I shall try,'' Elizabeth said, badly wanting to, but knowing that it would not be as easy practiced as spoken.

The sky was dark again when Elizabeth woke up beside Strong Heart in his longhouse. She had drifted asleep in his canoe again, and had not even been aware of when they had arrived at his village, nor of being carried to shore to his longhouse.

Now, as she awakened she felt a warm body lying behind hers. Strong Heart's nakedness against her own made a thrill shoot through her, for it seemed so long since they had been together intimately.

Elizabeth drew in a breath of joy and closed her eyes when she felt Strong Heart's hands moving over her back, down to cup her buttocks. Then they moved lower still, around to caress her at the juncture of her thighs where her heart seemed centered in its wild beatings. As one of his hands caressed her there, the other moved onto one of her breasts, pinching the nipple to a tight peak. Elizabeth's breath became short and raspy. Then his powerful hands were at her waist, turning her around to face him.

The fire's glow revealed that his eyes were heavy with passion. He reached for her hair and began slowly unbraiding it. She took this opportunity to run her own hands down the magnificence of his body—long, lithe, and aroused.

Her hair, now free of its plaits, drifted across the sleeping platform. Strong Heart moved to his knees and straddled her. She gazed up at his lean, bronze face, and touched one of his cheeks almost meditatively as she felt the strength of his manhood probing where she so unmercifully throbbed.

Filled with an overwhelming longing and need that felt like exquisite pain, she opened herself up to him and locked her legs around his waist and drew him deeply into her.

With a groan, Strong Heart pressed deeper. He circled his arms around her and lifted her closer to him, his mouth lowering toward her lips, kissing her urgently, eagerly, drugging her. Her own kisses were desperate and hungry.

His tongue sought through her lips until he touched her tongue. His hands were on her breasts, feverishly fondling her, as she wriggled her body against his in response to his wonderful ways of pleasuring her.

Again they kissed. Strong Heart's desire was a sharp, hot pain in his loins, surges of heat welling up in him, filling him, threatening to spill over.

His hips moved masterfully, faster and deeper. Feeling release so near, and wanting to postpone it because that would bring their lovemaking too quickly to a close, Elizabeth caught her breath, not daring to breathe, or to feel.

But the attempt to not give in to the ecstasy was in vain, because one more deep thrust within her, and one more flick of his tongue through her lips, and she was gone. Surges of euphoria flooded her through and through, making her feel as if for a moment she was spinning, deliciously spinning.

She clung tightly to Strong Heart as his body momentarily stiffened, and then he plunged one last time into her. Then he held her tightly to him as his body quivered and jolted against hers, his moans of pleasure mingling with her own as their lips slowly drifted apart.

Afterward, Strong Heart rolled away, and lay on his side, facing her. "Have I told you before that you are more beautiful than all the skies?" he said softly, placing a gentle hand to her cheek. "After the salmon harvest, we will be two hearts becoming one life, one flow. Ours will be a love everlasting."

Elizabeth nestled closer to him, as he moved his hands around to her back, caressing her. "Each moment with you is sweeter than the last," she whispered, sighing when his hand went to the most delicately tender spot at the meeting of her thighs, smoothing his fingers slowly back and forth, arousing passion inside her again.

"Perhaps Four Winds and this white woman named Maysie can find the same peace? The same paradise as we?" Strong Heart said, drawing his hands back up her body, now pressing her breasts. "This woman. She is surely the cause of Four Winds rethinking his future, and the direction that he was taking with his life. If she is at all like you, he is blessed—*doubly* blessed."

Elizabeth did not want to disappoint him by revealing to him that this woman was the woman he had dragged half drowned from the Sound. That Maysie had lived the life of a prostitute until lately, when she gave herself solely to Four Winds.

No. It was best not to reveal that Maysie had, in a sense, taken a similar road in her life as Four Winds—the *wrong* road. These two unfortunate people were finding salvation in each other's company, pulling themselves out of degradation into something that could be ideal, if they would only accept it.

The sound of people talking and moving anxiously outside the longhouse drew Elizabeth's attention toward the door. "Tomorrow we leave for the canyon?" she asked, raising up on an elbow. "I am so happy to be able to partake in the salmon harvest with you. It will be such an adventure."

"It won't begin the moment we arrive," Strong Heart said, rising from the platform and slipping into his fringed breeches. "After we reach the canyon, there could be several days of waiting for the right moment to start our harvest. And even then, we may have to wait awhile longer."

Elizabeth rose, stretched, then drew her buckskin dress over her head. "Why is that?" she asked, pulling the dress down her slender body, enjoying Strong Heart's look of admiration as he gazed at her.

Strong Heart admired her a moment longer, feeling the flicker of heat in his loins that Elizabeth's loveliness always sparked. Then he looked away from her and knelt on one knee beside the glowing embers of the coals in his firepit. "The salmon chief, Smiling Wolf, is the one who gives the signal for the beginning of fishing each season. No one dares approach the river to fish, unless he has given them permission."

He took a short stick and stirred the coals among the ashes. He scattered some wood shavings into the small, glowing embers. As they burst into flames, he placed more twigs on until the fire had grown enough for a larger piece of wood, which he quickly laid across it.

Elizabeth picked up her hairbrush and began brushing her hair in long, even strokes. "I have never heard of a salmon chief before," she murmured.

"The Suquamish salmon chief is a leader separate from the tribal chief," Strong Heart said, going to the door when he heard a faint knock. He said thank you to Many Stars when she handed him a huge, steaming pot of clam soup, then took it and hung it over the fire.

He turned to Elizabeth as she sat down beside him, handing him a wooden bowl and spoon, keeping one for herself. "Smiling Wolf is a shaman, a religious man," he explained further. "He is believed to have 'salmon power,' the ability to make the salmon reappear on schedule each year."

Elizabeth dipped soup into both of their bowls. She was always glad to learn more of his customs, knowing that was her true way of being totally accepted in his community.

Strong Heart gazed warmly at Elizabeth as she began sipping soup from her spoon. "*Ah-hah,* soon the gifts of the sea will bring prosperity to the tribe for one more long winter of cold moons," he said, then began eating too, thinking that finally everything was as it should be in his life, and especially his *la-daila*'s!

He would not allow himself to think of all of the ways that this could change, just in the blink of an eye. This was now, and in his heart, now was *forever*.

Later, when Elizabeth was comfortably asleep on the sleeping platform, a rug drawn snugly to her chin, Strong Heart placed a cloak around his shoulders. Lifting a heavy buckskin bag and slinging it across his shoulder, he took a long, lingering look at Elizabeth, then turned and left the longhouse.

The moon was only occasionally visible through the foliage overhead. Strong Heart ran through the forest, knowing where he must go to assure a bountiful harvest of salmon. This year it was more important than any other, because his people had already lost too much.

He would go to the medicine rock and honor it with tokens of worship. The medicine rock had the power to grant a wish to those who visited it. With their wishes they sought to bring back their health, or to heal a broken heart. Strong Heart sought to quicken the run of the salmon.

When Strong Heart reached farther along the banks of the Duwamish River, far from where his village slept silently during this midnight hour, he proceeded carefully up a steep embankment above the river. His gaze locked on the face of a brown, curving rock, and a tree that grew straight out of the rock. He could already see that others had come to honor the rock's powers, because many gifts hung from the bare limbs of the tree, like offerings placed upon the altar of a church.

Strong Heart moved carefully onward. The rock was exceedingly hard to reach. This was deliberate because a white man had destroyed one of the earlier altars of his people, and had taken the wampum and beadwork for himself. This special location of the rock was to discourage those who would easily avail themselves of the offerings of the people of his tribe.

After finally reaching the rock, he gazed in wonder at the preponderance of gifts. Hardly a space remained for Strong Heart's own offering. A broad smile touched his lips and he now knew that all would be blessed this season of the salmon run. It seemed that every able person of his village had come to the rock with their wishes.

Strong Heart knelt and placed the bag on the rock at the base of the tree and smiled heavenward.

29

When did morning ever break
And find such beaming eyes awake
As those that sparkle here!
    —THOMAS MOORE

The drums had throbbed and the chants had echoed to the heavens all night. It was now dawn on the river and the drums and chants had ceased. Elizabeth sat before the campfire, warming her hands as the sun rose slowly in the sky. She gazed around her at the faces of the Suquamish people as the women cooked over the hot coals of the fires, the braves scurried about preparing their methods of catching the salmon, and the children romped and played, their excitement evident in their eyes.

Two days ago they had arrived where the big river roared and foamed as it squeezed through the nearby canyon. They now waited for the Suquamish's most important event of the year, the time when salmon fought their way upstream through the canyon to reach their spawning riffles.

The sun now deliciously warming the air, Elizabeth turned from the fire and gazed at Strong Heart as he joined the others. He was sharpening the tip of a lightweight, short harpoon for throwing at the salmon.

Her gaze shifted, seeing others making nets of bark, and holding spears with various types of points. Some were preparing dip nets—bags of netting attached to a wooden frame on a handle.

Others were preparing a fence weir, to throw across the river later to block the salmon from traveling upstream after many had been allowed to pass by so they could spawn. From a platform on the weir, the Indians could easily catch the salmon with their dip nets and gaff hooks. Strong Heart had told her that these fence weirs were called fish-herding fences.

Elizabeth noticed that today, even though it was late autumn, Strong Heart and his braves wore only breechcloths and sported arm and leg bands twisted and woven of shredded bark.

Elizabeth's eyes were drawn elsewhere, as a heron with slow, flapping wings rose from one place along the shadowy banks of the river, skimming a few yards to settle again.

Farther up the river, a family of three black bears on a fishing expedition paused to look at the Suquamish intruders. They then ambled farther up the river, stopping again to wade into the water that was already teeming with hordes of silvery salmon. Soon they were feasting on their prime catches.

A movement overhead made Elizabeth look up. A red-tailed hawk soared, then landed on an old snag and surveyed his hunting territory, alert for a midmorning snack. Blue jays scolded from the riverbank trees. A kingfisher was a flashing arrow as he hustled upstream on some busy errand.

The hubbub around Elizabeth stilled. She turned wondering eyes to see why. She was filled with awe as the salmon chief made an appearance, walking slowly toward the riverbank. His long robe flowed around his legs, his gray hair dragged the ground behind him. The many winters of his age had bent him like an old tree.

Strong Heart's father followed, limping as Pretty Nose supported him by holding on to his elbow. Strong Heart joined them, their eyes on the salmon chief.

Elizabeth rose slowly to her feet and stood with the other women, behind the men and Pretty Nose. Many Stars moved silently to stand beside Elizabeth. They exchanged quick smiles, then Elizabeth became absorbed in the same ritual that she had now seen twice since their arrival at the swift waters of the canyon. Each day, she and the Suquamish had watched the salmon chief as he walked down to his special vantage point above the river. He had spent the other days motionless, staring at the fish passing upstream. Each time he had announced that the salmon were moving in the river, crowding into the quiet waters. He had said that more and more fish were passing upstream, and soon the harvest would begin.

Today Elizabeth felt the building anticipation of the Suquamish, hoping that today would be *the* day. Even now she could see the splashes of hundreds of salmon fins.

Many Stars clasped one of Elizabeth's hands and squeezed it affectionately as they awaited a response from the salmon chief.

Strong Heart had explained much of this ritual to her on their way to the canyon. He had said that his people assumed that as the salmon chief stood peering down into the river, the old man was talking to the fish, wishing them a safe journey, and thanking them for appearing in the river again. The people believed that he possessed salmon power, a special relationship with the fish.

Hadn't the salmon chief, as a young man, been selected by the salmon themselves?

Hadn't he, like his predecessors, struck a bargain with the salmon that they would crowd into the river at this time of the year?

And, at this special place, they would show themselves so that the people could harvest them.

The people knew that part of the bargain between the salmon and the old chief was that the fish would not be disturbed until many had swum on to the upper river, to provide food for other tribes at less favorable fishing stations.

This was true, but the old chief also knew—perhaps the salmon had told him—that fish must be allowed to escape farther upstream to spawn, to ensure that the runs would continue in future years.

Finally, after days of watching the river and meditating, Chief Smiling Wolf turned to face his people, to make the eagerly awaited announcement. ''My people, the first salmon can be taken today!'' he shouted, his old eyes gleaming.

There was an uproar of celebration reaching to the sky. Then there was silence again as Smiling Wolf turned to face the river, and in a low monotone, thanked the salmon for appearing again and allowing themselves to be taken, so that the Suquamish could live.

Then Chief Smiling Wolf moved aside, mingling with the watchers as everyone pushed forward to stand at the riverbank.

Elizabeth and Many Stars rushed to find an open space among those who were crowding together, their eager eyes watching something. After squeezing into the crowd, Elizabeth gasped with fear as she watched Strong Heart, one of the tribe's better fishermen, descend a wet, slippery cliff to a niche in the rock just above where the water cascaded through a chute in the canyon. She watched as one other brave followed, handing Strong Heart a spear. A line attached to the spear was piled neatly in front of Strong Heart's feet, where it could run out rapidly. The other end was tied to a stake that the brave drove into a crack in the rock.

Elizabeth placed a hand over her mouth to stifle another gasp. She had not known that Strong Heart was going to be doing this, or how dangerous and difficult spearing fish in the torrent was. Should he slip and fall into the churning waters or against the rocks below, he would not have hardly any chance of surviving. She now understood why he had not shared this part of the ceremony with her.

She breathed much easier when another brave handed a rope to the one who was standing just behind Strong Heart. She thought that this rope was to be tied around Strong Heart, in case he did lose his balance.

But, no! she groaned to herself. Strong Heart shook his head, refusing to use the lifeline. He was the chosen spearsman today. He stood intently watching the movement of the fish below him, his arm cocked.

Elizabeth took some relief that the brave who stood close behind him kept a watchful eye on Strong Heart, ready to use the safety rope in case he fell into the torrent.

Elizabeth glanced down at Many Stars as she edged closer.

"Strong Heart does not wear the safety rope on this special occasion today because he fears that the salmon might be offended if he appears too cautious," Many Stars whispered, smiling up at Elizabeth. "And do not fear. Strong Heart has been the lead fisherman for many years. He has not yet fallen into the waters."

Elizabeth weakly returned her smile, trying to take some reassurance from what she had told her.

Then she turned her eyes back to Strong Heart, and her heart did a great leap when suddenly his arm sprang forward, the spear flying to a fish struggling at the base of the canyon.

Everyone cheered when the spear went through the thick body of the salmon, just in back of the head. And as it flipped and flopped in the water, Strong Heart grabbed the line and quickly brought it in—the first catch of the salmon harvest.

One quick thump with a wooden club and the fish lay still on the rocks. Strong Heart removed the spear, and climbing away from the river, went to Smiling Wolf and lay the salmon at the feet of the chief.

The old man knelt on one knee and meditated a moment over the fish, then with a gesture signaled a woman to come to him.

Elizabeth watched as the woman picked up the fish and carried it to a place of scoured rock beside the river. The rock was pitted with kettle-sized depressions, a result of glaciers and floods in the distant past.

The woman proceeded to clean the fish with the traditional tools—short bone shafts edged with razor-sharp rock chips set in slots. As each one dulled, they were discarded and other blades were fitted in the slots.

"This form of tool that Brown Susan is using is as old as the beginnings of our people," Many Stars whispered, leaning closer to Elizabeth. "Our ancestors thousands of years before brought similar tools to the New World across a land bridge over the great sea."

Elizabeth smiled at Many Stars, glad that she was able to participate in the rituals of the Suquamish.

For a moment her thoughts drifted to her father, wondering how he had reacted when he found the nets destroyed. She could not help but smile smugly at the thought. Yet she was sad at the same time, for her father was now lost to her forever.

And she would never experience the wonderful joy of seeing her mother and father reunited. It most surely would not happen now.

She belonged to Strong Heart now—not her troubled parents.

Pulling herself out of her sad thoughts, she looked toward several women who had been tending a fire while waiting for Strong Heart to spear the first salmon. The women began using sticks to pick up hot rocks from the fire and took them to one of the depressions in the rock, which had been filled with water, and threw the rocks into it.

Elizabeth saw that the rock kettle was about four feet wide and fairly deep. And when the water in it began to boil, the women put the salmon in it. After it was cooked, they removed it and began cutting it in small pieces, and distributed it, until everyone had had a taste of the first salmon.

Then the true harvest began.

Elizabeth was relieved when Strong Heart came down from the high rock. She smiled sheepishly at him as he turned her way, his eyes dancing, his face split with a wide grin.

Then she stood back with the other women as all of the men and boys joined in the harvest.

When the red rim of the sun slipped over the western horizon, and the shimmering afterglow faded into night's darkness, the extent of the day's catch was counted. Chief Smiling Wolf began supervising the distribution of the fish to the women, the shares based on family size. Elizabeth had been told earlier that on an average day, twelve hundred fish, averaging sixteen pounds each, were caught.

Strong Heart came to Elizabeth, pride shining in his eyes. "Was it not a good day?" he boasted, slipping an elk-skin robe around his shoulders as the deep purple shadows of night brought with them the cooler temperatures of late autumn.

"A very good day," Elizabeth murmured. "And so interesting. I loved every minute of it, Strong Heart. Thank you for allowing me to be a part of it."

"Many moons ago, when the world was new, my ancestors discovered this fish which crowded into the rivers at the same time each year," he said, wrapping an elk-skin robe around Elizabeth's shoulders. "They discovered that salmon was an abundant, reliable, nutritious food, and that it could be stored for the winter when other food was scarce. After my people found the salmon, and knew how to process it for storage, we were freed from the necessity of following game. Permanent villages became possible.''

He swung an arm around Elizabeth's waist and began walking her toward the river, where he soon found a quiet place for them to sit in privacy. He drew her lips close to his, their eyes twinkling into each other's. ''A reliable food supply always makes possible more children,'' he said thickly. ''My *la-daila*, soon we must discuss how large a family we will add to our people's population.''

She thrilled at the thought of bearing his children, and at the thought of their sons being the mirror image of their father.

She twined her arms around his neck and accepted his gentle, sweet kiss. Afterward, she was not surprised when he stretched out beside her and lay his head in her lap and fell asleep, exhausted from the long day of fishing.

As he lay there, sleeping soundly, Elizabeth contentedly stroked his dark hair, the pool of water before her blooming with stars.

30

How delicious is the winning of a kiss!
—Thomas Campbell

Several days later the Suquamish were back at their village. This salmon harvest had been one of the largest in the history of Strong Heart's people. The salmon had been dried in the sun on huge racks, then smoked, and much of the dried salmon had been stored in baskets or wrapped in mats in food storage pits. The pits were six feet across and roofed with sticks and mats and then covered with rocks to protect them from animals.

Besides that which had been stored, baskets were filled with dried salmon stacked in and around the village. There were more than one hundred stacks. Each stack contained ten thousand pounds of dried fish. Some Indians from the foothills of the Rocky Mountains had arrived with horses and buffalo skins to trade for the preserved salmon.

With Strong Heart on one side of her, and Four Winds on the other, Elizabeth sat spellbound as she watched the male dancers. They celebrated the success of their salmon harvest, and welcomed the visitors who had come from far away to trade.

She had always loved the Fourth of July celebrations in San Francisco, with the fireworks bursting forth in the sky in various, blinding colors and shapes.

But tonight, as the moonlight flowed down from the sky with a white satiny sheen, she was more in awe of the dancers as they jumped and bounced in fast movements around the outdoor fire in time to the steady beats of the drums. They were only in breechcloths, their mantles trimmed with small bells, and they carried huge, beautifully flaked blades of red obsidian—a form of wealth to the Suquamish.

One by one, the braves leaped around the circle of fire, chanting their songs, their bare feet thumping, raising dust from the ground, their copper bodies gleaming in the light of the fire.

The rich smells of fish cooking drew her attention. There were large cooking kettles set over fires behind her, and fish were being broiled over the open fire and on beds of coals.

She smiled at Many Stars as she stood with the other women as food was steamed in large, shallow pits filled with hot stones. Elizabeth had helped place the food on the stones earlier in the evening. The whole affair had then been covered with leaves and mats, with hot water poured through to the stones. Soon after that, the wonderful fragrances had wafted upward, proving to Elizabeth that this strange method of cooking proved most effective.

She turned her eyes around quickly as the dancers stepped aside and one of them stepped close to the fire. When he poured large amounts of olachen oil on the fire, it blazed up fiercely, drawing sighs from the crowd who watched, their eyes wide.

And the dancers continued to dance, this time more wildly, more athletically, as their bodies turned and twisted, and their heads bobbed.

Elizabeth smiled to herself, deciding that, yes, tonight was a feast of sights, sounds, and smells—a night that she would never forget. Earlier, before the sun had set, there had been many contests—wrestling, shooting arrows and throwing lances at marks, foot and canoe races, and tugs-of-war. Strong Heart and Four Winds had participated in them all, the competition growing fierce between them. But in the end, they had fallen to the ground laughing, more amused than angered by whoever had won the most matches.

Elizabeth now turned her eyes to Strong Heart as he sat so proudly beside her. Like his father, who sat on a high platform with his wife presiding over the celebration, Strong Heart wore a headdress bearing carved figures, painted and inlaid with iridescent shells, spiked with sea lion whiskers, and hung with ermine tails.

His cloak was of costly sea otter fur and flakes of mica had been dusted on his face, glittering in the soft light of the fire.

To Elizabeth, he looked like some mythical god, so breathtakingly noble in appearance, a man of inscrutable self-poise and dignity. It was at this moment hard to believe that she had ever had the opportunity to meet him, let alone be *loved* by him.

And to think that soon she would become his wife was even more unbelievable, for he was not an ordinary man, by any means.

He was special. So very, very special.

Strong Heart felt Elizabeth's eyes on him. He reached over and took her hand in his, squeezing it lovingly. ''My *la-daila,* you look beautiful tonight,'' he whispered, his eyes admiring her. Many Stars had made the dress specially for Elizabeth out of white doeskin, fringed at the hem and at the ends of the long sleeves. Colorful beads and porcupine quills had been embroidered in intricate designs onto it.

His gaze moved to Elizabeth's hair, admiring the wreath of roses that Many Stars had also made for her, another token of her undying friendship for this woman whom Strong Heart had chosen to be his wife.

Elizabeth lowered her eyes, blushing as she felt herself being scrutinized with such admiration by the man she loved. She never wanted to disappoint him, and did not feel as if she had tonight. She felt especially lovely wearing the gifts made by Many Stars's delicate fingers. In time, when she learned the art of making these beautifully designed clothes, she would pay her friend back in kind.

Many Stars was suddenly before her, offering her a large, elaborately carved dish, decorated with the crest of Strong Heart's family, piled high with fish and cooked salmon on skewers.

Elizabeth accepted the offering of food, as other maidens offered the same to Strong Heart and Four Winds.

Long feast mats were unrolled before them to serve as a tablecloth, and for napkins, bundles of softly shredded cedar bark were distributed.

Having not eaten since breakfast, Elizabeth joined Strong Heart and Four Winds as they enjoyed the feast, washing down the assortment of fish with clam juice.

There was more dancing and merriment until the ghostly hour of midnight, delighting those who sat there. Then an elder of the village stepped forth, and began entertaining them with long, often humorous tales of the adventures or misadventures of such picturesque characters as the raven and mink, and of his own childhood, when he had been young, agile, and mischievous.

When he was done, everyone walked to him and gave him warm hugs, then went their separate ways to their longhouses.

Four Winds reached out and clapped a hand onto Strong Heart's shoulder. "It is time for my return to Seattle," he said. "My woman awaits me."

At this mention of Maysie, Elizabeth lowered her eyes, and thought of her mother. She would never understand how her mother could have chosen to be a prostitute. Yet who was Elizabeth to cast blame on anyone?

Everyone was driven by something—and her mother

had been forced to find a way to survive away from a man she had grown to loathe.

"And so you plan to marry her soon?" Strong Heart said, rising with Four Winds. Elizabeth rose slowly to stand beside Strong Heart, locking an arm through his, as a way of proving to herself that she had gained more in life than she had lost when she had fallen in love with Strong Heart.

"This is my intention, *ah-hah*," Four Winds said, nodding. He glanced over at Elizabeth and smiled, then looked into Strong Heart's eyes again. "And you? You will soon marry this woman whose hair is the color of flames?"

Strong Heart turned his eyes to Elizabeth. He smiled warmly at her. "*Ah-hah*, soon," he said, nodding. "Now that the salmon harvest is behind us, and my people are content with what life offers them, *ah-hah*, soon we will be celebrating a *potlatch* in our village. You will join the celebration? You will bring your woman so that she will celebrate, also, with us?"

"*Mah-sie*, thank you for the invitation, but I do not think so," Four Winds said, his face turning solemn. "You see, I must return to my people. I must prove to them that I am worthy of being called Suquamish again. They will sit in council and decide my fate, whether I live it as Suquamish among them, or whether I am destined to live as a white man, yet hidden away from the gang that I no longer belong to."

Strong Heart placed his hands on Four Winds's shoulders. "My friend, should you be turned away by those in your village, come to mine," he said passionately. "You will be welcome." He dropped a hand from Four Winds's shoulder and clenched it into a fist, placing it over his heart. "My *tum-tum*, heart, is warm toward you, forever."

Four Winds glanced over at Strong Heart's father, whose eyes seemed to be boring holes through him, then looked uncomfortably back at Strong Heart. "I do not believe your father shares the same sentiments as you about Four Winds," he said, his voice breaking. "Four Winds has made his past, so Four Winds will make his future. But, again thank you, my friend, for your offering to Four Winds. Never will your kindness be forgotten."

"That is good," Strong Heart said, nodding. "That is how it should be."

Four Winds hugged Strong Heart tightly. Then he stepped away from him to hug Elizabeth. Then he walked away, his chin lifted with dignity and pride.

"There goes a good man," Strong Heart said softly. As the drums drifted into silence in the distance, Strong Heart playfully lifted Elizabeth up into his arms and began carrying her toward his longhouse.

"The true celebration begins now," he said huskily, molding one of Elizabeth's breasts with his palm. "You are not too tired, my *la-daila,* to partake in our private celebration of life and love?"

Elizabeth lay her cheek against his chest. "I will never be too tired for you, my love," she murmured, knowing that was true. From the depths of her being, that was true.

As Four Winds made his way toward his horse that was waiting with the others in the corral beneath the stars, his steps were light, his heart filled with thanks, and much love toward his friend, Strong Heart. Never could any man find such devotion in a friend—such unwavering loyalty. And Four Winds knew that even if he tried until the day he died, he could never find enough ways to repay Strong Heart for his kindness to him.

Four Winds's footsteps suddenly faltered and his breath quickened when he heard muffled voices coming from somewhere close by. Since everyone had retired to their dwellings, this made him suspicious of anyone who might be outside.

He moved stealthily toward the sound of the voices, staying hidden behind trees until he found a group of braves huddled behind a boulder, the moon's glow not yet reaching them.

But Four Winds did not need the moon to identify the men. He knew their voices, each and every one of them.

He pressed his back against a towering elm tree, and leaned his head closer to the speakers, growing cold inside over what these men were plotting without the consent of their chief or his son.

It could bring the total wrath of the white community down on the Suquamish village.

He did not intervene, knowing they would not listen to him. He learned that the braves wanted to travel to Seattle, and once and for all burn the old house that sat on the hallowed ground of their ancestors. They were also going to rid the land of the fishery that was a threat to their future, and the white man who had brought so much sorrow into their lives.

Silkenly nude, Elizabeth reached her arms out for Strong Heart as he washed the last of the glittering mica from his face. "Come to me, my love," she said, her voice foreign to her in her need to touch his sleek body. His arousal was quite evident as his manhood stood erect, like a gleaming, velvet rod.

Strong Heart tossed the cloth aside, his heart pounding hard within his chest at the mere sight of Elizabeth. Her opened arms beckoning to him promised much that made his heart sing. Strong Heart paused a moment longer to take in the loveliness of her.

His gaze burned upon her bare skin as he looked at her perfect breasts with their taut nipples and tantalizing cleavage, her slim and exquisite waist, and her hips so invitingly rounded.

His eyes stopped and rested on her central tuft of hair at the seam of her thighs. His hand circled his throbbing shaft as he moved to his knees and straddled her.

"Place your hands where mine is," he said huskily, sucking in a breath of pleasure as she did as he asked. He withdrew his own hand and threw his head back and groaned as her fingers moved up and down, making him feel as though he might explode within her fingers, the longing was so powerful.

And when he felt her mouth on him, her tongue sensually stroking him, he stiffened and had to place his hands to her shoulders to urge her away from him, for another moment of such wonderful kisses and he would no longer be able to hold himself back.

Strong Heart settled himself over her, his tongue brushing her lips lightly. He then pressed his lips softly against hers as he entered her in one thrust. His lean, sinewy buttocks moved, her hips lifted to welcome their even strokes. His hands went to her breasts, stroking and kneading them, as his mouth seized hers, darting his moist tongue between her lips.

And then his mouth moved from her lips to her breasts, as he kissed first one nipple, and then the other. Then he sucked the nipples hungrily.

Overcome by passion, Elizabeth gave a little cry. Again his lips were on hers, silencing her with a fiery kiss, his thrusts becoming more heated, driving harder inside her.

She clung to him, this raging hunger that always came from being with him being wonderfully fed. She knew that his hunger was as great as hers, in the hard, seeking pressure of his lips as he continued kissing her, his steel arms enfolding her.

An incredible sweetness swept through her then, and

her body exploded in spasms of desire just as his own body quaked against hers.

After the tempest had subsided, they lay in each other's arms, their passion having given way to peace. Elizabeth scooted closer to him and kissed his brow. "After we are married, will you still find such bliss within my arms?" she whispered. "Can a love like ours last forever, Strong Heart? Can it?"

He caressed her skin lightly with his fingertips. "Even after thirty-seven winters I shall still desire you," he whispered huskily. "So shall you, Strong Heart."

"Even after we are grandparents of perhaps even a thirty-year-old grandson?" she said, giggling at the thought, hard to envision herself that old, and finding it even harder to envision Strong Heart as anything but young and virile. Even his father was still a handsome man in that he did not seem to be in his fifty-sixth winter of age.

Her man would remain ageless, especially within the deepest recesses of her heart.

"Even after we are grandparents of many grandchildren," Strong Heart said, drawing a blanket over them as the wind whipped suddenly down the smoke hole.

Elizabeth snuggled against him. "I had such a good time tonight," she said drowsily.

"That is good," Strong Heart said, smiling into the darkness as the fire had now burned down to low embers. "It is good, also, to know that our people will not lack for nourishment this long winter ahead."

He leaned up on an elbow, smiling down at Elizabeth. "But one must never forget that the wind, rain, and sun also nourishes the bodies of the Suquamish braves," he murmured. "There are many things that help sustain the body—food, pure air, water, and sun are our medicine."

A sound outside the longhouse, where the village now lay in a long past midnight slumber, made Strong Heart bolt to a sitting position. By instinct, he reached for the rifle that he kept on the floor beside the sleeping platform, then crept from his bed and moved stealthily toward the door.

"Strong Heart?"

The voice of Four Winds broke the silence, drawing Strong Heart's eyebrows up. "It is you, Four Winds?" Strong Heart said, jerking the door open. "I would have thought you would be many miles away by now. Why are you here?"

Elizabeth drew a blanket around her as she rose from the sleeping platform to stand beside Strong Heart as Four Winds entered. Something about his attitude and the worried expression on his face made her grow cold inside, and her pulse begin to race.

31

My lips are always touching thine,
At morning, noon and night.
                    —JOHN CLARE

"Tell me, my friend, what brings you back to Strong Heart's dwelling?" Strong Heart asked, frowning as he gazed into Four Winds's troubled eyes. "What keeps you from traveling on to Seattle, where your woman awaits your return?"

"What I have seen and heard delayed my journey," Four Winds said, his jaw tight.

"What did you see?" Strong Heart asked.

"I have uncovered a plan that includes some of your village's most devoted braves," Four Winds said, glancing over at Elizabeth. "These braves were in a secret council at the edge of the village, beside the corral. They have left to burn down the old house that sits on Suquamish hallowed ground and the fishery that has been built close to it. It is their plan to once and for all rid the Suquamish ancestral burial grounds of the evil white man who they feel is responsible for the raid on your village, along with the business that threatens to ruin the Suquamish's future salmon harvests."

Elizabeth gasped and paled. Four Winds had just described her father, his house, and fishery. Although she no longer loved her father as a daughter should, she did not want to see him murdered.

And what of Frannie? Sweet Frannie! She could be burned alive in the fire, or shot as she was trying to flee.

No!

It couldn't be allowed to happen!

She turned to Strong Heart and grabbed him by the arm. "Strong Heart, you've got to stop them," she said, her voice quavering. "Please go and stop the braves."

"It is probably too late," Four Winds said solemnly. "I came as soon as they left on their horses, but they have got such a head start, I doubt anyone could catch up with them."

Elizabeth lifted her chin stubbornly. "Strong Heart, I will go alone if you will not accompany me," she said' firmly.

When Strong Heart did not answer her, Elizabeth leaned up into his face. "I shall, Strong Heart," she cried. "Although my father may be guilty of many evil things, I can't allow him to be murdered. At least I shall try my damnedest to stop it from happening."

Having never heard Elizabeth speak a curse word before, Strong Heart realized just how determined she was to go to her father's rescue. And he was glad to see such a dedication to her parent, even though Earl did not deserve such loyalty. It was proof that her heart was not easily swayed. And that was good.

He gazed down at his woman for a moment longer, then turned to Four Winds. "I shall go and do what I can," he said grimly. "You will ride with me again, Four Winds? It will be like many moons ago, when you and I rode side by side on all sorts of adventures."

Elizabeth heaved a sigh of relief, and even before Four Winds had agreed to accompany Strong Heart on the journey, she had rushed to the curtain at the far end of the longhouse and lowered it. Standing behind it, she began dressing. She was going. No one could keep her from it. Not unless Strong Heart tied her to the sleeping platform.

"*Ah-hah,* my friend," Four Winds said, nodding. "Four Winds will ride with you. While you are getting dressed, do you wish that I go and awaken other braves to accompany us? Do you wish to travel by canoe or by horse? I shall ready whichever mode of travel you prefer.''

"It is best to go by horseback," Strong Heart said, walking briskly away from Four Winds. He flung the blanket from around his shoulders. He yanked on his breeches, and slipped his shirt over his head. "If we traveled by canoe, and the authorities began hunting for us, we would be too easily spied on the river. On horseback, we can be more elusive.''

He sat down and pulled on his moccasins. "And no other braves," he said flatly. "The journey will go more quickly with less.''

He rose to his feet, grabbing a headband, and placing it around his head. "Ready two horses," he said flatly. "Yours and mine. I will be at the corral soon, Four Winds. We will ride hard, hopefully to soon overtake those braves who have decided to do that which should have been debated in council.''

Fully clothed, Elizabeth stepped from behind the curtain. "Four Winds, prepare *three* horses for travel," she said, her hands on her hips. "I am also going.''

Strong Heart turned and faced her. He knew her stubborn nature, and her determination to stop the attack on her father, but he had not expected her to want to go.

And although she thought that what he was readying to do was solely for her benefit, it was not. His motive in this was a selfish one—to protect his *people*. He knew that if the Suquamish braves succeeded, the repercussions against their people would not be worth the victory. The white authorities would come to his village and take away those who were responsible for the fire and perhaps the murders of some white people. They would be hanged. And then the people of his village would be forced to move to a reservation, where they would lose all of their freedoms—all of their joys.

He did not want Elizabeth to slow him down. Already they had taken too much time in talking.

He went to her and gently took her face into his hands. "It is best that you do not go," he said, his voice slow and measured. "The journey will be done at a hard gallop so that we will be able to get there in time. My *la-daila,* it is late. Go to bed. This time tomorrow night I will be warming the blankets with you again."

Elizabeth stuck to her guns. "No matter what you say, I am going," she said. She stepped away from Strong Heart and glared at Four Winds. "Go and prepare *three* horses. If you don't, then your journey will be slowed by having to wait for me to get my horse ready, myself, for I am going!"

Strong Heart gave Elizabeth a long, frustrated stare, then turned and nodded to Four Winds. "Prepare three horses," he murmured. "We shall be there shortly."

Four Winds looked from Elizabeth to Strong Heart, then nodded and left with hurried steps.

Elizabeth turned to Strong Heart and flung herself into his arms. "Thank you," she cried. "Thank you for not ordering me to stay behind. If you had, I'm not sure what I would have done. I would not have wanted to embarrass you in front of Four Winds. Thank you for not giving me cause to."

Strong Heart stroked her long and flowing hair. "I do not embarrass all that easily," he said, chuckling. "But it is best that a woman does not show defiance to her man in front of friends. Tonight it came close to that, but I closed my eyes to it. Your reason for behaving this way was understandable. No matter how evil your father is, within your heart there will always be a corner reserved for the man who helped give you breath and life.''

Tears streamed from Elizabeth's eyes. She was so grateful to this man whose compassion ran so deep.

''But I do worry about how you can stay in the saddle through the long night when you have yet to have any sleep,'' Strong Heart said, easing her from his embrace, and holding her at arm's length.

''Do you not recall the nap you and I took early this afternoon, anticipating the late hours of the celebration?'' Elizabeth asked, wiping tears from her eyes. ''I rested well then, Strong Heart. I am fine for the whole night of travel. Honest, I am.''

''*Ah-hah,*'' he said, smiling down at her. ''I believe you are.'' He walked away from her and grabbed his rifle, then nodded toward her. ''Let us leave now. Let us hope that when we return it will be with a light heart.''

''Yes, let's,'' Elizabeth vowed, rushing from the longhouse with him.

Four Winds had brought the saddled horses to the house. As Strong Heart and Four Winds swung themselves into their saddles, Elizabeth leaped into her own, her heart pounding. She feared that they would be too late.

As they rode from the village, she tried to keep her spirits high. Courage was now needed as never before.

Elizabeth had known the ride would be excruciatingly hard, for she had been on this same journey enough times now to know how tiring it was to stay in the saddle for so long. She had managed to keep up with Strong Heart and Four Winds the long night through and soon they would be arriving at her father's place. To her chagrin, they had not caught up with the Suquamish who had left before them.

The sky was just lightening along the horizon when

Elizabeth's gaze was jerked upward. She was quickly overcome by a horror when she saw the flames of a great fire in the sky.

"No!" she cried. "We're too late!"

She broke away from Strong Heart and Four Winds and urged her horse into a hard gallop toward the dire signs in the heavens. The nightmares that had troubled her now rushed back into her consciousness. She recalled the fire, and how she had been trapped in it.

Surely the nightmare had been an omen. Yet those trapped within the flames were her father, and sweet, innocent Frannie, and all of the other servants. They must have been asleep when the fire had been set. Surely they had had no chance of getting out alive.

Guilt ate away at her for how she had turned her back on her father, even though he had deserved it.

Now she would never have a chance to tell him that, no matter what he did, she loved him.

And neither would he have a chance to redeem himself of his crimes.

When she reached the outskirts of her father's estate, she could see the flames engulfing both the house and the fishery. She almost fainted from the sight. Nobody could have survived the fire. And even though she had Strong Heart's devoted love, this was the worst moment in her life.

She quickly dismounted, and had to force herself not to go farther, but to stay hidden in the shadows of the forest. She couldn't allow anyone to see her or Strong Heart. She did not want Strong Heart to be blamed for the fire.

Elizabeth gnawed on her lower lip as she frantically looked for her father and Frannie among the spectators watching the fire. When she saw them both, as well as the other servants, clustered together outside the tall, old gate, she cried with relief.

Elizabeth then searched around her for those who

had set the fire. When she found no sign of Strong Heart's braves anywhere, she realized that they had left the minute they had seen that their fires had caught hold.

Breathlessly, Strong Heart and Four Winds dismounted close to Elizabeth, their eyes on the fire.

Strong Heart went to Elizabeth and swept an arm around her waist. Together they witnessed Morris Murdoch ride up, and dismount close to Earl.

Morris squinted his eyes as he gazed at the roaring flames and the falling walls of the house as it swayed in the brisk wind that blew across the Sound.

"I saw the smoke in the sky from my home," Morris said thickly. "Somehow I knew it was your house—and our fishery. I notified the firehouse. The fire wagon should be arriving soon." He turned wondering eyes to Earl. "Earl, what happened?"

"All I know is that the screams and shouts of my servants awakened me and then I smelled the smoke and saw flames leaping up to the second floor of the house," Earl said, nervously raking his hands through his hair. "I barely got out alive. If not for the rope bolted to the floor in my room, to be used as a fire escape, I . . . I . . . wouldn't be here to tell about it."

"You didn't see anybody?" Morris prodded. "You don't know how it got started?"

"The house is old," Earl said, his voice thin. "We've had a few problems with our fireplaces. Faulty flues. I guess that's how it started." He gazed down at the flaming fishery, his heart sinking as he watched the building collapse into a pile of burning rubble. His whole world was falling apart before his very eyes. "I . . . I . . . guess the wind carried sparks from the house to the fishery. It's gone, as well."

* * *

Elizabeth's head jerked as she saw a movement in the forest behind her out of the corner of her eye. She turned and grabbed Strong Heart's arm. "Darling, I just saw the elderly Indian again," she said in a rush of words. "Your grandfather. I saw him over there."

Her words trailed off when the old Indian stepped into full view, leaning on his staff, his faded old eyes gleaming happily as he watched the flames eating away at the house. At close range, Elizabeth saw that the man was short, thin, and bowlegged. His gray, unbraided hair was worn to his shoulders, and he had a benevolent face. He looked like an aging philosopher whose strength had waned, yet whose mind was still active.

Stunned by the sight of his grandfather, Strong Heart stared at him for a moment. But when Proud Beaver's eyes turned to him in recognition, the spell was broken and Strong Heart could not get to his grandfather quickly enough. He went to him and embraced him.

"My grandson, my deed is done," Proud Beaver said in a gravelly voice. "Please take me home—take me back to our people."

Strong Heart parted from his grandfather, an eyebrow lifted. "Deed?" he said, his eyes locked with his grandfather's. "What deed, Grandfather?"

As his grandfather's gaze shifted and stopped again on the raging flames that lit the night like daylight, he smiled triumphantly. Strong Heart followed his stare, and without being told, understood that it had not been the braves who had set the fire.

"The fire," Proud Beaver said, nodding. "It is my doing, not our braves who came shortly after I had set it, bearing their own lit torches. When they saw the burning house, they fled quickly. I did not allow them to see me. I did not yet want to leave. It pleasured me too much to see that which desecrated our hallowed ground for so long finally destroyed."

He smiled at Strong Heart. "I also destroyed the

fishery,'' he said happily. "It was easy. The fires burned swiftly. My heart sang while watching it.''

Fearing for his grandfather's life, Strong Heart whisked him away into the shelter of the forest. Elizabeth and Four Winds followed, leading the horses behind them.

Strong Heart turned his grandfather to face him again. He placed a gentle hand on his frail shoulder. "Grandfather, I have been searching for you for so long,'' he said. "Only recently did my search become a desperate one.'' Strong Heart lowered his eyes, hating to be the bearer of sad tidings.

But knowing that he had to do it, he began speaking again, but this time in a low, almost apologetic tone.

"Grandfather, in your absence there has been a raid causing much bloodshed and devastation at our village. But your daughter and Chief Moon Elk lived through the raid. I was not there at the time of the attack because I was searching for you. I then returned to find you and to take you back so that you could mourn the deaths of those you loved. Again, I did not find you. Yet here you are. How is it that you were so elusive, and now you are here, allowing yourself to be seen?''

"There is a cave that tunnels down through the earth, and stops at the far end beneath the house that I have set fire to tonight,'' Proud Beaver said softly. "I have been living there, finding the relics of the Suquamish dead, and burying them where they belong, in the earth of our people. Now our ancestors can finally rest in peace.''

"*Ah-hah*, that is so,'' Strong Heart said, drawing his grandfather into his arms, hugging him tightly.

Feeling the tears welling against her lower lids, Elizabeth placed a hand to her mouth, and stifled a sob that this tender scene between grandfather and grandson had evoked.

She then looked through a break in the trees at her father, glad that he was at least alive. She wondered what he was going to do now, now that his dream had died in flames.

But she didn't have much more time to think about it. Strong Heart was lifting his grandfather into his saddle. Then he helped her into her saddle and swung himself in front of her.

Strong Heart reached a hand out for Four Winds, their hands clasped tightly. "My friend, come soon to our village," Strong Heart invited. "Come and join the *potlatch* that precedes my marriage to my *la-daila*. Bring your woman. Let us be married together!"

Four Winds smiled over at Strong Heart. Elizabeth thought it a bashful sort of smile. Then Four Winds rode away toward Seattle without a word.

Elizabeth clung to Strong Heart's waist as he nudged his heels into the flanks of his horse, and they were quickly riding through the forest.

The firewagon made its arrival. But it was too late. And even though Morris suspected that Indians had set the fire, he didn't tell anyone. He had his own plans of revenge. He had found the destroyed nets in the river and he knew who was responsible.

He rode away without saying anything about it to Earl.

Downtrodden, with Frannie trailing behind him, her face sad and covered with ashes, Earl went to his ship, the only thing that he had left in the world. He had lost his daughter, his home, and business. He had lost his wife a second time, it seemed, for she had not made any more overtures toward him. And, except for faithful Frannie, he had dismissed his other servants.

He leaned against the ship's rail, staring up at the smoky remains of his house, and at what remained of his fishery. He had no reason to live now. His thoughts strayed to the small derringer that he kept hidden beneath his bunk in the master cabin.

That could end it for him, quickly.

Fearing his mood, Frannie hurried behind Earl as he entered his cabin. He was too quiet—his eyes seemed like a man's who no longer had hope. She didn't know what he might do in this state of mind, and hoped that she could stop it.

She almost ran into him when he stopped abruptly.

Earl was shocked by who he found standing in the shadows, a lantern giving off only a faint light to see by.

"Marilyn?" he gasped. "What are you doing here?"

Frannie said nothing, only stood by in surprised silence. She had never forgiven Marilyn for leaving Elizabeth, but now she hoped that Marilyn could be her master's salvation tonight—a night when she had seen him lose everything. The only other time, when they had met recently, Frannie had divined something in Marilyn's eyes and voice that proved that she still loved Earl.

"I saw the fire in the sky and since it seemed to be coming from here, I couldn't help but come to see for sure," Marilyn said, moving closer to Earl. She was lovely tonight in a flame-red velveteen dress with black lace at its high throat, and at the end of the long sleeves.

Her hair was hanging long and free down her back, seemingly an extension of the dress, with its brilliant red coloring.

"When I saw the house on fire, I realized just how much I still wanted you—how much I still love you," Marilyn continued softly. "Earl, if you can find a way to forgive me for what I have done since having left you, I promise that I will start all over again with you.

The life that I have been leading is not at all what I want. I . . . want to be with you. Under any circumstances, I want to be with you.''

''But I have nothing now,'' Earl said, his voice breaking. ''Nothing at all to offer you. All of my money, except for what I can get from the sale of this ship, was tied up in the fishery. And it is gone. I'm broke, Marilyn. Virtually broke. I have nothing left to offer. Nothing.''

''You have yourself,'' Marilyn said, placing a gentle hand to his ash-begrimed face. ''Darling, I will discharge all of my girls. The house can be a real home, where you and I can live as man and wife and grow old together.''

Feeling as if God had seen his remorse and, knowing that he was contemplating suicide, He had sent Marilyn to him for his salvation, Earl tearfully drew her into his arms.

Their tears mingled, they were so glad to have found each other again.

Frannie turned her own eyes away, hope now rising inside her for her own future. Without Master Easton, she had no future. She sure enough wasn't prepared to go and live with Elizabeth and her Indians. She feared Indians more than she feared living alone.

Daybreak came with a glorious sunrise, and also with the thundering of many hooves as the Suquamish braves' horses fell into stride on both sides of Strong Heart's and Proud Beaver's. They had obviously seen Strong Heart arrive to observe the fire, and had hidden in the forest, waiting for him to turn back toward the village, before joining him.

Strong Heart glared from man to man, silently condemning them for having gone behind their chief's back to do as they pleased, even though it was for the best of reasons.

But he was glad that they were blameless for the fire. Now there was only one man to blame, and no one would ever think he was the arsonist.

That made it easier to forgive the braves, and ride with them on toward their village.

"I'm so tired," Elizabeth said, laying her cheek on Strong Heart's back. "Strong Heart, I know that I said that I could withstand this long ride, but now I'm not sure if I can. Another half day on the horse will be too much for me. Please let's stop, Strong Heart. Please let me rest awhile."

Realizing that if Elizabeth complained, she was actually deadly tired, and he could not see himself forcing anything on her. He glanced up at his grandfather who rode proud and sure in his saddle, and then over at all of his braves. If they all stopped, the chances were that someone might come along and put two and two together, thinking they were all responsible for the fire.

But if only he and Elizabeth stopped, it would look less conspicuous; it would look innocent enough.

He raised a fist in the air and shouted to the braves to stop. And after explaining that the braves should go on, and accompany Proud Beaver back to their village, Elizabeth and Strong Heart were alone. A campfire was soon going by a meandering stream, and Elizabeth slept in Strong Heart's arms.

Strong Heart drifted off too and was not aware of a lone horseman riding his horse in a soft trot beside the campsite. The horseman's eyebrows raised as he saw Strong Heart and the white woman lying at his side—this was a strange sight, indeed.

He rode onward, his eyes gleaming. He had found something to laugh about when he reached Seattle and visited his favorite saloon.

32

If ever two were one, surely we,
If ever man were lov'd by wife, then thee.
                    —ANNE BRADSTREET

The afternoon was fading, the distant hills shaded in purple and gray when Elizabeth awakened. At first she was startled, wondering where she was, and then it came to her—she and Strong Heart had broken away from the others to rest.

The fire, she thought brooding to herself. It had taken away her father's dreams, but surely for only a while. As determined as he was, he would rebuild and then Strong Heart's grandfather would have placed himself in jeopardy for naught.

Then what? Would Proud Beaver return, to wreak destruction on her father again?

This time, would her father die?

The thought sent an involuntary shiver down her spine.

She forced herself to think of better things—of her future with Strong Heart, of being his wife, and the mother of his children. Soon that dream would become a reality, and she would let nothing or nobody stand in the way of the happiness that she had found with this wonderful man.

"My Suquamish *husband*," she whispered to herself, testing the words on her lips, loving them.

Rising up on one elbow, she gazed at Strong Heart. She smiled and reached a hand out toward him, yet did not touch him for fear of waking him. She had sorely needed sleep, but it appeared that Strong Heart had needed it worse than she. He still slept soundly, his breathing even, the artery at his throat pulsing with a steady beat.

Her mouth felt as if it was filled with cotton. Elizabeth turned and looked at the stream that caught the last flickering rays of the lowering sun in its rippling water. Careful not to disturb Strong Heart, she rose quietly to her feet and went to the stream and knelt beside it.

After taking several gulps from her cupped hands, she refreshed herself by splashing water onto her face. She rose slowly again, her stomach growling with hunger.

She turned and glanced at Strong Heart. He was still asleep.

She then spied a bush which displayed an array of bright red berries beside the stream, but it was quite a distance from the campsite.

Her hunger overpowering her caution, Elizabeth started walking toward the bush. When she nearly reached it, she stopped when she heard the sound of an approaching horseman.

Fear grabbed at her heart, for she had wandered too far from Strong Heart to get back to him quickly enough. She looked anxiously around her, searching for something large enough to hide behind.

But she found only a copse of birch trees with narrow trunks. She had no choice but to remain in the open, at the mercy of whoever was coming her way. Her only hope was that the horse's hoofbeats had awakened Strong Heart and he had found her gone. And he would come looking for her with the protection of his rifle.

Elizabeth's eyes widened when the horseman came into full view, quickly recognizing Four Winds. He had seen her just at the same moment she had seen him, it seemed, for he was now raising a hand in the air in silent greeting.

Elizabeth sighed with relief. Then her relief was replaced with apprehension. Four Winds had said that he was going to see Maysie, so why would he be this far from Seattle? Four Winds drew his horse to a skittering halt.

Elizabeth ran to him as Four Winds slid easily out of the saddle, facing her with a frown. "Four Winds, what is it?" she asked, her voice anxious. "What are you doing here? And where is Maysie?"

"I shall go for Maysie later," Four Winds said in a grumble. "Strong Heart's and your welfare came first." He looked past Elizabeth's shoulder, seeing Strong Heart asleep in the distance.

He then placed a hand on Elizabeth's shoulder. "I must go and warn Strong Heart," he said solemnly. "There is not that much time."

Elizabeth paled. "Warn him?" she murmured. "Warn him about what? And what do you mean by saying there is not that much time? Tell me, Four Winds. Tell me now."

"On my way to get Maysie, I saw a posse leaving Seattle," Four Winds explained. "I searched for my informant friend who knows everything about everyone to ask where the posse was going. He told me that a rider had come into town, and had been bragging and laughing during a poker game about seeing an Indian and a white woman asleep together in the forest. The new sheriff in town picked up on it and recalled the talk about a woman having escaped prison on the night of the prison's burning. He figured that this could be the one. He said that she fit the description of the missing woman." Four Winds paused for a second, and then continued. "The sheriff said that any woman who was sleeping with a low-down Indian would be the sort that would be an escaped fugitive," he hissed out. "The sheriff also said that the Indian was more than likely the one who had set the fire, and helped her escape. The sheriff gathered together a posse and rode out of town, heading in this direction. Knowing the paths of the forest so well, I took a short-cut, hoping to reach you before those who would like to hang you and Strong Heart.''

Elizabeth's head was spinning. What should she do? She turned and gazed at Strong Heart, a sob lodging in her throat at the thought of this wonderful man possibly being arrested. The thought of the hanging platform haunted her. She had to do something to protect Strong Heart from having to face such a ghastly end as that. His people depended on him. He was the future for his people. And although he was also her future, her *life,* she suddenly knew what she must do to save him.

She turned to Four Winds and grabbed him by the arm, her eyes pleading. ''Don't go to Strong Heart with this news. I have a plan that will spare him the humiliation of being arrested. Please cooperate with me, Four Winds. Will you?''

''What plan?'' Four Winds asked, raising an eyebrow. ''What do you have in mind?''

''I will leave Strong Heart while he sleeps, ride on and meet the posse, and draw them away from Strong Heart,'' Elizabeth said hurriedly. ''Four Winds, don't you see? It is the only way! It is best for Strong Heart. It is best for his people. Please trust me. Don't awaken Strong Heart. Let me go alone.''

Four Winds was torn, yet saw the logic in her plan. And even though he knew that Strong Heart might hate him for it, he decided that, *ah-hah,* he would do as the white woman asked.

''Take my horse,'' Four Winds said, handing the reins over to Elizabeth. ''It would wake Strong Heart if you went for his.''

Weak with fear, yet digging deep within herself to find the courage to make this sacrifice for her beloved,

Elizabeth nodded and lifted herself into the saddle. "Thank you," she said, gazing down at Four Winds. "Thank you for understanding. You see, Four Winds, I love your friend more than life itself. I only hope that this plan works."

Four Winds gave her the direction that she should take in order to run head-on with the posse. Then he stepped back and allowed her to leave, although he knew that the dangers were many in agreeing to the schemes of a woman. But for Strong Heart, he would do anything.

Turning slowly, he looked toward his sleeping friend, wondering how he would tell him. He knew that Strong Heart would become crazed with anger. Then, after he calmed down, hopefully he would understand both his woman's and his best friend's motives—which were for the benefit of the Suquamish.

It felt good to Four Winds to be doing something that was no longer selfish.

He waited for some time, to give Elizabeth a good start, then went to Strong Heart and knelt beside him. "Strong Heart, wake up," he said, touching his arm, and gently shaking it. "It is I, Four Winds. Wake up."

Strong Heart blinked his eyes as he stared blankly up at Four Winds. "Four Winds?" he said, rising to a sitting position. "What are you doing here?"

Then Strong Heart's eyebrows lifted when he looked at Elizabeth's empty blankets. He bolted to his feet and looked anxiously around him, then faced Four Winds as he rose to stand before him.

"Where is Elizabeth?" Strong Heart demanded, glaring at Four Winds. "She is not here and you *are*. Why is that, Four Winds? What have you done with my woman? When we last parted it was as friends— as trusting friends. And now I find my woman gone. Where is she, Four Winds?"

Four Winds placed both of his hands onto Strong

Heart's shoulders. "My friend . . ." he said, and went on to explain what he had heard, and what Elizabeth had decided to do.

Strong Heart was breathless with a building rage that Four Winds had allowed Elizabeth to do something as foolish as this.

"If my woman suffers at the hands of the white authorities, you will pay the price," Strong Heart said, jerking free of Four Winds's grip. "I must go and find her. If I am too late—"

Four Winds interrupted Strong Heart. "I pray that you listen to reason," he said, his voice low. "Ride on to your village. Consider the welfare of your people!"

"Do you not see that I am considering the welfare of my people by *not* going to my village without Elizabeth?" Strong Heart said between gritted teeth. "*Ah-hah*, it is true that I will one day be chief of my people. But do you not understand that a chief whose life is empty from the loss of his woman is no chief at all? And that my people would suffer because of it? I must go for Elizabeth. It is my duty to protect her—the woman who will one day be a Suquamish princess!"

"I beg of you to reconsider," Four Winds persisted. "Should the white woman be arrested, she would not be jailed for long. Her father would find a way to get her freed!"

"That is not so," Strong Heart grumbled. "Her father is a worthless man who thinks only of himself!"

He suddenly realized that they had only one horse between them, and he set his jaw as he glared at Four Winds. Strong Heart would not be the one who would be forced to walk. Four Winds had been foolish enough to give his horse to Elizabeth, so Four Winds would have to pay the price by going on by foot!

But even as Strong Heart was angrily thinking this, he knew that Four Winds would not suffer at all without a horse. The village was near, and Four Winds was known for his ability to beat anyone who challenged him in footraces. Tonight, Four Winds would use his skills well, it seemed.

"Which way do I go to find my *la-daila*?" Strong Heart said, scowling into Four Winds's face. When Four Winds did not respond and instead stubbornly set his jaw, Strong Heart placed his hand at Four Winds's throat and began softly squeezing. "Tell me, or . . . you . . . shall die!"

Knowing that Strong Heart was angry enough to do as he threatened, Four Winds gasped out the answer.

Strong Heart released his hold on Four Winds, and then without another word, not even a farewell, Strong Heart ran to his horse and was soon riding away through the darkness.

He prayed to the Great Spirit that he would not be too late.

Starlight, pale and cold, filled the black, velvety sky. The moon lit the meadow that stretched out before Elizabeth like lamplight, enough for her to see the men approaching her on horseback in the distance. Panic swept through her. For an instant she wanted to turn her horse around and retreat into the forest that she had just left.

But the haunting memory of the hanging platform coming quickly to her mind kept her urging Four Winds's horse into a steady gallop toward the posse, her chin held high. She would not let Strong Heart down, now or ever.

And this was the only way.

Elizabeth drew her rawhide reins tightly and waited. She was soon surrounded by the men, with their firearms drawn and aimed at her. Her gaze stayed on the man in the lead, his sheriff's badge reflecting the moon's glow back into her eyes.

Sheriff Ethan Dobbs tipped his wide-brimmed Stetson hat at her. ''Sheriff Dobbs at your service, ma'am,'' he said in a Texan drawl. ''Will you pleasure us men with your company into Seattle? Of course, you know we cain't take no for an answer.''

Deputy Franks, a youngish man with a spray of golden hair escaping the brim of his hat, edged his horse closer to the sheriff's. ''Sheriff, where's the Injun?'' he said, his dark eyes raking over Elizabeth, grinning at her from ear to ear.

''Ask the woman,'' Sheriff Dobbs said, nodding toward Elizabeth, who had not yet spoken a word for she was terrorized by the number of men and their weapons.

''Ma'am,'' Deputy Franks asked, now moving his horse closer to her. ''There was an Injun with you. Where is he now?''

''I don't know what you're talking about,'' Elizabeth finally said, hating it when her voice broke from fear. ''And may I ask why you have stopped me? I am on my way to Seattle. My father is waiting for me. Please allow me to pass.''

She knew that she had never been good at lying, but she was giving it her best. Yet she feared that no matter what she said, she was going to be arrested. Hopefully, she could talk them out of searching further for Strong Heart. If not, she had failed him miserably.

''It's too bad such a looker as you has to also be a cheat and a liar,'' Sheriff Dobbs said, nodding for Deputy Franks to rejoin the others. ''Come along peaceful-like, miss. Don't force me to put handcuffs on those pretty wrists of yours.''

Her hopes rising that they were more interested in her than Strong Heart at least for now, Elizabeth nodded. ''All right,'' she agreed. ''I'll cooperate. Just please don't handcuff me.''

''I said I wouldn't if you came along peacefully,''

Sheriff Dobbs growled, nodding an order for the men to holster their firearms.

But before they had a chance to, Strong Heart could be seen riding across the meadow in a fast gallop toward them.

Elizabeth turned with a start and felt faint when she saw that it was him, but understood why he had come. For the same reason as hers, he was ready to face the white authorities—to protect his love.

"It's the Injun!" Deputy Franks shouted, then rode on and met Strong Heart's approach. He soon returned with Strong Heart's weapons laid across his lap, and Strong Heart at his side. "By damn, Sheriff, he's come to give hisself up. Ain't that a hoot?"

Sheriff Dobbs rode up beside Strong Heart, slowly looking him up and down. "Do you have a name?" he asked, spitting over his shoulder.

"*Ah-hah,*" Strong Heart said stiffly, as he gazed lovingly at Elizabeth.

"And what the hell does that mumbo jumbo mean?" Sheriff Dobbs said in a feral snarl. "Speak English when you're speaking to me. Do you hear me, damn it? I ain't no heathen with a heathen's education."

Elizabeth paled as she saw the fire leap into Strong Heart's eyes as he turned them on the sheriff. And she blamed herself. If she had awakened Strong Heart and fled with him into the hills, instead of trying to take everything into her own hands, perhaps her beloved could have been spared this humiliation.

But, in time, they would have been found, and then how much worse would it have been for him? No matter what she would have done, it would have been wrong.

"Strong Heart," Strong Heart finally said, then turned his gaze back to Elizabeth. "The woman. Release her. She is innocent. I shall take her place in the jail cell."

"Hah, ain't that a laugh?" Sheriff Dobbs taunted. "Injun, you are both under arrest." He leaned his face into Strong Heart's. "But don't get any crazy ideas that you two'll share the same cell. We won't have no Injun fraternizing with any white woman, even if she is the criminal kind, herself."

Tears flooded Elizabeth's eyes and she had to look away from Strong Heart. Her heart was heavy from having failed the man she loved. She flinched when she heard the snap of handcuffs and knew that Strong Heart was not being treated as gently as she. In the heart of white men who did not understand the honor of an Indian, the Indian always posed a threat to them.

Hanging her head, Elizabeth rode off with the posse, Strong Heart somewhere behind her. She did not have to see him to know that he was even now a noble presence as he rode with his shoulders squared, and his head lifted high.

33

Thy love is such I can no way repay.
—ANNE BRADSTREET

The next day was gray, a light drizzle misting the air.
Maysie drew back a sheer curtain and peered up the
long avenue, disheartened. Four Winds had not come
for her as promised. She nervously wrung her hands,
fearing that the reason for his absence might be that
he had been gunned down by the outlaws that he had
abandoned.

Or perhaps the new sheriff had caught up with him
and had thrown him back in jail.

She would not allow herself to believe that he had
had second thoughts about taking her away to be his
wife. He had spoken with such sincerity when he had
talked about taking her to his village, so that they could
both begin a new life there.

He had talked about how one day he would be chief,
if his father had not yet chosen someone else to take
his place.

"My dear, hasn't he arrived yet?" Marilyn said,
moving to Maysie's side. She took Maysie's hand.
"Please quit worrying. He'll be here. I saw how he
looked at you, my dear. No man looks at a woman
like that unless he loves her."

"Oh?" Earl said, entering the parlor. "Does that
apply to me? Do you see me look at you in a special
way, darling?"

As Marilyn made her way toward him, her blue silk
dress and the many ruffled petticoats beneath it rustled
voluptuously. Earl gazed at her, then looked around

the room. Its decor had changed to something more modest. The red velveteen chairs, lounges, and drapes had been discarded. In their place was more simple furniture—that which matched Marilyn and Earl's finances.

Although Marilyn had had a roaring business during her reign as the renowned madam of Seattle, the man in charge of her ledgers *and* her money had fled, taking with him a good portion of what she had earned.

But there was enough money to last for many more years if they spent wisely, not wasting a cent of it.

Earl's heart warmed and his eyes twinkled as Marilyn locked her arm through his, gazing up at him as if she had never loathed or deserted him.

"My darling Earl, although it is dreary and gray outside, inside, where you are here with me, I see only sunshine," Marilyn murmured, rising on tiptoe to give him a soft kiss on his lips. "And don't you smell the delicious dinner Frannie is cooking for us? Your favorite, Earl—beef pot roast and for dessert, a mouthwatering rhubarb pie."

"You'd better keep an eye on that Frannie," Earl teased. "She's a woman after my heart."

Maysie was enjoying this scene of love and devotion between Marilyn and Earl. She smiled as Earl looked over Marilyn's shoulder and winked at her.

Then she turned her eyes back to the road. As a horseman turned into the lane that led to the house, she stepped closer to the window and placed her hands on the sill, her heart skipping a beat. Then it slowed to its regular pace when she saw that it was not Four Winds.

Earl heard the horse drawing close outside, and he bristled, thinking that perhaps it was a gentleman who did not yet know that this house was no longer a bordello. He eased away from Marilyn, ran a nervous finger around the white, tight collar at his throat, and walked toward the foyer.

With blinking eyes, Marilyn went after him. "Please don't think that every time a man arrives here, it's for the wrong reason," she pleaded, catching up with him as he reached the front door. "There are legitimate reasons why I have callers. And Earl, I have a friend who is looking for Thomas, my accountant. It might be Sam, Earl. He may have found Thomas."

Earl sucked in an uneasy breath and raked his fingers through his hair. Then he turned to the door and stared at it as the knocker sounded three knocks.

Stiff-legged, Earl jerked it open, Marilyn at his side. Both stared at a youthful, pockmarked face, and long, stringy hair hanging from beneath a sweat-stained Stetson. The boy's clothes were wet from the misty rain. Earl recognized him as one of the workers that he had hired for the fishery—now unemployed, thanks to the damnable fire.

"Well, hello, Brad," Earl said, extending a hand toward the lad. "What brings you here this time of day, and in the rain?"

"Mr. Easton, it's something I heard," Brad said, removing his hat, holding on to the brim and slowly turning it between his fingers. "I thought you should know. Or has someone else come and told you?"

"Told me what?" Earl said, raising an eyebrow.

Brad looked from Earl to Marilyn, and then back at Earl. "It's your daughter," he said, his voice weak. "She's-she's in jail. And so is that Indian that she ran off with."

Marilyn placed a hand over her heart.

Earl had to grab hold of the doorjamb, to steady himself in his alarm over what he had just heard. "Elizabeth?" he said, almost choking on the word. "My Elizabeth? She's in jail? Again?"

"The posse brought her in just a while ago," Brad

said, swallowing hard. "And they brought in the Indian, too. There's a rumor that there might be a hangin'. Maybe *two*."

"My Lord," Marilyn gasped, swaying as a nausea swept through her. Then she crumpled to the floor in a dead faint.

Earl was in a state of shock, but when Marilyn fainted, he came to life. "Marilyn!" he shouted, falling to a knee beside her.

He swept her into his arms and carried her to the parlor, stretching her out on the sofa. "Maysie, get some smelling salts," he shouted.

Wide-eyed, and numb from the news of Elizabeth's capture, Maysie hurried and got the smelling salts.

She went back to Marilyn and knelt beside her, waving the salts beneath her nose. Marilyn began and coughing and rolling her head from side to side. Her eyes flew open and she sat up on the couch.

"Are you going to be all right?" Earl asked, placing a hand to Marilyn's cheek. "I must go to Elizabeth. I've got to find a way to get her out of that place."

"But, how, Earl?" Marilyn cried, sniffling into a lacy handkerchief that she had taken from the pocket of her dress. "That requires money, Earl. We do not have that kind of money."

Earl began pacing back and forth across the carpeted floor in a frenzied manner. "There must be a way," he said, his throat tight.

Brad, forgotten in the doorway, overheard their dilemma. He took it upon himself to enter the parlor. "Sir, might I make a suggestion?" he asked, clasping his hands behind him.

Earl stopped. "Eh, what is that you said, lad?" he asked, staring at Brad.

"I know someone that's interested in purchasing your ship," Brad said. "This man came into town yesterday on a clipper ship. He's spread the word that he's prepared to buy anyone's ship, should they have any for sale. Seems he hit it rich panning for gold in San Francisco. He says he wants the ship to travel the high seas, more for pleasure than for business."

Earl listened with a quickly beating heart, his eyes anxious. "His name," he said, going to Brad. "Lad, give me his name. I think he may have found a buyer."

"He's stayin' at the Gooseneck Inn on Third Street," Brad said, placing his hat on his head as Earl took him by an elbow and began pulling him toward the door. "Should I go and fetch him for you, sir? I could have him back here to talk business with you quicker than you can wink your eye."

"That won't be necessary," Earl said, ushering Brad on outside. "I'll tend to it myself. Thanks, lad. Thanks a million."

"My pleasure," Brad said, tipping his hat and going to his horse.

Earl went to the hat rack and got his top hat, and gathered his white gloves from a table in the foyer. Then he turned and met Marilyn's approach. He embraced her. "I shouldn't be long," he tried to reassure her. "And when I return, by damn, Elizabeth will be with me."

Marilyn gazed up at him. "What about Strong Heart?" she asked softly. "You know how Elizabeth feels about him."

"Let Strong Heart take care of himself," Earl muttered, still resenting how the Suquamish had turned his offer down. He could not help but feel that if that deal had gone through, things would somehow be different.

Deep inside himself, where he weighed matters to find answers to whatever happened to him, he knew that somehow the fire had not started from a faulty flue.

A fire that fierce, one that had spread and burned that quickly, had surely been set.

But there was no proof, and his life was now changed because of it. He had to make the best of what he had left—and a big part of that was Elizabeth.

Marilyn watched Earl as he rushed out the door. Maysie came to her and slipped an arm around her waist, and they listened to Earl riding away on his horse.

Then Marilyn broke away from Maysie. Numbly, she closed the door and went back to the parlor and sat down, staring into space, feeling nothing but dread and impending doom.

Elizabeth shoved her breakfast tray aside, her appetite gone as she surveyed her surroundings. The cells were overcrowded with prisoners—men and women.

Although this was a new jail, smelling of fresh wood and plaster, it could not take away the feeling of terror that gripped her at the thought of what lay ahead. She had heard the sheriff and deputy laughing and talking about hangings—hers and Strong Heart's.

Yet she knew that they did not have the power to sentence anyone. A judge would be coming from a neighboring city to make that decision.

Hers and Strong Heart's futures were in the hands of that judge.

There may never be a marriage. There may never be children. There may never be a Chief Strong Heart.

Elizabeth's gaze shifted, and her heart ached when she saw Strong Heart sitting cross-legged on the floor of his cell across the way from hers. His hands rested on his knees, his eyes unwavering as he stared straight ahead. She had heard him chanting quietly only moments ago, and realized that he had been trying to reach his Great Spirit. Just as she had been trying to reach her own God with soft prayers to be set free from this place of degradation.

A commotion in the outer office took Elizabeth's breath away as she recognized her father's voice. Then there was only a hushed murmur of conversation between the sheriff and her father.

She waited eagerly. Soon they were coming toward her, a key in the sheriff's hand.

Elizabeth's eyes met her father's, seeing a twinkling in them and a smile that told her that somehow he had managed to get her free.

She could not believe it, even when the door creaked open and the sheriff gestured for her to step outside the cell.

"Elizabeth," Earl said, drawing her quickly into his arms, hugging her tightly. "I've come to take you home. Baby, I've come to take you home."

At this moment, Elizabeth cast aside all resentment toward her father. The fact that he had managed to get her free was all that mattered.

Then she blanched and looked over at Strong Heart, who was now standing in his cell, his hands gripping the bars. As their eyes locked, she felt torn with grief, knowing that whatever bargain her father struck, it did not include her beloved Suquamish brave.

"I can't," she said, moving quickly back inside the cell. She even closed the door. "If Strong Heart isn't going to be released, *I* shall not leave."

Earl frowned. He yanked the door open and placed a hand on Elizabeth's arm. "You're not going to stay here another minute," he said, his voice flat. "Elizabeth, damn it, let's get out of here while the getting is good." He leaned close to her ear. "I paid the sheriff under the table. If anyone figures it out, we'll both be locked up. Come on. We'll see to Strong Heart's release later."

Elizabeth's eyes wavered as she gazed with longing

at Strong Heart. But the thought came to her that there might be some benefit in her not being in jail. Strong Heart could be better served if she was free. Even though her father had said that he would see to Strong Heart's release later, she knew enough about the way things were between the Indians and the whites to realize that no matter how much her father paid, Strong Heart would not be set free without a trial.

And she doubted her father had any intention of getting Strong Heart out of there. It was all up to her, and she had a plan. She would speak up for Strong Heart at his trial. She would make sure that he was set free, for she already knew what she was going to say to ensure it.

"All right, I shall go with you," Elizabeth consented. Then she went to Strong Heart's cell and placed her fingers over his. "Darling, do not think that I am deserting you. I have a plan that will set both of us free. Please have faith in me. Soon, my darling. Soon we shall be married. Soon we shall see small footprints in the snows of winter—our children's footprints, my love. Our children's."

With many eyes on her, Elizabeth stood on tiptoe and kissed Strong Heart. Then, with tears burning at the corners of her eyes, she fled the jail with her father. She was numb as she rode the streets on horseback with him. She expected to be taken to his ship, where she supposed was his home until he could rebuild his fishery.

But her mouth dropped open and she emitted a low gasp of wonder when her father took her to her mother's stately house. She was speechless, until she was inside and she saw the changes—not only in the decor of the house, but also the sincere warmth between her mother and father.

"Elizabeth," Marilyn said, rushing to her after giving Earl a deep kiss. She touched Elizabeth's face, then seemed to be feeling for broken bones as she touched her all over, tears rushing down her cheeks.

"Oh, sweetheart, you *are* all right, *aren't* you?" Marilyn said, flinging herself into her daughter's arms.

"I'm fine," Elizabeth said, smiling at Maysie as she stepped into view. Then her smile faded when she realized that Maysie's exit from Seattle with Four Winds had been delayed because of his loyalty to Strong Heart.

She eased away from her mother and everything about her father and mother's reunion was explained to her, even the revelation of her father's bankruptcy in San Francisco, and his subsequent money problems.

Elizabeth suspected that her father had probably gone back to his wife only for the security that she offered him.

That suspicion was squelched when her mother explained her own money problems, and how Earl had managed to get enough money to set Elizabeth free.

"You sold your ship?" Elizabeth asked, astonished. "Father, that ship meant the world to you."

Earl went to Elizabeth and took her hands in his. "My daughter means even more than that to me," he said thickly.

Elizabeth's feelings were beginning to soften toward her father. Yet nothing could excuse the fact that he had plotted against Strong Heart's people.

No. She doubted if she could ever truly forgive him.

34

The heavens reward thee manifold I pray.
—ANNE BRADSTREET

The courtroom was packed with people who were curious to see an Indian put on trial. A strained hush came over the crowd as Strong Heart was escorted into the room and led to a chair at the front.

Elizabeth sat between her mother and father, looking sedate and prim in a plain cotton dress devoid of frilly trim, and wearing a matching bonnet. Her hair streamed long and free from beneath it across her shoulders and down her back. Frannie sat beside Marilyn.

Maysie sat on Earl's other side, wearing a dress as colorless as Elizabeth's, and sporting a bonnet where, beneath it, she had woven her hair into a tight bun. Her face was pale and lined with sadness. Maysie's gaze moved slowly around the room as she looked for Four Winds, even though she knew that he would not be there. He was still wanted and he could not take his place alongside Strong Heart. He had already had a trial, one which had condemned him to *death*.

At times, Maysie had grieved over Four Winds, thinking that he had forgotten her. She knew that she should hate him for his deception, but her very soul cried out to be with him again, and would not lose hope. It was this trial, which had brought lawmen from all corners of the Pacific Northwest, that had frightened Four Winds away.

Elizabeth strained her neck to see over the shoulder of a man in front of her. But she still could not see

Strong Heart easily. There were people blocking her view.

Nervously chewing on her lower lip, she settled back in her chair. Then she sat more erect and felt an anxious blush rise heatedly to her cheeks as the judge came into the room and took his place on the bench. He reached for his gavel and slammed it hard against the top of his desk.

"Let's have silence in the room and get on with this," Judge Cline said, looking soberly at Strong Heart, pausing as he studied him. Obviously he was assessing this man whom he would either set free or condemn to death.

Elizabeth watched the judge, seeing so much about him that hinted that his reputation for being a kind and considerate man could be true. Behind gold-rimmed glasses were dark eyes that looked gentle and caring. Although his thinning hair and bent shoulders indicated that he was perhaps in his early seventies, there were not many lines on his face. This man had smile wrinkles at the corners of his eyes and mouth. His color was good. His voice was pleasant when he talked to the two attorneys who sat on opposite sides of the room from each other. No jurors had been chosen for this particular trial. The judge would be judge *and* jury today.

"I have read the record of the accused," Judge Cline said, his voice smooth and even. "I see that he is accused of helping more than one person escape from Copper Hill Prison." He studied the papers that he was now laying out on the desk. "I see here that he is also blamed for the deaths of the sheriff and his deputy, and for setting fire to the prison."

He removed his glasses and sucked on one of the stems, again looking at Strong Heart intently. "That's an awful lot of meanness for one man to get into, wouldn't you say, young man?" he asked, laying his glasses aside, leaning forward, his eyes locked with Strong Heart's. "What do you have to say for yourself?"

Strong Heart rose to his feet and squared his shoulders. "Strong Heart is guilty for only two things of which he is accused," he said plainly, glancing over at Elizabeth. "My friend Four Winds had an unfair trial. Nothing was proven that should have condemned him to the hangman's noose. I saw no other choice but to set him free. Elizabeth Easton was unjustly arrested by the corrupt sheriff and was treated disrespectfully by the deputy. She did not deserve to be housed with criminals, under a sheriff and deputy whose respect for law and order was a mockery to the white community as well as the red. For this, I became her judge and jury. I set her free. These things I confess to, and it seems everything else which followed was by chance."

Judge Cline raised a shaggy, gray eyebrow, his gaze moving slowly to Elizabeth, whose testimony was to be heard today. He thought of her as nothing less than beautiful, and he could understand why any man would be pulled under her spell. Even an Indian.

Looking closer, he saw how frightened she was, and understood. Her testimony today was the only one, besides Strong Heart's, that he would listen to.

Judge Cline looked at Strong Heart again. "You may be seated," he said. "And thank you for your honesty. An honest man is hard to find these days. It is refreshing when I come across one." He smiled warmly at Strong Heart as he slowly sat down. "Lad, this trial won't take long, I can promise you that."

Hearing Judge Cline speak so kindly to Strong Heart gave Elizabeth cause to hope. The judge narrowed his eyes as he stared at her, again.

Then Judge Cline gently spoke her name, and gestured for her to come to the podium to take a seat.

Her legs trembled as she rose from her chair. The whole courtroom had fallen into a hushed silence, everyone shocked that she, a white woman, would testify on an Indian's behalf.

And she alone knew that they had not seen or heard anything yet. Before God and the town, she was going to openly defy all the unspoken laws that had been set down between the whites and Indians.

And she was going to do more than that.

She was going to reveal things to these gawking, high and mighty people that would set their tongues to wagging into the night and many days to follow.

When Maysie reached a comforting hand to her, Elizabeth took it and clung to it for a moment, then went to the podium. She sat down gingerly on the padded seat after swearing to tell the truth, and nothing but the truth.

"We won't bother with cross-examinations nor such bunk as that today," Judge Cline said, causing a stir in the courtroom which the judge ignored. He leaned to one side, eye to eye with Elizabeth as she turned to him. "Young lady, just tell me everything you know about what has brought Strong Heart to this courtroom. You are speaking on his behalf. I, as well as everyone else in this room, am prepared to listen. Begin speaking and you won't be interrupted until you are finished."

Elizabeth was amazed at the generosity of this judge, having feared the day that she would have to face him. The authorities whom she had already had dealings with in Seattle had neither been respectable nor honest.

But again, this man made her feel as if there was some hope—some reason to believe that justice would be served, and her love would be set free so that they could resume their lives together.

"Your Honor, I have never met a kinder or gentler

man than Strong Heart,'' she began softly, fighting
back tears as Strong Heart gazed devotedly up at her.
She wiped her hands on her skirt and continued. ''This
man has saved my life not once, but many times. He
did this at the risk of losing his own life. But do not
get me wrong, I do not sit here testifying in his behalf
because I feel as if I owe him for his kindness. It runs
deeper than that. I testify for him because I know him
to be innocent, and very wronged by the white community. This man, who will one day be a great chief,
has been humiliated before the whole town, and made
to sit in jail beside the most degenerate of criminals.''
She cleared her throat, then looked over at the judge.
''Your Honor, I was also wrongly jailed and placed
with hardened criminals. The sheriff and deputy
treated me as less than a lady by . . . by . . . trying
to rape me,'' she said, her voice growing in strength
as she spoke. She aimed her speech solely at the judge.
''Strong Heart knew that I was innocent. He released
me. It was after we fled Seattle that someone else went
to the prison and set it on fire. The deputy and sheriff
both died in the fire. So as you see, he is innocent of
that crime.''

The judge found her story plausible. For years, he
had known Sheriff Nolan's wicked reputation. He was
surprised no one had torched the prison before.

Elizabeth looked over at Strong Heart. ''He released
Four Winds from the prison because of loyalty to a
friend he did not believe was guilty of any crime. This
man, whom some would relish seeing hanging from a
noose, has a big, kind heart. There is surely no one
else quite like him on the face of the earth. Because
of his beliefs and loyalties, he has risked his life over
and over again these past weeks.''

Again, she looked at the judge. ''And for this he
might be condemned to die,'' she said, her voice
breaking. ''And, Judge Cline, if you need proof of his

whereabouts on the night of the fire and deaths of the sheriff and deputy, I can vouch for him. After he released me from the prison, we traveled quickly into the forest where we camped, so that we might rest before traveling on to his village. And by a campfire I made love with this man who will soon be my husband.''

The shock of this statement registered and the whole room seemed to reverberate with the gasps and exclamations of dismay.

Judge Cline's eyebrows shot up in amazement at Elizabeth. Then he picked up his gavel and slammed it against the desk. "Order in the court!" he shouted above the clamor. "We . . . shall . . . have order in this court!"

Everything became quiet, except for a few whisperings. The women's eyes rested accusingly on Elizabeth, apparently appalled by the thought of a white woman stepping forward and brazenly admitting to having slept with an Indian.

Yet she held her chin high, her eyes unwavering as the judge looked at her again.

"Continue," Judge Cline said, a quiet smile pulling at his lips.

"Judge Cline, I believe I have said my piece," Elizabeth murmured, smiling back at him.

"A testimony like I have never heard before, and perhaps won't hear again," Judge Cline announced, laying the gavel aside. He sat back in his chair, rocking slowly back and forth as he placed his fingertips together before him.

Then he leaned forward, his elbows on the desk, and began to speak again. "Never have I seen such courage as you have portrayed today, young lady," he said. "I'm inclined to believe you, for you knew the repercussions before speaking up—the way people would react to such a statement as this. That you could be shunned by the white community. Yes, young lady, it must be true, or you wouldn't have taken the chance of harming your reputation by telling a story like this—"

A sudden commotion at the back of the room made Judge Cline lose his train of thought. He stared at an Indian who was making his way down the aisle. A ripple of excitement flowed through the crowd at his presence.

Judge Cline slammed his gavel down, causing a quick silence to ensue. He glared down at Four Winds as he came to stand before the bench, his jaw set with determination.

"What is the meaning of this?" Judge Cline asked, leaning forward. "Do you not understand that you have just interrupted a court of law?"

"*Ah-hah,* yes, I understand," Four Winds said, folding his arms across his chest. "And that is why I am here—to speak for my friend, Strong Heart."

Four Winds glanced over at Strong Heart, relieved that he had not come too late. Then he smiled at Elizabeth.

He turned and found Maysie in the crowd, the hurt in the depths of her eyes making his heart ache. The knowledge of what he had to do to guarantee his friend's freedom had kept him away from Maysie.

She had to learn to live without him, for he would not be free to love her. His announcement today would condemn him in the eyes of the white community, and even his own people's eyes, forever. There would be no future for him.

"Well?" Judge Cline said, a touch of impatience in his voice. "Speak up and say what is on your mind so that we can get on with the proceedings at hand."

"I have come to tell the truth about everything," Four Winds said. "Strong Heart is innocent of all crimes. It is I who am responsible for everything that has happened—even my own escape from the prison.''

He held his gaze steady with the judge's, hoping that his lies would be convincing enough, for this was the last thing that he could do for his friend.

Tomorrow, they both would probably be swaying back and forth on the gallows for all to see.

''Continue,'' Judge Cline said, finding this hearing very interesting.

''When Strong Heart came to visit me in prison, I grabbed Strong Heart's pistol and forced him to get the keys to set me free,'' Four Winds said, knowing that his story would stand up because those who could refute it were dead. ''I abducted Strong Heart and Elizabeth that day. Hang me, not Strong Heart.''

Judge Cline leaned back in his chair, his eyes twinkling with amusement, for he could tell a lie when he heard it, and he knew damn well that Four Winds was lying to protect his friend.

Yet, that didn't matter. He had made his mind up already.

''Are you finished?'' Judge Cline asked Four Winds.

''*Ah-hah,*'' Four Winds said, nodding. ''That is all I have to say.''

Judge Cline leaned back in his chair for a moment, looking from Four Winds to Elizabeth, and then to Strong Heart. He smiled warmly at each of them. ''You are all free to go,'' he said finally. ''I have witnessed something here today that is rare. Loyalty. An intense loyalty between friends, and loved ones. Although the law has been broken by first one, and then another of you, the reasons for these actions have not been selfish ones. It was always because each of you saw a wrong that was being done to the other.''

Judge Cline rose from his chair and stood tall behind the bench. ''And,'' he said, his gaze moving about the room, silencing the commotion his verdict had stirred, ''prejudices are more to blame for what has happened here than anything. Because of my decision, perhaps prejudice can be lightened in this city.''

He grabbed up his gavel and pounded it one last time. ''Court is adjourned,'' he shouted. ''Clear the room. And good day.''

He picked up the stack of papers from the desk and paused to wink good-naturedly at Elizabeth. Then with long strides, he left the room.

No one left the courtroom. Everyone was shocked by the judge's decision. After a moment, the spectators stirred and began to leave. Some of them smiled and nodded at Elizabeth and Strong Heart, seeming more touched than disapproving of their love.

Elizabeth ran to Strong Heart, flinging herself into his arms. ''Darling, we're free,'' she cried. ''Free! Our dreams are going to come true after all!''

''Because of you,'' Strong Heart said, framing her face between his hands. Then he looked at Four Winds. ''And because of Four Winds. How will I ever be able to repay him?''

''No payment is needed, I am sure,'' Elizabeth said, turning just as Maysie stepped before Four Winds, gazing up at him with tear-filled eyes. Tears flowed from her own eyes when Four Winds suddenly grabbed Maysie into his arms and fled the courtroom with her.

''It seems all is forgiven between them, also,'' Elizabeth said, laughing softly. She wiped her face as her parents and Frannie approached her and Strong Heart.

''I . . . I . . . hope I didn't embarrass you too much today, by being so open,'' Elizabeth said, lowering her eyes.

''We're very proud of you, darling,'' Marilyn said, pulling Elizabeth into her embrace, and then giving Elizabeth up to Earl as he also hugged her.

For the moment Elizabeth relaxed in her father's

arms, then broke away from him. She looked from her mother to her father, knowing they had their own guilty secrets—especially her father. She felt lucky that Strong Heart would even accept her as his wife, with such a father as hers.

She then gave Frannie an affectionate hug. "Thank you for so much," she whispered, swallowing back a sob of happiness. "Had it not been for you, Frannie, I'm not sure what would have happened to me. You were all that kept me sane in my childhood. Thank you from the bottom of my heart."

Tears fell from Frannie's eyes. "Honey chil', you were my baby for so long, how can I say good-bye?" she said, clutching Elizabeth. "But you go on with that man of yours and Frannie understands. Be happy, Elizabeth. You deserves all the happiness in this world."

Elizabeth gave Frannie a kiss on her soft, round cheek, then stepped back and looked adoringly up at Strong Heart. "We really must go," she announced. She kissed her parents, then left the courtroom with Strong Heart at her side.

Once out on the wooden sidewalk, she laughed joyously as Four Winds rode past with Maysie sitting before him on the saddle. Two horses followed them. She waved at them. "Wait up!" she cried. "Wait up!"

"Four Winds works miracles, it seems," Strong Heart said, laughing. "He has brought my horse for me, and has also found one for you. Let us ride, my *la-daila*. We are free—free as the wind!"

Feeling giddy with happiness, Elizabeth and Strong Heart mounted up and rode away with Four Winds and Maysie.

They rode for a while, then wheeled their horses to a halt. "Four Winds, you are coming to my village?" Strong Heart asked, looking at Four Winds with the eyes of a boy, feeling humbled in his friend's presence.

"You can share in the wedding and *potlatch*. Friends should share everything." He laughed softly as he glanced over at Elizabeth. "Except, of course, wives."

Four Winds burst into laughter, then stopped. "No, I have thought it over and it is best that I go to my village and make things right with my people," he said seriously. "But I will ride with you as far as your village, then we shall say our farewells there."

Strong Heart nodded. "That is good enough," he said. He turned to Elizabeth. "Come, my love. There will be no more looking over your shoulder. We ride on open land in peace!"

Elizabeth inhaled a deep breath, loving the sound of those words, and how wonderful they made her feel inside.

35

While we live, in love let's so persevere,
That when we live no more, we may live ever.
—ANNE BRADSTREET

The sun was setting in the west behind the distant
mountains, sending off streaks in the sky that resembled streamers of orange satin.

A damp chill suffused the air as the three horses
rode from an open meadow into the forest where autumn blazed. Yellowed sycamore leaves dropped into
streams and sailed away. Elizabeth smiled and gazed
over at Strong Heart and Four Winds as they rode side
by side. Maysie was now behind Four Winds, holding
his waist.

Strong Heart and Four Winds were lost to the world
as they talked about their past—where they had gone
on their childhood adventures, or had challenged each
other in all kinds of games.

It touched Elizabeth deeply to see them goodheart-
edly joking between themselves. Strong Heart seemed
to have forgotten that Four Winds had for a while ridden with outlaws. Four Winds had redeemed himself
totally by helping Strong Heart become a free man
again.

Elizabeth felt such tenderness toward Four Winds,
for if not for him, there would have been no future for
her and Strong Heart. To her it had looked bleak these
past few days!

But now, she sighed to herself, everything was all
right and would soon be perfect, when she and Strong
Heart joined their hands and hearts in marriage.

She shifted her eyes to Maysie, glad that for her, life

was finally going to be good. There was a look of peace and contentment in Maysie's eyes as she sat in the saddle behind Four Winds, her lustrous long hair flowing in the wind.

Elizabeth shook her own hair so that it fell away from her face and shoulders. She had thrown her own bonnet into the wind shortly after their departure from Seattle. She lifted her eyes to the heavens where stars were just emerging in the twilight and the moon had risen over the mountain peaks to replace the sun. She closed her eyes, reveling in this new freedom which would last forever.

Her peace was shattered when horses suddenly appeared from behind the trees a short distance ahead, plunging toward them. For a moment she was too stunned to think, for she had not expected anybody to try and stop their journey to Strong Heart's village. He had been exonerated of all charges. She had thought they were free to ride without fear, or of having to defend themselves against—

Elizabeth's thoughts stopped still when she quickly recognized Morris Murdoch among those approaching.

Four Winds, too, recognized the members of the outlaw gang that he had been part of.

They saw that these men were not innocent passersby, but were intent on attack as they jerked their weapons from their holsters and opened fire.

''Find cover quickly!'' Strong Heart shouted, edging his horse back beside Elizabeth's. He snatched her reins and led her horse with his into a thicket of trees. Four Winds followed and he and Maysie slid quickly from the saddle.

Four Winds grabbed his rifle from its holster and tossed it toward Maysie. ''I hope you know how to use this,'' he shouted.

Maysie caught the rifle, paling as she stared down

at it. Then she positioned herself beside Four Winds as he started firing with a pistol at the attackers.

Elizabeth stood bravely beside Strong Heart, firing a pistol he had given her, while he used his repeating rifle. The outlaws sought cover. The shooting did not slow as gunblasts erupted from both sides.

Then there were the sounds of other horses coming, making Elizabeth and Strong Heart exchange worried glances. Elizabeth feared that this was the end, for surely those arriving were more outlaws. The attack made no sense to Elizabeth, unless it was revenge for Morris Murdoch on the Suquamish for thwarting his business plans. Or the attack could be for another reason—against Four Winds, for turning his back on the outlaws to live the life of an Indian brave again.

But then the outlaws ceased firing and mounted their horses, fleeing in the opposite direction of the arriving horses. Elizabeth knew that whoever was approaching was not coming to help the outlaws.

Lowering her pistol to her side, Elizabeth stepped out into the open with Strong Heart, Four Winds, and Maysie. They watched as several horsemen, the sheriff and her own father in the lead, rode on past. They heard gunfire erupt between the fleeing outlaws and the posse.

"My father?" Elizabeth whispered. "Fighting alongside the law?" She shook her head, having never been as confused as she was now.

She ran with Strong Heart toward the confrontation a short distance away. She paused to catch her breath, then saw the bodies that lay strewn along the ground, the stench of gunpowder lying heavy in the air—the fight was over.

Jerkily, and with an anxious heartbeat, Elizabeth's eyes moved from man to man on the ground, praying that her father was not among them.

But before she could find out, there was a noise in

the trees behind her. As she turned, she cried out a warning to Strong Heart. Morris Murdoch, on his horse, his eyes crazed, was trying to run Strong Heart down.

Strong Heart heeded her warning. He turned on a moccasined heel and leveled his rifle at Morris and fired. His aim was accurate as Morris's body lurched with the sudden impact of the bullet in his chest. His horse reared and threw him to the ground, where he lay, blood pouring from his wound.

Elizabeth could not stop the tears of relief when she saw her father step into sight from some bushes. Yet she did not go to him. Even now she still could not go to him and throw herself into his arms, declaring how happy she was that he was all right—and to thank him for having come when he did.

No.

A part of her held back, while another part of her fought the stubbornness that held her there.

Earl walked slowly toward Morris Murdoch, his pistol aimed at him, not trusting that even though he looked injured, he might not be.

Earl glanced over at Elizabeth, so glad that she was unhurt. Yet he ached inside when she did not come to him and welcome him. He had to correct that. Now!

Earl was going to see to it that Morris Murdoch cleared his name, or else. He saw that Morris was not mortally wounded, and that he would stand trial.

That is, if Earl did not kill him first.

Morris's chances were better in court than with Earl, and Morris surely knew that, for there was dread in the depths of his eyes as Earl knelt beside him. The fingers of Earl's free hand grabbed hold of Morris's hair, lifting his head up to look eye to eye with Earl.

"You son of a bitch, you tell my daughter the truth about everything, or so help me, Morris, I will take you and make you die a slow, torturous death,'' Earl said between gritted teeth. ''And don't think the law won't allow it. I'd be saving them money by not having to pay a judge to hand down your sentence.''

Morris coughed and clutched at his chest wound, blood seeping through his fingers. ''You bastard,'' he said, his eyes hazy with pain. ''You damn bastard. I should've known you'd be bad luck. You brought your bad luck with you from San Francisco. You threw it my way. Damn it, I should've known that you were a worthless dumb ass, unable to make things work right.''

''My daughter,'' Earl said, yanking harder on Morris's hair. ''Damn it, Morris, tell my daughter the truth. Tell her that I had nothing to do with the attack on the village. Tell her that the only thing I did that was underhanded was place the nets in the river.'' He leaned closer to Morris's face. ''Tell her now, or be sorry.''

''How'd you know about this ambush?'' Morris breathed out between gasps of pain. He closed his eyes wearily. ''Who doublecrossed me? Who?''

''You aren't as smart as you think you are,'' Earl said, laughing sarcastically. ''There are several among your gang who have turned informants to bargain for their freedom. They were smart enough to know that the end was near for your bastard gang of outlaws.''

''The dumb asses,'' Morris said, his eyes flashing with anger. ''How could they?''

''Enough of this,'' Earl said with a snarl. ''I'm waiting for you to tell the truth so that not only my daughter will know it, but also so that Strong Heart can hear you.''

When Morris stubbornly clamped his lips together, Strong Heart stepped forward and knelt on the other side of him. Elizabeth moved closer, her pulse racing.

Strong Heart yanked his knife from its sheath at his waist, and placed the sharp blade against Morris's throat. "You speak the truth now," he said, his eyes lit with fire. "Do it for my woman. She deserves all truths. She has earned them."

Fear creeped into Morris's eyes. He gulped hard and stared up at Strong Heart. "Her father is innocent of everything, except for putting the nets in the river," he cried out. "Please. Please . . . move that knife away. I . . . I . . . don't want to die."

Tears streamed from Elizabeth's eyes. She reproached herself for believing all of those ugly things about her father, when all along he was mostly innocent.

Innocent!

Now it was *his* turn to forgive, it seemed, for she had treated him callously instead of trusting him. In truth, her father had been as wronged as the Suquamish. He had been used by Morris Murdoch in the worst way.

Earl rose slowly to his feet. He flipped his pistol into its holster and turned to Elizabeth. His eyelids heavy, he beckoned for her with his arms to come to him.

"Baby, I'm sorry for all of this," he said thickly. "My choice of partners was bad, don't you agree?"

Elizabeth brushed tears from her cheeks and she swallowed back a sob as she broke into a run and flung herself into his arms. "I'm the one who is sorry," she sobbed, clinging to him. "Will you ever, ever be able to forgive me?"

"How can you ask that?" Earl said, holding her away from him, so that their eyes could meet. "Baby, you have done nothing to be forgiven for. It was your father who is to blame for everything. I'm sorry that I gave you cause to mistrust me. And I shan't ever cause you another moment's stress or worry. Your mother and I are going to start a new life together. My life will be centered around family, not business. Will you be a part of our new life, Elizabeth? It would make everything complete for me and your mother.''

"Are . . . are . . . you asking me not to marry Strong Heart?'' she asked, her voice wary.

"Not at all,'' Earl said, smiling down at her. "Your mother and I want to wish you much happiness with Strong Heart. And we would like to be invited to your wedding. Do you think that can be arranged?''

Fresh tears rose in Elizabeth's eyes—joyful tears. She again flung herself into her father's arms. "Yes, yes,'' she cried. "It can be arranged.''

Strong Heart looked on, his heart warm, his eyes smiling.

36

If ever wife was happy in a man,
Compare with me, ye women, if you can.
—ANNE BRADSTREET

On their wedding day, Elizabeth sat in the council house on a high platform piled comfortably with soft furs, overlooking their guests: Suquamish from this village and from the reservation. She watched wide-eyed as Strong Heart participated in what was known as a *potlatch*. She would have felt awkward except that she was not alone on the platform. Her parents sat on one side of her and Strong Heart's parents on the other side.

Even sweet Frannie had overcome her fear of Indians and had been persuaded to attend. She sat quietly beside Elizabeth's mother, casting Elizabeth occasional weak smiles.

Several Braves circled outside of the onlookers, dancing to the sound of drumming on a hollow box. Many of their steps consisted of springing into the air from squatting positions, or turning fast on their heels in a narrow circle. Their headdresses were wide bands of deerskin to which were attached the scarlet-feathered scalps of the pileated woodpeckers and they carried the skins of albino deer, their heads stuffed and also adorned with bright red woodpecker scalps.

There was choral singing in the background accompanying the drumming and dancing.

As Elizabeth watched, Strong Heart handed out gifts to guests who sat around the fire in the firepit. Her hands stroked her cloak of softly woven wool, trimmed with sea otter fur.

Beneath her cloak she wore a dress of doeskin, whitened with clay, and trimmed with the milk teeth of elks, and with tips of turkey feathers and porcupine quills. On her feet were knee-high moccasins, adorned with brightly painted beads.

She felt lovely, and Strong Heart was so handsome, in his own cloak of sea otter fur, the festive occasion marked by his wearing red cedar-bark head rings filled with loose white down, and a stiff, tire-like bark collar.

As they had dressed for today, she had watched him pull on leggings and a breechcloth painted with various colors in bright designs beneath his cloak.

She had then seen him as he added the sparkling flakes of mica to his face, which even now glittered under the fire's glow.

She knew that she had to grow used to these new customs, yet this *potlatch* did not seem appropriate for the occasion. In her culture, presents were given *to* the bride and groom—not to those who attended.

But Strong Heart had explained to her that sharing one's wealth was an honor. The more a person gave to others, the more important he was in their society. The *potlatch*, meaning 'gift giving,' was a way of celebrating important events—today a marriage of a most important man to the woman of his choice.

Strong Heart had warned her not to be alarmed by the amount of gifts that he would give away at the *potlatch*. He told her that in the coming years, there would be more such celebrations, to impress upon others the wealth that proved his worthiness of the title of chief. They were necessary, these times of spreading his wealth among those who were less fortunate than he or Elizabeth.

Elizabeth had not told him of her uneasiness about this, because she had no right to. She had chosen to live the life of the Suquamish. So she would have to accept all the ways *of* the Suquamish. And she would. In time, she would know as much as the other women.

Forcing herself not to think about how strange this gift giving was, Elizabeth watched and nodded her approval at Strong Heart each time he held up an object for her to see before he gave it away. Once this exhibition of wealth was over, they would finally join hands in marriage.

She still could not believe that all of the obstacles had been removed and that their lives were going to become normal, with the insanity of the past behind them.

And it had been the same for Four Winds and Maysie. A runner from his village had come to Strong Heart with the news that Four Winds had been accepted into his community, and that he and Maysie had shared their vows as man and wife already.

Elizabeth and Strong Heart had delayed their wedding day, giving Elizabeth's parents time to get there to be witnesses to their joyful marriage.

Still she sat patiently as she waited for Strong Heart to bring his gift giving to a close.

But he kept moving around the crowd, his generosity great today. Elizabeth could not help but covet the trade blanket that he was handing to one woman. It was beautiful—dark blue with a red border, embellished with heraldic beasts outlined in pearl buttons.

She also silently admired the baskets, beautifully carved boxes, and decorated hides that he gave away.

And then, surprising Elizabeth, Strong Heart stopped before her parents. "Come with me," he said, gesturing toward her father specifically. "Your gift awaits you at the river."

Earl's mouth opened in wonder. Then he left the platform as Strong Heart continued waving for him to follow.

The drumming, singing, and dancing ceased. Eliz-

abeth and everyone else followed Strong Heart and her
father outside, where the western mountains were
flushed a red gold, and down to the river.

Strong Heart went to the sandy beach and walked
toward a lone, intricately carved canoe. He went to it
and laid a hand on the prow, turning and smiling at
Earl. "This is my gift to you," he said. "This will
make it easier for you and your wife to come and see
your daughter from time to time. The rivers are more
gentle than a horse to a woman's behind."

Strong Heart glanced over at Elizabeth, his eyes
dancing. He hoped that she was remembering their
many adventures on horseback. He had silently mar-
veled at her tenacity to keep up with him. He had also
seen her grimace while rubbing her sore behind. How
her muscles must have ached when they had not been
able to stop and rest as often as she would have wished.

Ah-hah, a canoe would be better for her mother,
whose age matched Strong Heart's own mother's. His
mother would rather do anything than climb on a
horse.

Elizabeth was touched by Strong Heart's thought-
fulness. She went to him and linked an arm through
his, as she watched her father look over the canoe,
obviously moved by it.

"This is so kind of you," Earl finally said, looking
up at Strong Heart with grateful eyes. "I never expected a gift—especially one of this magnitude. I accept it heartily. Thank you." He gestured toward his
wife. "Marilyn, darlin', come and see this. The designs carved on this canoe are magnificent. So de-
tailed." He then noticed something else. Many pelts
were spread across the seats. "We shall return to Seattle in this canoe, and leave the horse and buggy in
exchange."

Earl shifted his gaze to Strong Heart. "That is, if
you don't mind taking the horse and buggy off our

hands," he said, knowing that this was the only way Strong Heart would accept anything in return for the generous gift.

"That will be acceptable," Strong Heart said, smiling back at Earl, realizing exactly what Elizabeth's father was up to and understanding.

Then Strong Heart clapped a hand to Earl's shoulder. "Now, I would share my life with your daughter," he said.

"I give her to you with my blessing," Earl said, his voice soft, emotion running through him that showed in his eyes as they were suddenly filled with tears.

Strong Heart nodded. "She will fill my days and nights with much gladness," he said.

Strong Heart dropped his hand from Earl and turned to Elizabeth. "My *la-daila,* it is time now for us to return to the council house and join our hands in marriage," he said, his eyes shining into hers.

He then leaned his lips close to her ear as he drew her into his arms. "And then, my darling, we shall celebrate in private," he said huskily. "Does that sound acceptable to you?"

"Yes, quite," Elizabeth whispered back, thrilled clear to the core with an intense joy.

Strong Heart knelt over Elizabeth beside the low, flickering flames of the fire in their longhouse. Her back was pressed into the soft pelts beneath her. She reached her hands to him and sought out the feel of his sleek body. His eyes swept over her with a silent, urgent message that she understood.

As if cast under some sensual spell, Elizabeth moved her hand to his pulsating hardness that he pressed toward her in an open invitation to caress it. Her fingers stroked him there. His breath came in short rasps, his eyes closed, as he began moving himself boldly within her fingers.

Feeling the heat of his manhood, and seeing the pleasure she was giving him, she raised up on an elbow and moved her lips to him, remembering the other times she had done this for him.

But this time, Strong Heart placed his fingers gently on her shoulders and urged her away from him, easing her back down onto the pelts. "My *la-daila,* your skill at giving me pleasure is almost more than I can bear," he said softly. "The art of restraint that I learned as a child almost becomes lost to me when your hands and lips are on me in such a way. If I were a selfish man, I would allow such caresses until my passion was fully spent. But because I love you so much, and want you to share the total ecstasy of our moments together, I cannot go further with this lovemaking until it is shared equally by the both of us."

"But I wanted to give you that sort of pleasure," Elizabeth said, reaching a hand to his face, softly touching it. "Don't you understand that giving you pleasure, pleasures me?"

"Pleasure?" Strong Heart said, a mischievous gleam in his eyes. "Let Strong Heart show you what true pleasure is, and then see if we either one has cause for complaint."

"All right," Elizabeth said, giggling as he leaned over her and his hot breath raced across her creamy skin. "Whatever you say. You are my husband. Do as you please with me."

Her soft laughter faded into moans when Strong Heart's hands and his tongue skillfully searched over her for her pleasure points, his engorged manhood pressing against her thigh, pulsing in its building need to find a home inside her, where she also so unmercifully throbbed.

When Strong Heart's mouth covered Elizabeth's with a fevered kiss, she ran her fingers along his satiny hardness, then spread her legs apart and placed the tip of his manhood where she was open and ready for him. She caught her breath and a lethargic feeling of floating claimed her when he thrust deeply inside her and began slowly stroking her, then moving faster in quick, sure movements.

As he held her in a torrid embrace, his mouth demanding and hungry, yet sweet, she writhed in response as his lean, sinewy buttocks moved. She began to move against him, her breasts now rising beneath his fingers, his tongue brushing her lips lightly.

He then buried his face next to her neck, breathing in the sweet smell of her, and cradling her in his arms, his passion cresting as she clung and rocked with him. His body turned to liquid fire as her fingers made a slow, sensuous descent along his spine, then splayed against his buttocks. Her fingernails sank into his flesh, urging him more deeply inside her.

His movements became maddeningly fast, sweat lacing his brow and back as he placed his hands on her buttocks, holding her in place as they continued to give and take pleasure from each other.

And then he drew away from her.

Elizabeth questioned him with her eyes, and when he drew her up on her hands and knees, she puzzled over what he might do next, yet was not afraid. This wonderful feeling that had risen inside her, had blotted out all other sensation, other than desire for more and more. Her thirst for her beloved was never quenched.

Strong Heart positioned himself behind her, parting her thighs, then pressed his pulsating hardness deeply within her again. As he held on to her waist, he drew her back to meet his thrusts, glad that she understood and began moving against him, moaning.

His hands crept around and found her heavy breasts, and cupped them with his warm fingers. With quick thrusts of his pelvis, he could feel his passion peaking.

Elizabeth felt a tremor begin deep within her, and

then it exploded in spasms of delight, matching his
own release as he clung to her, his body trembling
against hers.

Afterward, a great calm filled Elizabeth, but this
was not long lived. Strong Heart placed his hands at
her waist and lowered her onto her back on the furs,
his lips roving over her again, her every secret place
opening to his tongue.

Shaken anew with the intensity of her desire, Elizabeth welcomed him atop her, taking his mouth sav-
agely with hers as he plunged deeply within her.

She began to move against him, her hands clinging
to his sinewy shoulders, until once again they found
that precious moment of bliss, which passed much too
quickly, but was never, never forgotten.

Strong Heart rolled away from Elizabeth. Then he
drew a blanket over her up to her neck. He lay down
beside her, sharing the blanket. "Tomorrow we travel
to Seattle," he said, causing Elizabeth's eyebrows to
lift.

She raised up on an elbow, staring disbelievingly at
him. "I would think that would be the last place you
would want to be," she said. "Let us not tempt fate,
darling. We have finally found peace. I don't trust
leaving your village so soon after what happened in
Seattle."

She leaned closer to him. "And why on earth are
we going?" she asked, seeing an amused glint come
into his eyes.

"You will see," he said, with a low chuckle. "You
will see."

"Does that mean that you aren't going to tell me?"
Elizabeth said, annoyed by his laughter.

"That is so," Strong Heart said, turning so that
their bodies met beneath the blankets. He combed his
fingers through her hair. "*Ah-hah*, my *la-daila*, that
is so."

"Just tell me whether or not it is something that will add to our happiness, not take away from it," Elizabeth said, pouting.

"It is something wonderful," Strong Heart said, piquing her curiosity even more.

But her frustration did not last long, because his lips and body were sending her into another world of joyful bliss.

Tomorrow?

Who cares, she thought to herself? Right now was all that mattered. Tomorrow? Surely nothing could be as wonderful as *tonight*.

37

I love thee with the breath,
Smiles, tears, of all my life!
—ELIZABETH BARRETT BROWNING

It was not as amazing to Elizabeth that she would be
nearing the outskirts of Seattle with Strong Heart, but
that many of his people had accompanied them in their
large, beautiful canoes up the serene river with the
trees bent above it like lovers. And still Strong Heart
would not tell her why they were making the journey.

It seemed everyone knew, but her.

But she had quit asking and watched as Strong
Heart, sitting before her in their canoe, drew his oar
through the water with his muscular arms, an elk skin
coat snug against his lithe body. He made the chore
of manning the canoe look effortless, as did the other
braves accompanying him in his great vessel, each
man's oar moving in cadence with the other.

Elizabeth turned and looked at the other canoes following Strong Heart's down the long avenue of river.
She saw Many Stars, Strong Heart's grandfather, Proud
Beaver, and Strong Heart's parents. His father's leg
had healed. Many braves had been left behind to guard
the village, but many were here today on this puzzling
venture to Seattle.

When Many Stars saw Elizabeth looking her way,
she waved, her bearskin pelt drawn snugly around her
own shoulders.

Elizabeth returned the wave, then turned her eyes
ahead, forcing herself not to become impatient. Soon
they would arrive, and then she would know. She
hoped that Strong Heart would understand when she

asked to go and see her parents. It was wonderful to have a true family again, even though she was no longer a part of their world. She had prayed since their separation that they would come together again and make up for the long years lost to them and her.

And God had heard her prayers.

Oh, so often he had heard her prayers, and she was thankful!

The air, rich with the scent of cedar, had turned colder and brisker halfway from the Suquamish village. The wind whisked the leaves overhead, their rustlings similar to the sound of softly falling rain. A deer drinking thirstily at the riverbank, where the shallower water bubbled over white pebbles, was startled by the appearance of the canoes and darted to safety in the cedar's gloom. A woodpecker lightly beat a tattoo on a hollow tree.

Huddled beneath a warm bear pelt, the fur turned inside to give her more warmth, Elizabeth gazed up at the leaves of the trees, drinking in the beauty as if she were partaking of a vintage wine. She had never witnessed such breathtaking colors before as were displayed on these trees of late autumn.

There were orange-hued leaves, and purple and red. The most magnificent of all were the birches with their golden leaves clinging to the snow-white bark of the trees. The water was golden with the reflection of the trees.

A wind brought down a flotilla of leaves and they sailed off downstream in disarray, like a convoy without a commander.

It was so beautiful, Elizabeth almost forgot why she was there. Watching the seasons parade past filled her with peace.

She drew the fur more closely around her shoulders, lifting her nose to inhale the sweet, fresh fragrance of the air. Then she grew tense when she saw what ap-

peared to be a snowflake fluttering slowly from the
sky, sparkling like a miniature diamond against the
gray gloomy clouds that were battling the sun for
space, soon erasing it from the sky.

She looked anxiously at Strong Heart, wondering if
he had noticed the snowflake. She also wondered what
the chances were that a snowstorm might come from
those clouds overhead. Mount Rainier already had a
coat of snow enwrapping its great peak. This was her
first winter in the Pacific Northwest. She had cause to
fear the fierceness of the winds, the dangers of the
snows, and the long days and nights of isolation when
she would be confined to the longhouse.

But that latter thought made her relax from her wor-
ries. Not only would she be isolated in the longhouse,
so would her husband. They knew ways to pass the
long hours. It gave her a thrill even now to think about
how those hours would be spent.

Then her thoughts returned to their journey and
where Strong Heart was guiding his canoe. Her heart
seemed to leap into her throat and her eyes grew wide
as she watched the canoe sliding through the water in
the shadow of a sheer cliff, gnarled cedars clinging to
its sides, close to the land that was owned by her father. The reason she had not recognized it earlier was
because the house was no longer there.

When they passed the high hill that had once been
dominated by the old mansion, Strong Heart began
drawing his canoe even more closely to the shore. She
quickly saw the pier where her father had moored his
ship, and on that pier stood her parents.

"Mama?" Elizabeth gasped, sitting forward on the
seat. "Papa?"

She could not hold back her questions any longer.
She tossed aside the bearskin on her lap, and in her
long robe of rabbit fur went and squeezed herself between Strong Heart and the brave sitting next to him,

and sat down. "Why are my parents there on the pier as if waiting for us?" she asked, her words tumbling out in a rush. "Strong Heart, please tell me what is happening. It isn't fair that I am the only one who does not know!"

"*Ah-hah*, it *is* time that you should be told," Strong Heart said, turning a smiling face toward her. He paused from his paddling. The others rowed the canoe to shore.

"My *la-daila*, soon the hallowed ground of my people will be returned to us," he said feelingly. "Your father has given it back to us. After today, the ancestral burial grounds will not be disturbed by the presence of white men any longer."

He frowned at the towering, grotesque fence. "My people have come to witness the removal of the fence that glares like an enemy, standing for everything bad to the Suquamish." He looked over his shoulder at the canoes following close behind his. "In its place will be erected a massive totem pole, which will stand guard over the land that houses many Suquamish spirits!"

Elizabeth's lips parted with a slight gasp, everything he said flowing like a stream of sunlight into her, warming her through and through. "My father is doing this thing for you?" she finally said.

She turned her eyes to her father who was wrapped in a long robe of elk skin, beside her mother who was as warm in her own white rabbit fur coat.

Elizabeth cast Strong Heart another quick glance, knowing that the robes her parents wore had to be gifts from him, for they were identical to those that Strong Heart and Elizabeth wore. It was a wonderful thing—this amity that had grown between her husband and her parents. It could have been just the opposite—unbearable—and something that would have strained her marriage to Strong Heart.

But now everything was perfect. She prayed that it would continue to be this way.

She decided to accept things as they were now and count herself blessed.

After the canoe was moored and Strong Heart helped Elizabeth from it, she ran to her mother and embraced her, then turned to her father.

Her eyes filmed with tears as she hugged him. "Papa, thank you for what you are doing today," she said. She stepped away, yet held his gloved hands within hers. "Surely no one has ever been so generous. Especially now that you are poor. You could have sold the land for a profit. Instead, you are giving it to the Suquamish. Thank you. Oh, thank you."

"Yes, it seems that when I was searching to find a way to gather up enough money to pay your way out of the prison I forgot about what I could have got from the land, and only sold my ship," he said, chuckling. "It is good that I had that lapse of memory, baby, for it's doing your father's old heart good to see the beaming faces of these people whom you have joined." He cleared his throat nervously. "I . . . I . . . only wish that I had never gone to their village in the first place. If I hadn't, Morris Murdoch would have seen no need to do what he did, to cause Strong Heart's people such pain."

Marilyn stepped close to Earl. She placed her arm around his waist. "Darling Earl, that's in the past," she said softly. "Let us look now to the future. It will be as if our past never was. We are blessed, Earl, to be given this second chance. Let's not have any regrets, and spoil what should be a joyful day for everyone."

Earl dropped Elizabeth's hands and turned to his wife, giving her a soft kiss on the lips. Elizabeth watched them, glorying in the moment, then turned and watched the Suquamish make their way up the steep path, the braves carrying thick, heavy ropes. Others were toting a large totem pole, the designs carved into it bright and threatening. She had not noticed this pole earlier, for the canoe carrying it had stayed far behind the others.

Chief Moon Elk and Pretty Nose came to Elizabeth and her parents. After embracing one another, they all began ascending the steep path. Proud Beaver was assisted by two braves, his staff held proudly in one hand.

After they all reached the summit, they stood back in silence as the ropes were placed around the sharp pikes of the fence, and in one yank, the fence was toppled to the ground with a loud crash.

Many shouts and cheers rose into the air. The upturned faces were touched by the snowflakes that were falling thickly from the gray sky overhead. Elizabeth no longer feared the snow, for she saw that it had a purpose today. It was beautifying this land that had been dirtied so long ago by the first white man who had walked on the soil of the Suquamish ancestral burial grounds. It was covering the black ash remains of the house, and the destroyed fishery below.

Yes, it did seem a new beginning for these people, and Elizabeth was glad that she was able to be a part of it. What tales she and Strong Heart could tell their children!

Suddenly she felt nausea rising through her, threatening to spoil everything. She placed her hands over her stomach to steady it and smiled. She had been experiencing these feelings the past several days, and she understood why. She most definitely understood what missing a monthly flow meant. And she had missed hers! If everything stayed as sweet as now, she would be giving birth to Strong Heart's child before their next autumn salmon run.

"And what do you think of my surprise?" Strong Heart said, coming to Elizabeth with a broad smile.

She smiled impishly up at him, wondering what he would think about hers?

When Proud Beaver stepped into view, held on both sides by braves to steady him, Elizabeth forgot her surprise. It was so touching to see the elderly Indian watch the raising of the totem pole. He had achieved his goal, and even more, it seemed. His noble old face held great dignity, and his fading eyes were now able to watch for the last flickering of life's sunset in peace.

"I'm very pleased," she finally said, gulping back a sob. "So very pleased, Strong Heart."

"I knew that you would be," Strong Heart said, squaring his shoulders proudly. He circled an arm around her waist and drew her close beside him. Then he smiled a silent thank you to Earl as Earl turned his gaze his way.

Earl returned the smile.

38

Love is a circle that doth restless move
In the same sweet eternity of love.
—HERRICK

It was another autumn. Oaks that had glowed like hot
coals only two weeks before, now delivered up brown
leaves to a chill wind. Sycamores already raised bare,
white arms in surrender to winter's advance. The geese
had flown toward warmer climes, the frogs had buried
themselves two feet in mud, and the animals of the
forest had thicker fur.

The sun hung coldly in a western sky that was
streaked with long, uncertain bands of red, and the
dry, rich scent of the fallen leaves was almost painful
in its sweetness. Lakes gleamed like hand mirrors,
reflecting the gold of drooping willows.

Her three-month-old son in his little *guyou*, or cra-
dle basket, on the ground beside her, Elizabeth was
on a food-gathering trip. Wrapped in a warm fur coat,
she was digging roots and acorns in the oak groves.
When she returned home, she would soak and hull the
acorns, and grind them to meal in a shallow stone
mortar, leaching the bitter tannin out of the meal. Then
she would cook it into a nourishing gruel.

The Suquamish's main food was fish. And while it
was the men's duty to catch the salmon and bottom
fish, it was the duty of the women to dig clams and
collect shellfish from the beach.

Elizabeth had already gone by swift canoe to the
inlets and bays of the Sound, gathering enough shellfish for winter. Sticks of hardwood had been used to
dig up the mollusks. The shells provided useful ma-

terial for tools or utensils. Large mussel shells were ground sharp to form a woman's knife. Deep clamshells made convenient spoons for sipping broth.

On another journey, she had gone with other women to the prairies and mountain slopes and picked berries while their men had hunted.

Today her mind was not on her digging, or on the long winter ahead. It was on Maysie. A runner had carried the news to her and Strong Heart that Maysie was having trouble with the birthing of her first child, and may even lose it. It had been almost a week now since Elizabeth had heard anything else, and she was tempted to beg Strong Heart to take her north to see to Maysie herself.

For the sake of her own child, she set this thought aside. She had to think of her son's welfare first and foremost. She had been lucky with her own birthing. Her son had even come a month early, and was no less strong because of it.

"My woman works too hard today," Strong Heart suddenly said from behind her. He came to her and placed a hand at her elbow, urging her to her feet. "Come. Let us return home. Let us sit and watch our son as he grows."

Elizabeth laughed softly, loving how Strong Heart was so proud of his son. "*Ah-hah*, yes, let's go and watch our son grow," she said, lifting the heavy basket of roots up from the ground, proud of her work today.

She waited as Strong Heart went and picked up the *guyoo*. It had been brightly painted by him before the child's birth. When he very gently drew back a corner of the blanket, to peer down into his son's face, Elizabeth saw the pride in his eyes, and her thoughts went back to the day that their son had been born to them.

Elizabeth had been lying there for hours, struggling with her labor. Just before the final shove that had brought their son into the world, a red-tailed hawk had somehow managed to get into their longhouse, squawking desperately and flapping its great wings.

Strong Heart had managed to catch the hawk within the folds of a blanket and carry it outside to freedom.

Moments later their child's first cries filled the air, and their son was quickly given the name Red Hawk, for the bird that had come into their house as an omen.

"He is quite beautiful, isn't he?" Elizabeth asked, falling into step beside Strong Heart as they walked through the forest toward the village.

"A man or a boy is not beautiful," Strong Heart said, yet smiling at Elizabeth. "He is *handsome*. Is he not?"

"*Ah-hah,* handsome," Elizabeth said, humoring him. "Of course he would be, for you are his father."

Strong Heart did not have a chance to reply. In the distance a horseman was fast approaching them. Strong Heart quickly handed the *guyoo* to Elizabeth and reached for the knife at his waist. Then he relaxed his fingers and dropped his hand away from the weapon as he recognized the brave on the horse. It was Pale Squirrel, the cryer coming from Four Winds's village again.

Elizabeth grabbed Strong Heart's arm. "I hope the news is good," she murmured.

Pale Squirrel halted before them and raised a hand in greeting, his face wide with a grin. "A child was born to Four Winds and Maysie five sleeps ago," he proudly announced.

Elizabeth and Strong Heart felt a great relief flow through them, and then they asked whether the child was a son or a daughter.

"A son was born to them, his chosen name—Strong Winds—a name that is taken from the special friend-ship between Four Winds and Strong Heart," Pale

Squirrel said, his eyes shining as he looked at Strong Heart. "Do you approve, Strong Heart?"

"You take word back to Four Winds that Strong Heart accepts this honor with a warm and thankful heart," Strong Heart said feelingly.

"*Ah-hah,*" Pale Squirrel said, nodding.

"Before you leave on the long journey north again, come to our house and celebrate the birth of our friends' son with us," Elizabeth said, smiling up at Pale Squirrel.

"Your invitation is a gracious one, but Pale Squirrel cannot accept," he said softly. "I am eager to return to my people. They are celebrating now, but it will continue for many days, for I have another announcement for Strong Heart and his woman. Four Winds's father has given Four Winds the title of chief, himself worn and weary with an ailment that takes away his strength. Four Winds has accepted, and reigns even now as chief!"

At first, Strong Heart was stunned by the news—that Four Winds was chief. Then he felt a great happiness. If Four Winds had the duties of chief, husband, and father to attend to, he would not have the opportunity to return to an outlaw's life. *Ah-hah,* this news filled Strong Heart's heart with much gladness!

"How wonderful for Four Winds and Maysie," Elizabeth said, then lifted a hand to Pale Squirrel when he seemed anxious to leave. "Thank you for coming with the news. That was so kind of you."

Pale Squirrel accepted her hand, then accepted Strong Heart's hand, clasping it tightly. "Come soon and sit in council with my people," Pale Squirrel offered. "Send a runner to announce your arrival and we will feast and sing in your honor."

"The snows are near, but when spring arrives with its new grasses and warm winds, we will come north. The sons of Four Winds and Strong Heart will become friends, as their fathers have been for many, many moons,'' Strong Heart said, squeezing Pale Squirrel's hand.

''*Kla-how-ya,* good-bye, my friends,'' Pale Squirrel said, then wheeled his horse around and rode away.

Strong Heart turned to Elizabeth. He brushed a red lock of hair back inside her hood. ''My *la-daila,* my heart sings with happiness,'' he said softly. ''And so much is because of you. *Mah-sie,* thank you.''

''You are my happiness,'' Elizabeth whispered, leaning into the palm of his hand as he rested it against her cheek. ''You and our son, Strong Heart. *Mah-sie,* thank *you* for making it all possible. Had you not been there so often, I would not be alive. I don't feel as if I can ever find ways to truly repay you for risking your life to save mine.''

''You have already given me all that I ever want as payment,'' Strong Heart said, drawing her near to him as they walked on toward the village. ''I have you— and I have a son. Who could ever want for more than that?''

She stopped and turned to face him, smiling mischievously. ''Are you saying that you do not want a daughter?'' she teased.

Strong Heart's eyes lit up. ''Are you saying?'' he gasped out, almost speechless.

''*Ah-hah,* I do believe that I carry another child within my womb, my darling,'' Elizabeth said, nodding up at him. ''And I am almost certain it will be a girl, for I will wish upon stars every night to make it so.''

Strong Heart placed a fist over his heart. ''My *tum-tum,* heart, is filled with the joy of the moment,'' he said. Then, as Red Hawk began to cry, Strong Heart began rocking him in his arms as they went on to their longhouse.

After the baby had been fed and was soundly asleep

in his crib, and they lay beneath warm furs beside the fire, Elizabeth moved easily into Strong Heart's arms and welcomed his wild embrace as they made love more passionately than ever before.

Life was finally so *tsee,* sweet, for them, so very, very *tsee.*

Dear Reader:

I hope that you have enjoyed reading *Wild Embrace*. This is the third book of a major Indian series that I am writing for *New American Library*. The next book will be *Wild Splendor*, the story of Sage, a proud Navaho warrior, and the woman of his heart, Leonida. *Wild Splendor* promises more passion and adventure!

I would love to hear from you all. For my newsletter, please send a legal-size self-addressed, stamped envelope to:

CASSIE EDWARDS
Rt. 3, Box 60
Mattoon, IL 61938

Always,

Cassie Edwards